Feeding the Dragon
A correctional officer's story

A. Sappington II

Jadybug Press—Ararat, VA
ISBN: 979-8-218-35605-7
Library of Congress Control Number: 2024902228
Title: *Feeding the Dragon: A correctional officer's story*
Author: A. Sappington II
Digital distribution | 2024
Paperback | 2024

This is a work of fiction. The characters, names, incidents, places, and dialogue are products of the author's imagination, and are not to be construed as real.

Dedication

To God, the One who strengthens me.

To my girls, Faye, Ashley and Jayden, who walked with me as I looked my dragon in the eyes. You are my "why."

To my brothers and sisters who stood with me on the line. Of special note;

Warden Pat K., who led from the front and gave me the advice which carried me throughout my career.

Randy W., the toughest man I ever met, a stellar hack and my greatest teacher.

Bernie H., my mentor in the early years.

Paulie W., a great friend and teacher.

To Mike and Nancy O. for your honesty, insight and always having my six.

To my nieces Jordan and Megan.

Special thanks to Em and Alyssa W. from New Book Authors Publishing for taking me by the hand and guiding me on the journey to bring my words to the reader.

Introduction

On any given day in America, there is most assuredly a career day being conducted in at least one school somewhere. Students stand up in front of their peers and explain why they want to be a fireman or a doctor or policeman. I have never heard of or seen anyone stand up and espouse the dream of being a correctional officer. It is, beyond a doubt, a career that finds that special type of individual.

Correctional officers walk the toughest beat in law enforcement. Everyone the correctional officer engages with inside the prison is a felon capable of violence limited only to the imagination of the perpetrator. Throughout the correctional officer's career, he or she will spend every shift at a heightened state of awareness. Over time, a change occurs. To survive a career in corrections, the officer can never show weakness or fear. These human emotions must be locked tightly in a box and hidden deep inside. The correctional officer has only a radio, handcuffs, his or her cunning and, as a last resort their hands as they fulfill the duties of a police officer in a small violent city.

They will spend their entire career outnumbered by a hundred and twenty to one, working in a microcosm of society while enforcing regulations, ensuring the safe and orderly running of their institutions, protecting the inmates in their charge and protecting society from those deemed unfit to remain at large. They are a very special breed indeed.

The following is not a chronological tale, but rather a journey made up of individual moments which have the power, over time, to cause transformation. They are nothing more than silent ripples disturbing the surface of a pond before they are gone forever, important only to those who have spent time in these muddy waters. Argus is just one penitentiary correctional officer, but in some ways he is every penitentiary correctional officer. This is the story of the loss of naiveté and the heavy price it exacts.

Preface

Everyone has a dragon. Most people don't even know it's there. I mean, it never really shows itself to those who live protected orderly lives. Sure, every once in a while someone gets cut off in traffic and they smell the smoke from its nostrils but, they never, ever feel it's soul scorching breath. That privilege is reserved for those who stand on a line and look evil in the eye. For a dragon to get big and mean enough to show out like that, it has to be fed, and fed well.

Dragons are fed in dark places. Places made of steel and concrete, smelling of urine, sweat and fear. Places surrounded by razor wire, fences and gun towers where humanity is confined and lost. In these violent places the social contract has been adulterated creating a different set of rules which normalize the law of the jungle.

Once a dragon grows in you, it becomes part of you. You do not feel it grow. Dragons are insidious and they grow just a little at a time. Like dripping water filling a bucket. Dragons hook their claws deep in your soul. They belong to you for life. You can train your dragon. Manage it, or, you can let it eat you alive. The only way to manage a dragon like *that* is to face the darkness and look it in the eye.

Chapter 1
In peaceful blackness it sleeps

He walks into the city unemployment office. It is one of the many old brick office buildings in downtown Abhaile. It smells of old wood with a hint of mustiness that almost makes a person light headed if they take a full breath. It also smells of desperation in this particular building. There's a window in the partition that separates the lobby from the offices in back. As he enters, the lady behind the window doesn't look up. He's just one of many looking for a job and she'd lost interest long ago in the people who come through that door and their stories. As Argus walks through the doorway, he feels self-conscious in his sweat soaked work shirt and K-Mart work boots. The door closes almost catching his foot and makes a loud bang doing just what he doesn't want done which is to call attention to his arrival. The lobby is sparsely furnished. No comfortable couches here because this isn't a place of comfort. The city has predicted who the clientele will be and know that they won't complain. The furniture consists of several old schoolhouse chairs with desks attached. The kind you'd see in a 1950's era school. Argus isn't the only job hunter in the lobby but he might be one of the luckier ones because he already has a job. Like him, the others are looking for whatever they can get and they look the part. None of the job hunters speak or make eye contact. Under the glare of the sun from the windows and the fluorescent lights lies the shadow of a hint of shame.

He had been a United States Marine. While his service hadn't been extraordinary, he had served and is proud of that. He and Lynn, his wife had made a good life in the Marine Corps. They were young and happy and he'd made good money as an E-5 sergeant with BAQ and COMRATS and to top that off, the Corps had offered him a sizeable bonus to reenlist. They had a little trailer out in town that she'd made a home. He thinks back to those days and asks himself for the thousandth time, "How did I end up back here?"

As he stands in the lobby and looks around the room he feels a slight sadness. This isn't what he had envisioned when he and Lynn had loaded the small rental truck with their belongings to come home after his hitch. Back then, there was still a vision of a bright future in Abhaile for the couple. The last few years of humping furniture day in and day out to scrape together a meager existence where a twenty dollar tip was the mother lode had burned that vision from Argus' mind as surely as a bonfire burns dry wood shavings. Argus' mind goes back to an incident when his First Sergeant had told him, "You Marine, have piss poor planning."

Argus knows now without a doubt that the senior noncom was correct.

Argus had escaped this dreary place when he had enlisted and now he was back. When his hitch was coming to an end, the captain had summoned Argus to his office and asked if he was going to reenlist. He had declined. Argus hadn't been taught to think in terms of career and only knew, he was tired of being away from Lynn on so many deployments. Argus looks back now and realizes how immature his decision had been. So, the life he had left to follow his dream of being a Marine became the plan at the end, to come back home and work in the "family business." Four years had passed since then and in that time the "family business" had gone downhill and had finally closed because his grandmother, the patriarch had passed away. With no other choice, he and his father started their own "family business" but in truth, it wasn't Argus' business at all. From the day he left Camp Lejeune, he was destined to walk through these doors.

No long application or resume' needed here. It's 1989 but the future hasn't caught up with Abhaile, Indiana population 58,475. It's a good place to be from. He takes a pen from the cup and fills out the one page application he's retrieved from the stack on the counter. The information that they want isn't extensive and if Argus is going to be honest with himself his resume' isn't that impressive anyway.

After he turns the form in to the lady at the window she looks at the name and raises a thin painted eyebrow. "Argus Antrim?"

Argus replies, "It's Irish."

Not the first time he has received this reaction. The lady looks back down at her paperwork and says they'll be in touch. Abhaile has a reputation of being a little city with a big city attitude and Argus realizes that he could burst into flames right in front of this woman and she wouldn't care in the slightest. He misses his buddies from the Corps.

As he walks out of the building Argus thinks about the morning he gave Lynn the engagement ring. They were sitting on his parent's couch in the house he'd grown up in. It was early in the morning and everyone else was asleep. The house was quiet as he and Lynn sat on the couch looking at each other. She was beautiful in a tussled sort of way. He'd pulled the ring from the pocket of the gym shorts he was wearing and formally popped the question. He had promised her that she'd never want for anything and he's tried to live up to that promise but hasn't done a very good job at keeping it. A meager salary of $266.54 a week for as many hours as it takes to load that truck and get it unloaded doesn't make you a millionaire. Quitting time is when you are done with the job. There is no insurance and no retirement, period. His wife works as a waitress and caters at night to make extra money. He thinks, "I should have promised her she'd never *have* anything. It would have been more truthful."

He heads back to his truck to start the next job, his pride gone.

As he puts the truck in gear, his thoughts roam to when Lynn told him about the baby. She showed up at the "family business" wearing her waitress uniform and was drop dead gorgeous as usual. She looked at him and said, "Well, I guess you're going to be a daddy" and started crying.

He helped her into an old green vinyl chair by the door. It had a rip in the seat. He hugged her trying to let her know through his embrace that she is the love of his life. The baby was what made him wake up. Not the baby herself, but the situation opened his eyes to where he stood in the "family business." Argus regrets investing his entire savings into starting a business he'll soon leave.

He recalls the first appointment at the OB clinic. The doctor was a good one and Lynn liked him. Because Argus had no insurance, the doctor wanted $750.00 up front before he'd deliver the baby. It might as well have been a million. He approached his father and asked if he would mind if Argus took a loan from the business accounts, repayable with payroll deductions. His father said, "Argus, if you can't find any other way, okay, but I'd like you to find another way."

Argus couldn't take the money now, even if it killed him. He had spent his life chasing his father's approval but he wasn't about to beg. He humbled himself and got a job at night washing dishes at a local motel to make the money. The motel used to be a big deal in Abhaile but had degraded into a seedy overnight joint for truckers and patrons of the lounge that adjoined the dining room. It still had a reputation for its prime rib but that wouldn't draw enough customers to make it a thriving business again.

He worked all day at the "family business" and then rode the one speed bike his brother had put together for him out of spare parts across town and washed dishes until after midnight seven nights a week. Argus was already tired when he tied his apron on and the steam from the dishwasher sapped his strength like a vampire drains the blood of its victims. Argus rode the bicycle because he only had one car, a piss yellow nineteen seventy six Chevy Chevette that rattled when you first started it. The car wasn't much but his wife needed it to go to work. He would endure any hardship to take care of her because he was still a Marine and that's what Marines do, make it work no matter what, but the seed is planted that Lynn deserves much better than this. What he didn't realize was that no matter how hard he worked it wouldn't get any better. Every Marine knows that you can't assault through every ambush. Sometimes the only thing to do is back up and find another way.

Four years later he is leaving the unemployment office. That seed finally matured in an instant. There was nothing extraordinary about this particular job, but he will always remember it. You remember everything about a life choice. You go one way, your world crashes or go the other way and you have the chance to make things right. The job, as usual was taking longer than expected because the home was new construction and the owners didn't want the movers walking across the carpet with the furniture due to the mud. Understandable, but they wouldn't even allow Argus to put runners down to protect the carpet. It was raining and he was soaked and tired. He was tired of working for rich assholes like these people. The owners were taking the furniture at the door which had slowed everything to a crawl. Everything that went downstairs had to be carried around the house and down a muddy bank. He hated these people for the way they are treating him and his crew. Then out of nowhere Lynn showed up at the job site. He looked down from the tailgate and there she was, in the car. She was looking up at him. They had, had dinner plans and she was dressed for those plans. She had her hair and makeup done, ready for an evening with him. As usual, one more sacrifice to add to the hundreds she'd already made for "the business." There was a look in her eyes. The look said, "You're running out of chances buddy. How many sacrifices do you expect?"

She rolled down the window and said, "Get in."

At that moment, he had a choice to make. How many broken

promises did he expect her to accept? Argus couldn't blame her because this is not what he had promised.

Argus came to the realization in a second and looked at his brother. His brother had joined the "family business" a couple of years prior. Argus told his brother, "I've got to go."

His brother looked at him like he was crazy but Argus knew this train had been coming toward him since he had dragged her back to this place. There were only a couple of tiers left to unload anyway and he knew his wife was right. He knew she had justification to feel the way she did and she deserved better than this. Argus had promised her better and he wanted to be the one that provided that for her. Argus had looked back at the yellow moving truck receding in the side mirror of the car and thought, "Why the fuck didn't I reenlist."

He slumped in his seat and wondered if he looked like the failure that he felt he was. Lynn was looking straight ahead, concentrating on driving in the rain. There was no conversation between them as she drove. Argus wasn't sorry about leaving the job because he'd known for a long time that there was no viable future in this business, it was a dead end. At dinner Argus told Lynn, "I know there's no future in moving furniture. I should've reenlisted and stayed in the Corps. I'm leaving the company and doing something else for a living. I don't know what yet, but I shouldn't have come back here."

∞∞∞∞

A few days later, Argus pulls up to the house he grew up in. The house is located "down on the avenues" and the description of the location is indicative of the socioeconomic status of those who live there. The house is not as attractive as it used to be, whether the place has changed for the worse or the fact that it is no longer home, Argus doesn't know. All he knows is that it looks like a piece of rental property now which coincidently, it is. At some point the decision was made to paint the house brown, replacing the original white. It is no longer the cute little house of Argus' memory. It is hard to look at. His father owns several rentals in the neighborhood and this is one of them. The neighborhood was a nice place to raise a family if you had to live here when Argus was growing up but now, you're as likely to run into a meth addict as you are a little old lady carrying groceries into her house. Argus knows that before long, the little old ladies will all be gone leaving the neighborhood to the meth dealers. The house is a small cottage style structure with a front porch. The front porch swing and bushes are as long gone as the nice neighborhood. He follows the broken sidewalk around the house and goes through the gate to the back yard. Argus looks around and thinks, "Sometimes it's painful to go home."

Argus looks at the garage and sees his father standing on a step ladder, painting it once again. He steps up to his father and by the look on his face, company is not what he was expecting or wanting. Argus knows that his father has always used this busy work to get away from it all. Whether the "all" was four kids fighting over a box of cereal or the stack of unpaid bills on the dining room table, this was his escape. It is sort of his hobby. The soft slap of the latex laden brush ceases as his father looks at him.

Argus walks up to the ladder and makes small talk to delay what must be said, "Painting huh?"

His father looks at him and raises his eyebrows then looks at the paint can and then back at Argus. After all the roads he's been down, Argus is still chasing his father's approval but knows there's no way around this conversation. Argus tells him that he is leaving the company. His father is passively surprised but doesn't ask the reason for Argus' decision. He wonders if his father has suspected all along as he asks, "I know you've been unhappy. What are you going to do for a living?"

Argus looks around the yard. It needs to be cut. "I'm not really sure, maybe something in law enforcement or security. I'm not trained for much of anything else."

Argus thinks as he answers, "There aren't many jobs in the civilian world that entail crawling through the bush and calling in high explosive artillery shells."

In true Antrim fashion his father really doesn't have much to say and goes back to painting. Argus says, "Well, I'll see ya tomorrow," turns around and walks away.

∞∞∞∞∞

Argus goes to work like every other morning. He's the first one there, as usual. This annoys him as he looks around the dilapidated office area. It isn't much to look at unless you're fond of scavenged office furniture and a filing system that isn't a system at all. He thinks, "No fucking discipline from anybody."

He misses the Marines as he puts his keys back in his pocket and grabs an assortment of pens off the desk, finding one that works on the third try. He checks the work book and makes the bills of lading out for the day then goes out and starts the trucks to get them warmed up. He cleans some trash out of the cabs and looks in the back to make sure they're clean, then goes back in and finishes his coffee. Today is a day of light deliveries. Pickup here, drop there, local work inside the city. He takes the last drink of his coffee and checks the answering machine for messages. The agent from the unemployment office has left a message and wants Argus to call him.

Later on in the day, he's in between appointments. Driving down a street he's driven down a thousand times before and spots a payphone. He thinks, "Stop and call, why not. It's time to move on."

The phone is answered almost immediately by Miss Eyebrow, "Unemployment Office, may I help you?"

Argus gives her his name and is connected with the agent working on his job search.

The agent says, "Yeah, I've got you an interview."

He is excited but controls himself. The agent asks why he's not more excited. Argus guesses that the composed response is not what the agent is used too. The agent tells him it's with a contract security company and the rate is ten dollars per hour. Is he interested?

"Absolutely," Argus replies.

This is almost double what he is making with the "family business." The agent gives him the interview information. It's an hour drive to the place which won't be a problem now that Argus has been able to get himself a small pickup truck on his salary. Nothing special but it is better than a bicycle. This is totally due to Lynn's ability to stretch every penny to its limit. It is one of her many talents. This job will give them some breathing room and he is excited to share the news with Lynn. He starts to see a light at the end of the tunnel.

∞∞∞∞

The drive to the ammunition plant is indeed a long one. The route takes Argus out of the city of Abhaile and north for thirty miles along a two lane highway which winds through rural Indiana. The road was a main thoroughfare at one time but that time has long past. The grass along the side of the road is high and the pavement is cracked as Argus presses the gas pedal to get there on time. He is nervous and he doesn't want to be late. Argus hates to be late. He doesn't have much interviewing experience and no security experience. He makes the turn off the highway and travels along an old black topped lane for a quarter mile. He is almost to the guard house at the end of a long driveway, when a guard steps out. The guard is well armed with an M-16 A1 rifle and a 38 caliber revolver which gives Argus a boost of confidence as he thinks, "Well at least I'll be familiar with the weapons they issue."

The guard isn't very squared away and wouldn't come close to passing a Marine Corps inspection but he seems like he's on his job. Argus stops his truck and puts it in park as the guard steps up to his driver's side window. His eyes take a tour of the cab and bed of Argus' truck before asking, "Can I help you?"

Argus smiles at the guard. "Hi, uh, my name is Argus Antrim. I have an appointment for an interview."

The guard checks his clip board after getting Argus' driver's license and makes him sign in. The guard leans on the window sill of Argus' truck and looks down the lane toward the inside of the facility. "You're going to want to follow this road all the way until you see a three story building. It's the only building with more than one floor on the place. Pull into the parking lot and go to door 107. I'll tell the sergeant you're on the way."

Argus pulls away and follows the directions the guard has given him. On the way, Argus takes in the scenery of the place and doesn't know what to think. The place looks abandoned with old rusting manufacturing warehouses, ammunition bunkers with weeds in front of the doors and some of the roads are not paved. Not what you'd call a thriving place to work, but Argus isn't picky at this point. The whole place is surrounded by a chain link fence at least twelve foot high. Argus looks toward the North and notices a man in the distance jogging. The man is wearing shorts and a t-shirt. He is also wearing a gas mask. Argus pulls up to the building and parks. When he gets to the door, he's met by a sergeant holding the door open. He wears a white shirt with the sergeant insignia and is pretty squared away. Shirt pressed and shoes shined. He follows the sergeant up to the second floor. On the way, the sergeant is friendly and makes small talk while Argus is sweating in his dress clothes.

The Captain enters the room and introduces himself as Captain Lakes. He is tall and has the lean and athletic physique of a basketball player. He has a kindly demeanor which is relaxed and self-assured. Argus likes him immediately and perceives that he's comfortable in his role as a Captain. The interview questions are mostly run of the mill. Captain Lakes focuses on Argus' experience or lack thereof. He questions him at length regarding his military service and weighs each of his answers carefully. This is something Argus takes notice of. It occurs to Argus that his lack of experience is tipping the scales against him. He feels like a general laborer posing as something else in a suit.

The Captain asks why he should hire him. "What can you bring to the company?"

This is a hard question for Argus. He doesn't have much to answer with but he needs this job. Simply needs it, "I know I don't have much experience but, I know I can do a good job for you if you'll just give me a chance."

This is as close to begging as he can come to without getting on his knees and grabbing the Captain's legs.

Argus thinks, "Proud Marine to this."

Argus is glad there are no mirrors in here. He couldn't bear the thought of looking in one right now. The Captain tells him that he thinks he might do a good job and asks if there is anything in his past that would stop him from getting a security clearance. Argus sits up straight in his chair. "No, nothing. I had a clearance in the Marines."

Argus can't tell if the Captain is being sincere or just letting him down easy. The smell of desperation is thick in the room. The Captain concludes the interview by standing up and thanking Argus for his time. Argus shakes his hand like you're supposed to do and thanks him as well, adding one last, "I really think I could do a good job for you."

Captain Lakes tells him that they'll contact him and let him know. He isn't sure how it went and he doesn't want to hope. The thought of loading and unloading a truck until he's too old to do it anymore depresses him. It is a longer ride home.

∞∞∞∞

It only takes a few days for him to receive the call. They've decided to give him a chance and Argus is ecstatic. The next guard class begins in two weeks and will last a total of six weeks of onsite training. If he passes the training, he will be assigned to a shift. Lynn is very happy when Argus gives her the news and throws her arms around his neck and kisses him. He wants her to be proud of him. He also wants to be proud of himself again. Since returning to Abhaile, Argus has been on a slippery slope carrying him slowly away from that feeling. As he stands in the kitchen, Argus thinks back to a job he did for his old newspaper route manager. The truck was loaded and unloaded as usual with no damages.

The newspaper route manager told him that he did a great job. Then he said, "So this is what you're doing now huh? Strong back, weak mind?"

It is an insult he would always remember. Argus didn't set him straight because the customer is always right.

He goes to work as usual the next day and his father shows up shortly after Argus arrives but none of the other employees have arrived yet. The office is quiet which intensifies the tension between the two. Argus tells his father about landing the job and that he'll stay on part time to help out. His father looks at him with a look of resignation and walks out the door to check on the trucks. Argus can tell that he's not looking for company while he does this. The helpers and his brothers arrive and the work plan for the day is formulated. After fifteen minutes of bitching about the assignments, the trucks leave the parking lot and Argus knows he has left the fold. He can't help but think that he left a long time ago and should never have returned.

∞∞∞∞

He reports for training at the same building he interviewed in. He's excited about the new challenge and the chance to move forward. This will be something better for him, his wife and daughter. There are a dozen potential guards sitting at the tables in the room. Argus looks around as do the others and nods are exchanged. The Training Officer, Mr. Baxter enters the room and introduces himself. He is a man of medium height and build with a boisterous personality. He is likeable and a skilled speaker, presenting the material in a way that confirms his command of the subject matter. He is the only member of the security cadre who doesn't wear a uniform.

On this first day, the administrative tasks are to be completed. Uniform issue, paperwork and an overview of the reason for the guard force. The facility used to manufacture TNT back in the day but these processes were discontinued long ago. Now, the plant is solely staffed by an administrative cadre and a guard force. All maintenance tasks and support functions are performed by an army of contractors who enter and leave the plant daily for this purpose. Some of the land is leased to farmers as tillable farmland. The sole mission of the security complement is facility security, access control and guarding the highly lethal substances stored there. To reinforce the importance of this mission a movie is shown about what he will be guarding. The movie shows the death of a horse exposed to a minute amount of the substance. It is sobering and painful for Argus to watch. It is meant to inform beyond the shadow of a doubt what the guards will be dealing with. Argus already knows because he was trained in the Marine Corps to direct artillery rounds on target loaded with this substance.

∞∞∞∞

The bags are big OD green monsters. Something you'd carry football equipment in. They are waiting on the tables when the recruits arrive for training. The training officer makes sure each guard gets the proper bag. Clothing sizes were obtained the first day of training to help with this issue. Inside the bags are several items, all made of thick rubber. A full length apron that ties in the back, boots that come to just below the knee, rubber gloves reaching almost to the elbow and an M-17A1 gas mask with hood. Inside the gas mask carrier are two atropine and two pralidoxime auto injectors. These are to be self-administered in case of exposure. Death is almost certain, but with the medications, you can function longer. Argus thinks, "Expendable for the mission once again."

The guards are taught to don the equipment efficiently and the method for staging it in the bag to rapidly put it on. The standard for successfully passing this test is to put the equipment on and decontaminate a person with chlorine bleach in five minutes or less. Argus thinks this is ludicrous and can't see how it can be done, but then a guard from the force does just that in a demonstration. Mr. Baxter looks at the class. "These bags will be with you wherever you go. No one is to ever be without your bag. Consider this the cardinal rule gentlemen."

The guard class gives donning the equipment a try, with all initial attempts ending in abysmal failure. This worries Argus. Mr. Baxter informs the class that whenever he yells, "gas", the guards are to don the equipment. Making the time cutoff is mandatory to maintain employment. They have six weeks to get it right.

The rifle range is simply an area in a secluded part of the plant. No crosswind flags and range markers like he is used too. Argus shot at a range of five hundred meters in the Marines and qualified expert each year. Today he'll shoot at fifty meters with the same type of weapon. He smiles as he lies down on the soft earth because this is his wheel house. The class is just zeroing the rifles in and qualifying with one magazine of 30 rounds in the prone position. Not surprisingly, he shoots a perfect score and the grouping is tight. Argus knows the M-16A1 like he knows his hand. The weapon feels like an old friend in his hands. With each pull of the trigger, the rifle dances against his shoulder and the sights jump and fall right back onto the target. His body positioning is flawless which makes all the difference.

He thinks back to when he hunted squirrels as a teenager. His rule was head shots or nothing. The goal wasn't to get the bag limit of five squirrels, the goal was the pleasure of the stalk. His marksmanship skills were honed in the forests surrounding his hometown. He was always at peace, alone in these places and looked forward to August each year and the start of squirrel season. On opening day, Argus would rise early and go to a patch of woods where he could find a good hardwood tree then he would become a ghost and wait. His rifle was a Ruger 10/22 with a telescopic sight. He would often give the squirrels to his grandmother when he hunted in the woods behind her house. She, in turn would make him breakfast, squirrel or no squirrel. She made delicious eggs and bacon. Argus can still recall the smell of the meal mixed with a slight tang of cigarette smoke and coffee. It is a good memory that he will always cherish.

The next phase of qualification is the 38 caliber revolver. The class shoots standing, kneeling and off hand. Once again, he does very well. He is well acquainted with the revolver and has always been an excellent shot. As a teenager, he hunted raccoon at the edges of the corn fields near his home town at night. He would shine his headlamp at the treed animal and shoot it between the eyes. They always looked at his light unless it was a full moon. He never hunted on a full moon. As a lifelong hunter, Argus was very careful never to wound an animal. If he didn't have a shot, he didn't pull the trigger. He hunted with a Harrington Richardson nine shot revolver in 22 caliber. The gun was one of two notable gifts from his father. Qualification day has been cool and windy but not uncomfortable. He knows winter is not far off.

He picks up the brass shell casings from his qualification and feels a sense of pride again.

∞∞∞∞

He is still in training. He has been assigned to one of the guard shifts to shadow the guards and observe. The twelve hour shifts are broken up into three hour increments totaling four different assignments during the shift. These changes are designed to keep the guards alert because routine breeds complacency. The busiest increment, inner facility patrol consists of patrolling the buildings and physically walking through the administrative building to check each office door. Argus learns that some of the guards are superstitious and believe the administrative building is haunted. A few years prior, a guard who was being disciplined, pulled his side arm and killed several people in the building before he was shot by the sergeant who had first greeted Argus. Some guards think that the ghosts of the dead still remain in the administrative building and are scared to walk through it but he is not afraid of ghosts. His grandmother used to say, "Don't fear the dead, fear the living."

As he and his partner patrol the building, the phones in the offices begin to ring. He learns later that this is a game played by the officer in the radio room to mess with the guard patrolling the building. At every building, before entering, the guards must radio their position to the radio room. He finds this amusing. Argus likes a good practical joke but the female guard he is with does not. She is one of the ones afraid of the building.

The next increment is the ready reaction force. This duty is the hardest for Argus because he likes to stay busy. A contingent of guards sits in a break room in case a guard needs backup on one of the other patrols. Argus doesn't play cards or have a book to read and, he is tired. He needs to move, not sit. He is glad when the three hours are complete. Next, he is assigned to the radio room with an officer and learns the radio protocol. He finds this three hour stretch interesting and the fact that he can type is a welcome surprise for the radio room guard. He has Argus type the shift report from the shift before. It's an old electric typewriter and he doesn't type fast. This takes up a lot of the three hour stretch. The guard lets him perform the radio checks with the patrolling units and log everything in a log book. Argus decides that he likes the radio room because it is busy and he likes busy.

The final three hours are spent patrolling the fence line and checking gates. He likes this duty as well. The guard he is with is a middle aged man and has been with the company for a long time. He has all the ear marks of a man who has been riding in a patrol vehicle for years. He is overweight and tired. The guard tells him, "We can do this how they taught you, or we can do it the smart way."

This sets off alarm bells for Argus, but he is just a trainee. Argus tells the guard to show him how he does it. The way Argus was trained is to patrol the fence line looking for cuts or holes. When you arrive at a gate, you get out of the vehicle and physically touch the lock, pull it and shake the chain. That's the right way. The way this guard does it, is pull up to the gate, shine the headlights on it and, that's it. No pull, no shake, no touch.

Every security procedure has a way for the supervisor to check if it's being done correctly. This procedure is no different. The way the supervisor audits the patrol is by affixing a red padlock to the gate on or near the chain. When a guard finds a red lock, he must radio the supervisor who has the key. A simple procedure really if you're doing your job. The guard is not and he has Argus with him. The red lock is missed completely. The guard is in trouble and even though Argus is just a trainee and not responsible, he is pissed that he was a part of it. It's a valuable lesson learned. He decides, no matter what the rule, he'll follow it to the letter.

Opening and closing the guard house is also part of the perimeter patrol. It is a small ten by ten foot shack with a built in counter, a chair and a bathroom. Another guard is assigned to train Argus in gatehouse operations to check in contractors and visitors to the plant. This will be part of his duties when he does get assigned to a shift. The counter is waist high and made of Formica and plywood. From the counter to the ceiling are windows which could use a sound cleaning. It is made of old wood construction dating to the Korean War probably. The guard who is training him is squared away and a big guy. He is all business, and interested in training Argus the right way. The guard shows him all of the logs and different forms to be filled out before entry into the plant. Different forms for visitors and contractors and cursory inspections of vehicles as they enter. Argus learns that seat belts must be worn on the plant unless the vehicle doesn't have any. Employees have stickers for their vehicles and identification badges.

He practices getting all of the vehicle and personal information from each visitor and contractor respectively. The line to get into the plant

14

grows because he isn't efficient yet and there are a myriad of forms he has to learn. Each contractor must sign a log book. This is because everyone must be accounted for on the plant. The guard explains that this is in case of an emergency and possible evacuation. There are only two gates to gain access to the plant. The front and the back gate. There are also static access points which must maintain accountability for "hot work" at various maintenance sites throughout the facility. Any work involving an open flame must be compartmentalized and controlled. This is an old TNT plant and there is still residue present. The risk of explosion still exists.

∞∞∞∞

Argus has completed training and has done very well. He has been assigned to D-Shift. The first day on shift, to his surprise, the shift supervisor wants to confirm that Argus can don the protective gear. Although it is just due diligence on the part of the supervisor, this annoys Argus. He thought since he had passed the training, there shouldn't be a need to test him again. As it turns out, it takes him two tries to make the time limit. Argus thinks as he wipes the sweat from his brow, "This is something I'll have to keep practicing."

The guard testing him provides valuable pointers on how to stage the gear in the bag to which Argus is grateful. He is wringing wet with sweat by the time the testing is completed. It will be a long twelve hours.

After he's proven himself with the gear, the shift supervisor gives him a set of keys and instructs him to take a patrol vehicle out and learn the interior roads of the plant because it is expansive. The patrol vehicles are old, white pickup trucks with a double light bar on the top. Argus gets in the truck and turns the key. It starts with a low throated rumble and a cloud of blue smoke. He puts the truck in gear and signs on the radio as vehicle patrol number seven which is the number on the side of the truck. He decides to approach this task in a grid pattern and guides the truck in the direction of the South corner of the facility. Argus learns quickly to notice what intersection he is located at or has just passed when the first radio check is announced. The radio room calls Argus, "Central to Patrol Seven, what is your position?"

Argus looks around for any kind of road sign to tell him where he is located but there isn't any close enough to read. He asks the radio room to standby as he presses the gas pedal. The radio room officer

15

knows what has happened and presses the rookie for a location. He has to hurry to an intersection. He calls his location in and pictures the radio operator laughing. He smiles and is glad they are messing with him. He knows this means they already like him.

∞∞∞∞

He has been on the job for a few months and has settled in to the shift. It is night shift and he has been paired with a female guard. They are patrolling the outlying sheds in the area of the fields the farmers use for tillable ground. They spot a door ajar. The only lights are the overheads on the vehicle and the headlights which do a poor job of piercing the inky blackness. The area of the fields is deserted and dark at night. His partner is experienced but this is out of the ordinary. She calls it in to the radio room and announces a foot patrol to investigate. They both exit the truck and walk toward the shed. When they near the building his partner covers him while Argus walks up to the door of the shed from the side. As he nears, a gust of wind catches the door, moving it with a rusty creak. His rifle is held at low cover as he looks back at his partner. She has a worried look in her eyes but he is smiling. He eases the door open, staying behind the door. The shed is empty. Just a door left unlatched. This is the most excitement he has had in months.

∞∞∞∞

He is working as the radio operator on the first three hour increment of the shift. Argus pulls this duty regularly because he can type halfway efficiently. The radio operator at the first of the shift types the blotter from the previous shift. This is not sought after duty in the guard force but Argus goes throughout his duties in this post with a good attitude. He is happy to have the job. The telephone rings on an outside line and he answers it, "Initium Army Ammunition Plant. Officer Antrim, may I help you?"

The person on the other end of the line says, "Listen up asshole, there's a bomb. It's going to go off soon."

This is followed by a disclaimer, "This has been a test exercise message."

Mr. Baxter has played a recorded message to test the bomb threat protocol. Argus has filled out the form with all the required information correctly and hits the red button located on the wall for emergencies. This is called the "panic button."

The shift supervisor arrives almost instantly from his office down the short hallway. "What's going on Antrim?"

Argus gives him the form and smiles triumphantly. "It was a test exercise message from Mr. Baxter."

The supervisor smiles and tells him he did exactly what he was supposed to do. Argus is wide awake now.

The lift station is where the sewage goes from the plant. It is the only check that must be performed off site. It is a short drive down the highway which seems like miles when you're half asleep at the end of the shift. This check is performed once every twenty four hours at the end of the midnight to noon shift. The shifts run from midnight to noon and noon to midnight. The schedule rotation is four days on, three days off. Then three days on, four days off. Every week, the guards switch from nights to days and back to nights. Argus and his partner are tasked with this check. They call the radio room and announce the beginning of this inspection and that they will be off the plant property. A short drive later and they are on the dirt road to the lift station. The sun seems particularly bright today and Argus has to squint. He knows this is just fatigue and maybe a little eye strain. He makes a note to buy some sunglasses.

They pull up to the lift station and circle the truck around the small dirt turn around, grown up with weeds except where the tires of various patrol vehicles regularly mash them down. Argus looks over at the station building. It is a small white elevated building with a gated door. The building is dirty, the white color only serving to showcase this fact. They exit the vehicle and check the chain on the gate looking for any suspicious activity. There is a large field of what looks like gray mud approximately thirty yards at its widest point. This is the sewage after it has been "lifted" through the soil. He notices, to his amusement, a few tomato plants growing in the middle of the gray mud and thinks, "No matter what kind of shit you go through, you can still grow."

Argus passes on picking the tomatoes. It's amazing what becomes amusing when you're dead tired.

∞∞∞∞∞

The season is late summer and the middle of the night. He has been on a regular shift for about nine months and has begun to feel the beginnings of brain damage from the boredom. Argus and his partner are patrolling the inner perimeter of the plant. The word abandoned truly fits this place at this hour. They might as well be patrolling the moon. Argus looks to his left through the driver's side window of the truck at the deer just standing and looking at his vehicle as he rolls by so close he could just about reach out and touch them. The deer are safe inside the fence and they know it. There is no hunting allowed on the plant, period. Argus speaks to them as if they might answer but they don't understand or seem to care what he's saying.

The giant tractors stand silent in the fields. They are huge machines with two large wheels at each corner of the tractor designed to pull great loads without effort. As part of his duties, Argus can, at his discretion check the tractors for keys in the ignitions. It is a regulation that all keys must be removed from the tractors by the farmers so no one can use the tractor to breach the perimeter fence. He thinks, "Why not take a walk."

Argus parks the vehicle at the edge of the field and walks out to where two tractors are parked. The ground is rough having been plowed and turned. His partner stays in the truck because he's not interested in taking a walk. He reaches the first tractor and climbs the ladder to get into the cab, seeing a set of keys hanging from the ignition. Argus pulls the keys free and sticks them in his pocket. The process is repeated for the second tractor with the same results. He gets back to the truck and drives to headquarters. He turns the keys in to the supervisor with a description of both tractors and location. His supervisor looks surprised. Most guards are not interested in walking across a field in the middle of the night. The farmers will have to retrieve the keys from the shift supervisor in the morning. This is an inconvenience for the farmers. They may be upset, but they can't argue with the rule.

∞∞∞∞

Argus arrives for his shift as usual at a little before noon to a room full of guards partaking in the usual pre-shift banter and ribbing. All the guards line up in formation for uniform inspection and to receive the shift briefing. After the briefing, the guards line up at the armory to receive their weapons and ammunition. Ammunition for the rifle magazines and pistol are stored in wooden blocks. This makes it easier to count the rounds in and out. Argus loads his rifle magazine and inserts the magazine into his rifle. He loads his 38 revolver and holsters the weapon before grabbing two speed loaders for the pistol and three magazines for the rifle. Argus is assigned to a static post in charge of entry to a hot work. He is given a log book and location of the hot work. One of the ready room guards drives him to the post and drops him off. The work cannot start until a guard is on duty.

He arrives and checks each worker into the area, making notations of workers in and out. He has to know the exact number of workers in the area at all times. As he makes the first notation in the log, Argus realizes he has made a bonehead mistake by forgetting his watch at home. Every time a worker goes in or out, Argus has to call the radio room for a time hack. This gets old quickly for Argus and the radio room operator. Before long the radio room guard realizes what has happened. Not the first time apparently, so he sends his personal watch out to Argus to use while he is on this post. Argus considers the radio room officer a friend after this gesture. Argus does not call many people "friend."

∞∞∞∞

The room is dark and cool. So dark he can barely see his hand in front of his face. It is just an eight by ten room located in his basement which was an old pantry Lynn had converted into a bedroom by just adding a bed and not much else. Someplace to sleep during the day so his wife can actually live life like a normal human being without waking him. They've converted this room into his bedroom for the midnight to noon shifts. Four days of twelve long hours on and twelve short hours off with an hour drive each way, every day.

That's the thing about shift work. You're separated from the normal rhythm of life. Argus has become accustomed to this schedule, but the circadian clock never fully adjusts. Argus fights constant fatigue that he pushes himself through to support his family. He will have to leave by 10:30 pm to make guard muster so Lynn gently wakes him at around 8:00 pm to get ready. This gives him barely six hours of broken sleep between shifts. Argus looks at his boots, trying to will himself to put them on and thinks, "It's worth it to spend a little time with Lynn and Olivia."

He eats a meal she has prepared. She does her best to support him and take care of him. She is a good wife. All too soon, it's time to head out. He kisses her goodbye and makes sure she locks the door behind him. He gets in his truck and starts it up with one last glance at the

19

front door. Argus puts the truck in gear and takes off making one circle of the block to make sure no scumbags are hanging out in the neighborhood. Not that he could do anything about it. This just makes him feel better. He gets on the highway and heads north for another shift on the moon. Twelve hours later and he's heading home. The world safe for one more day from a poison someone created. He is bleary eyed and has adopted the habit of buying a soda from the machine in the break room for the ride home. He holds it against the back of his neck until it gets warm, then he drinks it. The cold bites his skin. This keeps him alert on the drive. He pulls up in front of the house Lynn has made a home, gets out of his truck, showers, eats and heads back to the basement. Like a vampire retiring to his native earth, separated from the living for three more days.

∞∞∞∞

The patrol vehicle bounces down one of the many dirt roads on the facility. He and his partner, Jim Kettle have drawn the inner perimeter tour for the first three hour slot. Jim is driving the vehicle and Argus is riding shotgun in the passenger seat. Although the shift is just starting Argus is already tired. This shift is the last night of a four day stretch. Midnight to noon. The sound of the motor is background noise for his thoughts. Argus and Jim do not speak, both preferring to fill the space in the cab with their personal thoughts. Argus knows his partner is tired too. They drive for miles like this round and round, watching for suspicious activity. The windows are down so they can stay alert. It is September and there is a chill in the air which is not unpleasant. The dirt roads are anything but smooth and the gentle rocking of the truck causes Argus to nod off. "Holy shit! Stop the truck, I've got to stretch."

His partner stops the truck and Argus gets out. He walks around and shakes his head like a dog thinking, "I definitely need some coffee, no make that a lot of coffee."

He steps to the back of the truck and takes a leak. They're in a deserted area of the plant. No one to see but the deer and they're guilty of the same thing. Argus has been on "D" shift for eleven months. The shifts started running together months ago. He's still grateful for the job because it has given him and his family a leg up. The money is good for the area and there are actually benefits with this company. Argus walks back to the passenger's door and gets back in the truck. He looks over at Jim and sees that he is looking at him with eyebrows raised as he asks, "You get any sleep at all Argus. You look like shit."

They have become friends over the many months. He tells his partner, "I'm going brain dead in this place."

Jim is just a little older than he is, both guards being in their late twenties. They take off again and patrol the abandoned ammunition plant as Argus works on the problem of staying awake for the next twelve hours. Jim says, "I know how you feel brother. I'm tired as hell too."

He doesn't look at Argus but just concentrates on the windshield. Argus can sense some hesitancy in the silence. He looks at his friend and asks, "You got something on your mind?"

Jim turns toward Argus with a grin. "I don't know if you'd be interested but, I've got this uncle. He works at Tarragon Penitentiary in town."

Argus knows where the place is. He'd delivered a copying machine to the Education Department when he was still moving furniture. Jim continues with the recruiting pitch, "They're having a big hiring push and are looking for correctional officers. I think you'd be good at it, Argus."

Argus has never even been inside a jail before and in the penitentiary only once. He has absolutely no experience and asks his partner, "What about you?"

Jim laughs, "No man, not my bag but you ought to apply. I'll see if you can use my uncle as a reference. It's a steady job. Good career if you can get your foot in the door."

Argus doesn't think in those terms. But if the pay is better, he's interested. The rest of the shift is as uneventful as the first. His thoughts are consumed with this new opportunity. It takes discipline to follow the security protocols in a place like this where nothing ever happens until it does. So, Argus dots his "I's" and crosses his "T's." Grabs the lock and always shakes the chain.

∞∞∞∞

A search in the telephone book and one phone call. That's all it took. Now Argus is looking at an application the size of a short novel. It came in the mail in a manila envelope with a return envelope included, all the way from the Maximum Security Penitentiary Tarragon, Abhaile, Indiana. He sits down to fill it out at the small Duncan Fife dining room table he'd bought on a moving job for his wife. They want, simply put, every aspect of his life from graduating high school until the present moment written down on the provided pages. Argus sits next to a twelve inch pile of personal records to provide his financial history, work history, past residences, high school diploma, marriage license, birth certificate and DD-214. His military service information to include every country he visited while in the Marines. Does he still maintain contact with anyone from those countries? Has he ever declared bankruptcy? Argus looks at the application and realizes, he'll have to prove his whole life.

His wife helps him because she's much more organized than he is. It's one of her many gifts. He fills the application out by hand in black ink. No other color allowed but black. Argus does this carefully because he only has one copy of the application. It takes all of the three days he has off work to get it filled out. He drops it by the post office and tells the clerk he'd like someone to sign for it when it gets there. The mail clerk looks at Argus and smirks before he sends it, certified, signature receipt. It costs Argus close to ten dollars but the extra money is worth it. Argus takes a deep breath because he realizes how big this is. Argus has learned that the starting pay for a correctional officer makes the penitentiary one of the highest paying employers in his hometown besides the college or the hospitals. He's not a college graduate or a doctor so he'll take the one that's left.

∞∞∞∞

The conference table is long and polished to a glassy shine. It is a heavy wooden one made of oak or mahogany. Argus is glad he doesn't have to load it on a truck. The table has twenty chairs around it. Nice, upholstered, comfortable chairs on wheels. The room is expansive with plaques and pictures of the penitentiary, group photos of correctional officers in uniform and men in suits. A flag stands in each corner. He wears the same suit and tie to this interview that he wore to the interview for the ammunition plant. He only has one. It's a pinstripe, conservative with wing tip dress shoes. The room is cool but he is sweating. This is the first of two interviews he'll have to complete before they'll make their decision. This is the panel interview. He has never taken part in an interview like this and he's uneasy. He enters the room and is directed to a chair at the close end of the table. At the far end on both sides sit a psychologist, an associate warden and a woman from the Personnel Office. Sitting directly opposite Argus at the other end of the table is a man in a white shirt with lieutenant insignia on his collar. The woman from the Personnel Office is friendly and greets Argus. She introduces the members of the panel who nod at him as they're introduced. They thank him for joining them and look at him inquisitively with friendly eyes and smiling faces.

That is, all except the lieutenant. Argus has seen those eyes before. He had a good friend in high school and had met his friend's father only once. The man had been a foreman in the construction shops at the penitentiary. He was a big, solidly built man and he had those eyes. They were hard and direct with a shine to them that barely concealed something smoldering beneath the surface. His friend's father had barely spoken to Argus when they met. He was working on something and wasn't looking for company. It was obvious he wanted to be left alone. The lieutenant is using those same eyes to size him up. He had never thought of himself as small, but at five foot six and a hundred and seventy pounds he isn't a big man by any means. This lieutenant is doing the math. Was he cut out for the penitentiary? Could the lieutenant trust him with his life? He finds that he cannot hold the lieutenant's gaze. His eyes are cold. The lieutenant is a serious man whose eyes have seen too much. Argus' drill instructors had been Vietnam Veterans. They also had those eyes.

The panelists take turns asking standard interview questions. "Tell us about yourself. What is your greatest strength and weakness? What would you do if you caught a co-worker peddling contraband to inmates? Why should we hire you?"

Predictable questions easily rehearsed. Argus catches himself looking up at the ceiling for the answer to each question as if the perfect answer was up there, somewhere. They see that he recognizes this and find it amusing. He feels like an idiot and makes a mental note not to do it again. The lieutenant goes last. He asks only one question as he looks at Argus directly with those eyes. "Mr. Antrim, what would you do if an inmate had me cornered in a housing unit and was holding a mop ringer like a baseball bat and was going to cave my head in with it?"

There is no bullshitting this. All of a sudden, the reality of where he is sitting becomes apparent. He swallows the dryness in his throat and replies, "Well, first I would yell at the inmate and make verbal contact. Try to get his attention off of you."

"Okay," the lieutenant says, "What if he's intent on taking my head off and comes at me?"

He knows what the lieutenant is looking for, but there's a

psychologist at the table. It's a tight rope.

"Well, I would take the inmate down. I'd tackle him." Argus quickly adds, "But only as a last resort."

The lieutenant seems satisfied. The psychologist nods and makes a notation and that's it. The interview is over as quickly as it had begun. The panel thanks him for coming in and shakes his hand. Argus thanks them for the opportunity to interview. The woman from Personnel escorts him out and says she'll be in touch. He thanks her again. He walks out to his truck, gets in, starts it up and thinks as he breathes the first relaxed breath he's taken in an hour, "A mop wringer? What the fuck."

∞∞∞∞

The office is much smaller than the large conference room the panel interview was held in. He supposes that someone is letting the investigator use their office for this interview. Some of the same pictures adorn these walls as the conference room but there isn't much else on the walls. No personal effects or pictures on the desk besides a computer with not much else other than a stapler and piles of paperwork indicating someone had a lot of work on their plate. He doesn't notice these things. His attention is on the investigator and the file he has open in front of him. Argus is nervous. This is the integrity interview and the place where he will bare his soul. The investigator has investigated every piece of information Argus had provided in his application. He had interviewed each reference, his neighbors and co-workers. His financial records have also been reviewed. The investigator is well dressed in a suit but he looks tired. He is probably mid-forties. Well-groomed but his shoulders slump. He has the mannerisms of a man who has put in a lot of hours on the road. A big hiring push means more work for the background investigator.

The one thing Argus has to remember is that the investigator knows the answer to every question he will be asking. Total honesty, no matter how brutal or embarrassing is the only way to get through. The investigator asks his questions with several points needing to be expanded upon.

"I see you've got a lot of traffic violations relating to being a motor carrier. Care to tell me about that?" the investigator asks.

So, Argus explains to the investigator that when he and his father started his father's business, to get the permits, they had to have customers willing to say they provided a good service. To get the statements, they had to operate without the permits. It was a catch twenty two. When the state police caught him operating, they wrote the ticket. The investigator seems satisfied with this answer. He continues answering questions and expanding on facts for the investigator for what seems like hours. Confessing all of your sins causes time to slow. Right now in this office, a minute has become an hour. He doesn't omit anything. He expands on every fact. He knows the investigator is waiting for a lie but he will not get it from Argus.

Then the final question "Is there anything that you can think of that you've not provided information on in your application?"

How could he answer this question with certainty? Argus racks his brain trying to think of anything he'd missed. Did the investigator know about the Jesus figurine he had stolen from the fifth grade teacher's desk? He decided to step off the cliff. "No. I can't think of anything."

He waits. The investigator looks at him for a second, and then he stands and puts out his hand. The interview is over. The investigator thanks him for coming in and says, "Someone will be in touch."

Argus is escorted out again and walks to his truck. He is completely drained. Argus accepts the fact he has done his best. It will either happen or it won't. He decides not to want it too much.

∞∞∞∞∞

He looks at the cake and smiles. Argus thinks, "Somebody's idea of a joke."

The cake is chocolate with white frosting. There is a cartoon picture made of icing depicting a man with his pants sagging below his butt. The caption reads, "Good luck in prison." Two weeks before tonight, the lady from the penitentiary had called and offered him a position. Argus wasted no time in accepting. The money was a ten thousand dollar a year pay increase. That was just at the base pay rate. Who knew how much overtime he could get. He is overjoyed and notified the security company management of his good fortune by submitting his two week notice.

He has been with these people on D-Shift for a year. They accepted him early on and he has made friends here. He showed up and did the job and they know he is dependable. Argus wasn't expecting it but for his final shift, his friends have planned a surprise party. The shift is, as usual, uneventful. Required patrols are completed and security checks are made. During the three hour increment when Argus is stationed in the break room, the cake is brought out. All planned out so everyone can share in his going away. This makes him feel good. Everyone likes to think they are valued by the people they work with. As noon rolls around and the shift change is completed Argus feels a little sadness at leaving the people here. This is what he has known for a year. The unknown is no longer abstract, but looms at the doorway. He never thought about being a correctional officer. He doesn't think that anyone dreams of being one. Hell, he doesn't even know what the job entails specifically. He's excited about the money, that's all. His dream was to be a Marine. He made the team and then left.

He thinks, "You can't change the past so you keep moving forward."

That's exactly what he'll do. Move forward, travel light and face whatever comes, for his wife and kid. He gets in his truck and leaves the plant for the last time with a cold soda pressed against the back of his neck.

∞∞∞∞∞

He is waiting just inside the main doorway to the Staff Training Center. The surroundings are looking more familiar to him, this being the third time he has been in this place. While still nervous, the angst has left him. He has crossed the first hurdles to making the team and gotten his foot in the door. Argus plans on keeping it there. There are three other new hires standing with him. They are all taller than he is by at least two inches and outweigh him by ten pounds. All are athletic. He realizes he is the runt of the group as he thinks to himself, "Only four. Just four recruits out of how many interviews?"

This could be good or bad. Good if the job is sought after and he and the others are the cream of the crop but bad if they were the only ones crazy enough to accept the job. He shrugs and thinks, "The money is too good to second guess. Time will tell I suppose."

While they are standing there, a correctional officer enters wearing a side arm. He goes up the stairs, looks around and then goes downstairs. In a short time, he returns. He looks them over but doesn't speak. Just nods and walks past. He exits, gets in his patrol vehicle parked just outside and drives off. The lady from the Personnel Office comes out of her office and introduces herself, "Come with me gentlemen. My name is Jenny Phan. We're going to get you on board today."

26

She ushers the four into the large conference room and shows everyone where to sit. The table is not so imposing to him now. On the table are four stacks of paperwork. Each stack is to be filled out by the numbers as she guides the new hires through them. Before starting the process, she gives the group instructions, "Don't get ahead or behind. Work on the form I have in my hand. Use black ink only."

She makes sure of this by providing the pens. It is a lengthy, tedious process that takes almost two hours.

On boarding is extensive and as Argus learns on day one, the Agency loves paperwork. Finally, the last sheet of paper is completed. The new hires will be required to purchase their uniforms. The rookies are given general guidelines as to what to buy. White long sleeved dress shirt or light blue, short sleeve dress shirt. Navy blue-clip on tie for the long-sleeved shirt. No tie with the short sleeve. Grey polyester trousers, a black leather belt and black boots. They are given name tags that hook to the pocket of the shirt. They are also given small daily planners and white pocket protectors. She recommends JC Penny for the uniform purchase. Argus thinks, "I'll have Lynn help me pick out the clothes. She has a knack for this."

With the paperwork completed, Mrs. Phan gives the new hires a bathroom break as she gathers the packets. She comes out of the conference room, packets in hand after double checking each one. She drops them by her office and says, "Okay guys let's take a tour of the training center."

The offices are first which hold nothing out of the ordinary. Next a large room where meetings and classes are held. The room is expansive and must be five times the size of the conference room. It's dark and cool and has the feel of a chapel. There is a podium with two flags in the corners behind the raised stage. Everything is finished in a dark wood. The impression is expensive and professional. Argus is impressed. The lady explains this is where institution meetings and training are held. Monthly meetings are called, "Recalls."

The final part of the tour is the basement which houses the weight room. He is no expert on gyms, but this room is impressive. Three Olympic weight sets, a full set of dumbbells up to one hundred pounds, squat rack, smith machine, leg press, stair climbers and treadmills. In a separate smaller area is a speed bag and heavy bag. This is a power lifter's paradise. There is also a sauna and showers. She excuses herself to go make a phone call and tells the new hires to try the place out. He and the others stand and talk by the Smith machine.

She returns a short time later and as she enters, her demeanor changes. She seems angry as she faces the new hires. The friendly smile has vanished maybe because they haven't so much as lifted a weight. She says, "Do you men know where you are? You do realize that you'll be expected to fight these inmates. You'll be expected to use this place regularly so that you're prepared to do that."

Argus thinks, "Actually, I didn't know that."

He realizes, he hasn't a clue about this job.

∞∞∞∞

Lynn is excited and her excitement is infectious. She is smiling and talking a mile a minute as they enter JC Penny's Department Store. His wife loves to clothes shop, especially for him. He'll never understand it. He smiles just watching her. They don't have a lot of money to spare, so three trousers, three shirts and a blue tie will be the limit for today. It will be just enough uniforms to get started. It was explained that the tie had to be clip on, so the inmates wouldn't be able to grab it and choke you with it. This sounded reasonable to him. Argus recalls a story his father had told him about his grandfather. His grandfather was a taxi driver during the great depression in Abhaile and wore a uniform with a tie. Back in those days, Abhaile, Indiana was a rough town where the gangsters from Illinois came to hide out. He had a disagreement with a rider over the fare which turned into a fight. The rider had used his grandfather's tie to choke him. This was the last time his grandfather ever wore a tie at work.

Argus suffers through trying on everything prior to leaving the store. Shopping is not his favorite thing to do but Lynn is good at it. She is accomplished at finding a deal if there is one. Luckily for them, he already has boots from the ammunition plant, so that isn't a cost they will have to endure. As they leave the store, he looks at his wife. She is smiling, excited and her eyes are bright. She's looking at him with those eyes and it makes him happy.

Chapter 2
With yellowed eyes wide, it waits.

The new hires have two weeks of institutional familiarization before they go to the Agency Training Center in Georgia. This is to teach them about the penitentiary and its specific idiosyncrasies. This is where he finds himself with the other new hires today. One week of classroom instruction. They are in the conference room again. Class after class, the various speakers offer presentations on key control, use of force, inmate accountability and counting procedures. The list goes on and on. It's like drinking from a fire hose.

Each speaker has all kinds of stories and examples to illustrate the subject which makes it more interesting than just reading out of a book. The new hires watch a movie about the history of the institution. The place is steeped in tradition and the staff members are proud to work here. He is proud to have been selected. With every presentation, he realizes this is a place set apart. Not everyone makes this team which is appealing to him because the mission is an important one that only a select group can fulfill. He feels like he did as a Marine. This place will give him purpose and he'll be able to provide for his family like they deserve. He is part of something special again.

∞∞∞∞

Argus pulls up to the speaker box at the front of the Maximum Security Penitentiary Tarragon and presses the button. A metallic voice comes on, "Can I help you?"

"Um, I'm one of the new hires. My name is Argus Antrim. I was told to report here this morning for institutional familiarization."

The metallic voice, "Stand by."

He is within site of the tower. A single structure approximately 40 feet tall overlooking a sally port gate. A sally port is a controlled entry point which allows entry and exit without the fence line ever being compromised. The two gates are never opened at the same time. The steel fence is high with multiple rows of razor wire. He waits.

A few minutes later the metallic voice comes back, all business. "Okay, do you have any alcohol, narcotics, firearms, explosives, weapons or ammunition of any kind in your vehicle or on your person?"

This was rattled off with practiced speed. He answers, "No," immediately.

"Pull around to the visitor parking to your left, exit your vehicle, lock it and step to the base of the tower with a photo identification."

He is wearing his newly purchased uniform. The polyester trousers are already making his legs itch. They are tight in the legs which is usual for clothes bought in his actual waist size. He has also worn his white shirt and tie because he wants to make a good impression. He feels like he stands out with the new clothes on and thinks, "A new rookie just off the rack."

He makes it to the tower and the officer sticks his head out the window and looks down from his perch. He is an older man who doesn't look friendly at all. The gate buzzes. "Well, push on the gate you fuckin' rookie! Jesus Christ!"

He thinks, "Welcome to the pen," and walks through. He doesn't take it personal. This is standard hazing the Marine Corps is famous for. It's part of making the team.

A different lady from the Personnel Office stands in the lobby of the penitentiary. She has a friendly smile and introduces herself as Liz Crawford. She reaches out to shake Argus' hand with a firm grip. She has short brown hair and is wearing a pantsuit with low heeled dress shoes. She looks professional. Everything about this place has been professional so far, well, except the tower officer. This is a different world from what he's used too. She will be the escort for the new hires today. After showing the officer at the desk his identification and filling out the contraband form, he is escorted to the Personnel Office to wait for the other new hires. The office is a large room, separated by gray partitions. The partitions are made of metal and fabric. This gives the appearance of many separate offices. He hears one of the women in the office tell another as he enters, "Uh oh, baby doll alert."

He feels his face flush. There is already one new hire waiting. They sit at a table in the back of the office. As he steps up to the table, they nod but don't speak. His compatriot at the table is a tall man about Argus' age with blonde hair and an unfriendly demeanor. Argus thinks, "This guy should be working the tower. He's got asshole written all over him."

The second week of institutional familiarization will be completed inside the institution. They'll learn hands on under the supervision of seasoned correctional officers. They'll also get a feel for what the job is like, in case they want to quit before the agency spends the money to train them. Up to now, the realities of this job have been abstract. He feels some tightness in his gut. They won't be abstract after today.

The four rookies are now present and accounted for. Mrs. Crawford gives them their official credentials bearing the title, "Correctional Officer" and a picture. This is their passport to get in and out of the prison. The credentials are to be carried at all times. The first thing on the agenda is a full tour of the institution. They're led out of the Personnel Office and down a breezeway to another sally port. To the left is a large glass window with bars in front. He looks through the glass. It is dark inside. He sees that this is so the officers can see out but anyone on the outside cannot see exactly what is inside. Argus notices that the glass is at least one inch thick. He thinks, "A fortress inside a fortress."

Mrs. Crawford gives the rookies one final set of instructions. "This is the Main Control Room. If anything happens, you are to stay with me. If we get separated, you come here."

There is a barred gate made of heavy steel. It slides open with a mechanical grinding. The rookies and their escort enter the sally port. They show the Control Room Officer their newly obtained identifications. Argus can see a correctional officer on the other side of the second gate. He is a big man with a hard look on his face as he stands close to the gate facing toward the inside of the corridor. Argus notices that the officer's head never stops scanning. The officer is on high alert and there is tenseness to his body. Mrs. Crawford draws a radio from the Control Room and tells the officer inside about the tour. The officer tells her that he has the memorandum. He looks the rookies over skeptically. The first gate has closed and now the second gate is sliding open. He can see the inmates moving past in the large corridor on the other side and there are lots of inmates. The corridor is full. The rookies and their escort step through and the gate slides closed behind them. He thinks he will always remember the sound of that gate slamming shut.

The rookies stand against the wall of the corridor. It is ten yards wide and one hundred yards long. Argus looks up at the ceiling fans rotating twenty feet above his head. The corridor is full of activity and full of inmates. You can tell they are inmates by their uniforms. Olive drab green fatigues with side pockets on the trousers. Some in Olive

31

drab shirts or white t-shirts and some in gray sweat shirts. The sunlight from the windows at the top of the corridor wall streams in, reminding everyone that the sun still shines outside this place. Argus takes notice of the dust particles from the fans floating in the sunlight. The walls are painted an off white. No wood here, just concrete and steel. The floor is waxed and polished to a shine. He smells the food being prepared for the noon meal in the Dining Hall located across the corridor from Control. Argus has trouble identifying what is being cooked from the smell as the inmates file past, some walking with purpose, some with a lazy saunter. All have the facial expression of men who have nothing better to look forward to than another day just like the last one. You don't start your incarceration in this penitentiary. You work your way up to it. It is a maximum security level penitentiary and the inmates look the part. Some of the inmates have their heads up looking around and some have their heads down, just trying to get to their next destination without trouble.

The Corridor Officer greets each one of the rookies with a handshake as Mrs. Crawford introduces them to him. He has a crushing grip. The Corridor Officer explains that this is an open movement for the inmates to move from one area of the institution to another for various reasons. This occurs each hour on the hour for ten minutes. The Corridor Officer excuses himself and pulls his radio from his hip. "Corridor to the housing units, clear the corridor and lock your doors. This movement is over. They missed it."

Control mimics this announcement over the loud speakers. The corridor begins to clear as the officers at both ends of the institution begin to usher the inmates inside the units and close the unit doors. In just two or three minutes, the corridor is clear of inmates. The officers are practiced at what they do.

The tour continues through the housing units, Education, Chapel, Gymnasium, Recreation Yard, Linen Factories and Construction Shops. Mrs. Crawford explains that they won't be touring the segregation units. This takes most of the morning. The prison is expansive and Argus has trouble keeping track of where they are. The prison was originally designed to house nine hundred men. The current inmate count is sixteen hundred.

"So this is the reason for the hiring push," Argus thinks.

The tour ends at the Dining Hall where the rookies will eat lunch in a side area, "The Staff Dining Hall."

The food is the same as what the inmates are eating and is served by inmates under the supervision of a Food Service Foreman. Argus gets a tray and sidesteps through the line. At each station, he holds his tray forward and an inmate spoons food on to it. He finds a seat with his fellow new hires and begins to eat. To Argus' surprise, the food tastes pretty good. Several times Argus looks around and catches inmates staring at the group. He and the other rookies do not speak much. They are all still trying to get their bearings in this new environment. Their tour guide eats with a group of men in suits. After the meal, the rookies take their trays and silverware to the scullery and drop them off. An inmate is cleaning the trays off, sorting the silverware and stacking the trays. The inmate moves with speed and efficiency and does not acknowledge Argus as he drops his tray off. The rookies wait at their table for Mrs. Crawford to finish her meal.

∞∞∞∞

Argus stands in the Lieutenant's Office. The Operation's Lieutenant is leaning back in his chair behind the desk. After the first day, Argus and the rest of the new hires were instructed to report to the Lieutenant's Office as assigned to shadow various officers on different shifts. The lieutenant assigns Argus to Unit 2 with the day shift officer for the next eight hours. Smiling, he stands and steps around the desk. Argus notices that he is wearing cowboy boots. His name is Lieutenant Jennings and he is a thin man who is maybe six foot tall. His demeanor is relaxed. He looks at Argus and says, "Antrim, you just go on down to the West End. Those fellas are gonna show you the ropes."

The first rule Argus has learned is to use last names only. The inmates don't need your first name. That's reserved for friends. It is never okay for an inmate to call you by your first name. Argus follows the Corridor Officer down to the West End where Unit Two is located. He is the officer who was running the corridor on the day of the tour. His name is Benell. He is a legend at the penitentiary and his crushing grip is part of that legend. On the way, they stop by Control where Argus trades one of his new brass "chits" for a body alarm. It looks like a red radio with a button on top. If he needs help, he hits the button and help is on the way. The Control Room Officer notes the unit where the body alarm is going to be located.

Officer Benell tells Argus, "That's not a radio. You can't talk on it. If you hit the button it becomes an open microphone and Control can hear what's going on. Don't leave the unit without notifying Control where you're going. Better yet, just don't leave the fucking unit."

Argus' wife has packed him a lunch. He's got his lunch bag with him. He thinks, "I got food. No reason to leave the unit."

The unit officer keys open the door and smiles. He's in his early thirties and is one of the officers that they use to train new hires. Argus enters his first housing unit. The officer says, "Hey man, welcome. My name's Kelp. Let me show you around."

The walls are the same off white as the corridor. Everything else is battleship gray. The floor is bare concrete, waxed and shined. There are two tiers, a bottom one with cells down each side and a top one that mirrors the bottom. There is a railing around the top tier. A switch back staircase leads from the bottom to the top. There's a staircase on each side.

Argus learns that the bottom is called the "flat." The doors are solid steel with a small window with cross bars in the window. The doors slide open and closed on heavy metal tracks. There are large range fans on pedestals standing at the near and far end of the flat. The noise is deafening. It's like having a single engine airplane, idling in the same room with you. The whole place, not just this unit but, everywhere Argus has gone behind the grill has the same underlying smell of confined humans. Body odor mixed with the odor of food and soured linen. There is no air conditioning and the heat is steam heat from a radiator in the cell. This is an "honor unit" which means the inmates who live here have a relatively clean disciplinary record. It also means the inmates here have enough juice not to get their hands dirty. The unit seems quiet to Argus. There are just a few inmates at a table on the flat playing cards, a few more standing around the upper tier watching. Argus realizes they are always watching. The officer closes his unit door and locks it with a practiced twist of the large door key. Argus comments on the way the officer twisted the key with a snapping motion.

Officer Kelp tells him that there's a technique to it. He adds, "You'll get plenty of practice rookie" and laughs.

Kelp leads him to the officer's office which is just a cell with the bunks and sink removed. A desk and chair have been added. Argus and the officer take a few minutes to get to know each other.

Kelp shows Argus all of the logs and forms he'll use each day and gives him a short rundown of what they'll be doing today. An inmate comes down to the office and pokes his head around the door. "Can I get a razor, boss?"

Kelp gives the inmate a safety razor and the inmate just stands there. He asks the officer what he thought about the game last night. Officer Kelp responds, "C'mon man. You know I don't follow it."

The inmate then asks Argus, "How 'bout you officer?"

Argus follows Kelp's lead. "Naw man, I don't follow it either."

The funny thing is, Argus really doesn't follow sports. The inmate says, "Okay boss man" and leaves.

Kelp looks at Argus and grins. "That dude was fishing. They're already trying to figure you out."

∞∞∞∞

Argus is wearing a light, navy blue wind breaker. It does little to guard against the October chill in the air. He walks briskly to keep pace with the officer who he has been assigned to this evening. The schedule has him on evening watch with the Rear Yard Officer, 4:00 pm to midnight. Tonight the Rear Yard Officer is doing an interior fence check and fire door check. This is outside work. Argus wishes he had worn a heavier jacket. He won't make the mistake of under dressing again. The officer sets a good pace as he talks to Argus about the prison and asks him about what experience he has. They are walking a well-worn path around the interior perimeter fence. The evening sun glints off of the razor wire between the inner and outer fences. There are two fences and at least 15 rolls of razor wire.

Argus thinks, "A man would bleed to death before he got through it."

Every so often, they veer away from the fence and check an exterior fire door. The officer is experienced and follows a practiced pattern. He has been with the penitentiary for over eighteen years and knows everything about it. Argus is trying to absorb as much insight as he can, peppering the officer with questions. The officer is in his mid-forties. He's just a little taller than Argus but thirty pounds heavier. His face is pock marked and weather beaten. His name is Vale. Argus admits that he has no correctional experience but he does have the Marine Corps in his favor. Officer Vale is an old jar head himself. He can tell that Vale is very interested in training him by the way he is explaining everything in great detail.

Periodically, Officer Vale will call Control on the radio and report their position. This is to let the next tower know they will be coming into view. The towers are manned and armed. It makes good sense to let them know you're coming. As they near Tower Four, Vale stops and turns to Argus and says, "Look, I can tell you're new to this, so I'm gonna cut to the chase and I hope you don't take it personal, but we've got to know we can depend on you. That you can handle yourself. We're going to let these inmates run at you. We're not going to let them hurt you, but we've got to know if you've got what it takes."

This surprises Argus. It makes him wonder if he is really prepared for this job. He shrugs his shoulders, smiles and says, "I guess we'll see."

He is sure he looks a lot more confident on the outside than he feels on the inside. They finish the check and Argus is a little less talkative as Officer Vale continues to explain the operations of the penitentiary. His thoughts are occupied by what Vale had shared with him. At evening mainline, Argus is taught how to do a proper pat search. The officers pick the inmates out randomly and call them over for the search as they exit the chow hall. Argus has not developed the eyes that the officers have for picking out the inmates with extra food, etc. He practices his new found skill throughout the evening meal. Later, he watches as Officer Vale and his inmate work detail do the evening trash run to the compactor, collecting trash from all the units in large wheeled bins. He is busy for the whole shift moving throughout the institution completing tasks with the Rear Yard Officer.

At the end of the shift, Argus has one more task to complete and that is assisting the Linen Factory Foremen in counting the inmates from the factory back into the main institution. Argus is positioned at a barred gate right across from the Visiting Room and is mentally exhausted. This gate controls access to the Linen Factory and Construction Shops and as the inmates are released from work, they are counted as they come through this gate. The inmates are lined up outside the gate already, waiting to be let into the corridor. Argus thinks back to the class on inmate accountability. He knows the count has to be agreed upon by both staff members that do the count.

He thinks, "Okay, don't fuck this up."

The factory staff member asks Argus if he's ready. Argus nods and they throw the gate open. The inmates are moving through the door quickly, trying to get back to the housing units for showers and maybe some television time before lockdown. Argus is trying to focus and keep an accurate count in his head. The inmates come through the gate two and three at a time. They go right to get to the West end and left to get to the East end. All focused on getting back to the units. They aren't searched because they have already gone through a metal detector and been searched at the West Yard Officer station. Argus tries to keep his focus on the door, but there are distractions. Inmates further down the corridor, talking loudly and staff members speaking to his left and right. Finally, the last inmate passes through the gate.

The factory foreman asks, "Okay, what's your count?"

Argus gives him the number. "Two hundred thirty two."

The foreman looks at Argus, then at his scratch paper. "You sure you don't mean two thirty three?"

Argus remembers from the class, your count is your count. "The foreman tells Argus, I got two thirty three."

Argus tells the foreman, "You guys do what you want too, but I got two thirty two."

The foreman reports the discrepancy to Control. The rookie's count is one under what Control has on their paperwork. The Operations Lieutenant calls an emergency count immediately. The inmates are locked down early for this count and won't be let out of their cells until morning. The institution is counted and clears with a good count approximately thirty minutes later. The factory foremen have had to stay over until the count cleared. Argus was off by one. He's expecting the foremen to be angry, but instead, they tell him not to worry about it. It happens to everyone. "The important thing is that you stuck to your guns."

Argus has passed another test. They know he won't be persuaded to change his count.

∞∞∞∞

Argus has two more days of institutional familiarization. Two more days and he'll be on a flight to Georgia to begin three weeks of training. The penitentiary is covering the travel costs and even his meals. Argus is assigned to shadow the Unit One Officer from 8 am to 4 pm, "Day Watch." The officer has been with the prison for a long time and is within a few years of retirement. He takes Argus on a tour of the unit. He is not enthused about dragging a rookie around with him all day. The officer climbs the stairs, ascending each step as if he is completely worn out yet he does not use the handrail.

He tells Argus, "Never use the handrail in any unit. The inmates sometimes tape razor blades on the back side so you'll slice your hand open."

He also tells Argus never take a corner close. Always go wide around a blind corner in case an inmate is waiting to ambush you. Argus watches the inmates as they pass going up and down the stairs and notices they follow these rules too. Unit One has three floors. The first floor holds the counselor's and secretary's office as well as the unit officer's office. The unit officer's office is just inside the large steel restraining door of the unit. If you walk down the hallway past the unit management offices, you come to an inmate television room. Just inside the unit doorway is a wide switch back stairway. Two short flights between each floor. Four turns. Four blind corners to go around.

There are one hundred twenty five inmates housed on the second and third floors. The housing unit is not made up of cells, but rather each floor is like the squad bays Argus remembers from his days in the Corps. The dorm is separated into cubes by the same style dividers as the Personnel Office. Two bunk beds to a cube. Each inmate has a small locker, four lockers to a cube. This is supposed to be an honor dorm. It is anything but. The inmates housed here are just not the worst of the worst.

Argus and the officer enter the second floor. It is literally a whole room of blind corners. Makeshift clothes lines hanging in the cubes. In multiple cubes there are blankets hanging from the end of the bunks in an attempt at providing a semblance of privacy where privacy is a detriment to supervision. The third floor is the same. Argus can't see how one officer can run this unit. Throughout the day, the officer shows Argus how to do a cell search. The officer explains, "I only look for hard contraband. Wine, weapons and drugs."

He shows Argus the same forms as his first day in Unit Two. Inmates come to the officer for passes to different parts of the institution. These passes allow the inmate to move about the institution between regular movements. Inmate work crews come to the unit and must be checked in. Inmates come to office requesting supplies. Constant movement in and out, up and down all day. Argus can see why the officer is tired. Eight hours of walking stairs.

Toward the end of the shift, Argus and the officer make a tour through the unit. Second and third floors first, then back down to the first floor television room. The television room is dark with only the light of the television stabbing through the darkness. Three inmates are sitting in a semicircle in front of the television on folding metal chairs. As they walk toward the center of the room, Argus glances to his right and sees two inmates in a corner. One inmate is much smaller than the other. The smaller inmate has a paper bag covering his nose and mouth and is inhaling to the point the bag collapses. Argus knows what this is.

They are sniffing paint or glue. Argus readies himself for the unit officer to react. The officer turns around and walks back out of the television room without looking in the corner. Argus follows him out and looks back toward the television room. The larger inmate is looking out of the small window at Argus. There is no friendliness in his eyes.

When they are almost back to the officer's office, Argus asks, "Hey, did you see those guys huffing in there?"

The officer says, "Yeah."

Argus is incredulous. "Well, aren't we supposed to do something about that?"

Argus doesn't have a clue what to do.

The officer answers, "Look, there's no way to test if they've been huffing. You've got to learn to pick your battles around here."

Argus has learned many things the past two weeks. The most important is what type of officer he wants to be. Now, he has seen both ends of the spectrum.

∞∞∞∞

The corridor is filled with inmates creating a solid mass of humanity in olive drab. It is an open ten minute movement and it is the final few hours of Argus' institutional familiarization. He has used this week to learn all he can before going to Georgia. He stands in the corridor on the West End with the officers and pat searches the inmates that they pick out. They watch him and critique each performance. "Always keep one foot between his legs. Keep one hand at the base of his spine. Never look down, always look at the inmate. Crush and feel the pockets. Make the inmate empty the pockets. You don't want to catch a needle do you?"

Argus starts to see the pattern. He sees the inmates running cover for the mules. The cover inmates try to look guilty so you'll pick them instead of the mule. Then the mule just walks on by. He enjoys the mind game. There is an inmate coming down the corridor. One of the officers leans over and says, "That one. Search that one."

Argus thinks the officer must have seen something. The inmate is overweight with a beard and long hair coming out from under a green stocking cap. He is wearing an OD green field jacket. There are plenty of places to hide contraband on this guy. The officer calls the inmate by name. "Come over here and grab the wall so this rookie can search you."

When he says it, he puts an emphasis on the "rookie."

The inmate says, "Oh, yes sir boss."

The inmate smiles and places both hands on the wall and spreads his feet. Argus thinks, "This guy's done this before."

He steps up behind the inmate, and places a foot between the legs, and against the inmate's foot. He places a hand on the inmate's lower back. The inmate takes a long breath and says, "Oh yeah, that's it."

Argus starts at the end of the inmate's arm and works his way down one side like he has been taught. The inmate takes another long breath and says whimsically, "Oh boss, you're really good at this."

Argus continues the search. The inmate begins to moan, "Oh boss, I wish you'd rob a bank. I'd love to have you for a cellie."

Argus realizes now. It's a set up. The inmate is famous for doing this to rookie officers. He looks at the officers behind him. They're laughing. Argus laughs too. "You assholes."

Argus likes a good practical joke.

∞∞∞∞

The fledgling correctional officers sit in the classroom awaiting their Agency Training Center uniform issue. The flight to Georgia had been a short one courtesy of the Agency. White panel vans had been waiting to take the new recruits to the training center. This is where new correctional workers from across the Agency come together for their basic training. Anyone working in a prison has to undergo basic training as a correctional officer. Argus looks around the classroom at his fellow students. All of the officers he had been hired with at the penitentiary are there along with twenty other trainees. Dorm assignments are given out and Argus draws as a roommate one of the new hires from the penitentiary. He is a quiet sort that doesn't say much and smiles less but seems to be a good guy and is always sitting back and observing. Argus likes this. He is a people watcher too. His name is Ken Shelter. He is taller than Argus with about the same build. Argus forms the impression that Ken is very comfortable with himself and doesn't need other people to keep him company. Argus likes him immediately, maybe because he is a loner too.

The lead instructor introduces herself and presents the training outline. Also provided is a manual three inches thick. The Agency does love its paperwork. For the next three weeks the students will be instructed and tested on the information presented through classroom and hands on training. They will participate in real life scenarios to test how they'll handle various situations. The Training Facility employs actors to play the antagonists in these scenarios. Also, as a requirement to pass the training, a physical fitness test, self-defense and firearms qualification will have to be completed. The Agency Training Center is modern, clean and exudes professionalism. Argus hasn't been involved in training like this since leaving the Marines. He is happy to be here, although, he already misses his wife and daughter. He pushes these thoughts from his mind. Argus thinks, "I need to focus. Don't want to blow this."

The campus is expansive and self-contained. There are student quarters, a gym, shooting range, chow hall, driving range and classrooms located here. There is even a place to play pool and get a beer if you like. After the initial administrative requirements are completed, the instructors release the students to find their quarters and get ready for the start of training the next day. The room where Argus will spend the next three weeks is nice. It has the basic conveniences you would expect. Two single beds and a bathroom with two desks. It is one of many in a building surrounded by pine trees and resembles a rural college dorm. The room itself is nothing fancy but livable. Argus notices an ironing board. He's still a Marine and happy he'll be able to square away these wrinkled uniforms. Ken suggests they go down and have a beer after chow to unwind. This sounds good to Argus and they head out to find the chow hall, making the quarter mile walk and finding the building in about fifteen minutes. The chow hall is a large room filled with tables and chairs and is unremarkable from any other buffet style restaurant. He is pleasantly surprised to find that the food is good. Argus approaches the cash register prepared to pay for the meal, but the lady at the register simply hands him a clipboard and says, "Name and last four of your social."

After dinner, they find the local pub. It is dark and cool inside with lots of dark wood trim. Tables and chairs are spaced around the pool tables like most of the establishments of its kind. In the back are booths where several students are already well on their way to inebriation. Argus and his roommate grab a beer at the bar and head to an open pool table. Ken turns out to be quite a challenge on a pool table. Whether it's Argus' lack of skill or his roommate's skill is anyone's guess. The pub is already full and it seems that the rest of the students have had the same idea. By the second beer, Argus is already down three games of eight ball, but he's enjoying himself. The crowd in the bar is getting louder with the occasional whoops and laughter. Argus has seen this before and thinks as he looks around, "There's going to be a lot of headaches tomorrow in class."

In the Marines, he'd spent plenty of time in bars and knows the signs and the signs say nothing but trouble. One of the other new hires from the penitentiary approaches the table Argus and his roommate are playing on. He is the blonde new hire with the bad attitude from the first day of institutional familiarization. His name is Sam Line. He is six foot and weighs probably 215 pounds by Argus' estimation. He is also obviously drunk and not smiling. Argus smiles as he approaches. He looks at Argus and says, "You a Mareeeen?"

Argus replies, "I am."

Sam says, "Well I'm a Ranger."

Argus has been here before. He knows what comes next. Argus replies, "Your parents must be very proud," and smiles a relaxed smile.

Sam takes a step forward and says, "They are and I'm the better man and you're going to say so, right now!"

Argus smiles at the absurdity. "No, I don't think I'll be saying anything like that, right now."

He mimics Sam in his best slurry voice.

Argus is holding the pool stick in his right hand at his side and Sam is going to wear it across his temple in about one more step. Out of nowhere Ken steps in between the two. "Come on man, we don't need this kind of trouble," and leads Sam away looking over his shoulder on the way to the bar.

Argus gets the feeling that he and Sam are not going to be friends. Argus sits down at the table and thinks, "What a fucking asshole."

His roommate returns a short time later with a smile on his face. He shakes his head and laughs. Argus tells Ken, "Thanks, I owe you a beer, but I'm going to get in trouble in here and I don't need any of that. I'm going back to the room."

Ken looks at him and raises his eyebrows, "Yeah, probably a good idea. You might be an asshole magnet. I'll see ya later Antrim."

Argus steps out the door knowing two things. He won't be back to the pub and he has at least one person at the pen that'll have his back. He might even be a friend.

∞∞∞∞

The trainees are in a different classroom than they were on the first day. They have been at the facility for over a week struggling through class after class on Agency policy and procedure. At times they just struggle to stay awake. Argus and his roommate have become friendly, but are not running buddies. Like Argus, Ken is a loner and stays to himself. Argus does the same so the bunking arrangement works to their favor. The exercise in class today involves hands on demonstrations regarding counseling an inmate. Line is picked as the guinea pig and sits at a table in front of the class. An actor will play the inmate. The only information that is given is that the inmate has a problem and Line, as the unit officer, must counsel him on it. The actor enters and sits down at a chair opposite Line who is sitting upright with a tense scowl on his face. The inmate is 300 pounds and around five foot ten inches tall. Argus sits back and prepares to enjoy the show. Line starts off by asking the inmate what the problem is in his most empathetic voice which comes off as totally fake. The inmate says that he has a problem but doesn't know how to tell him. Line leans forward in his chair and says, "Just spit it out."

He's getting animated. Argus thinks, "This guy has no business in security work. Way too short a fuse."

The actor says, "Well officer, I've tried to fight it but, I've developed feelings for you," as he puts his hand on Line's hand. Line reacts as if he's been electrocuted.

Argus can't contain himself and begins to laugh hysterically under his breath. Line yanks his hand back and yells, "What the fuck!"

The inmate reaches for his hand again and Line stands up, knocking the chair over backwards. The instructor yells, "Out of roll!" Stopping the scenario.

Line's face is beet red and he looks like he's going to hit the actor. Everyone is snickering. Argus is bent over trying not to choke. The instructor explains that you always reply to any approach by an inmate with a professional demeanor. Argus thinks, "Damn, this is fun."

He loves a good joke.

∞∞∞∞

The class is being held in a mock cell-house. The flat is only 20 feet long with only eight cells. The students have been separated out into groups of eleven for better manageability. Argus stands and listens to the instructor explain the exercise, "This will be a critique of the student's ability to search a cell properly. Some of the cells have no contraband while others have hard contraband hidden in them. It is the student's job to find the contraband."

Argus feels cocky. He's been trained by the Tarragon Officers on how to search a cell. This will be a piece of cake as far as he is concerned. The cells are normal size cells with a bunk-bed, toilet, sink and two lockers. The doors of the cells are sliders with bars not unlike the cells in the segregation units at the penitentiary. The cells are empty of any inmate property, so as far as Argus can see, there isn't much to search.

He steps into his assigned cell and starts in one corner just like he's been taught and moves around the cell systematically. Opening the lockers and feeling behind the ridges. Argus looks under the shelves for contraband taped to the underside and checks the steel rod to make sure it is attached and not sharpened and just put back in place. He checks under the lockers with no luck. He rolls the mattresses too. He squats down and checks around the underside of the sink and toilet. Nothing taped to the bunks and they're secured to the floor as well. He looks for any areas where the walls have been patched with toilet paper and toothpaste. Argus feels like he's gone through the cell with a fine tooth comb. He thinks as he looks around. "This must be a cell with nothing in it."

Argus steps out of the cell confident that he's done a good search. The instructor asks him if he's sure he's done. Argus nods his head and that is when the instructor begins to smile.

"That's not good," thinks Argus.

The instructor steps into the cell and Argus begins to sweat. "Also not good."

The instructor exits the cell with two bone crusher shanks that were taped under the slider door. This is the first shank Argus has ever seen firsthand. He sees that they are just as deadly as any bayonet he'd ever placed on the end of his rifle in the Corps. The one thing the Marines had made a part of his DNA was duty and honor. He thinks back to what Officer Vale had said, "We need to know we can count on you."

Argus went into the cell cocky and is now humbled. He takes it personal, mentally chastising himself, "Two shanks that could end up in a staff member's chest because I failed to find them. This will not happen again. This is serious man. You have got to get up to speed."

The students are back in the mock cell house today. There is an actor at the far end of the flat playing the inmate. A male student is selected to play the part of the unit officer and enters through the unit restraining door. The only instructions for the scenario are that the student is the unit officer and he is to work his unit and manage whatever transpires. The student stands at the restraining door and monitors the one inmate in his charge. The inmate is pacing back and forth, muttering under his breath and becoming more animated. He stops and stares an angry hard stare at the student. Then he begins to pace and talk to himself again. The inmate always stays at the back of the flat, well inside the unit.

After five minutes of this, the student walks to the back of the unit and approaches the inmate and says, "Hey buddy, is something bothering you?"

The inmate looks up quickly and yells, "What!"

The officer repeats the question. The inmate clenches his fists and holds them down at his sides. His whole body is taught. He advances on the student and starts screaming, "Buddy? Buddy? You think I'm your fuckin' buddy? What the fuck do you know about my problems motherfucker!"

The student puts his hands up, palms out and starts backing away but the inmate angles around and circles him, cutting him off. Now the inmate is between the door and the student.

The inmate becomes more and more aggressive until the officer is backed into a corner. The instructor calls, "Out of role."

Immediately the inmate turns back into the actor and smiles. The student is shaken. Argus is impressed by the actor. That was definitely a realistic performance. The instructor asks the student why he didn't call for assistance as soon as the inmate started advancing on him. He critiques the student at length in front of the class to make it a valuable learning experience.

The student thankfully blends back into the group of students as the instructor says, "Okay, your first mistake was calling the inmate buddy. Next time, just ask the question. Don't give them anything to feed into. The inmate was obviously upset and already exhibiting signs of imminent disruptive behavior. His fists were clenched, he was talking to himself and he was glaring at you. You all have got to get good at reading body language. That's really important. Secondly, your distancing was wrong. You were way to close when you first engaged this guy. I mean he is in your unit and you're going to have to deal with this situation, but you've got to do it safely. Your posture was really good with your hands up and you tried to deescalate the situation but you let him get between you and the door. That is a very, very bad thing to let happen. You should have hit the button on him the minute he started after you."

Argus enjoys the scenarios. He is a hands on learner and even though this very subject was covered in class, to see it played out was a great learning experience. Argus makes a mental note to remember the body language of the actor. He doesn't want to make any of the mistakes he's just witnessed when he gets back to the institution. There is no such thing as "out of role" in real life.

∞∞∞∞

Argus stands facing the female student on the mat for self-defense training. She is slightly overweight and one of the few students that is shorter than he is. When they were paired up at the beginning of the class, she'd volunteered that she is a unit secretary at one of the lower security institutions. Now she is standing across from Argus, waiting for him to grab her lapel. The self-defense discipline of choice for the Agency is Aikido. The instructor called it, the "gentle art." All week long the students have been learning to let the force pass. Some wrist locks are practiced with names Argus tries to remember like kotegaieshi, nikyo and sankajo, as well as the defense against the two hand grab, one hand grab and how to fall correctly. Argus has been in a few scrapes. Not many, but a few. He never had anyone just grab his lapel and stop. No matter, he learns the techniques and practices with enthusiasm because this is what the Agency wants him to use for defense. It doesn't look anything like what they taught in boot camp. Argus grabs the secretary and she cross grabs pausing to make sure her hand placement is correct, pivots and twists his wrist. Argus falls to the mat dutifully.

He gets up, shakes his wrist and tells her, "Good one."

She smiles. He thinks as he takes a step back to get his distancing again, "Nothing wrong with giving her a little self-confidence."

Now it's his turn. He was raised as a gentleman, so he does the technique gently trying to make sure he does not injure her. The more Argus practices the techniques, the more he realizes they will take years

46

of practice to perfect. He only has one more week before he returns to the penitentiary.

∞∞∞∞

The evenings are the worst. He misses his wife and daughter. Argus and his wife met while he was on a ninety six hour pass when he was in the Corps. It was truly love at first sight. They were married a year and a half later after his overseas deployment to Japan. His military occupational specialty was artillery scout which meant that he was deployed all of the time and although he loved being a Marine, he loved his wife more. That's the main reason he had not reenlisted. Now, he tries to fill up the evenings so he doesn't have to think about missing her. He studies his Agency manual over and over because he wants to do well on the final exam but, you can only study so much and keep your focus. His roommate has found his own program, out doing something. Argus has no idea what. He's bored and needs to burn off some steam so he gets dressed out in shorts and a sweat shirt and leaves to hit the strength and endurance course before the sun goes down. The S&E course is a one mile sandy wooded path through the pine trees with obstacles spaced strategically throughout the run. He has been running this course regularly over the last couple of weeks to get ready for the physical fitness test in a few days. Argus was never a natural athlete and knows he has to work extra hard to maintain his physical fitness. He enjoys the solitude of the path, so to Argus, it's much better than the gym. After an hour of pull ups, pushups and sit ups during the run, he is dirty, sweaty and tired. He heads back to the room and takes a quick shower. He thinks about studying some more, but instead, dials his home telephone number. He wants to hear Lynn's voice.

∞∞∞∞

He sits in his assigned seat on the plane and looks out as the Georgia landscape passes by far below. Argus is no stranger to flying, but most of his experience was at tree top level in a chopper. The window seat is nice. It gives him something to watch as he thinks. Argus had passed all of the requirements to be a correctional officer and has done very well. He hadn't set out to be an honor graduate of the academy but, here he is with a certificate saying just that. He'd just done what he always seems to do, which is, put everything you have in to the task. He guesses that is the Marine in him. So, a short graduation ceremony, a scramble to get the vans loaded and a race to get to the gate at the airport. First hurdle completed. This will be a short flight back to Indianapolis. Abhaile, the little town he is from doesn't have an airport big enough for a passenger jet. His thoughts wander to the penitentiary. Argus has done well in training, but none of the scenarios have been real, with real consequences. If he fails in an interaction inside the prison, the consequences can be swift and painful. He thinks back to a class on hostage situations in which the students had been the hostages during a riot. It was a sobering class. After the role play, the students had watched a film on a riot in Louisiana that had happened many years before.

The instructor had advised the students to have the conversation with their families on the realities of the career they were starting. "Ladies and gentlemen, it is a fact that you might leave for your shift one morning and not come home. That's reality. You need to prepare your families for that eventuality."

Argus tried to picture that conversation but couldn't even imagine how one would start. He also wondered if he was ready.

The training was abstract. During institutional familiarization, he had always had a training officer with him. Although training would not stop in Georgia, he would be expected to do the job from day one. The fact that he was an honor graduate meant, the men and women depending on him would expect him to be on point. As the Rear Yard Officer had warned, "We're going to let these inmates run at you to see what you're made of."

He is given a respite from these thoughts as the plane touches down with two hops and a strong deceleration of the massive engines on each wing. Argus thinks as the deceleration pulls him forward in his seat, "This pilot knows what he is doing."

Argus deplanes along with the rest of the herd and walks down the gangway to where Lynn is waiting. He kisses and hugs her tightly. She smells and feels wonderful. She has always worn "Vanilla Fields" cologne and he loves her scent. They get his bag from the luggage carousel and head out into the November wind for the seventy mile drive home. On the drive home, they talk about all the things that have gone on while he was away. She drives and the conversation is relaxing. As always, she carries the conversation and it is nice to watch her as she talks. As he watches her, he feels a resolve deep inside. Whatever he has to face, he'll do it head on and do it well. She and his little girl deserve to be taken care of and this is how he is going to do it. Time for thinking is finished. Whatever is to come, will come.

∞∞∞∞

He is a Sergeant in the United States Marine Corps and he's good at what he does. Although he has never seen combat, he wrote the blank check to his country. He will go without hesitation if called. He is lying on his back in the bed he and Lynn share in their little trailer near Camp Lejeune. It is dark in the bedroom. The dark paneling making the darkness even deeper than the ambient light from the window suggests. His eyes open for some unknown reason, his body tense. He listens to his wife's soft breaths as she sleeps. He feels a dread in his stomach. He has been training to kill the enemy for three years with a rifle, a bayonet, explosives and his bare hands. He doesn't scare easily, but he is afraid. He rises up and listens intently for any unusual noise but hears nothing. There is only silence except for the normal cracks and pops of the trailer as the wind blows. The bedroom door is closed. This is odd because they never close this door at night. He looks at the door and instinctively knows something is on the other side. He is sweating profusely.

The door opens slowly and there, standing in the door are two Rottweiler hounds. Side by side in the doorway they stand and look at him. Their eyes shine with the light from the window. They are big and muscled and he has nothing to defend himself with. The feeling of dread is overwhelming. Then he hears a voice. Not from the hounds, but from somewhere else. It's his voice and it says, "You will not be eaten, you will eat."

The hounds turn to leave. He wakes up covered in sweat. He never shares this dream with anyone. On the eve of his first day in the prison, his dream comes back to him.

∞∞∞∞

He stands at the unit corridor door with a handful of brass chits and a door key to the Visiting Room. He has been assigned to Unit Six on his first day in the penitentiary. Total inmate count of one hundred thirty eight inmates. The total staff count in the unit is one. This unit is directly across from Unit One and is also a dorm style unit. There are

49

three floors to this unit. The first floor is a second adjacent unit of eighteen single cells with slider doors and bars. The cells are open and have been since the 5:00 am count cleared. Argus will also be responsible for a small adjacent unit in the other direction which is also a dorm with twenty geriatric inmates. He was informed by the Operations Lieutenant that due to staffing, he would also be responsible for letting inmates into the Visiting Room shakedown area located right across the corridor. The Corridor Officer keys Argus into the unit then he ascends the two short flights of stairs to the second floor where the unit officer's office is located. The unit officer and his number two have been on since midnight and are ready to go home. They aren't interested in training a rookie before they leave. The Unit OIC is overweight and balding. He looks at Argus with tired eyes as Argus gives him the chits. The officer gives Argus the keys to the unit and asks if he knows what he's doing. Argus does not but realizes the admission will do him no good. He'll have to make the best of it. The officer shows Argus the call-out sheet with inmate appointments on it, the bed-book with inmate photos and bed assignments and the various logs which he has seen before as the Number Two looks on. After the short class, they grab their things and Argus walks down to key them out of the unit. Argus then ascends the stairs for the second time, unlocks his office and enters, wondering what to do first.

He checks the call-out sheet and finds only a handful of inmate appointments for his unit. He's grateful for that. He exits the office and rifles through the keys on the ring to find the key to the door again and locks it. Argus starts the day with a tour of the unit. Before entering the third floor, he finds the key to the large restraining door that separates the floor from the stairwell. He gets halfway through the floor when the Corridor Officer calls him on the radio to come down and let an inmate in the Visiting Room. He runs the stairs to complete this task and goes back up to finish touring the third floor. He does the same for the second floor. Then down two more flights to the adjacent units. The unit with the sliders has eighteen cells. Seventeen of the cells are open. One is closed and still has inmate property inside along with a lot of dried blood. He has no idea what to do with this wrinkle. The officer hadn't told him about this. Before he can study this problem, he's called to the Visiting Room again. After keying that door, he tours the Geriatric Unit and then returns to the adjacent unit on the first floor. It is 8:55 am and the first move of the day is called.

Argus opens all three unit doors and stands in the corridor

monitoring the inmate traffic. Several inmates approach him for a pass to go to their call outs. The pass will allow them to return to the unit in between moves when the appointment is completed. Argus hasn't learned to carry the pass book with him yet. He climbs the stairs to the office with the inmates behind him. Argus writes the passes after looking at the inmate identification cards and checking the call-out sheet. The Corridor Officer calls the move closed. Argus locks the office door and heads back down to the corridor to help clear it of inmates. Two inmates are standing at the Visiting Room door. The Visiting Room Shakedown Officer calls him on the radio to open the door. Argus crosses the corridor and completes this task, then goes back to the unit and secures his doors. He realizes he hasn't started notations in his unit log or completed any cell searches yet. He has been on duty for one hour.

The day progresses at the same pace as the first hour. Argus does his best to keep pace with the day. After noon mainline, the Administrative Segregation Unit calls the Corridor Officer and announces they'll be releasing an inmate to the Unit Six first floor adjacent unit. Argus knows that the unit is full except for the closed cell with the property in it. He has learned quickly to carry the small phone directory and pass book with him. He calls "ADSEG" on the telephone and tells the officer about the property in the cell. He receives no mercy.

"Well, you better get it out of there rookie, because your inmate is on his way."

This is when Argus comes to the terrible realization that he doesn't know how to run the old Alcatraz style lock box which opens and closes the cells in the unit. He was told by the training officers that he should run his unit and not bother the lieutenant. "If the LT has to run your unit, what does he need you for? Only call him if it's something you absolutely can't handle."

Argus gets on the telephone with Officer Kelp, the officer he'd first shadowed and explains the problem. Kelp laughs and tells Argus he'll walk down and help him out. Argus is grateful to see him coming the short distance down the corridor. Kelp shows Argus the operation of the cell door control and has him practice a couple of times. He has even brought two property bags so Argus can pack the property in the bags and carry it up the two flights to inventory it in the officer's office on the proper form.

By the time Argus gets the property into his office, the Corridor Officer is calling on the radio with his gravelly voice, "Corridor to Unit

6, you've got one on your door."

Argus heads back downstairs and lets the inmate into the unit. The Corridor Officer brings him the inmate's bed book card.

The orderlies in the unit like their job and want to keep it. They are already cleaning the blood out of the cell. It takes Argus the rest of the shift to inventory the property in addition to his other duties. He isn't proud of his cell searches. He knows they weren't thorough, but it would never fail that he would just get started only to be called down to key a door, run a movement, write a pass or God knows what. The inmates in the unit know that a rookie is on duty because it is completely obvious. Argus will be assigned to the rookie roster for the next year. Instead of changing posts every ninety days, he'll change every thirty days to get a feel for all the units. Argus ends his shift like he began, with a handful of chits.

The relieving officer has arrived early by thirty minutes. Argus thanks him for this. The officer tells him no thanks are needed, "We relieve on the half hour around here. The last thing you want is to be labeled a minute man."

Argus makes a mental note to arrive thirty minutes early from now on. The relieving officer is in his mid-thirties, muscular and friendly. He asks Argus' how the shift went.

He replies, "Busy, but I'm still learning."

The officer laughs and tells him, "Don't sweat it. You'll get it Antrim. Just keep doing what you're doing."

Argus grabs his lunch box still containing his uneaten lunch and heads down the stairs. The relieving officer comes down with him and keys open the corridor door. Argus walks down to the Lieutenant's Office, enters and asks the LT if he needs anything before he leaves. The LT tells him, "No Antrim. See you tomorrow."

Argus is mentally exhausted but somehow feels good. He's made it through his first day.

∞∞∞∞

Argus is in the officer's office of Unit Six on the second floor of the unit. He's auditing his passes to ensure the inmates have returned them as policy directs. He has been in this unit a week as the Day Watch OIC and he's finally getting used to the work flow. This unit is preferred housing and the inmate behavior reflects that. An incident report can lead to a housing change back to the cell houses. No inmate wants that. Argus finishes the audit, updates his logs and prepares to eat the can of tuna he's brought for lunch. He learned days ago that you eat on the run in this job, so he reverts back to eating like he did in the field while in the Corps. Canned goods consumed from the can. Argus uses the P-38 can opener he's been carrying on his key ring since the Marines and starts working on the can lid.

Halfway through opening the can, Control announces on the radio, "Control to all portable radio units, we have a fight in Unit Thirteen. A fight in Unit Thirteen."

Argus jumps to his feet, puts his personal keys back in his pocket and sprints out of the office, stopping only long enough to lock the door. When Control announces an emergency, designated units respond. Unit Six is one of those units today. While Argus is gone, the Unit One officer will be responsible for watching Argus' unit. Argus sprints down two flights of stairs and hits the corridor door. He fumbles for the door key and gets it unlocked. The Unit One officer is in the corridor and waves him on. Argus sprints a football field length to Unit Thirteen in the East End. When he is thirty yards away, an inmate staggers from the unit. The inmate has a golf ball sized lump on his forehead. He makes it three quarters of the way across the corridor, pirouettes and falls onto his side, saying, "Damn."

The inmate lies there, unable to get up.

It is the afternoon and the unit lights are off but the afternoon sun coming from the windows high above illuminates the scene as Argus glances into the unit. Folding chairs and tables turned over and a range fan is lying on its side. The fight occurred right out on the flat. Argus goes for the inmate who has fallen and securing a wrist, rolls the inmate onto his stomach and applies handcuff restraints behind his back with the assistance of another officer. They then get the inmate to his feet and place him facing the corridor wall. Three other officers are placing the second combatant in handcuff restraints behind his back. The second combatant inside the unit is yelling, "Motherfucker cain't fight! That motherfucker cain't fight worth shit!"

He has blood streaming from his nose.

The inmate Argus has in custody is large but paunchy. He is unsteady on his feet. Argus is not surprised judging from the lump on the inmate's forehead. The other inmate is also large but muscled with little body fat. The inmates have to be kept separated so Argus and his partner escort their inmate to the Lieutenant's Office, while the other inmate is held across the corridor, face to the wall. Argus' inmate is begging the Operation's Lieutenant not to send him to ADSEG. "Please boss, I'll give you heroin, wine, weapons, whatever you want. I know where it's at. Please boss."

Argus ignores the inmate. He's going to ADSEG, no question about it. The Activities Lieutenant instructs Argus to come with him to the unit and help out with a search of the flat to ensure no weapons were used. The inmate is left with the other officer who helped Argus escort the inmate to the Lieutenant's Office.

The inmates of the unit have been placed in their cells and are locked down. Argus begins by pulling the end caps off the legs of the folding chairs and then turning them upright and banging them on the floor. Since his first day, Argus has had some practice at performing searches. His skills have improved. As Argus bangs the third chair on the floor his efforts are rewarded with a nine inch pick shank that simply falls out of the chair leg onto the floor. The weapon is a steel rod, sharpened to a spear point. Argus has learned from the old timers that a pick shank is more dangerous than a bone crusher (knife type shank) because the puncture wound will close around itself and life threatening injuries aren't readily apparent. The victim is much more apt to bleed out internally. Argus secures the weapon and continues his search. No other weapons are discovered as a result of the search. After the search, Argus returns to the Lieutenant's Office and is cleared to return to his unit. The inmates have been escorted to ADSEG and staff members have one less shank to worry about. The institution resumes normal operations and Argus climbs the two flights of stairs to his office. The adrenaline is still pumping, so he is unable to sit still. Argus dumps the tuna in the unit trash can, his appetite gone, washes the can and puts it back in his lunchbox. You don't leave any sharp metal for the inmates to get hold of, so the tuna can will leave the institution with him. He makes a tour of his unit like nothing happened. His pulse would tell a different story.

∞∞∞∞

Argus finds himself running to an emergency at least once a week. In fact, in his mind, an emergency has become the norm rather than an exception. He has been back from Georgia three weeks and sees why this penitentiary is known as one of the most violent. These thoughts occupy his mind as he patrols the first floor adjacent unit of Unit Six. What he has learned so far is that the rules here are different. On the outside of the penitentiary, if someone cuts in front of you in the grocery checkout line, you might say, "Hey, the line's back here."

You might even exchange some harsh words. In here, if an inmate cuts the line, it will most definitely end in a fight, usually with a blade. It is Argus' job to intervene in these altercations. Most of the inmates in this place are serving what one would consider a life sentence. Even if the sentence isn't natural life, the inmate will be an old man when he leaves. Violence is a way of life here. It is the rule.

Argus takes his job seriously. He conducts more pat searches and cell searches than are required to deny the inmates the means to hurt one another or his fellow officers. He's getting good at it and has started to think like these men already. He can look at the inmates in the corridor and actually see the pattern of the game. With that comes something he can't explain. Argus feels it, just under the surface. He has begun to smell the smoke from the dragon's nostrils all the time. As he thinks these thoughts, scans his six, walks a little farther and scans again Control announces a fight in Unit Two. This is unusual. Unit Two is an honor unit. His friend, Kelp is the officer working the unit.

Argus sprints off the range and locks the restraining door behind him. He runs the thirty yards to Unit Two. The restraining door to the unit is already open. The officers from the West End have beaten him into the unit. As he enters the unit, he looks to his right and sees two officers trying to wrestle an inmate to the ground. The inmate is resisting. The other inmate in the fight is standing a short distance away in a corner with his fists up. He doesn't realize the fight is over. Argus sidesteps the first melee and drives forward with a forearm into the other inmate's chest, driving him back into the corner. Another officer arrives and together they force the inmate to the ground on his stomach. The inmate refuses to be cuffed and the officers have to force his arms behind his back. The inmates are finally cuffed and removed from the unit headed for ADSEG. The same Activities Lieutenant who responded to the fight in Unit Thirteen has responded to this incident.

He looks at Argus as he escorts the inmate from the unit, laughs and says, "Damn Antrim, you just got here and already you been in some shit."

Argus looks down and sees blood on his shirt again and thinks, "Consistency is a beautiful thing."

∞∞∞∞

He is tired. The kind of tired you are when you've tried to sleep, but sleep eludes you. He's showered in an attempt to jog himself awake but this only resulted in being clean and tired. It is his first night on midnight to 8:00 am as the MW Number Two Officer in Unit Six. The Number One Officer is a man in his mid-thirties with black hair and a lean physique. He is a member of the penitentiary SWAT team. When things go bad, he's one of the men who sort it out. When Argus arrives, he introduces himself, "Antrim? I'm Nash. Heard I had a rookie for the month. Any questions, don't hesitate to ask. I've already heard good things about you."

Argus is glad to hear people are giving good reports. Two officers work Unit Six on night shift. Argus' partner for the night is eager to train him and shares anything and everything he can in regard to procedures, tips and tricks. The restraining doors are locked at the beginning of the shift, but behind the doors, the inmates are roaming freely in the dorm. There are no restraining doors on the cubicles. There are roughly sixty inmates to the second and third floors each and eighteen inmates to the first floor. Nash lets Argus practice closing and dead locking the cells on the first floor. Argus has all kinds of trouble with cells not latching and the wrong cells engaging. No wonder, the locking mechanism is fifty years old and Argus hasn't had a lot of practice.

Lock down is finally accomplished. He and Nash have arrived thirty minutes early to get this done before the midnight count. Argus follows Nash's lead in counting this unit. The officers enter the floor and yell, "Count, find your bunks!"

Once the inmates are in place, one officer goes through and counts the inmates while the other officer covers him from the door. The hard fast rule is, you count living, breathing flesh. The counting officer returns to the door and then the second officer counts. Once the floor is counted, the two officers compare counts. If they agree, they move to the next floor. If they don't agree, they recount. Each floor is filled with blind corners to negotiate as the officer must enter each cubicle to see the inmates for the count. Argus and his partner successfully count each floor the first time. They call the counts in to Control to be verified. If Control agrees with their counts, the count has been fully verified. He likes working with this officer. Nash is all business. After the count clears, they open the restraining doors and announce lights

56

out. Then they re-secure the doors and turn the main lights out at a locked breaker box outside of the floor restraining door. Now the only light in the dorm comes from the book lights the inmates have purchased from commissary and the lights from the restroom at the far end of the unit. This accomplished, both officers go back to the office to scan the outgoing inmate mail, seal it and place it in a mail bag to go out on the next business day.

Midway through these duties, an inmate begins pounding on the third floor restraining door. Nash says, "Antrim, go up and see what he wants, would ya."

Argus climbs the two flights up to the third floor and looks through the six by six window in the door. An inmate is looking back at him through the glass. Argus shines his flashlight on the inmate. The first thing that registers is the blood on the front of the inmate's shirt. The second thing Argus sees as he follows the blood with his eyes is the three inch laceration on the inmate's throat. Argus calls down to Nash, "Hey man, this dude's throat is cut!"

Nash yells back, "Don't open that fuckin' door!" Then he calls Control, "Unit Six to Control, I need assistance in Unit Six, third floor, inmate assault."

The Operations Lieutenant arrives with several other officers and the door is breached. The inmate is removed and taken to Medical where the cut is deemed superficial. Argus and the other officers go through the unit checking each inmate for signs of a struggle. Some of the inmates were asleep and are in no mood to stand in front of the officers without shirts and have their hands, face and torso checked for wounds or blood. No other suspects are found. Argus and Nash go to the inmate's cube and secure his personal property for inventorying. His housing assignment has now changed to ADSEG. The next count will be at 3:00 am.

Counting the dorms at this hour is much different than the midnight count. This count is conducted in the dark with only a flashlight and the ambient light from the bathroom at the far end of the dorm. The aisles in between the cubicles are only three feet wide with the openings to the cubes staggered on each side of the aisle. The sounds of humanity come to Argus through the blackness as he thinks about the inmate whose throat had been slashed just a few hours earlier. The perpetrator is still in the unit and he has a blade. The blind corners are much more ominous as he negotiates his way through the cubes, flashlight in hand. It is cool in the unit but Argus doesn't notice as he feels a bead of sweat snake down his spine and stop at his duty belt. He has been taught to count the dorms holding the lighted end of the flashlight with the battery end up on his shoulder. Whichever way Argus turns, the illumination from the three cell flashlight follows. If he is attacked, it will be an economical movement to bring the weighted end of the light down on the attacker. He never shines the light in a sleeping inmate's face. That according to the training officers is disrespectful and unneeded. The light is shown at the inmate's solar plexus which provides the needed illumination.

As Argus enters each cube to count the inmates, he looks left and right to clear the hard corners. The hard corner is where danger could be waiting. There are two or three inmates to each cube. Nash is by the door, covering Argus. So the count goes two, four, seven, nine, twelve and so on. Argus writes the number on a piece of scratch paper at the end of each aisle. Every officer has a different method. This is what works for Argus. As he counts, every sense is heightened and Argus is completely focused on the task. Counting a dorm at night in a penitentiary is inherently dangerous and Argus has no misconceptions. He moves slowly, cuts no corners and counts living, breathing flesh.

It is 5:45 am. Argus and Nash have opened the cell doors on the first floor and the floor restraining doors for the second and third floors. Mainline will start soon. Inmates are starting to filter down to the corridor restraining doors of the unit. Nash puts down the telephone and says, "LT wants you to help out with pat searches at mainline cause he's short staff."

Argus says okay and picks up his lunchbox saying as he leaves, "See you tonight Nash."

Argus walks down the corridor and puts his lunchbox and jacket in the Lieutenant's Office, then heads down and positions himself in front of the exit door to the chow hall. He has a paper cup with a paper towel wadded up inside to serve as a spittoon. He puts a dip of Copenhagen snuff in his bottom lip and waits.

At 6:00 am, like clockwork, the Corridor Officer opens morning mainline. It will last for one hour. The corridor doors to the housing units are opened and the inmates converge on the chow hall. Inmates are never allowed to run in the corridor and the Corridor Officer has to slow a few hard heads down. Inmates go in one door and get in line for breakfast then they exit the chow hall by another door. There are several other officers doing pat searches as well. Argus is better at spotting inmates carrying extra items from the chow hall than he used

58

to be and has pretty good luck with his pat downs. He finds a piece of extra fruit, a bread wrapper full of pasta and a bread wrapper of bacon hidden in the inmate's crotch that the inmate had planned to sell for stamps. All of it goes in the trash can outside the chow hall. Then Argus sees one of the inmates that was huffing glue in the television room of Unit One come out of the exit door. He is the larger inmate that looked at Argus with such hate in his eyes.

Argus calls him over, "You! Yeah you, step over here and turn around for a pat down."

The inmate saunters over. There is disdain in his eyes. He steps up to Argus and doesn't turn around. He is four inches taller than Argus and has him by twenty pounds. Argus and the inmate have locked eyes. A test of will has begun.

The inmate starts the parley, "So, you think you're some kinda super cop or somthin'?"

Argus' heart rate is elevated. He's still new to this game. "No, just doing my job. Go ahead and turn around."

Argus smells the faint aroma of alcohol and realizes the inmate is slightly intoxicated. The inmate responds, "No, no, you think you're some kinda super cop."

The inmate edges closer. Argus stands his ground. If he steps back one inch, he might as well leave and never come back. Argus lowers his voice and his chin. His body tenses. Somewhere inside Argus the dragon has broken the lock on his little black box. The lid moves, a crack appears and a wisp of acrid smoke escapes.

Argus says, "Last chance. You better turn around for this search." His voice is low with menace.

The conversation reaches its apex. Argus is completely focused on the inmate as he leans in toward Argus. So much so, that he doesn't see the two officers converge on the inmate from both sides and grab him by the arms and lead him to the Lieutenant's Office. The other officers had recognized the body language immediately and had let the situation play out to see if Argus would knuckle under.

Vale's words come back to him. "We're going to let these inmates run at you to see if you've got what it takes."

Argus has been trained by these men that you give no order unless you're willing to back it up with force. He feels a change occurring but he has no words for it. The other officers step up to Argus and explain that he was doing fine and the only reason they pulled the inmate away from him was because they realized the inmate was drunk. Everything is a test in this place and Argus has just passed one. He spits his snuff in the cup and puts a fresh dip in. Some of the snuff lands on his shirt. He brushes the snuff off of his shirt, puts his spit cup on the floor behind him and calls another inmate over.

∞∞∞∞

Argus stands in the doorway of the Staff Training Center gym located in the basement of the building. He looks around at the well-lighted room. There are three individuals working out. Argus will make four. Lieutenant Grant and Atkins are working on lifting every weight in the gym on the bench press. Officer Thoms is in the back working a speed bag over. Argus watches as Grant and Atkins rep six wheels for ten without obvious effort. This is what he is here to work on. Nash had asked him about the incident in front of the chow hall. Word travels fast in the pen. He tells Argus, "Antrim, you did okay but frankly man, you've got to get bigger. These inmates understand only one thing. That guy was way too comfortable facing off with you. They only respect size and strength. You have to be big and strong enough to make them think twice about stepping to you like that."

So, Argus had listened intently to the SWAT member give him a class on what supplements to purchase and how to adjust his diet to put on muscle fast. Things he had never heard of and some he had. Creatine, protein powder, amino acids and testosterone enhancers. All over the counter and readily available at any health food store. Argus had stopped the morning after his shift at the local supplement retailer and purchased the list Nash had given him.

The items were expensive but Argus considered it an investment in himself. If it gave him a physique like Nash's, then that would definitely be a good thing. Nash had also given him some basic guidelines for working out to gain mass. Lift heavy, and then lift heavier. Work the muscle until it won't work anymore. Argus is here today to do just that. He watches the lieutenants working out. They are obviously friends. Lieutenant Atkins is about five-ten with a back so muscled his head won't even touch the bench as he lifts. Lieutenant Grant is built the same at an even six foot Argus guesses. He thinks about walking over and getting some advice, but these guys are lieutenants and he is just a rookie. Better to just stay away. He walks back to the rear of the gym where the heavy and speed bags are located. Officer Thoms is making the speed bag sound like a machine gun. He is bald with a long handlebar mustache and has a reputation with the inmates that he is not to be trifled with. He is Argus' height with a compact physique and it is obvious he is good with his hands. As Argus enters the area, Thoms gives him a side glance without missing a beat. There is no welcome in his eyes. Argus touches the heavy bag and throws a few barehanded punches. He feels clumsy and out of place hitting a two hundred pound leather bag without gloves. He leaves the room and heads back to the weights.

Argus decides to work his chest and triceps today beginning with some dumbbell flies and triceps extensions until his chest and arms scream. The weight he is using isn't impressive compared to the others in the gym and his arms shake because his mechanics are terrible, but Argus figures, at least I'm here. He knows Nash's advice is on point. These inmates work out every day and Argus will have to do the same. After leaving the gym, Argus feels sore and tired but it's a good tired. Not the usual night shift fatigue. He has one more stop to make before going home. The local sporting goods store where he buys his first set of heavy bag gloves. He's sure he'll need the practice.

Chapter 3
In the blackness, it smiles

The Unit Four Day Watch OIC is sitting on a large trash can at the end of the flat by the corridor restraining door of the unit. He's been at the game a long time and his demeanor is incredibly relaxed. He insists that everyone, staff and inmate address him as Mr. Wilt. Argus liked him immediately when they first met two weeks ago. Argus is the Evening Watch OIC and is Mr. Wilt's relief. Every time Argus arrives to relieve Mr. Wilt, he can be found on his trash can. He is one of the few officers that are as vertically challenged as Argus. Mr. Wilt seems to command the respect of the inmates and Argus wishes he knew Mr. Wilt's secret because he is anything but intimidating.

Argus gives Mr. Wilt his chits and the two perform shift change on the flat. Mr. Wilt leaves and Argus goes to the office and places his lunch box and thermos behind the desk away from the door. He spots the mail bag in the office, but he won't do mail call until after the 4:00 pm stand up count. For this count, once in a twenty four hour period, the inmates must stand and face the door so the officer can make sure they are healthy, unmarked and able to stand. It is an accountability check and a welfare check all in one. Argus locks his office door and makes a cursory tour of the unit as the inmates from the various work details return to the unit for count.

Unit Four is a classic cell house like Unit Two, but without the honor unit status. The doors in this unit lock. The recall movement is complete so Argus locks his unit door and at five minutes to four he announces in his best drill instructor's voice, "Count! Count time! Cell up!"

At two minutes to four, Argus starts closing the cell doors with the inmates inside. Each door closes with a slam and click. He pulls the door to make sure it latches. He starts on the top tier because he feels this is safer. This method leaves no one above his head to drop anything on him. He then clears the flat and locks the lower tier. At 4:00 pm, Control announces over the radio, "Control to all housing units, count time, count time. This will be the official 4:00 pm stand up count. Count your inmates and call Control with your count."

The Unit Three OIC will assist Argus with the count, and then Argus will assist him with Unit Three. Argus steps to each cell and pulls the door once more as he counts. He keeps a tally in his head as he goes and looks each inmate over to make sure they are not injured. Most of the inmates are standing when he reaches their cell. Some are not. Argus just stands and waits. He does not tell them to stand because he might lose count. The inmates know, until you stand, the count cannot proceed. Until the count is finished, they are locked in their cells. No one wants the rest of the block to think they held up the count.

Once Argus has finished counting, he goes to the corridor restraining door where the Unit Three OIC has been covering him. Unit Three begins his count of Argus' Unit. Both compare their totals and call Control with the total. Then they cross over to Unit Three and count in the same fashion. It takes around thirty minutes to count the entire institution. Once Control announces a clear count, the doors are unlocked and the inmates prepare for mainline. In the half hour before mainline, Argus does mail call on the flat right outside his office. He calls the name of each inmate and the inmate steps up or his mail is passed back. Nobody fucks around with mail call either. Two hard rules, you don't cause someone to be locked down any longer than they have too and you don't mess with the mail.

When he'd first taken over the unit a few weeks ago, the inmates had tried him. They were just little games at first. They'd even tried to pick his office door lock with a broken bed spring, leaving the bed spring in the lock so Argus would know they had tried. Over time they had come to the realization Argus would do his job according to the policy and always be firm, fair and consistent. It wasn't personal to Argus as he had told them early on. "It's not personal it's just policy."

The inmates were getting used to him by now. He treats them all the same and does his job. Argus completes mail call and goes into his office to complete his logs.

This is the only time during the shift he will be in the office for more than a few seconds. Argus has developed the habit of standing out on the flat by the door and spitting Copenhagen in the trash can Mr. Wilt sits on. He has found, if you stay out of your office, the night is quieter. The Corridor Officer opens evening mainline but unlike breakfast, each unit will be called to mainline in order according to how well they did on the monthly unit inspection performed by the Associate Warden of Custody. The dirtier the unit, the later they eat. It is just another way to manage the behavior of someone doing a lot of time. Argus' keys the door to his unit as they are finally called to chow. He performs the pat searches as usual, throwing the contraband in the same trash can he spits in.

After mainline, it is time to start his cell searches. He is required to do at least five searches during his shift. He will get at least five, sometimes more according to what occurs during the evening. He has six hours to go until scheduled quitting time. Argus is getting better at cell searches through practice and introspection. He has found, he can think like an inmate. Argus takes a slow, easy tour of the unit, smelling the air. Watching the inmates to see who is watching him. There is a card game going on at a table on the flat. The "scribe" is standing behind the inmate running the card game, keeping score on a piece of paper. Gambling is against the rules, but no chips are on the table and the notations are just tick marks anyway. Argus knows this without even seeing the paper. No way to make a case from that.

"Just a friendly game," Argus thinks.

Several inmates are watching the game. Argus has caught one of the inmates keeping track of him as he walks the unit. Argus has always been a student of human behavior. What you might call a people watcher. With each passing shift, Argus is getting more comfortable in this place. He thinks to himself, "You shouldn't stare at me you shifty little fucker. It's not polite."

Argus already knows where the inmate lives because he stands out. The inmate is a loud mouth and usually flies way above the radar. Argus goes to his cell about halfway down the flat on the left side. As he prepares to enter the cell, the inmate yells in a tropical accent, "Hey officer, what are you going in my cell for?"

The inmate leaves the card game and walks over to where Argus is standing. Argus smiles and tells the inmate that he knows why he's going into the cell and, "No, you can't watch me search so take a walk."

The inmate tells Argus, "You're messing with my worm officer. That's no good."

Argus is intrigued now. "Wait a minute, your worm?"

The inmate turns back around, "Yeah officer. Everybody has a worm in them and you're messing with mine. Bad things happen to people who mess with my worm."

The inmate turns and walks back to the card game.

Argus enters the cell and sees that the inmate is the only occupant. That means anything in the cell is the inmate's. As is his practice, Argus just stands in the middle of the cell and thinks about where he would hide something if he was locked in here. Argus starts in the corner and works his way around the cell, searching meticulously. His goal is to replace everything exactly the way he found it. It's a respect thing. Respect is everything in the penitentiary. Argus comes up with very little to show for his efforts. Just a few pieces of nuisance contraband are discovered and aren't anything to get excited about. So why did the inmate show out like he did? Argus knows he's missed something. He looks at the mattress. He's already rolled the mattress and it was empty. Then it hits him. What about rolling it cross ways. It's labor intensive but pays off immediately. Something hard is keeping Argus from rolling the mattress this way. Argus inspects the mattress and finds a pencil sized hole in the side. He braces the mattress against the bed frame and pushes down. The end of a steel rod pops through the hole. Argus pulls the pick shank out of the mattress. It is a pencil sized metal rod, six inches long and sharpened to a point on one end. A shoe string is taped to the other end. This is what the inmate was worried about Argus finding. He sticks the shank into his belt and exits the cell, satisfied with his search. He deadlocks the cell and the inmate knows he's found the shank.

Argus asks the inmate, "Well, c'mon. You gonna walk down there like a man or do I have to cuff you?"

The inmate tells Argus, "I'll walk Antrim, but you're upsetting my worm. Something bad is going to happen to you."

Argus pulls his radio from his belt and calls the Corridor Officer, "Unit Four to Corridor, I have one I'll be bringing to the Lieutenant's Office. The Unit Three OIC steps out in the corridor so he can monitor both units while Argus is gone. Once Argus and the inmate arrive at the Lieutenant's Office, Argus pat searches the inmate, puts handcuffs on him and opens the door. Argus shows the Operations Lieutenant the shank and says, "He's the only inmate in the cell boss. It was in his mattress."

Argus fills out an evidence form, photographs the shank and puts everything in an evidence bag. The code for the offense is 104, possession of a weapon and must be referred for prosecution but shanks are rarely picked up by the Prosecuting Attorney. There are just too many. The Corridor Officer clears the corridor and locks it down.

Argus thinks, "One more customer for ADSEG."

Now Argus will return to his unit, write the incident report and pack the inmate's property. Argus has been getting a lot of practice packing and inventorying property.

Later in the evening, the inmates are out on the tiers and flat. There are loud conversations throughout the unit as the inmates try to be heard above the range fans. Argus looks down from the upper tier at the line for the microwave where the washers and dryers are located. Inmates holding their microwave bowls full of ramen noodles or whatever else they're stacking with. So far, everyone has played nice tonight. It sends a message when you walk one out at the beginning of the shift on a one hundred level offense. Nobody else wants to follow if it can be helped. Argus has made quite a few rounds of the unit tonight after packing property and doing all but one of his cell searches. He circles the unit for one more cell to search. He's on the top tier, all the way to the front of the unit on the same side as his office below. It is a blind spot for those officers who stay in their office. Not for Argus. He decides on the end cell for no particular reason. That's how random cell searches work. Argus steps up to the cell door. There are two inmates in the cell talking but they stop when they see Argus. "Fellas, I need you to step out of the cell so I can shake it down."

They step out with sullen glances and huffs while walking fifteen feet down the tier to lean on the railing. Argus is good with that. He won't allow them to stand right outside as he searches. The inmates both have long hair in ponytails. Both are around the same size and look like they should be on motorcycles. Neither one looks like a monster.

Argus enters the cell and stands for a second, just thinking. Then he starts in one corner as usual and works his way around the cell. He rolls the mattresses, checks under the bed, inside the shoes and bends the soles. He searches one locker, finding nothing so far except the normal nuisance stuff. He looks under the first locker by tipping it slightly and propping it on his three cell flashlight then he starts on the second locker. He opens the combination lock with the universal key he has on the unit keys and opens the doors. Argus immediately sees the pictures hanging on the inside of the door. He will never un-see them. They are cut outs from a magazine and are what one of the inmates considers pornography. They picture nude women laying across stone slabs and stainless steel tables in provocative poses. Standard poses for any porn magazine, but these women have been butchered. One has a deep cut on her thigh and her throat has been cut. The others have been

66

mutilated in like fashion. They look off to the left or right with unseeing eyes as they lay in pools of bright red blood. Argus gets back on track and finishes the search of the locker, but then he stops again and looks at the pictures. Argus thinks, "This is what gives this guy sexual gratification."

It is incomprehensible to Argus who was raised to protect women. From this moment on Argus is certain that this penitentiary is where evil resides.

∞∞∞∞

Argus opens his eyes to the sight of his bedroom ceiling. He is slightly disoriented and sweating as he blinks the sleep from his eyes. He feels his heart beating in his chest as he tells himself, "You're at home. There is no cell house. Relax, it was just a dream."

He looks around the bedroom and feels the tension in his muscles as he swings his legs over the side of the bed. He thinks to himself, "You can't just turn it off."

He doesn't know why, but he feels angry. It is the dream, he knows but knowing doesn't help. Argus rubs his face with both hands and looks at himself in the vanity mirror. He hears Olivia playing in the living room and the sun is shining through the curtains from the outside. He thinks it must be mid-morning. Lynn has let him sleep in. He walks out of the bedroom into the living room of their tiny home and feels the warmth of the sun on his face. Theirs is a cottage style house with two bedrooms and a basement. The kitchen is small but they don't need much. There are windows all along the front and alley side of the house which let in a good amount of sunlight. The sun streams through these windows providing plenty of ambient light to the West side of the house. There is an enclosed front porch and a nice quiet neighborhood. Shortly after buying the place, Argus had built a privacy fence around the yard. All in all, it's a great starter house which Lynn has made a home.

His daughter is playing in the living room floor and Lynn is sitting on the couch with one leg tucked underneath her. She looks at him with a smile expecting some appreciative gesture for letting him sleep. Argus knows he should give her this, but, something inside him is off. He feels, "mean." He would call it anger, but there is absolutely nothing to be angry about and he knows this. He sits down in the recliner and looks out the window with bleary eyes. There is a gnawing in his gut. His daughter has been playing with a tiny baby carriage. She is only a toddler and is glad to see that daddy is awake. She smiles as she pushes the baby carriage toward him. Argus looks down as it lightly bumps the side of his leg. Olivia is giggling, just wanting to play but something takes control of Argus' leg and he can't stop it. He lifts his foot and pushes the carriage away with his toe. A voice is in the back of his head screaming for him to stop but the deed is done before he hears.

His daughter starts crying as Lynn jumps to her defense saying, "Don't you dare do that to her!"

He is immediately sorry and ashamed of himself. He looks at his wife holding their little girl and thinks, "Argus! What the fuck is wrong with you!"

He tries to apologize but his wife is the comfort zone for his little girl and a beast has no place there. Argus stands and looks at them with no words and really, what the hell would he say? He goes into the bathroom and washes his face in cold water. The bad dreams have started.

∞∞∞∞

The unit looks abandoned but there is someone else here. Argus instinctively knows this. He is moving down the upper tier. The concrete is battleship gray and the glass from the windows litters the floor. Argus looks to his left at the shattered windows and the torn plastic blowing with the cold wind from the windows in the back of the cells. He is cold and alone. The t-shirt he is wearing is no protection from the icy wind and he feels it on his arms. His boots crunch the broken glass as he carefully moves down the tier, trying to be as quiet as possible. He knows his enemy is here, somewhere. He knows he can't run or hide. He must find the enemy and face them. There is a sick feeling in the pit of his stomach. He has no weapons but still he moves forward. As he approaches the stairwell, Argus hears the wind blowing through the windows to his left and the crunch of the glass. His eyes are locked on the blind corner that he must go around. He starts around slowly, hands up, taking the corner as wide as the upper tier railing allows. He's just about at the apex of the turn. He looks to his left and sees his reflection in a broken window pane. The building disappears as he opens his eyes in the dark. He is sweating as he listens to Lynn's soft rhythmic breathing.

Argus bends at the waist and puts his hands on his knees. His lungs strain to take in precious oxygen. His clothes are soaked through with sweat to include the socks inside his duty boots. The only thing that isn't soaked is his uniform shirt which he has pulled off and hung on the wrought iron divider that separates the weights from the heavy bag. He has adopted the habit of working the heavy bag for an hour after his shift. No matter how long the shift is, he will not go home to his wife and daughter without exhausting himself on the bag. Argus doesn't bother changing clothes. He just drives to the Training Center from the prison, takes his shirt off and puts his bag gloves on. He looks at his watch on the ledge of the divider. "I've got time for one more round."

He had been called to the Warden's office after he'd responded to the fight in Unit Two. At first he thought he was in trouble, but it turned out to be the exact opposite. The Activities Lieutenant had recommended him for a special act award. The Warden had presented him with the small cardboard plaque and shook his hand. Argus liked the Warden. He had risen through the ranks from correctional officer so he knew the stressors in working a cell house. Argus had smiled during the photo so his eyes were half closed when the shutter clicked. The photographer from Personnel had to take another.

As they shook hands the Warden had given him two pieces of wisdom which to Argus was much more valuable than the plaque. He said, "Keep smiling Mr. Antrim and find someone to talk too if you need to talk. Not your wife though. She doesn't need to know anything about this place."

Argus took that advice to heart, but even though he is friendly with everyone, he doesn't trust anyone enough to open up like that. At heart, he has always been a loner. The heavy bag has filled that void. After every shift, day or night, he comes here and punishes it mercilessly and in so doing, cleanses himself of this thing that he never wants his wife and daughter to see again.

He checks his watch again. She knows he'll be late because she knows what he is doing. She knows he is doing what he needs to do. He thinks, "therapy," and almost laughs.

For one last round, he pounds the bag. He throws a jab, cross, hook, hook, then an elbow and another. He hits the bag hard and rocks it. His knuckles have become callous and where there is no callous, there is blood. Each time he strikes, electricity shoots up his arms. The pain is weakness leaving the body. He hits until he has no more breath and then he's done until tomorrow. Argus looks at his bag gloves and sees the padding is almost worn through. He'll need a new pair soon. The instructor who gave the hostage class told the students at the Training Facility to talk with their families about the fact that they might not come home. He has never had that conversation with his wife and he never will. The Warden is right and Argus is thankful he was given this insight by the much more experienced man. Lynn will never know about this place.

∞∞∞∞

Argus is working Unit Four and has just made a round in the unit. He stops by his office, keys the door and gets a drink of his coffee then steps back out on the flat. He turns and locks his door and heads for his giant spit can at the door of the unit. It's late in the evening. The counts and mainline have been completed. Now it's a waiting game. He thinks, "Just play nice for a little while longer fellas."

He's standing with his back to the corridor restraining door watching the inmates on the flats when Officer Tarry shows up at the door. He is older than Argus by ten years and has medicated himself with food for the better part of his career. Over the past months, Argus has come to the realization that every correctional officer medicates themselves in some way. Whether it is food, exercise, alcohol or something else everyone has something to help them cope. Argus' drug of choice is the punching bag and his addiction has benefits. He has gained ten pounds of muscle in the past few months and his hands have become hard with the constant pounding. He can rep his body weight for fifteen on the bench which is a big improvement and he has no plans to stop. He wonders if he even could.

Argus keys the door for Tarry who's looking at him expectantly. "Antrim, the LT wants you to report to Disciplinary Seg for a move."

A calculated use of force AKA forced cell move. They usually use SWAT for that. Tarry hands Argus his chits as he hands Tarry the equipment for the unit. Argus starts out the door and Tarry stops him. "Grab your stuff, you won't be back tonight. It'll take a while."

Argus heads down the corridor to the Lieutenant's Office and drops his lunchbox and thermos off then he heads across the corridor to Disciplinary Segregation.

The West SEG officer keys the outer door and yells, "Staff on the door!"

The Disciplinary Seg Officer pokes his head around the corner and says, "Yeah, give me a minute."

Argus thinks, "He's not having a good night."

Argus is keyed into the unit through the sally port and finds himself in the middle of a flurry of activity. As soon as he walks in, a fetid stench strikes his nostrils. There is a half inch of water on the floor and it is already soaking through his boots. His boots squish as he heads into the laundry room where several members of the SWAT Team are getting suited up in Vietnam era flak vests and football helmets. There aren't enough SWAT members on duty, so Argus has been picked to fill the gap. He feels a fleeting sense of pride. Nash is one of the officers suiting up and Argus bets he had something to do with this. They hand Argus a football helmet and flak vest so he can suit up. It's hard to put a shank through a flak vest.

To a lay person, a calculated use of force looks like five guys going in to tackle one inmate but in reality, it is a use of force technique designed to protect the inmate from injury. Each member of the team has a specific duty. Acting in concert, they overpower the disruptive inmate quickly using physical control techniques. The number one man on the team will pin the inmate against the wall and control the inmate's head ensuring he isn't injured. The number two man controls the left arm. Argus will be the number three man. He will control the inmate's right arm and apply the handcuff restraints. The fourth and fifth man will control the inmate's legs and apply the leg irons. Once the inmate is restrained, he will be carried to a clean cell and placed in handcuffs, black box, belly chain and leg irons until his disruptive behavior ceases.

The team is suited up and ready. The Operations Lieutenant briefs the team prior to going down range to the cell. It is hard to hear the briefing over the screaming and taunting of the inmates on the range. Everything is filmed. Argus knows that there is to be no talking from the team members unless a weapon is spotted. The lieutenant is the only one who speaks. From the briefing the team learns that the inmate has assaulted staff by throwing urine and is refusing to submit to handcuff restraints. He has also blocked the toilet and flooded the range. Nash asks Argus if he's comfortable applying the restraints. Argus tensely nods his head.

Nash says, "I know this is your first one so, listen, there is no wrong way to put the cuffs on in this situation. The goal is to get them on his wrists okay."

Argus smiles and nods again. Nash lightly punches him in the chest. Nash will be the number one on the move. The team lines up and each team member states their name and duties for the camera, then the lieutenant gives the same briefing on camera. It's time to move. The team follows the lieutenant down to the inmate's cell. Seven sets of boots splash through the toilet water.

The inmates start yelling at the inmate who is going to be moved, "Better not bitch up man! Here they come! Go hard motherfucker!"

Argus looks into the cells as they pass. The inmates have put all of their property on the bottom bunks to keep it out of the water. They're keyed up and anxious for a show. As they arrive at the cell, the lieutenant tells the inmate that this is his last chance to cuff up. The inmate says, "Go fuck yourself bitch."

The other inmates on the range explode with taunts and insults directed at the officers. The lieutenant yells, "On the box! Open seven!"

The inmate moves to the left and then right in the cell trying to confuse the team as to where he'll be when the door is racked. These doors are sliders with bars like the first floor in unit six. Before the door is fully open the force cell team enters as one unit. Nash makes contact with the inmate without slowing down. The other team members are right behind Nash, driving him forward. The inmate is trying to stop a thousand pounds of correctional officer and he has no chance. Argus grabs the right wrist of the inmate, twists and locks the elbow. The number two man does the same with the left arm. They bring the inmate down to the floor and apply the restraints. He splashes in the water as he goes down. The inmate has quit the fight but he's now screaming bloody murder for the benefit of the camera. The team picks the inmate up and exits the cell. He starts wriggling in their grasp, trying to fight again. He wants to put on a good show for the rest of the inmates on the range. The sound in the unit is deafening as other inmates scream taunts and profanity laden insults.

After the team gets the inmate in the clean cell, they search the inmate and adjust his restraints. Once the inmate is secure, the Physician's Assistant examines the inmate for injuries and asks if he is injured. The inmate tells the P.A., "I'm titanium steel motherfuckers. You can't hurt me."

Argus smiles at this as he and the others back out of the cell. The camera is still recording as the team exits the range to more insults. The team lines up like before. When it is Argus' turn he says into the camera, "My name is Argus Antrim, correctional officer. I was the number three man on the team. I controlled the upper right appendage and applied the handcuff restraints. I have no injuries."

After the lieutenant's brief, the recording is stopped. Argus is sweating in the gear and sheds the flak vest. He wore the same kind in the Corps. Nash tells him, "You did good Antrim. Your year is almost up isn't it?"

Argus tells him, "Yeah, another couple months."

Nash smiles. "I'd like to see you try out for the SWAT team when you get your year in, if you're interested."

Argus looks at Nash, the weight of the compliment is not lost on him. "Yeah man, you know I'm interested."

Nash hits him in the chest again and smiles. "Let's get these memos done."

Argus is thinking about his two hundred pound friend at the Training Center. He has a lot to share.

∞∞∞∞

Unit Three is the unit where all disciplinary transfers are housed when they first arrive at the penitentiary. The powers that be at some point in the past decided that it would be a good idea to put all of the troublemakers in one unit and let them work their way out. Tarragon is where troublemakers are sent to learn to program.

"They earn their way here," he thinks. He is standing in his usual spot at the corridor restraining door, spitting into the trash can and the inmates are used to him by now. He's been in the unit two weeks. Argus starts to reflect on the past months and all he's learned.

His instincts have definitely improved as he's gotten a feel for the job. Argus was always a borderline introvert and always enjoyed watching people and their mannerisms. This has served him well here. He can feel the mood in the units soon after walking in the door. He can feel tension in a unit just like a dog can feel an approaching storm long before the rain comes. As he watches the inmates move about the unit, he can almost see the game and all of its angles. Make no mistake, there's always an angle to everything. He can tell by the way an inmate carries himself if he is a punk or a predator. He can smell fear on a man. It is an acrid smell, almost like wet, muted skunk. As he takes a tally of the past months, this is what he finds himself doing out of instinct, studying the inmates in this block. He spits his Copenhagen out and immediately puts another dip in. Argus has learned more here about human behavior at the basal level than in all the previous years of his life. Humans simplified to basic instinctual behavior. He has made some mistakes along the way since arriving. After all he thinks, "I'm human."

One mistake occurred right in this very unit. An inmate was showing out by mouthing off on the flat. Argus had gone in his cell to search it. The inmate had just arrived. There wasn't much inside the cell, so it didn't take long for Argus to complete the search. Argus exited the cell and waved the inmate over. His intention was to counsel the inmate on his behavior off the flat like he'd seen more experienced officers do. His mistake was an example of a lesson learned in Georgia. It was a simple tactical mistake that could have ended badly. He had entered the cell first. Now the inmate was between him and the door. The inmate had no respect for himself, let alone Argus. Argus told the inmate the disrespect wouldn't be tolerated. The inmate screamed at Argus, "I'm not following your orders 'cause I don't give a fuck about you or your authority! I DON'T GIVE A FUCK!"

It was almost like the inmate wanted Argus to lock him up. Argus just shook his head and walked out of the cell past the inmate. It was a no win situation inside the cell and Argus knew it. He hadn't pressed the button on the inmate because, doing that would be to admit he'd run into something he couldn't solve on his own. If the LT had to run his block, what did he need Argus for? The inmate ended up getting himself locked up the next shift anyway and Argus figured that's what he wanted. To check in protective custody without it looking like that's what he was doing.

But, word travels fast in the pen and the next day when Argus checked in with the lieutenant at the beginning of his shift, Lieutenant Atkins pulled him up, "Antrim, you don't wanna let one of these inmates get you in a cell like that, especially in Unit Three. There's radio dead spots down there where your portable won't transmit to Control."

Argus knew he was dead wrong in what he did and told the lieutenant, "Your right boss. It won't happen again," and he meant it.

As he thinks, Argus notices a lot of traffic going in and out of the end cell on the right. Guys coming out are carrying a coffee cake or some type of food item from the Commissary. He thinks, "That dude's running a store."

Argus makes a mental note. "That could be valuable if I have problems with that guy later on or need to send a message."

Popping a store inconveniences every inmate in the unit. Argus makes a routine round of the unit to get a closer look while not looking. It amazes him at how these inmates tell on themselves. Argus stops by his office on the way back to his post and gets a drink of coffee. He logs his round into the log book, exits the office, locks the door and assumes his spot at the trash can.

As he stands there, he thinks about inmate Coffee Cup. The inmate was his unit orderly in Unit Eleven. Argus was fairly new and hadn't learned even a small portion of the game yet. Inmate Coffee Cup showed up at Argus' office and asked, "Anything else you need me to do boss?"

Argus had no idea what else might need to be done so he told the inmate, "No, not right now."

But, the inmate didn't leave. Instead he started talking about coffee and how much he liked a cup in the morning. Then, the inmate noticed Argus' cup of fast food coffee and the styrofoam cup with the orange lid that it was contained in. Inmate Coffee Cup said, "Hey boss, when your done with that cup can I have it? I could use a bigger cup to put my coffee in while I'm working around here."

Add one big smile. Argus thought he's fishing and the cup was just a sideline. "You know that's not gonna happen. Now if you don't mind, I got work to do."

Inmate Coffee Cup took the hint. "Oh yeah, no problem boss."

He left and Argus didn't think any more about it. He had read the book they gave the trainees in Georgia called, "The Games Inmates Play," and should have seen the angle but Argus missed it.

As far as he was concerned, it was just another inmate trying to figure him out to find a weakness. Argus finished his cup of coffee out in the corridor, mashed the cup and threw the whole thing away. The lid was hard plastic and couldn't be mashed.

During noon mainline, Officer Grai, the Corridor Officer came down to Argus' unit with inmate Coffee Cup in tow. Officer Grai asked Argus, "This look familiar to you?"

Argus replied, "It looks like my coffee cup lid from this morning on a different cup."

Officer Grai looked hard at Argus. "He says you gave it to him."

Argus looked at the inmate and he realized information wasn't the goal. The goal was to get Argus to give him a small piece of contraband he would use to try and turn Argus. It became clear and it showed on Argus' face. Trafficking in contraband equals immediate dismissal. Argus thought about his wife and daughter. It angered him that this inmate thought he would be weak enough to be turned. The inmate didn't know who Argus was.

He looked at Officer Grai as he barely controlled his anger and said, "I didn't give this piece of shit a motherfucking thing. I threw that shit in the trash."

He looked at inmate Coffee Cup with dead eyes. Officer Grai knew him. Argus had bought a leather duty belt from him. Officer Grai trained Argus on proper pat search techniques.

Grai was satisfied and told Argus, "Watch what you put in the fuckin' trash from now on and handed it to Argus."

The inmate made his exit into the unit.

Argus thought, "Alright motherfucker. We're both gonna be here for a while and I won't forget this shit."

Argus has always carried everything out that he brings in since. The only thing that goes in the trash can now is tobacco spit. Argus' thoughts are interrupted by yelling coming from the Unit Counselor's Office. It sounds like a one sided, heated argument. The Unit Counselor steps out of his office and makes it to the center of the flat about ten feet in front of Argus before the inmate catches up with him, circles around and heads him off. The inmate is nicknamed "Half Pint" because he is about a buck fifty soaking wet and shorter than Argus. He is also volatile, crazy and he reeks because he doesn't shower. Argus believes this is a defense against sexual predators.

"Half Pint's" MO is to act out and get handcuffed in the unit like a tough guy then be taken to ADSEG when he wants a vacation. The counselor has his hands up in a conciliatory gesture as "Half Pint" tells him all the things he plans to do to him sexually. It's a long list.

He says, "You gonna be my bitch, motherfucker!"

Argus sees that the inmates are starting to take notice and gather for the show and he's had enough. He decides he's not going to give "Half Pint" what he wants this time.

Argus steps forward and calls the inmate by name. "Half Pint" turns on Argus and steps toward him yelling "Put the cuffs on me big man! Put the cuffs on me!"

After the incident in the cell, Argus saw the writing on the wall and had stepped into his first dojo. Since that time, he had studied Kenpo Karate and Kyusho Jitsu religiously. He knew no matter how much muscle he was able to put on, with his stature, he would always need an edge. The inmate was standing arm's length from Argus now, fists clenched, face forward and Argus had, had enough.

Argus says, "Fuck them cuffs," and grabs "Half Pint" at a point just above the elbow, digging his thumb into the pressure point. "Half Pint" grimaces and leans in to Argus to try and relieve the pressure.

Argus guides the inmate out of the unit like a petulant child as he yells over his shoulder, "Lock my door for me counselor."

All the way down the corridor to the Lieutenant's Office "Half Pint's" other arm is making circular motions in the air as he yells, "Put the cuffs on me! Put the cuffs on me, big man!"

When they get to the Lieutenant's Office, the Operations Lieutenant just rolls his eyes and grabs a detention order. "Half Pint" is on another vacation.

Chapter Four
The lock is broken as acrid smoke begins to rise

Unit Ten has a relaxed atmosphere tonight. This is the final night of Argus' tour on the rookie roster. He is working the 4:00 pm to midnight shift. The counts have cleared, the weather is cool and most of the inmates are on the flats or in the television room. Next quarter he will be on sick and annual for ninety days. Sick and annual post is a fill in post. He will work one or two weeks here and there in the institution filling in for people who've called out sick or are on vacation. It will be a good opportunity to gain experience although the post isn't a sought after one. Every officer has to fill sick and annual at least once a year. Argus is doing what he always does with the same results. Watching his unit and being visible so the inmates know he's there and on watch. It makes for a quieter night. No inmate will admit it, but they want him on that door, spitting Copenhagen in the trash can. His presence allows them to relax a little bit. They know he'll be there to handle the wrecks when they come.

It was commissary day for the unit and the inmates are walking around eating the small container of ice cream they purchase once a week. The card game is friendly and the inmates at the table are laughing at some unknown joke or are ribbing one of the players. Argus figures, if they're laughing, they're not fighting. The line for the microwave is a long one tonight. Argus is continually amazed at what they can cook in that small white box. Yelling erupts from the television room. Argus steps to the door and sees the inmates are watching a game. No trouble, just avid sports fans. The trouble usually comes after the game when the bookie starts calling in the bets. Betting is against the rules and Argus busts a bookie when he finds the master betting slips, but he can't catch all the fish. He does his best. Usually at least one inmate won't be able to pay and will have to request protective custody until his family can put the money on his commissary account. Then he'll send word through the inmate grapevine that he can pay the tab and the interest. Sometimes the bookie will let him come back to the yard and then again sometimes not.

Argus leaves the television room door. He doesn't watch sports, he watches humans so that game doesn't interest him. Argus thinks, "It's time for a round in the unit anyway."

The inmates act like they're ignoring him for the most part. He's just another part of doing hard time. He decides he'll check the inmate's drink containers when he clears the television room at lock down to make sure they haven't made any hooch for the game. If he finds anything, he'll check the inmate for intoxication. The bust will either be intoxication or possession. The charge is the same level offense so it doesn't really matter. You can't drink and drive in a penitentiary without consequences. He'll have the Corridor Officer back him from the door when he does this. Argus makes it back to his spot at the door, throws in a fresh dip and spits.

He notices an inmate standing in the microwave line. The inmate has a homemade microwave bowl he's holding with both hands and he's white knuckling it. The bowl is completely full of ramen noodles and water. The inmate probably bought the bowl from an inmate who works in food service for stamps. It looks like a bulk food container which has been cut down to around five inches tall. Its nuisance contraband Argus could take if the inmate was an asshole but he's not. Argus files it away for future reference. He starts watching the inmate's focus on the bowl. Argus studies these guys for the same reason they study him. Find out what is most important to them and use it to manage them. When you're doing as much time as they are, an incident report for nuisance contraband means little to nothing. It all comes down to running your block and Argus has gotten fairly good at it.

Argus had no experience at all when he first entered this place, but he's been a dedicated student and learned the lessons the older hacks have taught him. He's also learned a great deal from the inmates, although they didn't know they were teaching him. Argus' checks his watch and sees that its 2315, time to clear the television room for lockdown. He steps inside the television room and announces, "Ten minutes to lockdown fellas."

The inmates start folding up their chairs and heading past. Argus checks their containers with no luck. No scent of hooch as they pass either. He picks three out and pat searches them. He finds two betting slips that he takes. The inmates realize he could write the incident report but it's petty. It would be like writing a report for an extra banana and really not worth the paper. At 2325 he starts shutting cell doors as the inmates race from the ice machine to their cells. Two inmates have missed the first pull on the doors and have to wait until

Argus has secured the unit, then he comes back around and lets them in their cells.

Argus makes another round and pulls the doors again just to make sure. The oncoming officer should go around and pull doors when he gets there but some don't. Argus won't turn over an unsecure unit. His relief arrives at the corridor door and Argus lets him in. They go to the office and exchange chits for equipment. The only inmates still out of their cells are the two orderlies sweeping the flat and television room. Argus stays an extra five minutes and gives the oncoming officer his brief. The night was quiet but Argus will never say the "Q" word. It's bad luck. He tells his relief it was uneventful, leaves the unit and heads through the Control sally port.

Argus thinks about his evening as he makes his way out of the institution, mentally retracing his steps. Seventy five percent of the time, an uneventful shift is just what a correctional officer experiences. Minor encounters with the inmates which evolve into nothing. It's the other twenty five percent that can result in an officer being hurt or killed and the trouble is, the officer never can tell when the twenty five percent will happen. During the past year, Argus has learned that you never let your guard down. Every pat search is a felony stop. Every cell search is a high risk warrant. The inmates are all felons and they've earned their way here some way or the other.

He reaches Tower One and is let in the first gate of the sally port, looks up at the tower so the officer can see his face and is then let out the other gate. As he walks to his truck, Argus thinks, "Hyper vigilance is what is required all the time on the inside."

There's a price to be paid for that type of mental focus but the price is greater if you don't have it. It's not an easy switch to turn off completely and it has changed him. Unlike before, Argus always sits in a room with his back to the wall now. He looks at waist lines in the grocery store for signs of a weapon. He walks a half step behind his wife and to the side to cover the back and scan the front. He trusts absolutely no one completely except his wife and his fellow hacks.

He reaches his truck, starts it up and heads to the Staff Training Center to punish the heavy bag once again. Argus has to admit that he is good at this job and he loves it. The job has given him a mission, like the Marine Corps had. He can think like the men he keeps inside the wire and he is proud to be a worthy opponent in the game. In the past year, the constant hyper vigilance has caused something to awaken in him. The inmate in Unit Four had called it his "worm." Argus calls it a dragon.

∞∞∞∞

At the penitentiary, the segregation units are Administrative Detention or "ADSEG" and Disciplinary Segregation or simply "DS." If the penitentiary is a small violent city, the segregation units serve as the jail inside the jail. Inmates in ADSEG have been placed there for an allegation of an infraction in the rules which is serious enough to prohibit them from staying in the general population because they pose a risk to the orderly running of the place. The Operations Lieutenant makes the determination as to whether to place them there using the greater weight of evidence. As an officer, Argus must make the case each time he brings an inmate before the lieutenant. Other reasons for an inmate to be sent to ADSEG are protective custody and being under investigation by the prison Investigative Office. While in ADSEG, an inmate has almost the same privileges as general population inmates because they haven't been sentenced by the Disciplinary Hearing Officer for the alleged offense.

The inmates in ADSEG receive one hour of outside recreation every twenty four hours, commissary orders delivered to their cell, Law Library privileges located in the unit and various other privileges. In any segregation unit, security is tighter. The inmates are locked in the cells and only moved from the cell to the shower, Law Library of other location after being handcuffed behind the back or in front with a belly chain attached to the cuffs. They are escorted hands on at all times. "Hands on escort" is simply the officer's hand on their elbow as they walk.

Disciplinary Segregation is different. The inmates in DS have been seen by the Disciplinary Hearing Officer and been sanctioned under the Agency's inmate discipline codes. They may be sanctioned to various forms of punishment, such as, time in DS, Commissary restriction or loss of good time earned. The inmates will also be allowed less personal property in DS. They will still be afforded recreation every twenty four hours, Law Library and showers. All inmates in ADSEG and DS receive the same food as inmates in general population or "GP." The food is served in plastic trays and brought to the unit by the # 3 Officer in ADSEG from Food Service. When compiling the food list, an inmate's religious or health concerns are taken into account. The inmate is afforded the opportunity to pick his meal type. Meal types include but are not limited to, Regular, Kosher, No Pork or Soft Tray for those with this medical need.

The segregation units are run by a Segregation Lieutenant. He has sole responsibility for the safe and orderly running of the unit. Not everyone works the segregation units. The "SEG LT" is allowed to pick his "crew." Argus is working the #2 position in DS for the week and he is proud that he has been picked. You don't work in DS unless you're deemed to be a solid officer by the SEG LT. Argus is new to SEG and is anxious to learn this aspect of the job that he loves. He arrives at 5:30 am for his 6:00 am to 2:00 pm shift and is keyed through the DS sally port by the WEST SEG Officer with a yell, "Yo! Staff on the door!"

The midnight to 8:00 am DS Officer in Charge lets Argus into the unit. The DS OIC is an Officer by the name of Grange and he looks tired. He is within two hours of getting off shift. He is taller than Argus but about the same age. He also has a rough sense of humor which Argus likes immediately. Grange tells Argus, "Well put your stuff in the office and you can serve this coffee I made. I'll sort the meals while you're doing that. Don't turn your back to the cells. Only give out two cups of coffee for each inmate. That's it. If you can't give everyone extra, you don't, got it?"

Argus replies, "10-4" and nods.

Grange says, "Oh, and watch the guy in the box cars. He's there for a reason."

Argus has only a faint idea of what to expect once he reaches the box cars.

The DS range has eighteen cells. Sixteen are on the main flat. Two of the cells, "17 and 18" are behind a second restraining door. All of the cells are sliders with bars like Unit Six. Argus grabs the handle of the small brown plastic cart with the coffee carafe riding on top and starts down the range. Grange locks the restraining door behind him and leaves to sort the food. Argus has to admit he is nervous and doesn't want to mess up. This is completely new, but he decides, inmates are inmates. Argus looks down the range and sees the green handles of the small plastic cups sitting on the bars of the cells and he makes his first mistake. Argus starts at cell number one.

There's a very good reason for starting at the last cell when serving drinks or food. By starting at the first cell, Argus gave the inmates a chance to drink one of the cups of coffee and ask for an additional one on his way back. Frankly, it's a pain to have to tell 30 inmates, "no" right in a row because they'll ask just to aggravate. That's part of the game, to see if you'll break weak and give in. Argus doesn't know this pearl of wisdom so at cell number one, the orderly's cell, he starts pouring coffee. He takes the cup from the bars and fills it almost to the brim and puts it back the same way he got it.

The orderly is there by the bars and says in a low voice, "Boss, put the cups back with the handle facing in. We put them out with the handle facing out. You put them back with the handle facing in. It's a respect thing."

Argus looks at the inmate and sees the logic. Unless he does it this way, the inmate has to grab the hot cup of coffee from the top. The chance of spilling is greater. It's just common courtesy. Argus nods thanks to the inmate and switches the cups. He fills the cups like this all the way down the range to cell 16.

Argus slides the box car restraining door open and pushes the cart through the narrow hall to cells 17 and 18. Cell 17 is occupied, cell 18 is empty. There is another solid sliding door in front of cell 17, a three foot by four foot area and then the slider with bars that keeps the inmate in the cell. This slider consists of bars like the others. These two cells are reserved for the most assaultive inmates. Argus looks in the cell. It is dark and smells like a tiger's cage. Argus can see an outline of the inmate sitting on the bunk. The cups are on the bars. Argus knows that this inmate is a former military and has special training by the notes on the dry erase board in the office. He steps up to the bars and pours the two cups of hot coffee and replaces them back on the bars, handles in. The inmate steps up to the cell door and Argus looks into the inmate's eyes. What he sees there is violence and insanity.

The inmate takes a cup from the bars, takes a drink, looks at Argus and says, "Wear this motherfucker."

Then the inmate throws the hot coffee on Argus. He is just able to turn enough so the liquid hits the side of his neck and back. It doesn't miss his face and eyes by much.

Argus is stunned at first. The inmate just stands there without saying anything. Argus backs out of the enclosure and slides the solid door shut. He pushes the cart back out on the regular tier and shuts the restraining door to the box cars, then pushes the cart back down the range. The inmates see the wet uniform and red skin. They know what has happened. They do not ask for a second cup of coffee.

When Argus gets back to the range restraining grill he yells, "On the grill!"

Grange walks over and says, "What the fuck happened to you?"

Argus tells him what happened.

Grange says, "Well get used to it, you'll have to write him up for assault on a staff member. Are you hurt?"

Argus tells him, "No," but wouldn't admit it if he was.

Argus is angry but can't show it. He knows from working the units, you get more respect from the inmates if you show no emotion. Nothing they can do phases you. Emotion is weakness. It's called, letting them get you out of the box and when it happens, they have gained the knowledge of what bothers you. It's a bad thing to have happen. Argus becomes stoic, grabs the food cart and feeds the range from back to front giving cell 17 his two trays first. The inmate steps to the bars and takes the trays from Argus' hands. Argus stares into the inmate's eyes until the inmate turns away. His message, "Nothing you do can break me."

Argus counts the trays that go into each cell and makes sure of the tray and lid count. The trays are made of hard plastic and could be fashioned into a knife.

Argus goes into the office and Grange helps him write the report on the inmate in cell 17. Because there was no serious injury, it is deemed a minor assault, code 224. He's told that it will be one of many already written. That's why the inmate is in the box cars. Argus signs the report and gives it to the WEST SEG Officer to take to the Lieutenant's Office then he grabs the cart and picks up the food trays. The trays and lids are waiting on the handcuff slot when Argus gets to cell 17. The inmate just sits on the bunk in the cell and looks at Argus. Argus gets the trays and finishes collecting the rest of the range, making sure of the tray and lid count at each cell. Argus gets to the grill and yells, "On the grill!"

After he exits the range, Argus sees that the inmate orderly is out of his cell and in the laundry room sorting clothing. Today is shower day for the unit. Argus will wear his wet uniform for the rest of the shift as he escorts the inmates to receive a shower and a fresh clothing exchange. It is Argus' first day in the unit and he thinks as he works, "The dragon is hungry in this place."

∞∞∞∞

Unit Thirteen is one of the larger units at the penitentiary with a base count of 150 and is located on the east end of the corridor. It is a standard cell house with the standard duties, just more inmates. It is the unit where Argus responded to his first fight and afterwards found a

84

pick shank in a folding chair. Argus is working the 4:00 pm to midnight shift in the unit. He hasn't worked the East End very much so the inmates are unfamiliar with him. Argus has worked the unit for a couple of evenings and has had to deal with some of the same things he dealt with as a rookie in the west end.

Argus thinks, "Well at least I know the games they're trying to run on me."

The first night, the inmates wanted mail call prior to the count. That's not how Argus does it. They want him to call the Corridor Officer and get permission to send them to work when they miss the movement for that very purpose. Again, that's not how it works. Argus tells them, "It's not personal, it's just policy."

He isn't making friends.

Argus stands out on the flat for his whole shift, this bothers the inmates. Apparently they're not used to this type of supervision. Argus puts a dip of Copenhagen in and spits in the trash can by the door. Several inmates approach Argus for an "Inmate Request to Staff Form," AKA, "Copout" or a razor or some other supply they need. Each time Argus goes to his office and gets whatever the inmate needs and steps right back out. Argus knows they've got contraband they're trying to move but like a bad penny, he's always there. Argus makes a round in the unit. As he reaches the midway point of the upper right tier, he looks at his watch and thinks, "I've got time for a search before the next movement." So he steps into a cell.

As always, Argus stands in the cell for a second and thinks. He looks around to try and get a feel for the inmate who occupies this cell. The cell is cluttered and unorganized. An extremely organized cell is a good indicator of hard contraband. Someone who is meticulous usually has secrets. Argus starts in one corner and works his way around the cell. He's working around the back corner when suddenly the door flies open and an inmate steps in. Argus stands in the back of the cell with a slight grin. His gaze is direct as he waits on the inmate to show his intentions. The inmate seems confused that he hasn't startled the new officer.

Finally, the inmate says, "I'm getting a cigarette."

Argus has already searched the cigarette pack on the top of the locker, so he steps forward, grabs the pack of cigarettes and hands them to the inmate. Now the inmate is totally confused. Not only has he not startled the officer, but the officer isn't intimidated. Argus has closed the distance.

Argus knows that in the penitentiary, there is never a time when an inmate is speaking with an officer that there isn't another inmate close by listening to make sure the inmate isn't snitching. He does the math and suspects that there's another inmate outside the door within earshot. So, is this inmate trying to check in without formally requesting protective custody or is he trying to intimidate Argus? One thing is for certain as far as Argus is concerned, he wants Argus to overreact and engage in a verbal with him so he can escalate. Argus reads him in an instant. The inmate is holding the pack of cigarettes indecisively.

Argus looks at the inmate and smiles. "Okay, you've got your cigarette, now get the fuck out of the cell."

The inmate looks at the pack of cigarettes, then at Argus who is still smiling, then at the door, then at Argus and then exits the cell. Argus looks out the door window and sees the inmate standing a few feet down the tier talking to another inmate. Whatever their plan was had not worked. If it was to intimidate, "Inmate Cigarette" has lost face. Argus finishes the search and confiscates a good amount of nuisance contraband. Nuisance contraband is anything the inmate is not authorized to have, made from stolen government property. No confiscation form is required. Argus doesn't know it, but he's just made an enemy.

∞∞∞∞

The inmates are used to him now. His week in Unit Thirteen is almost complete. Being consistent in following policies takes the guess work out of the things for the inmates. When they know what to expect from an officer, it makes for a smoother shift. The petty games have almost stopped. They still try Argus but it doesn't go anywhere. As always, from just watching the inmates, he has been fairly successful in his cell searches. Careful study of the inmates in his unit lets him know who is who. Then it's just a matter of the search. Of course, sometimes "Mr. Murphy" steps in and smiles on Argus.

Argus is standing at his post by the trash can when the range telephone rings. The range telephone is a phone mounted to the wall on the flat near the corridor restraining door of the unit. This phone is an internal telephone only. No outside calls can be made on it. It is a phone placed outside of the officer's office to provide convenience for officers like Argus who spend their shift actually watching the inmates.

86

Argus answers the phone, "Unit Thirteen."

On the other end of the line is the Operation's Lieutenant. "Antrim, I've got an incident report on one of your inmates I need to investigate. Will you grab him and send him down?"

"10-4 Boss." Argus goes to his office and looks in the bed-book for the inmate's cell number. He exits the office and heads down to the last cell on the left off of the flat. Argus opens the cell and finds the inmate asleep on the top bunk. He addresses the inmate by name and tells him, "LT wants to see you."

The inmate gets up and hops down off the rack. Argus will keep an eye on him now that he's made contact. The inmate stands for a second in his socks as if he's trying to clear his head or deciding on something. Argus' sixth sense kicks in as he watches the inmate look around the cell.

Argus thinks, "Something's off about this dude."

The inmate outweighs Argus and is slightly taller but frankly, he's used to this. The inmate bends down to get his boots. Argus tells him, "Hold up. Hand me your shoes."

The inmate complies. Argus searches the boots. They stink but are clear of contraband. Argus hands the boots back to the inmate and he puts them on. The inmate reaches on top of the locker and retrieves a wallet. Again Argus tells the inmate to hand him the item. Again the inmate complies.

Argus begins to search the wallet. He goes through all the little compartments and in the center one finds a small plastic baggie filled with a brown powder. Argus instinctively knows what this is even though he's never seen it in real life. He puts the baggie back where he found it and sticks the wallet in his belt. Then he gets ready to fight. If the inmate is smart, he will rush Argus and attempt to flush the narcotics. Minor assault on an officer will be much less of a charge than a 100 level narcotics offense. To Argus' surprise, the inmate just stands there.

Argus says, "Okay, come on out here so I can pat you down."

The inmate complies. Argus is on high alert. The inmate has a cell mate but that inmate is not in the cell and wherever he's at in the block, he's not coming anywhere near this train wreck. He deadlocks the cell and pat searches the inmate. Argus calls the Corridor Officer on the radio and informs him that he will be escorting one to the Lieutenant's Office. Unit Ten comes out into the corridor to cover Argus' unit. When they arrive at the Lieutenant's Office, Argus handcuffs the inmate and enters the office. He shows the lieutenant the brown powder and informs him that he took it straight from the inmate's hand.

The lieutenant tests the brown powder using a NIK testing kit. It tests positive for heroin. Argus fills out an evidence chain of custody form, photographs the baggie with the powder and places everything in an evidence bag.

The lieutenant calls the Corridor Officer on the radio and says, "Operations to the Corridor Officer, lock the corridor down. I've got one in cuffs going to ADSEG."

Argus returns to his unit to write his first narcotics incident report and pack the inmate's property. But before he does that, he searches the cell with a fine tooth comb. He doesn't find anymore hard contraband. Argus has the cellmate identify what is his from the common property lying around the cell and then gets to work. Argus tells the cell mate to wait out on the flat while he secures the property. All the time he's securing the property, he can't believe that he didn't have to fight the inmate.

He thinks, "Some shit you just can't explain."

∞∞∞∞

It is Argus' night off. His mother has agreed to babysit and he and Lynn are out for a few drinks at the VFW with her friend and husband. They are a nice couple. He is a pipefitter and her friend is a waitress at the same restaurant as Lynn. There is a band playing music and Lynn loves to dance. Argus and Lynn have been dancing together for nine years and he still enjoys being with her. The bar is crowded and everyone is having a good time. Argus sees that Lynn's seven and seven is almost empty. He asks her if she'd like a refill. She looks at him and nods emphatically with that beautiful smile. Argus gets up and weaves his way across the room through the partiers to the bar. The bartender looks over at him and nods in a question.

Argus yells, "Two seven and sevens please!"

The bartender gets on it as Argus waits.

A man steps up to the bar next to Argus as he looks over. The man is Counselor Camden from the penitentiary. He had retired during Argus' rookie year and probably doesn't even recognize him. Mr. Camden was always kind to Argus when he worked the counselor's unit.

Argus says, "Hey Mr. Camden, it's Antrim from the pen. How're you doing man?"

Mr. Camden replies, "Oh, hey Antrim, I'm doing fine. You look like you're doing okay," as he nods to the drinks on the bar.

Argus looks at the man. He seems kindly as ever. Argus asks, "How's retirement treating you sir?"

Mr. Camden looks at the mirror behind the bar and says, "Good. It's good. No more inmates. No more grills and no more bad dreams."

Then more introspectively, "No more dreams."

He looks down at his hands then at Argus and the smile returns. Argus looks him in the eyes but says nothing. He thinks, "I'm glad I'm not the only one."

Mr. Camden says, "Well Antrim, it was nice seeing you. I'm gonna get back to my table. Good luck young man," and then he's gone, making his way through the crowd with a beer until Argus can't see him anymore. Argus pays for his drinks and thinks about what the man had said.

So, he's not alone in having the dreams. He thinks, "That's good. I'm not weak or going crazy."

He grabs his drinks and heads back to Lynn.

"Took long enough," she says with a laugh. "I want to dance."

The band is a good one so Argus and Lynn head for the dance floor to do what they love to do.

∞∞∞∞

Argus has been picking up overtime shifts when he can since his rookie year was up. The money is better than he could have hoped for and it has put him and his family in a better financial position. Argus has made enough so Lynn can go back to school for a secretarial degree. Every night, she studies short hand or some other subject while he lies in bed beside her. The Segregation Lieutenant likes him and knows he's a solid officer, so he's been able to pick up some overtime in ADSEG for a 2:00 pm to 10:00 pm shift on his day off. Argus reports to the Lieutenant's Office at 1:30 pm and then heads over to Segregation. He is keyed in through the DS sally port then heads up the four short flights to ADSEG. When Argus enters the unit, he finds the officer he'll be relieving and they exchange equipment for chits in the SEG Officer's Station.

There are four ranges in ADSEG with eighteen cells per range. Each cell can hold two inmates and the unit is always at capacity. So much so that many times when an inmate is discovered to be intoxicated in GP, he'll be placed in a holding cell for the night and then released the next morning with a 200 level incident report for intoxication. He'll stay in general population until the Disciplinary Hearing Officer sees him and hands out the sanctions. An officer that works SEG never stops for the whole shift. Argus carries a hand towel draped over his radio to wipe sweat from his arms and face. The SEG Unit is sweltering and like a sauna when showers are being conducted. Two ranges each day have showers. Upper ranges one day, lower ranges the next. Today the lower ranges are showering.

Argus jumps into the mix and is keyed on to B range to handcuff the inmates in the shower near the restraining door and escort them back to their cell. An officer is covering him from the end of the range and will operate the electronic door to the cell. Argus yells, "On the box, open 11!"

The door grinds open with a mechanical whine. The inmates walk in the cell. Argus yells, "On the box, close 11!"

The door closes and Argus removes the handcuff restraints. He then steps to cell 12 and asks, "Are you fellas ready?"

The inmates back up to the bars and Argus applies the restraints. "On the box, open 12!"

The inmates back out onto the range and Argus puts a hand on an elbow each. The officer on the box closes the cell and Argus gets the inmates in the shower. Clean clothes are on a small gray cart just outside the shower. The inmates place their dirty laundry in a plastic bag hanging on the cart. Once the inmates are in the shower and the door is secure, Argus and his partner go to the next range and change the shower. This is how it goes on every shower day.

Argus is working with a friend today. His name is Brown but everyone calls him Brownie. Many of the officers have nicknames. The inmates have started calling Argus "Snoop" because he is always searching. His friends call him "Ant." Argus trusts Brownie with his life and the feeling is mutual. That is a rarity reserved for men who share danger daily. The SEG OIC catches Argus and Brownie after the showers have been changed and detail them to go upstairs to D-Range and search the cell of an inmate who is in the Law Library. This is a standard practice to make sure the required cell searches are completed. Argus and Brown head upstairs. Brownie will be on the box and Argus will go down range and search the cell.

Argus says, "On the box, open 5."

Brownie flips the required switch and the cell opens.

Argus enters the cell and begins his search as always. Immediately he smells the unmistakable odor of hooch or homemade wine. Inmates are given everything they need to make wine. They are given one piece of acidic fruit daily. They are given sugar with their coffee and they are given bread with their meals. A little water and three days to ferment and they have hooch. Not in great quantities but still enough to cause intoxication. The inmate who lives in this cell is in ADSEG because he had taped a shank to his hand and attempted to stab another inmate to death. The shank was taped to his hand so that when it became bloody from repeatedly stabbing the other inmate he wouldn't lose his grip on the knife. His mistake came when he chased the other inmate down the main corridor and the other inmate hid behind Officer Benell. This fact didn't stop the pursuing inmate and he kept coming. Officer Benell dropped him with a right cross and secured the weapon with his crushing grip. So, he still hadn't learned anything because now, Snoop had found his wine. Argus goes through the cell and soon finds two pints of the liquid. It's held in a plastic bag which was probably obtained from the orderly. Argus comes out of the cell and holds it up for Brownie to see. All the inmates on the range also see with the small plastic mirrors they use to watch the officers. The cell is closed and they exit the range with the wine. Argus puts the wine in the office and informs the OIC of the find. Argus and Brownie go and get the inmate from the Law Library. The inmate is part of a disruptive group. He is in his early forties and as most serious convicts, he is in good shape.

He looks at Argus and there is no friendliness in his eyes. He's been kept waiting in the Law Library and he knows why. Argus puts a belly chain around the inmate's waist and handcuffs him in front because the inmate has a bad shoulder and can't be handcuffed behind the back. Argus and Brownie escort Inmate "Bellychain" up to the range and Brownie keys Argus and "Bellychain" on to the range. Brownie is once again on the control box.

Argus says, "On the box, open 5."

The door grinds open. At about that time, an inmate from down range yells, "They found your shit man!"

"Bellychain" steps into the cell and the door is closed. Argus begins to remove the belly chain by first removing the cuffs from the inmate's left wrist. Inmate "Bellychain" begins breathing faster. Argus watches his chest rise and fall. "Bellychain" takes his free hand and starts to

91

quickly feed the handcuff through the belly chain.

Argus is still somewhat inexperienced and he sees what is happening too late. He grabs the end of the chain just as "Bellychain" gets the cuff free and now Argus is in a tug of war for the chain. Inmate "Bellychain" gets his foot up on the bars and pulls back with both hands. Argus' arm is pulled into the handcuff slot all the way to the shoulder. Argus tightens his grip but feels his shoulder start to give. The inmate has all of his weight on the chain. Argus' grip weakens against the weight and the chain rips through his grasp, lacerating his hand. Argus is focused on the inmate but he sees Brownie grab for his radio. Argus holds up his hand to signal Brownie to wait. Argus needs to deescalate this situation. His brother officers are going to have to face the sharp ratchet end of a handcuff protruding from "Bellychain's" fist and the chain he now has in the cell. Argus takes a deep breath while blood drips from his right hand on to the range floor. The inmate has wrapped the chain around his left hand and is swinging it back and forth.

The inmate tells Argus, "If you roll on me man, I'll get you back. I'll get you back motherfucker."

Argus intentionally puts his bloody hand up in a conciliatory gesture. "Look dude, you got my word, if you give me my iron back, nobody will roll on you. Nobody's coming if you give me my shit back."

The inmate looks at Argus' hand. There is a pregnant pause as "Bellychain" decides if Argus can be trusted.

Argus puts his hand down. "Look, all we got is our word in here. You'll wear an incident report and that's it."

Another minute as "Bellychain" decides. The inmate steps forward and puts the hand with the cuff through the slot. Argus removes the handcuff and the inmate hands him the chain. Argus and Brownie go downstairs and report the incident to the OIC. Argus tells him that he gave his word that no team would be formed in exchange for the iron.

The OIC calls the SEG Lieutenant and explains what happened, "Look boss, he got the iron back on his word. If we roll on the dude, his word's no good. That'll get around."

The SEG Lieutenant agrees and Argus is sent down to the Lieutenant's Office to get his hand photographed, bandaged and a medical assessment completed. He'll write two incident reports, one incident report for the wine and one for the assault. Inmate "Bellychain" will never see general population at Tarragon again. As he crosses the main corridor, hand dripping blood, he hears the West SEG Officer tell the Corridor Officer, "He'll either get tough or he'll quit."

Argus thinks, "Well, I sure as hell ain't gonna quit."

∞∞∞∞

The corridor is full of inmates. Argus is working Unit Ten as the Day Watch OIC on the 8:00 am to 4:00 pm shift. He is doing what he usually does during an open movement, monitoring the inmate traffic in and out of his unit and performing random pat searches. It has been a month since the incident in ADSEG. Argus really doesn't think about it too much except to tuck the lesson away for the future. It was just another day as far as he's concerned. The laceration was very superficial and healed long ago. Every day Argus comes through the grills he learns something new to make him a better officer.

His efforts have not been unnoticed by the powers that be. He has received three sustained superior performance awards and two special act awards so far. Additionally, two members of the SWAT Team have approached him about joining. Tryouts are in a month. Argus is just doing what he does, putting everything into a career he's found that he loves. He is standing by his unit door when ADSEG calls the Corridor Officer on the radio and informs him they are releasing an inmate to Unit Eleven. Within minutes, Argus sees the inmate coming down the corridor with his bag of property. As he passes Argus, he slows slightly and without looking at Argus simply says, "Bellychain says he apologizes. Nothing personal."

The inmate keeps walking and Argus does not acknowledge the inmate at all. So there it was. In one short sentence, his credibility with the inmates has been established. Argus' actions in SEG hadn't been for the inmate at all. The motivation in his actions had been to protect his fellow officers and in so doing, he will now be more effective in managing the inmates. The open movement ends and Argus clears his area of the corridor of inmates. As he turns to enter his unit he thinks, "Respect begets respect and in here, respect is everything."

∞∞∞∞

Argus calls Control from his office in Unit Ten and explains that he just got off the telephone with the lieutenant and has picked up a shift of overtime and needs to let his wife know, "Can I get an outside line?"

The Control Officer laughs and says, "Yeah, stand by Ant. You're turning in to an OT hound brother. What's the number?"

Argus gives the officer his home telephone number and he's connected within a few seconds. Lynn answers the telephone and as soon as he says, "Hello sweetie," she knows.

"You've got overtime."

Argus says, "I couldn't pass it up. It's a tower and easy money."

She asks if he has enough food and Argus assures her that he'll be okay. He has adopted the habit of carrying extra in his truck for just this type of situation.

Argus' relief arrives and he does a quick exchange, letting the oncoming officer know about anything pertinent then he heads out the door for the second eight in a sixteen hour shift. It will be one of many already. The money is good and he and Lynn are planning on selling their tiny home and moving into a better neighborhood. For the first time in his life, he can actually look at nicer houses in a serious way. He is proud of this and of himself. Maybe he can make good on the promise he made Lynn when he proposed. Not that it matters to her, but it does to him. Argus still doesn't have a lot of time in with the Agency and working a tower is a rarity for a "rookie." This will be Argus' first tower duty since starting at the penitentiary.

Towers are usually reserved for old timers getting ready for retirement. They are also places that the occasional new guy is hazed. He has heard the stories and is ready for the games to begin, but getting paid to sit for the whole shift with no inmates is just too appealing. Almost like a paid vacation. Argus stops in the Control Sally Port and tells the officer, "I need the key for Tower Two."

The officer in Control is Officer Omar. He is an experienced officer with a lot of game. Argus no longer wears a tie because Officer Omar had advised him as a rookie, "You better get rid of that cum bib rookie. These convicts will choke the life out of you with it."

Argus knows when an officer like Omar gives you advice, you take it. Omar just smiles at Argus and says, "Oh, you get that key from Officer Laundry in Tower One." Then he leaves the Control window.

Argus heads through the sally port and heads for Tower One not wanting to be late for his relief at Tower Two. He stops ten feet from the Tower One Sally Port and yells up to Officer Laundry. Laundry sticks his head out of the window. He is the officer that greeted Argus on his first day of institutional familiarization from the tower. Officer Laundry has made the towers his home. He is close to retirement, is grumpy and everyone loves the guy. Argus yells, "Officer Laundry, I need to draw the key to Tower Two!"

Officer Laundry replies in his usual manner, "Oh my God! Antrim you've been here all this time and you're still a rookie! There is no key, the guy you're relieving lets you in, you stupid motherfucker!"

Argus smiles, shakes his head and thinks, "They got me already and the shift hasn't even started."

Mr. Laundry lets Argus out through the sally port and he heads to his truck for the short drive to Tower Two. Argus pulls into the parking space and heads for the door at the bottom of the tower. The officer sitting forty feet above him is waiting and buzzes him in the door. Argus closes the door behind him and climbs multiple flights in the switchback stairway to one flight below the tower floor. There in front of him is a thin ladder leading to a trap door. The tower officer opens the door and greets him with a smile from above, "Welcome to my house rookie. Don't fuck it up while I'm gone."

Argus negotiates his newly replenished lunch box up the ladder and through the trap door. The shift change is brief. No chits to exchange and very little to pass on. Argus looks around at his perch for the next eight hours.

The officer tells Argus that he is to monitor ten inmate telephone calls this evening. The lines he is to listen to are written on a sticker attached to the intercom box. "The forms you fill out are right there on the clipboard. Be as detailed as you can. The Perimeter Patrol will be around to pick them up after lockdown. Just lower them down in the bag. If you need anything else, just ask on the intercom and read the post orders and sign them. Okay my man, I'm out."

The officer grabs his large lunchbox and wriggles through the trap door. Argus looks out the window as the officer leaves the tower with a bang as the heavy metal door shuts and locks.

So, this would be his post for the next eight hours. Argus picks up the log book and makes his initial notations. He looks at the previous notes to make sure he covers everything that he is supposed to. He makes sure his weapons are in the proper condition, counts the rounds and makes sure the long gun is in "duty carry." Argus keeps one eye on the fence line as he does this. It is definitely a different view from up here. Argus is impressed at the placement of the towers. Interlocking fields of fire just like a Marine Corps defensive perimeter. He hears his name on the intercom and tries to answer. It's the LT and he's asking if Argus is in the tower but he can't hear Argus answer. The LT again, "Hey Antrim. Are you in Tower Two?"

The telephone rings. "Hey Ant, you got your intercom muted."

Argus hits the mute button and sounds off, "Here lieutenant, sorry."

The lieutenant laughs, "Okay thanks."

Argus is reading the post orders when his telephone rings again. It's Officer Tarp. He is around Argus' age but has been a correctional officer for a while. He mentored Argus in the Main Control Room during his rookie year. Argus likes Tarp and he thinks the feeling is mutual. Tarp never treated him like a rookie and was a great teacher. Tarp says, "Hey Ant, if you need anything, give me a call, I'm in tower four. There should be a list of tower numbers on the wall up there. Mute your box unless you've got something to say, okay? Oh, and if you start to get sleepy, hold the metal dustpan in your hand. If you fall asleep it'll drop and wake you up. Just a tip."

Argus thanks him for the heads up and they get off the phone.

Argus continues looking around the tower to familiarize himself with his post. The tower itself isn't very roomy measuring at around six by eight feet in all. In that space, a captain's stool, counter and commode take up most of the room. The trap door is closed, but when open, there isn't much floor left. Argus looks at the telephone monitoring equipment. He punches the extension to be monitored and immediately an inmate's voice comes on the line. Somebody says, "Mute your box rookie."

Argus mutes the intercom box. He gets a form and starts filling it out. Argus sees immediately that this is going to be completely different than working a cell house. The intercom box reminds him of the CB in the moving truck. Officers talking about all sorts of things just like a bunch of truckers. Argus is bored already. He almost wishes for the harassment to start. Argus has heard stories of the games the other tower officers play on rookies up here.

There's the water pressure game where the Tower One Officer will announce that there is too much water pressure in the area of the rookie's tower. In this case, he would call Argus and tell him to flush his toilet every hour during the shift. Then there's the window accountability game where the Tower One Officer announces, "Okay towers, time to count your windows. Call your counts in to extension...."

The extension given is the Warden's reservation housing telephone. The rookie calls in his window count to the Warden after hours and since the Warden is a former hack, he tells the rookie good count and then tells the rookie who he is, playing along with the joke. Finally, there's the chair inspection routine where the Perimeter Patrol pulls around to the rookie's tower and has him lower his chair out the window on the rope attached to the small paperwork bag so it can be inspected. It is a wonderful night for a tower hack if he can get the rookie flushing the toilet with his foot while he has the chair out the window on a rope.

Argus decides to get his telephone calls out of the way. This takes him almost two hours. Then Argus realizes, his work is done except for monitoring the fence line. He decides to put the time to good use and finds that he can do pushups off of the counter and still see the fence line. He thinks, "I should be able to get a thousand in before midnight."

The other officers try to bait him over the next several hours on the intercom. "How do you like the job so far? Tell us about yourself. Have you counted your windows yet?"

Argus just takes it in stride. He's happy they're giving him a try. It means he's made the team. Argus' tower covers the area behind the West End. In between sets of pushups, he looks at the cell blocks through his binoculars but finds there is nothing to see except an occasional glimpse of an inmate, here and there inside the block. Before the shift has ended, Argus has reached his goal of a thousand in sets of ten and fifteen. He has also decided towers are good for overtime, but he'll never put in for one as a regular post. He enjoys the game inside the pen too much and thinks, "What sane person wants to be inside a prison?"

∞∞∞∞

All of the hard work is finally paying off for Lynn and Argus. The overtime has provided the financial resources to purchase a new home in the south end of town. Lynn has been hired at a manufacturing plant in town as a secretary thanks to her new degree. The home is located in a quiet little neighborhood just off of one of the main streets in town. It isn't much bigger than the one they've sold, but it is so much nicer. The home is a little brick ranch with an in ground pool and sun room. It has two bedrooms and a basement with a pool table. Lynn fell in love with the sun room immediately and has made it a place to read her books. She loves to read and the room provides natural light and warmth, making it a comfortable nook for her to fall into a favorite book. The master bedroom has more closet space and the kitchen is big enough for entertaining. Argus is happy he's been able to provide this nicer home for his wife and daughter. Argus loves to swim and was on the swim team in high school. The pool is a luxury he never envisioned for his family. As far as Argus is concerned, joining the Agency has been one of the better choices he's made for Lynn and his daughter Olivia. He has started thinking in terms of career. A career he has started to love.

Chapter 5
The Dragon is loose

Argus is working on the East End of the institution in Unit Eleven as the 4:00 pm to Midnight Officer. He likes working the East End better than the West End simply because he knows the inmates better. Unit Eleven is a good unit to work. The unit team is solid and he works well with them. Argus is standing at his usual spot by the door of the unit, spitting Copenhagen into the trash can. It is around 7:00 pm and the inmates are out on the flat doing what inmates do, playing cards, waiting for the microwave and standing on the tiers talking. Argus notices that though the mood in the unit is calm, there is a lot of activity. He dismisses this as the inmates not wanting to spend any more time in their cells than they have to. The range fans are going full blast but Argus still hears what sounds like a verbal altercation in one of the cells on the right top tier. He starts to move in that direction to check on what might be a fight in the making when an inmate quickly comes out of cell forty seven. Argus then sees an arm emerge and try to grab the inmate but it misses.

As he sees this, he hears someone say, "Come on back in here then bitch."

Argus yells at the two inmates. The skinny inmate that exited the cell looks at Argus and then heads down the stairs and enters his cell on the lower left tier. Argus thinks, "Okay that one's diffused for now. Let's go see what's going on."

Argus walks up the staircase and goes to cell forty seven where the verbal occurred. Inside the cell he finds an inmate he has interacted with before. The inmate hasn't caused Argus trouble in the past. Argus asks the inmate, "You're not planning on wrecking my shift tonight are you?"

The inmate is visibly angry and doesn't look at Argus as he says, "Snoop, I ain't got no conversation for you. If you want anything else, step up in the cell."

The message is clear. Something is going on and it will need to be addressed before it escalates. Before Argus can respond to this obvious challenge, the other inmate in the argument comes back out of his cell yelling, "C'mon then bitch!"

He was wearing a t-shirt when he entered the cell, now he's wearing a field jacket. Argus knows then that he has probably strapped up. The inmate is running for the staircase as is Argus. The inmate and Argus meet at the turn in the staircase but the inmate cuts inside Argus just as he hits the landing and gets past him. Now Argus is chasing the inmate up the stairs in an attempt to stop him before he reaches cell forty seven. When Argus reaches the top of the stairs, he sees Inmate "Skinny" standing just to the side of cell forty seven yelling for the other inmate to come out. Inmate "Skinny" has a metal dust pan that has been sharpened by years of being dragged across the concrete floor. He is holding it above his head, waiting for the inmate in cell forty seven to come out. When he does, Inmate "Skinny" will split his head open. For now, the other inmate stays in the cell and Argus grabs his radio.

Up until now, he has handled his cell block and realizes in a fleeting second of clarity, this will be the first time he has called for assistance. "Unit Eleven to Control, I believe I'm going to need some help down here in Eleven, cell forty seven."

The Control Room Officer is Omar. Before Argus can put his radio back in the metal holder on his belt, Omar is on the radio, "Control to all portable radio units, staff needs assistance in Unit Eleven. Staff needs assistance in Unit Eleven, cell forty seven."

Argus thinks, "I've got to do something. This is not going to happen right in front of me."

Argus won't let it happen. He is a Marine and Marines aren't built that way. Argus holsters his radio and moves quickly up behind Inmate "Skinny" trying for a half nelson but misses and ends up with a bear hug on the inmate's chest and one arm. The inmate is still swinging the dust pan as he and Argus tumble backwards toward the staircase. They hit the concrete together as Argus' radio slides away and the metal case is flattened against his right side. He feels a stab of pain as flesh and metal vie for the same space but the fight is on now and he knows he has to win. Inmate "Skinny" is trying to get up when Argus tackles him and drives him into the stairway upside down. Argus is also upside down but still on top.

The adrenaline has dumped and Argus is trying to control it before tunnel vision sets in when he sees two large hands grab Inmate "Skinny" by the shoulders of the field jacket and yank him right out from underneath Argus. He looks and sees Lieutenant Atkins holding Inmate "Skinny" by the shoulders as if he weighs nothing. Additional staff members are handcuffing the other inmate in cell forty seven. The inmate is being held face first against the wall as he's cuffed.

He looks over at Argus and yells, "Snoop you know I didn't do anything! I didn't come out of the cell! Snoop! You know!"

Argus yells above the noise, "Settle down. I'll straighten it out!"

The inmates are in the corridor, facing the wall. Argus is in the Lieutenant's Office explaining to Lieutenant Atkins what occurred.

Argus tells the lieutenant, "It was an attempted assault boss. They had a verbal, then "Skinny" went to his cell and strapped up. I had to jump him so he didn't split the other guy's skull. The dude in forty seven didn't even come out of his cell."

Argus and Lieutenant Atkins come back out in the corridor. Lieutenant Atkins signals with his hand for the officer holding the inmate from forty seven to take the restraints off and take him back to the unit. Inmate "Skinny" will wear a shot for possession of a weapon and attempted serious assault. His housing unit is changed to ADSEG.

Argus goes back to his unit and tries to straighten his radio carrier out but it is a lost cause. He sticks the radio in his pocket, goes to Skinny's cell, locks his locker and tells his cell mate to separate out their common property. "Skinny" won't be back for a while. It is about count time so Argus cells the inmates up and prepares for count. His side hurts but he's still got work to do so he brushes the pain aside. After count, Argus goes to "Skinny's" cell and collects his property. He'll note on the property inventory that common property was separated by his cell mate. Argus will spend the rest of his evening writing the incident report and inventorying the property. The property will stay in his office until the Property Officer picks it up tomorrow. Argus drops the incident reports off at the Lieutenant's Office on his way out of the institution.

He skips the heavy bag tonight and when he arrives at home, he realizes how much he depends on his hour with his friend. Lynn is asleep and he tries not to wake her as he comes in. He takes his shirt off and sees the purple goose egg on his side. His knee is also turning a nice shade of blue. Tomorrow is his day off, but he'll have to go in and get a medical assessment and fill out a report of the injuries. As he's contemplating this at the kitchen table, his phone rings. It's Lieutenant Atkins. "Antrim, I didn't know you had a fight with that inmate. You gotta come in and fix this."

Argus thought it had been obvious.

He's tired, sore and pissed off. "I had to jump the guy LT. He wasn't fighting with me, he was trying to split the other guy's head open. I was restraining him from doing that. I've got to come in tomorrow and get an assessment anyway. I've got some minor dings. I'll come in tomorrow first thing on my own time."

The lieutenant hangs up.

Argus thinks, "I don't give a fuck if he likes it or not. What the fuck does being upside down in a stairwell on top of an inmate look like."

He has a lump in his throat as Lynn comes into the kitchen. "Honey, is everything alright?"

She can tell he is pissed. "Yeah babe just a little excitement tonight. I've got to go in and finish up some paperwork tomorrow morning."

He's shirtless and she sees the goose egg. "What happened?"

Argus doesn't elaborate, "Just a fight. No big deal. It won't take me long."

The Warden's words come back to him, "Your wife doesn't need to know anything about this place."

He knows Lynn knows a little of what goes on at Tarragon. You can't come home with blood on your shirt at least once a week and not have your wife figure some of it out. He's just going to keep her as far away from most of it as he can. That's what the heavy bag is for. Argus will go in tomorrow and tie up the loose ends. That's what he does. There's not much more he'll say about it and Lynn knows this. She goes back to bed. Argus goes into the bathroom and takes a hot shower. He throws on some sweats and sits on the couch in their living room. He should sleep but sleep won't find him tonight. The dragon is still hungry.

∞∞∞∞

He stands in the mulch and dust at the starting line taking shallow breaths, his eyes focused on the telephone poles lying horizontally in front of him at chest level. Argus looks to his left at Big Franks as he heaves on the brink of vomiting. Franks' eyes do not leave the first obstacle as he does this. Franks is a stone mason and works in the Masonry Shop at the institution. He's six foot three inches tall and built like an oak tree from working with rock for years. He is also a senior member of the SWAT Team and consistently vomits every time he runs the obstacle course. The rest of the team is just as focused, standing around Argus, each, dealing with the intensity in his own way.

The SWAT Team is the best of the best at the facility. They are the men called in to adjudicate hostage situations, special escorts, high risk entry and major disturbances. Now, Argus is one of them. He had tried out for the team a month ago and did pretty good.

Argus isn't a natural athlete and his physical performance wasn't stellar but, like Hibben had said, "We're no track team."

The thing the team members were looking for was the fact that Argus put everything into the tryout without letting off for a second. It doesn't matter what kind of shape you're in if you're a quitter. That is one thing Argus is not. He benched his bodyweight fifteen times and ran the mile in a respectable nine minutes while wearing boots and when he was done, he was exhausted. The administration didn't decide who made the team. The team decided in a blackball vote. One blackball and the answer was no. It had to be unanimous if these men were to be expected to trust you with their lives.

Argus feels privileged to be standing here this morning, waiting for Lieutenant Sena to blow the whistle and send the team down range through the obstacle course. Argus stands with eighteen type "A" personalities. They are tactical operators with one goal, to be the best at whatever they are tasked with. The whistle sounds and the team takes off. Hibben takes the lead early. He is a legend on the team and holds the obstacle course record. The first obstacle is telephone poles placed horizontally that must be jumped or rolled over. Eight in all and elevated to chest height. They are three feet apart and Argus clears these like he's jumping a fence. He is no stranger to an "O" course. There were plenty in the Marine Corps. Argus clears this obstacle and finds that his breathing is already out of control. He cuts speed just a little to try and correct this as he mounts the four by four timbers situated in a "Z" pattern that must be successfully negotiated before mounting the horizontal ladders.

Argus thinks, "Fuck, that sun's hot, breath in, breath out. Shit!"

He steps off the timber and has to go around to the beginning and start over. He looks and sees Hibben is already at the rope and climbing fast. "How in the hell can he do that?"

Argus gets past the timbers and jumps for the first rung on the ladder. Hand over hand he makes his way across twenty feet of metal rungs, touches the last one and drops six feet to the ground. Sweat is pouring into his eyes as he climbs an inverted telephone pole ladder twenty feet into the air and then swings over.

He can't breathe at this point. "Don't fucking stop. Don't fucking stop!"

There it is the rope. Argus hits it at a full sprint and jumps as high as he can to reduce the amount he has to climb. He's fifteen feet in the air and pulling hard when he looks up and something happens. His arms are toast. Argus locks his legs on the rope and tries to rest his grip.

Lieutenant Sena is screaming at him, "ANT! GET THE FUCK UP THAT ROPE! GET UP! GET THE FUCK UP THERE!"

Argus has five feet to go, but he doesn't have five feet in his biceps. He thinks, "Fuck me man" and lowers back down, his arms giving out three foot from the bottom as he drops and rolls.

Lieutenant Sena is screaming for Argus to go around. Argus takes off and goes around the rope obstacle starting again on the course where he would've come down the other side. He hits the next obstacle, and pulls himself along the inverted rope bridge while his arms scream. On the other side, he swings across a ditch on a rope and mounts the telephone pole balancing obstacle. This obstacle is the last one and is made up of several poles shaped in a "Z" pattern the operator must run on top of. Argus is almost dizzy when he starts the thirty yard sprint to the finish. The other team members are yelling for him to hurry. He hits the finish at full speed. Argus isn't the only one that doesn't make the rope but that doesn't soften the blow.

Argus thinks, "I'm going to live on that rope. It won't happen again. It's time to get to work."

He's pissed at himself and disappointed in his body. Hibben comes over as Argus crouches in the shade of the rappelling tower and claps him on the back. "Don't sweat it Ant, everybody has trouble with the rope at first. I'll show you some tricks on climbing it later."

Argus will gladly take the instruction but he knows that the only fix for this problem is going to be some sweat and blood on these obstacles.

∞∞∞∞

Unit Three never fails to live up to its reputation as the unit with the worst inmates in the institution. After all, it's the unit where inmates coming to the penitentiary on disciplinary transfers are housed when they arrive. An inmate must work their way out of this unit by displaying a pattern of good behavior or at least clean conduct for a period of time before being moved to one of the other units in the institution. Argus has drawn this unit on the roster for the quarter. It is the zoo that Argus remembers from his rookie year and the unit lives up to its nickname of "three dagger" consistently but it does come with good days off for the 8:00 am to 4:00 pm shift so Argus doesn't mind. Also, he likes the fact that he can work any block, even this one successfully.

Argus walks up to the unit at 7:25 am and bangs on the door with his three cell flashlight and waits. The officer he's relieving comes out of the office on the left of the flat and keys him into the unit. As Argus follows the officer to the office, he looks around the unit and notices an inmate standing on the top tier near the far corner. The inmate is bird dogging. He's either a lookout or he's running a game himself. Argus thinks, "I'll figure you out my man" and smiles.

The officer Argus is relieving is Officer Morris. He's a good officer, hired after Argus. Morris tells Argus, "There's been some thieving going on in the unit. Two guys have reported their radios stolen. Somebody is locker knocking."

Argus says, "Okay, I'll keep a lookout, anything else?"

Morris picks his lunchbox up. "Just the usual bullshit down here. Watch your back today brother."

Argus keys him out of the door and turns to face the unit. "First things first, I'll walk the range and see what I can see."

Argus strolls the unit, walking the flat first and then the upper tier. As he gets to the end of the upper left tier, the inmate he'd noticed standing on the right corner of the tier starts walking away and enters a cell halfway down the range. As Argus walks the cross over from the left to the right, he passes a large metal range trash can like the one by the door he'll be spitting into and notices a shoestring sticking out of the trash. Argus has learned that inmates will hide their weapons in the cell at night but move them to a readily accessible common area during the day because officers search cells during the day and common areas at night. This is why Argus searches common areas during the day in addition to cells. He thinks like an inmate.

Argus reaches down and pulls the shoe string. On the end of the shoestring is an eight inch pick shank. Argus thinks, "This trash is going to be emptied soon. Either someone is incredibly stupid or this has been put here to use this morning." He sticks the shank in his belt and smiles. Someone yells from one of the cells, "Hey! Give that back!"

Argus shakes his head and says loud enough to be heard, "You all got one and now I got one too."

Then he just keeps walking the tier until he reaches the stairs and heads toward his office. As he walks Argus thinks, "A knife within the first fifteen minutes of the quarter. Let the games begin."

Argus keys his office open and starts his logs. He also writes a short memorandum detailing where and when he found the knife. He calls the Corridor Officer on the telephone and asks him to step down when he gets a chance to take the weapon and memorandum to the Operations Lieutenant. Argus' radio doesn't transmit from his office. It is one of the dead zones Lieutenant Atkins was talking about.

The Corridor Officer shows up, Argus gives him the weapon and says, "Found in the trash can. I can't put it on anybody. Would you give it to the LT?"

Officer Skim, the Corridor Officer says he will. Argus walks the unit once more and then assumes his position at the door to watch and spit. Argus thinks, "Ninety days. I'm gonna be busy."

∞∞∞∞

Segregation is full. When Argus finds wine in an inmate's cell, he takes the wine and the inmate to the Lieutenant's Office, tests the wine with an alco-sensor, then takes the inmate back to the unit and writes an incident report for possession of intoxicants. The inmate will stay in GP until the DHO sees him. Inmates are allowed to retain one piece of fruit. Argus confiscates any extra citrus fruit as nuisance contraband. If he finds more than ten packets of sugar, he takes it. Any bread in the cell is his as well. The inmates start spreading the ingredients of the hooch into multiple cells. It is a hooch war and Argus only has eight hours to fight it each day. Argus finds wine in the mattresses of inmates using their body heat to cook it. He finds it in heating vents. He finds it in toilets covered in dry breakfast cereal and a blanket. Anyplace there is a heat source to cook it, he finds it. Argus has an excellent nose for finding wine. If it hasn't fermented yet but is just the start of the makings, Argus pours it down the deep sink.

Argus likes to keep busy and part of that is shaking down. Every knife or batch of wine he finds is one less armed drunk he and his fellow officers will have to fight. There is a reason the inmates call him "Snoop."

That's what Argus is doing when Control announces on the radio, "Control to all radio units there is a fight in unit six, first floor shower. Weapons involved."

106

Argus exits the cell he is searching and bolts down the stairs. He hits the corridor door, keys it and is running the thirty yards to unit six at a sprint. Argus' friend, Officer Stepford is the unit officer. Stepford is an anomaly as far as Argus is concerned. He knows the inmates in the institution better than anyone and has the uncanny ability to memorize the inmate's registration numbers. Argus has seen him rattle off an inmate's number from memory when interacting with the inmate. It is, in a word, spooky. Stepford along with another officer are already escorting one naked inmate out with what looks like superficial stab wounds to his arms and legs. The other naked inmate is handcuffed and being held against the wall just outside the shower. It is clear to Argus what has happened, the larger stabbed inmate has pressed the smaller un-stabbed inmate for sex but he misjudged his prey. The shank is small but wicked and sharp. The shower in the unit is a one man shower which supports Argus' theory. Argus goes down range with another officer to do upper body checks making sure the two naked inmates are the only participants. Argus finds an inmate washing his hands and orders him out of the cell. The inmate has a cut on the ring finger of the left hand. Argus tells him to turn around and face the wall as he pulls his handcuffs from their pouch.

The inmate complies and says over his shoulder as Argus puts on the handcuffs, "I was just in the wrong place at the wrong time."

Argus replies, "Ain't we all my man, ain't we all."

∞∞∞∞

Seventy-five percent of an officer's career is showing up for his or her shift and following the policies in supervising the inmates wherever the post is. It's that twenty-five percent that can be life and career changing. This is the knowledge Argus carries with him just like every other CO as he enters cell fifty on the upper right tier of Unit Three. The morning has been uneventful. He has had the usual daily interactions with the inmates in Unit Three and the hooch war continues. Argus doesn't have any misconceptions about winning. With a full Segregation Unit, the inmates are going to continue to try and make the wine at a greater pace but Argus can't let the pressure off. He's no quitter so he tries to mitigate the danger that must be faced by performing searches to confiscate the means of making it. The inmates know that SEG is full and push the discipline envelope, requiring unit officers to know the policies and become creative in managing their

107

units. Argus knows the policies like the back of his hand and he's very creative.

Argus stands just inside the doorway of cell fifty and looks around calmly. He doesn't know who lives in the cell. That's how random searches work. The cell is a standard six foot by eight foot cell with a metal bunk bed and two small metal lockers. This doesn't leave much room for personal property and only about eighteen inches from the bunk to the lockers to walk between. At the outset, Argus decides to speak with the inmates regarding the cleanliness of the cell. It is a mess. Laundry bags of dirty laundry are hanging from both inside bed posts. The smell in the cell is musty with a strong odor of unwashed humanity.

The tops of the lockers are covered with trash and unorganized and without even checking, Argus can tell they have much more property than policy allows. "There's definitely some work to do here."

Argus catches movement in his peripheral vision. An inmate was standing at the door looking through the window. Argus moves to the back of the cell and waits. The inmate passes by again, stops then moves on. The inmate is worried about something. Argus always closes a cell door when searching a cell. It's a safeguard against being bum rushed in the cell. Argus opens the door and finds an inmate about his size standing just out of window view, leaning against the upper tier railing. Argus asks the inmate, "Is this your cell?"

The inmate nods. Argus says, "Well, I'm shaking it. Take a walk, I'll be done in a few minutes."

The inmate walks away and Argus continues the search. Argus dumps the laundry and goes through it piece by piece. Inmates will hide contraband anywhere they think an officer is too squeamish to search. He recalls searching a shower drain for shanks at one point in the past when an inmate passing the shower grimaced and said, "Boss, you do know the punks douche in there?"

Argus just looked at the inmate and said, "My hands wash."

The inmate just shook his head and walked on. Argus rolls the mattresses both ways and works his way around the shoes under the rack. There's clothing all the way under the rack that he has to get on one knee and reach for. Finally, Argus gets to the lockers and opens them. They are both packed full. Argus searches skillfully moving the contents and clothing. There's a great amount of nuisance contraband. He thinks, "That'll come in handy when I tell them to square this cell away. They can clean it or I will."

The inmate is back and passes the cell again. Argus thinks, "That dude's sweating something."

Argus keeps looking for the hard contraband he knows has to be there just by the way the inmate is acting. He lifts the clothing in the second locker and finds an athletic sock with a knot tied in the top. Inside the sock are three radios with different registration numbers engraved in them. The inmates are not allowed to have large radios. The radios they are allowed to retain are small pocket sized battery powered radios that can only be listened to with headphones. The inmates purchase these from the Commissary. When they make the purchase, the Commissary Foreman engraves their registration number onto the side of the radio with an engraver.

Argus is looking at three different numbers and knows he has found his locker knocker. Inmates who steal from other inmates end up wearing a piece of steel in their chest especially in this unit. Argus thinks, "What the fuck is this guy thinking. This inmate will have to go to SEG even if he sleeps on the floor."

Argus takes the sock with the radios still inside and wraps them in a towel. As he leaves the cell he doesn't deadlock it. Thus making it look like he didn't find a thing.

Argus enters his office and sits down at the desk. The office is just a converted cell and the desk has to be positioned against one of the side walls. In this unit, the desk is positioned to the left as you enter the office. He grabs an incident report and a confiscation form and begins to write. When he comes to the description of contraband, Argus takes the radios out of the sock to notate the registration numbers which are engraved on the radios. The radios are laid out on the desk when the inmate appears at the office door.

He is approximately thirty six inches from Argus and asks in a Spanish accent, "Why you take my radios, boss?" Argus knows a few phrases in Spanish and replies, "Tu numero?" while holding each radio up.

The inmate replies, "No" all three times.

Argus explains that the radios are contraband and that he knows exactly why Argus took them. Argus adds, "I'm confiscating them, I'll be with you in a minute."

The inmate leaves and Argus continues to write. Three minutes pass and Argus has almost completed the confiscation form when he sees the inmate explode into the office out of the corner of his eye. Argus only has time to raise his arm in a block before the club the inmate is holding crashes down across Argus' forearm. Electricity jolts through

Argus as the realization hits him that he is being attacked. He stands and quickly backs the two steps to the back of the office to get into a better fighting position. All of this happens in an instant as the inmate swings the club again in an upward angled back swing which Argus catches across the shin as he raises his leg in a low block. The Kenpo Karate is paying off and Argus does not have to think about these movements. Argus is trying to get his radio off of his right hip and defend himself at the same time but the radio is a new one with a tight clip attached to the radio. Argus takes a blow to the left rib cage but his adrenaline is free flowing and he only feels the impact.

Argus turns his head, keys the radio and yells, "Staff needs assistance Unit Three!"

Just as he finishes this transmission, the club lands across his left ear and jaw. After Argus told the inmate he was confiscating the radios, the inmate had gone to the Laundry Room and broken off an industrial mop handle to a length of about forty inches and now is doing his best to beat Argus to death with it.

Argus is mad and he's done what policy dictates. A voice in his head screams, "THAT IS ENOUGH MOTHERFUCKER!"

He charges inside of the weapon using both forearms against the inmate's chest and muscles him out of the office, shoving as hard as he can to gain some distance. Argus throws a front snap kick but misses. His ears are ringing and he doesn't notice Control has not called for staff to respond. The inmate comes at Argus again with a downward arcing swing aimed at his head. Argus counters by moving quickly inside the blow, slamming into the inmate with his full body weight, causing the club to fly over Argus' right shoulder and clatter against the wall of the flat near his office. Argus grapples with the inmate and pushes him into the corner near the unit television room and there, he puts his forearm against the inmate's throat and begins throwing hooks into the inmate's ribcage. The inmate is holding tight to Argus, still trying to gain the advantage. With each punch Argus hears the inmate grunt.

Argus hears someone behind him yell, "Hey, Hey, HEY!" as he realizes there were at least thirty inmates on the flat and he has no idea where they are.

He also knows there are no staff members behind him. He is fighting for his life and knows he is outnumbered. Argus has to end this and quickly. He grabs the inmate by the hair with both hands and drags his face down the wall smashing his head into the staff telephone on the wall of the flat. Then Argus sees in slow motion the receiver of the telephone come out of the cradle and drop to the floor as the cord comes out of the back of the receiver and bounces back up into the air.

Argus hears Control on the radio as if far away, "Unit Three, you have a no dial."

A no dial alarm is received in Control when a staff telephone is left off the cradle for a certain number of seconds. It makes the receiver an open microphone so Control can hear what is going on near the telephone. Because the receiver isn't connected to Argus' phone, there is no open microphone.

Most no dials are false alarms. Today it isn't.

Argus hears this and thinks, "No shit! I just called for assistance!" as he remembers that his office is a radio dead zone.

No help is coming. Argus' training is tipping the scales in his favor. The inmate and Argus are wrestling for position as Argus palm heal strikes the inmate's chin which weakens the neck muscles, reaches around and grabs the inmate's hair, jerking hard as he scoops the inmate's leg and throws him to the concrete. The inmate sprawls on the concrete floor face down.

Argus puts his palm in between the inmate's shoulder blades to hold him down, keys his radio and yells, "I need assistance in three NOW!"

He is trying to keep track of the inmate he is holding and the other inmates on the flat. Other staff members arrive within seconds and order the inmates into their cells.

They ask Argus, "Where's the other one, Ant."

Argus answers, "I'm the other one. Get that club, its evidence."

While staff members search the flat, the inmate is escorted down to the Lieutenant's Office in handcuffs. Argus enters the Lieutenant's Office while other staff members hold the inmate in the main corridor.

The Operations Lieutenant asks him what happened and Argus begins speaking rapidly as the adrenaline still pounds through his veins, "Lieutenant, don't you fucking pull me out of that unit. Don't you dare fucking pull me!"

Lieutenant Mack is the Operations Lieutenant and holds his hands up, "We'll deal with that in a minute. Take a breath Ant and think carefully about everything you say. Now, tell me what happened."

Argus gives the Operations Lieutenant the account of the incident. Lieutenant Mack assures Argus he's not being pulled but he will have to go to the hospital to get assessed and treated for any injuries, then he'll be given a couple days off with pay. The Warden will call Lynn and let her know that he's okay. The Physician's Assistant will treat the inmate's injuries.

Argus sits in the examination room at the hospital and thinks about the inmate. He was told before being driven to the hospital that the inmate is serving an eighty-eight year sentence for serial rape and sodomy. Argus will write an incident report for possession of a weapon and serious assault. The inmate is already doing life. Argus has a purple goose egg on his left forearm but no bones are broken. His left ear is also turning blue. He still has a berserker rage in his belly. The Warden arrives at the examination room and checks on him. Argus decides that he would follow this man anywhere. He's just a GS-7 hack and the Warden's here checking on him. Argus knows that he's joined a small club in the Agency. He's fought toe to toe for his life with no help coming and has come out on top.

Argus arrives home as darkness is cloaking his neighborhood. Lynn and Olivia are waiting for him as he pulls up. He doesn't tell her the details. "An inmate came at me. I did what I had to do. I'm okay. No worries."

She knows that's all she'll get. Argus will have to go in tomorrow and write the reports. The attack will be referred for prosecution and the inmate will be temporarily transferred to another institution pending trial. Argus goes in to work the next day and types the incident reports on the typewriter in the Lieutenant's Office. This will look better for the prosecutor to use in court. Then Argus returns home to spend some time with his girls by the pool. Three days later Argus walks up the main walk toward the prison lobby with cold determination in his heart.

As he enters the lobby, the Lobby Officer says, "Hey man, they want you in Personnel before you go back."

Argus raises an eyebrow and says, "Okay, thanks" as he heads to the right for the Personnel Office.

Waiting for him there is an Internal Affairs Agent. The agent is smartly dressed in a suit and tie. He has a direct look in his eyes and a firm handshake. Argus smiles as he shows him his credentials. The agent asks Argus to recount the events leading up to the assault, what transpired during and what happened after.

Before Argus begins he leans forward in his chair and says, "Can I ask a question, you aren't coming after me for excessive use of force are you?"

The agent shakes his head, "Hell no, he had a weapon. If you were carrying a gun, you could've shot him. No, the inmate had some injuries. I want to know how he got them. Specifically, did you give them to him or did some of your buddies?"

Argus realizes what this is now. Contrary to popular belief, that never happens. Argus details how the inmate got each one of his injuries. The bruised ribs, the bruising and lump on his head and the abrasion on his forehead all explained.

"What a crock," thinks Argus. His friends wouldn't do that to him.

The agent thanks Argus and he reports to the Lieutenant's Office to let them know he's here to work his unit. His dragon is here too.

∞∞∞

He stands in the corridor between Unit Two and Unit Three as the open movement is going on. It is Argus' first day back on shift after the incident with Inmate "Radio". Since arriving, the inmates have acted normal in the unit. Argus has done his job as always. The attack was just another day on the job and he's determined to look at it that way. An inmate is heading into the unit and stops in front of Argus.

The inmate is laughing which makes Argus' sixth sense awaken. "Officer that was some shit the other day. Every time you hit that dude his feet came off the floor. I ain't never seen no shit like that. Everybody knows when you go after somebody like that you don't let them take your piece from you. Hahaha! That was definitely some shit."

Another inmate is walking past and joins in, "You got some shit with you Snoop. I told these dudes you had some shit with you."

Argus just nods and tells the inmates, "Nah fellas. Just another day at the office."

Both of them know he won't talk about the incident. That's all they'll get. Inmate "Radio" has been transferred to another institution. Argus doesn't know where, nor does he care.

Argus goes throughout the day as he always does, just doing his job. At 3:30 pm his relief arrives to find him standing by the restraining door monitoring inmate movement into the unit for the recall move. They go to the office and exchange chits for equipment. The shift has been uneventful. Argus picks up his lunchbox and leaves the unit. As he walks down the corridor, he thinks about the incident with Inmate "Radio". He's heard through the grapevine that the older hacks are saying they're proud of him and how he handled himself. They're also supposedly saying that he gained ten years of respect with staff and inmates from this one incident. Some good always comes from the bad. Argus always tries to learn from everything in here and he learned a great deal from this. He's proud of himself but not prideful.

He thinks, "I made a mistake in not removing the inmate from the unit immediately, but it was just a fucking radio."

He'll not make that mistake again. He's sure he'll make others because that's the nature of this game. This mistake could have cost him. Had he not been training and hitting the bag after every shift, things might have turned out differently. Argus thinks about bouncing some of these ideas off of somebody but he has no idea who that might be. It's not his way to talk with people about things like this. That's the price of being a loner. He pulls into the Training Center parking lot for his session with the heavy bag after a few days away. He is glad to be here.

∞∞∞∞

"Step over and grab the wall so I can pat search you." Argus is standing outside of Unit Three, pat searching inmates as they return from noon mainline. Inside the penitentiary, every pat search is conducted with the inmate facing the wall with arms extended and hands on the wall. Argus pats the inmates down following the rules the hacks who trained him insisted on. So far he has confiscated a few food items as usual that are nothing to get excited about. A big part of contraband interdiction is performing pat searches in volume. If an inmate thinks he might be patted down, he's less likely to try and move the contraband. It's all a numbers game. Argus is just finishing up a pat search when he hears a familiar accent from across the corridor. It is inmate "Worm" returning to Unit Four from mainline.

Argus turns to face the inmate as he walks toward the unit. "I told you if you keep messing with people's worms something bad will happen to you! HAHA!"

Argus just shakes his head as the inmate enters the unit. Argus thinks, "Bad things happen when you awaken a dragon too."

∞∞∞∞

The ninety day quarter is coming to an end for Argus and there is a staff recall in the Chapel of the penitentiary to give out awards to staff. The counselor assumes the supervision of Unit Three so Argus can attend. Apparently, he is receiving another award. Argus enters the Chapel and sits toward the back behind his friend and mentor Officer Oak. They exchange the usual lighthearted greeting as Argus sits down. Officer Oak is the best officer that Argus has ever worked with and has given Argus a wealth of knowledge on how to be a stellar hack. Oak has taught Argus many things by just watching how he works. Oak is a Vietnam Veteran and never gets rattled. Argus wishes he had half the self-discipline Oak has as he interacts with the inmates in his stoic way. If there is one correctional officer that Argus tries to emulate, it is Oak. Oak always carries two pieces of gum in his daily planner, one piece for the first four hours of the shift and one for the second four hours of the shift.

Argus asked Oak about this practice one time and Oak just replied, "Self-discipline Ant. You should never stop working on it."

The Chapel is just what you'd expect a chapel in a prison to look like. There is a steel restraining door to the main corridor, a few offices, a library with multidenominational literature and a pulpit. The decorations are very generic because all faiths worship here. It is painted in the same color as the main corridor. Argus is looking around the room noticing these details when his name is called to come to the front and receive his award from the Warden. When he gets to the front of the Chapel, he is both surprised and humbled to learn that he has been chosen as Correctional Officer of the Year in addition to the special act award for his actions in Unit Three. The Correctional Officer of the Year is voted on by the officers at the penitentiary. It is not an award given by the administration, making it very special to Argus. His fellow hacks have given this gift to him and he hopes he can continue to live up to the honor.

He's thinking about these things as he returns to his seat when Oak leans over and whispers, "Keep playing ball with the Agency Ant and someday they'll stick the bat up your ass."

This surprises Argus but he can't get into the conversation in the middle of the award ceremony and ask Oak what he means by that. It won't be long before it becomes clear on its own.

∞∞∞∞

Argus sits in the courtroom thirty feet behind Inmate "Radio". The inmate has pled guilty to the charges of assaulting a correctional officer with a weapon.

Today is his sentencing hearing and Argus listens as the inmate's lawyer explains to the judge why the assault is minor because, "It was just a broom handle. How can you really injure someone with something like that? I mean, c'mon."

There are three bailiffs standing in between Argus and the inmate. This is something he doesn't fail to notice. This amuses Argus as he thinks, "What do they think I'm going to do?"

He just smiles and shakes his head slightly. Argus didn't have to attend the sentencing but was asked by the Warden to attend and he readily said yes. He felt he should be there. He'd provided a victim's witness statement detailing the assault and the angle of the strikes which were intended to injure. The first of which was aimed at the back of his neck. Argus was also struck on the head. If the inmate had knocked Argus unconscious, there is no telling what might have happened. He is certain with all he knows, he could have been killed. The inmate's lawyer is making it sound like the inmate hit Argus with a plastic drinking straw.

Argus thinks, "This punk lawyer ought to have to work a housing unit. These inmates would break him like spaghetti."

Argus is proud to be a correctional officer. It is a job very few can do effectively. The inmate is serving an eighty-eight year sentence for serial rape and sodomy. It might as well be life. He has demonstrated that he will resort to violence over nothing. Argus looks at the inmate and is proud that he is the one who keeps men like this behind a fence away from society. The inmate is sitting in the defendant's chair, slumped down with his head down looking meek as a kitten. The judge delivers the sentence. Seventy-seven months to run consecutively with the sentence he is already serving.

Argus thinks, "Twelve months of commissary restriction would have had more impact on that fucker. I wish I would have hit him harder."

As for Argus, he just stands and walks out of the courtroom. He exits the building and looks back toward the gold colored dome of the courthouse and thinks, "Justice". He makes it to his truck and starts the engine. As he puts the truck in reverse he looks in the rear view mirror and what he sees there causes him to pause and put the truck back into park. The man he sees in the mirror is not the man who started at Tarragon. Argus sees the lieutenant who interviewed him. He sees his friend's father and he sees his Marine Corps drill instructors. It's Argus' eyes. They are eyes that have seen too much already and have a look that indicates something just under the surface.

116

Carl Jung said, "No tree, it is said, can grow to heaven unless its roots reach down to hell."

His dragon is fully grown now with razor sharp teeth. He backs out of the parking spot, puts the truck in drive and heads home to his girls.

∞∞∞∞

At any given time there are enough inmates being transported around the country to fill an institution. Some inmates are going to lower level institutions and some to higher security levels. Inmates are transported for a variety reasons throughout the Agency. Each one of these inmates must be properly identified and their personal property packed for shipping. They must also be strip searched and given new clothes to wear during transportation. Once this occurs, someone must apply restraints according to their custody level, and once the prisoner exchange is made with the different agencies, someone must receive the proper amount of restraints in return for the inmate. This is where Argus has distinguished himself. The Transportation Lieutenant assigned Argus the duties of keeping the "iron" accounted for on his first overtime shift during transportation operations and he has fulfilled these duties ever since. Argus likes the job and the overtime is steady. Prisoner transport occurs weekly.

This is what he is doing today as the "Ironman," applying restraints to inmates prior to loading them on to a prison bus for transport. Argus checks the list and looks at the inmate picture card. The inmate standing in front of him is a high/in inmate. He'll be restrained with a belly chain, handcuffs and leg irons. If he were a high/max, he would also have a black box applied to the handcuffs to impede any manipulation of the handcuff restraints. Argus applies the restraints as always in a professional manner not to cause the inmate any undo discomfort. He wants the other transport crews to have a good impression of Tarragon.

Argus looks up and sees a familiar inmate approaching him to have restraints applied. It is Inmate "Radio". Word travels fast in a penitentiary and what Inmate "Radio" did is no secret. The inmates in the holding cell are watching what Argus will do as well as the staff members controlling the movement of the inmates in Receiving and Discharge. Inmate "Radio" steps up in front of Argus but he will not look at Argus. His head is bowed. It is his worst nightmare. The officer that he attacked is the one who decides how tight his restraints will be applied.

Inmate "Radio" is a high/max inmate. Argus double checks the roster and applies the handcuffs, making certain to put the tip of his thumb against the inmate's wrist before ratcheting them down. He then moves the cuff over the inmate's wrist ensuring the sizing is correct. Argus is focused on the inmate as he does this. Inmate "Radio" doesn't look up and neither of them speaks. Argus reaches to his right without taking his eyes off of "Radio" and retrieves a black box from the iron box and applies it to the handcuffs. Inmate "Radio" continues to look at the floor. Argus steps to the side of the inmate and wraps the belly chain around the inmate's waist ensuring that the sizing is right by keeping his fingers in the chain. He steps back to the front of the inmate and feeds the belly chain grommet through the black box and feeds the chain through the grommet over the top of the box. Then Argus puts the padlock through the chain and locks it. Argus doesn't speak as he puts his hand at waist level so the inmate can see it and rotates his finger, signaling the inmate to turn around. The inmate doesn't look up and turns around as instructed. Argus then applies the leg irons in the same fashion. Once the leg irons are applied, Argus tells the inmate to turn back around and face him. The inmate continues to look at the floor. Argus keeps his hand at waist level and points to the holding cell. Inmate "Radio" shuffles away into the holding cell and sits on the bench. Everything at Tarragon is a test but as far as Argus is concerned this wasn't something to be proven to his fellow hacks, nor to the inmates. This test was personal. It was a test of what he would see when he looks in the mirror and in the end, that's all that matters.

∞∞∞∞

It is early evening on his day off as Argus stands in the mulch and dust at the starting line of the obstacle course and looks at Lynn standing off to the left. He smiles and she smiles back. She's always supported his crazy ideas. Hibben had given Argus some pointers on getting his time down in completing the obstacle course but, Argus had to practice somehow before the next SWAT training.

Lieutenant Sena told Argus when he asked to practice on his own time, "Sorry Ant, you can't run it alone. You gotta have someone there in case you fall off."

So Argus asked if his wife could come and watch him as he practiced and Sena had agreed with the stipulation that he didn't climb the rope. Argus promised him he wouldn't. Sena even loaned him an old beat up flak vest so he could do it with some extra weight.

118

Now, here Argus stands with the flak vest strapped up and Lynn smiling that pretty smile at her crazy husband. Hibben had told Argus not to concentrate on the whole course.

"Break it down into each obstacle and attack that one obstacle. Don't think about what's next."

Argus looks at the sky and the waning light."We've only got about an hour to do this."

His plan is to run each obstacle three times in the vest. That should be a good workout. He looks at Lynn one more time and then takes off to the first obstacle. He hooks a leg over each pole and vaults his body to clear the chest high obstacle. Two more times and he knows this is the right plan. This is putting his mind in the frame to attack a single obstacle and not the whole course. Next the ladders which turn out to be more challenging.

Argus runs the obstacle one time, drops down and looks at Lynn, shaking his head. This one is smoking my grip."

Lynn takes a few steps forward and says, "What if you use your legs more? Also try going faster. You're spending too much time on the obstacle and it's wearing your arms out."

The rungs are slick but he gets his body into a rhythm by kicking his legs as he reaches for the next rung. His forearms are aching by the third time around but Lynn's advice has paid off. He moves on to the inverted ladder which is no problem until the third time. Argus grip is flagging and he has to kick hard on the last rung to make the swing over the top.

He's breathing hard but having a ball. Lynn is watching and cheering him on. Argus likes to show off for her. Argus hits the rope and wraps his feet like Hibben had shown him then he does ten pull ups in place at the bottom of the rope. This toasts his arms but he knows it will only make him stronger. Argus pulls the inverted rope bridge three times and ends it there. It's getting dark anyway and there's a chill in the air. Argus and Lynn walk the short distance back to the Staff Training Center holding hands. He wonders if she knows how much he appreciates her. This is a part of Tarragon that he can share with her and they make plans to start jogging the back road behind the penitentiary. Argus and Lynn have been jogging together since he was stationed at Camp Lejeune. They would jog around the short loop in the trailer park they lived in. Who would've thought back then that they would be considering a five mile loop behind a penitentiary.

As he looks at her, he thinks, "I'm going to run with you forever."

119

∞∞∞∞

Argus stands at the restraining door of Unit Three and spits into the trash can. He's studying his daily planner, trying to figure out which days he can work some overtime. There are plenty of types of overtime to choose from for an officer like Argus. Since arriving at Tarragon, he has volunteered for a myriad of assignments and has gained the trust of the supervisory staff as well as his fellow officers. He is a member of the SWAT team which opens up the high risk escorts that occasionally become available and the weekly transportation crew is always a steady option. With that and the occasional call in, he decides to let the lieutenant's know about the two days he can definitely work. Argus loves his job and is proud to be here at Tarragon. As he contemplates what might come open, his mind drifts back to the roughest shift of overtime he's done so far and the one he is proudest of. The inmate was a high level, maximum custody inmate with ties to the local community and had to be escorted for an overnight stay at the local hospital. As a SWAT member, Argus donned his tactical gear and accompanied the escort. He carried his sidearm and a nine millimeter submachine gun slung across his body with a tactical sling. Argus road shotgun and when they had arrived at the hospital, he walked point from the vehicles to the room making sure the way was clear. It was slow going down the corridors of the hospital because the inmate was shackled in the usual iron appropriate for his custody level and couldn't move at more than a shuffle.

As they moved down the corridors, the hospital staff gave them plenty of room as they passed. They finally made it to the room and Argus unlocked the outer door and then the inner door. He stepped into the room and made sure it was unoccupied and secure, he motioned for the crew to bring the inmate in. Once the crew and the inmate were in the room, Argus stepped out of the inner room and locked both doors. Argus was now in the space between the inner and outer doors which amounted to a four foot by four foot area with a small bathroom directly behind him. There was a folding chair included for his comfort. For the next sixteen hours Argus stood this post. It was grueling and required an amazing amount of mental discipline. To keep himself alert, Argus stood for ten minutes and then sat for ten. He did this for the full sixteen hours until another SWAT member arrived at midnight to relieve him. Argus was never so glad to breathe open air in his life.

120

Argus' thoughts are interrupted by the ringing of the range telephone on the flat.

He walks over and answers the phone. "Unit Three, Antrim."

His friend Tim Lantern's cheerful voice comes through the receiver.

"Hey Ant, you'll never guess what we got in the investigative office."

He and Tim became friends shortly after Argus started at Tarragon and have worked many long hours together. Tim has been on loan to the Investigative Office and is working hard to make the loan permanent.

"You got me, what have you got?"

Tim starts to laugh and says, "You aren't going to believe this but we got an inmate complaint that says you threatened him."

Argus thinks, "What the fuck. I don't have to threaten inmates. Tim knows this. Its policy, they either comply or not."

Argus is a little confused and asks who he supposedly threatened. "It's Inmate 'Coal.' Says you threatened to bust him up and I told them up here that sounds just like Ant. You did that didn't you?"

Argus sixth sense lights up. Something isn't right but he can't put his finger on it. Tim knows that's not how Argus operates. He has all sorts of policies he can use to manage inmates. Any inmate knows you can't just "bust him up".

Argus thinks to himself, "Why would I throw an empty threat like that? It's stupid."

Then it hits Argus. He doesn't want to think it but, Argus' gut is telling him that his friend is trying to sell him out. He is silent for a moment as Tim repeats the accusation in a jovial voice.

"C'mon Ant, you did that didn't you man."

Argus knows for certain now. There is a new Senior Investigative Agent at the prison. His name is Wiggle and he is a head hunter. The word is when he puts a case on you, there's no wiggle room. His friend wants to work full time in Wiggle's investigative office and this call is how he's earning his thirty pieces of silver.

Argus should be angry, but instead he's sad. His friend is a traitor. Wiggle is listening in on the call, Argus is sure of it.

His voice flat, Argus says, "I don't know what you're talking about Timmy. Don't ever talk to me again" as he hangs up the phone.

Now Argus will wait. If he's wrong, Tim will be calling him back telling Argus that it's a mistake and he's got it all wrong. If he's right, he won't receive a call because he's seen through the ruse and Timmy is indeed, a traitor. Argus waits for a few minutes by the phone hoping for it to ring. It doesn't. He moves back to the door to spit. Oak's words in the Prison Chapel come back to Argus. So after all the hours away from his family that he can never get back, they're now trying to shove the bat up his ass.

Now Argus begins to get angry.

"Why didn't they just ask me? Why the sneaky bull shit? How much of my personal time have I devoted to this motherfucker?"

Argus doesn't know who to trust now. His SWAT brothers for sure but other than that he doesn't know. He'll have to be on guard now. They're trying to put something on him. "As if the pressure of this place wasn't enough now I have to watch which staff member has my back. Well fuck Tim Lantern. I hope he enjoys his shiny new job."

Argus' mood is sour as he stands by the restraining door spitting. He decides to start bidding for posts with weekends off. There aren't many and for hacks like him with just a few years in, the posts won't be great but he can work anywhere in this joint. Argus finishes out the day without much enthusiasm. His relief shows up at 3:30 pm like clockwork and finds Argus ready to head out which is unusual. Argus mentions something about an appointment, gives a brief update on the unit and then leaves. He barely speaks to anyone on his way out. The appointment is with the heavy bag and it's one he dare not miss.

Chapter Six
Snake's venom will never kill a dragon

He is walking across a grassy field as the sun shines on his back. It is incredibly hot as his boots sink into the sandy soil. Argus looks down and sees that he is in uniform as he tastes the salt and moisture in the wind. He thinks, "I must be close to the sea shore."

He stops and looks around for the water but there is none in sight. The sky is cloudless and a beautiful blue. It is hot as he looks at the thigh high grass moving with the wind. That's when the first viper strikes, burying its fangs into the meat at the back of his leg. Argus reaches down on instinct and grabs the snake by the throat and squeezes with all he has. Another one strikes, hitting him on the thigh and Argus begins to run as he throws the first snake away.

He's running now as his breath comes in ragged gasps and his legs feel like heavy weights. "It must be the venom."

The snakes are hitting him from all sides now. They're hidden in the grass and leap in the air to strike.

Argus can't even begin to try mounting a defense because the snakes are hidden in the thick grass. "I have to get out of this grass."

The field is endless. He digs in and keeps running but he knows it is hopeless. There are too many strikes and too much venom. He begins to weep as he feels her hand on his shoulder.

He opens his eyes as Lynn says," Honey, are you alright?"

He clears his throat and rises up in bed, "Yeah, I'm fine baby."

He wipes his eyes with the back of his hand and goes into the kitchen to make some coffee.

∞∞∞∞

Argus comes through the Front Lobby on his way toward Tower One. His shift today in Unit Three was like most shifts, uneventful. His thoughts are on what post he is going to bid on for next quarter. The bids are due tomorrow so he'll have to make his choices tonight and turn the form in at the Lieutenant's Office.

As he reaches the desk, the Lobby Officer says into the telephone, "Yes sir, he just rolled up. Okay sir, I'll tell him. Hey Ant, Unit Manager Gaylon wants you to hold here for a second. He's on his way from the back."

Unit Manager Gaylon is in charge of Units Ten and Eleven. Argus has worked those units many times and wonders what he wants. Argus moves to the lobby chairs, sets his lunch box down and waits. A few minutes later, Mr. Gaylon steps into the lobby from the direction Argus had just come from. "Antrim, I'm glad I caught you. How've you been?"

Argus stands and shakes his hand, "Good sir, how about you?"

Gaylon continues, "I'm doing well. Have you got a few minutes? I've got something I want to talk to you about."

Argus shrugs his shoulders, "Yeah, what can I do for you?"

Mr. Gaylon looks at Argus. "Let's walk" as he motions with his head toward the direction of Tower One.

Mr. Gaylon talks as they head that way, "Have you put your shift request in yet?"

Argus shakes his head and raises his eyebrows. Mr. Gaylon continues, "Good, good. Look, I've got some things going on down in Unit Eleven that I need to clean up. There are some heavy hitters down there and I need someone who can run the unit that follows policy and will hold the inmates accountable. Are you interested?"

Argus can't believe it. A couple of weeks ago, the administration is trying to put a case on him and now he's being recruited to run a unit. Admittedly, Mr. Gaylon has nothing to do with the Investigative Branch but still, Argus finds it kind of poetic.

He almost laughs. "Sir, I was planning on trying to get weekends off next quarter."

Argus likes Mr. Gaylon and the Counselor in the unit, Mr. Blanco but frankly, he's still feeling the sting from Tim's call.

Mr. Gaylon puts his hand on Argus' shoulder as they reach Tower One. "Look, I could really use you down there. The days off for the Day Watch OIC are Sunday and Monday. I'll give you the information on every inmate in the unit so you'll already be ahead of the game."

If Argus is honest, he's flattered by this and frankly likes a challenge. "Okay Sir, I'll put in for it. Thanks for the opportunity."

Gaylon looks at Argus quizzically, "You're the one doing me the favor. Thanks Antrim."

They shake hands and head their separate ways, Argus out and

Gaylon back to the institution. He reaches his truck and starts it up, his mental gears running through the possibilities of what might be going on in Unit Eleven. Argus knows that they have at least one gang in the unit with notable numbers. Argus will put the paperwork in and if he's assigned to the unit, he'll see when he gets there. When he reaches the Training Center, Argus realizes that putting in for the post will knock him out of the transportation overtime. He'll have to make it up somewhere else. Maybe call outs or medical escorts. He'll make it work. Argus heads downstairs and peels his shirt off like so many times before. He looks at his worn bag gloves. It is definitely time for a new pair. The area that protects his knuckles is almost worn through. Oh well, the callous' will pick up the slack. He squares off, checks his watch and begins his one hour therapy session, completely free of charge.

∞∞∞

He makes his relief, keys the off going officer out of the unit and heads back to his office to acclimatize himself. It is the first day of the new quarterly roster and Argus finds himself in Unit Eleven. This unit is a standard cell house with the officer's office on the right side of the flat. When the roster committee had completed their quarterly meeting and it was determined Argus would be in Eleven, Mr. Gaylon had provided him with information on every inmate in the unit. Now it was just a matter of seeing who was who. This is the unit where Argus had taken inmate "Dustpan" down so the inmates are familiar with him. The same inmate is living in cell forty seven. Inmate "Dustpan" is no longer at Tarragon. Argus starts his logs and looks through the desk to get rid of any leftover contraband and trash. It's always the same when you take over a unit. First day is cleaning day. An inmate stops by the office for a copout and Argus gives him the form.

The inmate says, "Hey boss, you need anything let me know. This is a quiet unit. You probably won't even need to leave your office for too much."

Argus looks at the inmate, "We'll see. You know my job just like I do."

The inmate isn't a familiar face. Argus figures that the inmate will figure it out soon enough. He finishes up his paperwork and walks out on the flat. As he looks around, he sees that the unit is fairly clean on the surface. There are two orderlies working at the end of the flat, sweeping and mopping. Argus is pleased to see one of the orderlies is Inmate "Coffee Cup" and he has a new friend working with him. Inmate "Red" is small. Maybe five foot two with shoulder length red hair and it's obvious as Argus watches, the two are connected at the hip.

He steps back into his office and checks the bed book cards to identify the orderlies in the unit and what their duties are, gets his pass book, steps out of the office and locks the door. He heads to the corridor restraining door and pulls the trash can near the door, puts a dip of Copenhagen in and spits. Argus walks the tiers looking in each cell at how clean they are while making notations on a three by five card. Two cells are a complete wreck with the beds unmade and trash everywhere. Argus goes back to the office and finds the work assignments of the inmates in the cells and calls their shop foremen on the telephone. He has the foremen send the inmates back to the unit on the next move to clean the cells. They'll be docked an hour pay for this. It's not personal, just policy. Beds have to be made and cells have to be clean. This is what Argus has been recruited to do, manage the unit.

The first ten minute movement is called by the Corridor Officer. Argus opens his unit door and monitors the inmate movement while doing pat searches. His friend Dane Pickle is working Unit Thirteen. Argus stands with him halfway between the units and talks as they pat search and watch the inmates. It's nice to have a friend working a unit next door. Argus sees an inmate pass a carton of cigarettes to another inmate and he calls the inmate over. He tells the inmate to open the carton so that he can see inside. Argus doesn't care about the cigarettes as long as its only cigarettes in the carton

Another inmate passes by and starts complaining about what Argus is doing. "Why you harrasin' that man? I wish those was my cigarettes. You wouldn't be lookin' at um."

The inmate keeps walking and enters Unit Ten. Argus hands the carton of cigarettes back to the inmate and doesn't bother with the mouthy inmate. He thinks, "You can keep talking as long as you keep walking."

Argus is used to the inmates running their mouths. He figures its part of their job as inmates. Their troubles begin when they stop and confront. That can't be tolerated if you want to maintain some semblance of order.

The movement ends and Argus goes back to his unit. He sees that Counselor Blanco is in his office and steps over to say hello. "Hey Mr.

Blanco, how's things going for you?"

Blanco looks up from his paperwork with a smile, "Snoop! Man I'm glad to see you. You need anything? If you do, let me know okay."

Argus tells him that he will and leaves to make another round in the unit. He completes his round and writes a couple of passes for inmate appointments then calls the Corridor Officer and sends the inmates on their way. Argus makes another tour of the unit to identify which cells he'll start his searches in. As he walks the tiers, he sees the inmates with the dirty cells are in them cleaning. They look at him as he passes the cells but don't speak. Somehow, Argus doesn't think they want any conversation. Argus picks a cell on the upper left tier and steps inside. He closes the door behind him and stands in the middle of the cell thinking. Once again, he starts in one corner and works his way around the cell, searching each item. He makes note of some nuisance contraband but nothing that he is going to confiscate. Argus is using his first few days to find out who is who and what's important to them. He's just getting to know the inmates. He'll use this to manage them. The rest of the shift is as uneventful as the first. Argus knows this is a marathon, not a sprint.

∞∞∞∞

Unit Eleven is a pretty good unit to work and Argus is getting comfortable in the routine he has set. The inmates are also starting to get used to the program. Basically, if they have it coming according to policy, they'll get it. If not, don't ask. It's been two weeks since Argus took over the unit and he's done his job like he always does. He's also been watching from his giant spit can and knows who is who now.

He looks down the flat and thinks, "It's always better to watch and listen for a while. You're so much more effective in the end."

The inmates have been cutting the range telephone cord and Argus has already replaced it once. This morning he showed up at work and the telephone cord was cut again. As the day watch OIC, its Argus' job to take care of these maintenance issues. He calls the Communications Shop and puts in a request for a new telephone cord.

The foreman asks him, "What'd you do to those inmates? This is the second time I'm fixing the phone."

Argus tells him, "Not sure what the beef is. I'm going to find out though."

Argus steps down to the last cell on the right off the flat and finds

Inmate "Television" sitting in his cell. "Television" is the leader of one of the gangs in the unit. Argus stands at the door and doesn't enter the cell. He wants other inmates to hear what is said. He just needs to say it to someone and the other inmates will listen to what he is saying to this inmate. It's a status thing. Argus is taking a roundabout way of making an announcement in the unit.

"Television,' why are you guys cutting the range phone?"

Inmate "Television" looks at Argus with an innocent look. "I ain't cut nothin' Snoop. I think somebody might be mad at the evening watch OIC. Not sure though."

Argus looks at "Television" sideways and says, "Well, this is the second time and I'd appreciate it if it didn't happen again. You all are starting to inconvenience me."

"Television" shrugs his shoulders as he replies nonchalantly, "I ain't got no control over that."

Argus walks away thinking, "Word travels fast in a penitentiary. My message was clear. They better cut the crap."

Argus enters the unit and locks the corridor restraining door. The ten o'clock movement has just ended. He scans the unit and realizes something is out of place.

That little voice in the back of his head says, "Take notice, something is off."

Argus can't place it at first but then it hits him. Inmates "Coffee Cup" and "Red" are not out cleaning. In fact, they're nowhere in sight and they didn't leave on the move. Argus walks over to the television room and peers in. They aren't in there watching television. As he walks past the laundry room, he sees they aren't in there either. Argus walks midway down the flat to where their cell is located on the right side. Just as Argus sees that the window of their cell is covered, an inmate whistles on the top left tier. Their lookout didn't do a very good job and Argus is ahead of them. He takes the three large steps to the cell door and yanks it open. There on the bottom bunk are Inmates "Coffee Cup" and "Red" without a stitch of clothing on. The inmates are so surprised and flustered that they jump out of the bunk and put each other's underwear on. "Coffee Cup" standing with the extremely small underwear belonging to "Red" and "Red" holding the very large underwear belonging to "Coffee Cup" bunched up in his right hand so that they stay up. Argus hasn't seen what he needs to see to make the case for a sexual act, IE "erect penis inserted into fill in the blank" but the inmates don't know this.

128

Argus almost laughs at the ludicrous scene and thinks, "Now the reckoning for that dirty shit you tried to do to me so long ago with the coffee cup."

All Argus had to do was wait. Argus takes a deep breath and decides to play this smart. By the time it's all over Inmate "Coffee Cup" will be in his back pocket.

His voice is flat as he says, "Step out of the cell I'm going to shake it down."

Argus sees the panic on their faces immediately. Inmate "Red" almost begs in his whiny voice. "Please boss no, we're embarrassed."

Argus raises his eyebrows and says, "Yeah I can see that. You should be. Get dressed and step out."

The inmates get dressed while Argus stands at the door. When they are clothed they step out of the cell past him. Argus goes in and closes the door. These inmates are orderlies and there is a myriad of nuisance contraband but the cell is neat as a pin.

Argus thinks, "What a good little wife" and smiles.

All the cards are in Argus' favor for making these two his snitches. Argus doesn't have enough to send them to ADSEG but they don't know that.

He calls them down to his office after the search. His voice is low and direct. "If I ever catch you again, you'll go to the hole and I'll see to it you're placed in different cells. When I pack your property there won't be one speck of contraband left and you'll get reports for that too."

Then he looks directly at "Coffee Cup" as his voice lowers a bit. "Let me know what I need to know. Now get back to work and keep that window uncovered."

The message to both inmates is clear but Argus doesn't have to say it out loud. His eyes say it loud and clear. "I know what is most important to you in your whole little world and I can take it if you don't provide the information I want."

The inmates thank him profusely and leave.

Argus thinks, "Karma is a fickle bitch" and smiles.

∞∞∞∞

There's something to be said for being able to think like these men. It is as if Argus was meant to be here doing this kind of work. He has studied them over the many months and has the instincts as if he is doing time himself.

In some ways Argus thinks, "I am, just on the installment plan."

His instincts are attuned to this environment and when he is here, he uses those instincts to his advantage. He steps into a cell midway down the flat on the right side for a random search. The searches are random and Argus usually does his mandated five per shift but being who he is, his averages are pretty good as far as hard contraband is concerned. Argus knows his inmates.

The cell is neither dirty nor exceptionally clean. The inmates who live in the cell work in the Construction Shops which automatically gives them access to weapons grade material. They are both at work and will be until the 3:30 pm recall movement. Argus closes the door and stands in the cell just looking around for a second. On the bottom bunk is a pornographic magazine opened to a page depicting a naked woman with her legs spread in a seductive pose. The look on her face is standard for this kind of picture. She is in the throes of passion.

Argus smiles as he thinks, "You got the wrong hack boys."

There are correctional officers who have a weakness for this sort of stuff and would sit on the rack looking at the magazine instead of shaking the cell. Argus recognizes this for what it is a decoy. This tells Argus something is in this cell and he is going to find it.

He starts in one corner of the cell and starts working his way around meticulously. He searches the lockers first and finds a small container of white latex paint and the remains of a roll of tape. Argus sets the container and tape to the side and exits the cell, dead locking it. He goes to his office and retrieves the bar tap mallet from the expanded metal cage hanging on the wall in his office and returns to the cell. He taps the window bars to make sure they're secure then he taps the base of each wall to make sure nothing has been secreted there and painted over. Argus doesn't find anything out of place.

He thinks, "So, why the tape and paint?"

The 1:00 pm ten minute move is called so Argus exits the cell and deadlocks it. He'll return to the search after the move. By now an inmate from his unit has probably caught a work crew heading back out to the shops and sent a message to the inmates living in the cell. "Snoop is working your cell over hard."

It won't do any good because Argus is on the hunt and his instincts are telling him something isn't right. The move ends and Argus goes back to the cell, unlocks it and resumes his search. He rolls the mattresses and checks the shoes under the bunk. He goes through the laundry bags and finds nothing. He takes the fluorescent light apart and examines the area where the ballast is located still finding nothing. For a moment Argus is out of ideas.

He sits down on the bunk and looks around thinking, "What have I missed?"

Two minutes pass and then he sees it. The vertical steam pipes have insulation around them that is painted white. He is so used to seeing the pipes in the cells that he's looked right over them. Argus stands and goes to the pipes in the back of the cell. An inmate knocks on the cell door and Argus turns. "Hey boss, I got an appointment in Medical. Can I get a pass?"

Argus goes to the cell door, reaches in his pocket and checks his call out sheet. He gets the inmate's identification card and matches the ID with the sheet.

Argus locks the cell and says, "Okay, c'mon."

Argus writes the pass at the door to the unit and calls the Corridor Officer letting him know he will be sending one to Medical on a call out. The Corridor Officer authorizes the move and Argus keys the door. He heads back and enters the cell again. Each cell has a set of vertical steam pipes in the back corner near the radiator which provides heat to the cell. These pipes are covered with a round tube like insulation from the floor to the ceiling. The insulation covering is the off white color of the corridor and soft. Argus grabs the insulation and shakes it against the pipe. What he expects to hear is a dull thump. As he shakes the insulation, he hears a "ping". Argus turns the insulation around the pipe until he's looking at what once was the back. There, almost indistinguishable from the surrounding insulation is a six inch long piece of tape that is well painted to blend right in. Argus removes his "Uncle Henry" pen knife from his pocket and cuts a slit in the tape. He spreads the insulation apart and reveals a metal rod set in a wooden dowel and sharpened to a spear point. Argus admires the workmanship. It looks like an ice pick you would get at the hardware store. He double checks the pipe insulation and finds another piece of tape.

Argus opens this one in the same manner and comes up with three more steel rods that are not sharpened.

Argus thinks, "A shank factory. I'll be damned."

He takes a towel and wraps the shank and metal in it, picks up the paint and tape then deadlocks the cell. He goes to his office and calls the Operations Lieutenant explaining what he's found. Lieutenant Grant is on duty today and Argus makes his case for not only possession of a weapon but also manufacture of a weapon as well. He explains why both inmates will have to wear the shots because the weapon and steel rods were found in a common area of the cell and hidden with the tape and paint. Lieutenant Grant agrees with Argus. The case is solid. Argus calls Unit Ten and asks the officer if he'll watch the unit while he takes the shanks down to the Lieutenant's Office and processes the evidence.

Officer Grass says, "Sure old buddy, I'd love too."

Officer Grass is the happiest officer at Tarragon. Argus has never seen him without a smile on his face. He steps out with the shanks and paint as Grass steps out in the Main Corridor with a big smile. Once he gets to the Lieutenant's Office Argus photographs everything and places it in an evidence bag then heads back to Unit Eleven to write the incident reports and pack the property.

As Argus exits the Lieutenant's Office, Lieutenant Grant says, "Outstanding work Antrim. Do you need any help with the property?"

Argus declines, "Nah LT. I got it."

Lieutenant Grant will call the Construction Shops and have the inmates escorted to the Lieutenant's Office where they'll be given copies of the lockup order and escorted to ADSEG. This probably won't come as a surprise to them. Argus will spend the rest of the shift on the paperwork and property. He decides to wrap the inmate's copy of the property inventory around the porn magazine and put it at the top of the bag. After he's done, he'll put the vacancy sign out. There's an open cell in his unit.

∞∞∞∞

Argus is standing by the corridor restraining door of his unit. He has been on duty for one hour and after completing the morning paperwork has assumed his position by the door to watch the inmates. He sees Inmate "Red" come out of Counselor Blanco's Office and head his way.

Inmate "Red" steps up and asks in his whiny voice, "I've got to go to Safety and pick up some supplies for the counselor. Can I get a pass boss?"

Argus walks over to Counselor Blanco's Office and asks, "Hey Mr. Blanco, you sending "Red" to Safety?"

Blanco answers, "Yeah Snoop. He's getting supplies."

Argus returns to the door where "Red" is waiting and says, "Give me your ID."

"Red" hands it over and Argus writes the pass. As Argus is writing,

"Red" says, "Rig in 19."

Argus doesn't acknowledge that the inmate has said anything and calls the Corridor Officer on the radio, "Eleven to Corridor, one to Safety on a pass."

The Corridor responds. "Send him" and Argus keys the door.

Argus thinks, "So, cell nineteen has a needle in the cell. That'll take some time and I'll have to let our little interaction be forgotten before I move on it. I'll work it in after lunch."

He puts a fresh chew in and spits in the trash can. Argus is watching the main gang in the unit standing around a table on the flat. There are five members standing around the table and one younger inmate standing there but it's clear he hasn't got enough standing to get right up to the table.

Argus thinks, "He must be rushing the fraternity. That pledge will be the one holding their contraband."

Argus knows from experience, the newest member of a group is the one holding for the group. That's just the way it works. The ten minute move is called by the Corridor Officer. Argus keys the door and steps out into the corridor taking a deep breath. He'll be busy when the move ends.

∞∞∞∞∞

He walks the flat in a relaxed way. Noon mainline is complete and Argus is now just counting down until 4:00 pm. He stops at cell nineteen and checks his watch for theatrical purposes. Something the inmates have seen him do a hundred times before.

The action says, "Looks like I got time for one more search."

Argus knows the inmates are always watching and does little things to throw them off. It's a big mind game. He enters the cell and closes the door behind him. A heroine setup is not something you can usually find quickly. The truth is that most of the time it's just dumb luck. Argus sits on the lower bunk and tries to put himself in the inmate's place.

"Okay, I'm a junky and the only way I can fill my habit is with this hype kit. I'm probably going to fix after lockdown so it won't be out in the open. I'm going to bury my rig deep someplace that I won't be opening lockers and dragging all my personal stuff out."

Argus starts in one corner and works his way around the cell starting with the bunks first. He rolls the mattresses and pulls the blankets back

133

to check for rips. He checks the shoes and bends the soles. He looks through the lockers and under them but doesn't have high hopes. The lockers just don't figure into what the inmate needs to fix silently.

Argus removes the tops of the talcum powder and looks inside. He tips the shampoo and conditioner bottles up and puts his flashlight behind them to look for a rig shaped shadow with no luck.

Argus looks around and thinks, "Okay, where the fuck did he put it?"

Argus is almost to the end of the cell and he's searched through it with a fine tooth comb. There's a small red cooler about four by six inches sitting on the floor. Argus looks inside and finds it empty. He closes the lid and stands up but then he stops. He opens the cooler again and sees a small crack with a tiny bit of white Styrofoam insulation peeking through. Argus tries to pull the plastic insert out of the cooler but it's wedged tight.

Argus thinks, "Somebody's had this thing apart."

He pulls again and it starts to move. Back and forth Argus moves the plastic until the insert pops free and he is rewarded with a heroin rig. The inmate has carved a small space out of the Styrofoam in the side wall of the cooler. His hype kit fits neatly into the space. It is what Argus expected to find. A small gage needle melted into the cutoff barrel of an ink pen. There is a small rubber bulb on the other end of the pen barrel. Argus suspects the inmate got the needle from a diabetic inmate. It looks like an insulin needle and the diabetic inmates sometimes try to leave the needle in their stomach at pill line and walk away with it. The diabetic injections the inmates give themselves are monitored but if the officer or nurse gets distracted it's possible. The rarity makes the needle all the more valuable.

Argus leaves the rig where it's at and puts the insert back down in the cooler part ways. He exits the cell and deadlocks it until he can secure the inmate's property.

Argus thinks as he walks to his office with the cooler, "It was so nice of this guy to write his number on the cooler."

Argus calls Lieutenant Grant once again and explains what he has.

Lieutenant Grant just laughs, "Fuck Snoop! You're workin' those dudes over down there ain't ya."

Argus laughs too, "Just trying to make you look good LT. I'll be down in a second with the stuff."

Once Argus gets to the Lieutenant's Office, he processes everything as evidence. Lieutenant Grant has the inmate escorted off of his work site in the Laundry and brought to the office.

He wants Argus there when he confronts the inmate. "Stick around Antrim. He may cop to it and you'll only have to pack one inmate's property."

Once the inmate arrives, he's patted down and enters the office.

Lieutenant Grant says, "Your luck just ran out convict. Look what Officer Antrim found in the cooler with your number on it. You gonna man up?"

The inmate's eyes haven't left the cooler since he walked in. He huffs and looks at the ceiling then at Argus. "Yeah man, it's mine. My cellie's got nothing to do with it."

Argus says, "Fair enough. I'll just pack the one out LT."

Lieutenant Grant just raises his eyebrows, nods and smiles. Argus leaves to go back to Eleven to secure the property. He won't get it inventoried before his shift ends but he'll get it secured. He'll stop by the Lieutenant's Office and write the incident report before he goes to the Training Center once he's relieved. Argus doesn't mind putting in the extra time. He knows now, this is what he was meant to do.

∞∞∞∞

Lynn is busy getting Olivia ready for daycare, putting her little jacket on and filling her Ninja Turtles backpack for the day.

Argus looks appreciatively at his wife and thinks, "How does she do it?"

Lynn is dressed to the nines as usual. She's recently landed a job as a high end executive assistant for the general manager of a jet engine manufacturing facility in town. It didn't surprise Argus when she got the job. A naturally organized woman, Lynn was perfect for the position.

Argus thinks, "She's way out of my league."

He gets his jacket, lunchbox and thermos and kisses his girls goodbye then heads out the door.

When he gets the truck started, he looks in the mirror and says to himself, "Watch yourself today."

Argus can tell that he had one of the dreams last night. Sometimes he remembers them and sometimes not but he can always tell by the empty feeling he has in his stomach when he wakes up. It's like a black hole in his soul that evokes a feeling of impending doom. He shakes it off and backs out of the drive. The drive to work is a short thirty minutes and ends with him pulling into the staff parking lot as usual.

The scene is all too familiar. Past Tower One and the Lobby, then Control and to the Lieutenant's Office to check in. "Hey boss, I'm here."

Lieutenant Mack is the Operations Lieutenant today. Argus likes Mack. He is a solid lieutenant with good judgment and a confident demeanor. Argus has been in some pretty serious situations with the lieutenant and knows Mack doesn't get rattled. Mack is on the short list of people Argus trusts.

He looks up from the roster and says, "Gotcha Antrim."

Argus heads to the East End and Unit Eleven. It is 7:25 am. Argus makes his relief and the Morning Watch OIC lets him know the inmates have cut the range telephone cord again and this time have stolen the whole receiver.

He finishes by saying, "The button is taped down so you don't get any no-dials. It happened on evening watch last night."

He then heads down the corridor without looking back. Argus gets the tape dispenser and goes to the telephone where he puts more tape on the button. He starts his logs as usual, gets the callout sheet and notes the inmate appointments on a three by five card then puts his pass book in his pocket and exits the office for his first tour of the unit. Argus locks the office door and just stands there for a second, looking around. The orderlies are cleaning, the dryer is running and there are around twelve inmates on the flat and tiers. Everything looks normal. Argus starts walking the unit and checking fire hoses and extinguishers making sure they are full. The inmates sometimes use the extinguishers to cook hooch. Argus hasn't been able to figure out how they accomplish this but he's found at least two in the past full of wine.

Argus thinks, "Sometimes you see the damndest things in here."

Argus walks the unit looking in each cell as he passes. The cell sanitation has improved since he adopted the practice of calling inmates off of their work assignments to come back to the unit and clean the cells up.

Argus always tells them when he has to do this, "You clean it this time, if it happens again, I'll clean it."

He can see that he's going to have to be creative in handling this telephone situation. The inmates can't blame him, he did warn them. The range telephone is not only a convenience for the unit officer it is also a convenience for the inmates. If someone wants to summon an inmate to their area, they can call the unit on the telephone. If the officer is out on the flat, he can answer the telephone out there instead of going to the office and get the inmate sent on his way. Argus decides he's not going to go to his office today and he's not going to replace the telephone today either.

Argus thinks, "Sometimes it's more effective to show someone they're being discourteous than to try and tell them. Argus will pass it on to his relief that he's handling the telephone situation and not to get it replaced. He'll do it.

Argus goes to his spot at the corridor door then spits in the trash can and decides to let things play out. He has a feeling it won't take long but that's how this game is played.

The Corridor Officer announces over the radio, "Corridor to the housing units, send your food service workers to the Dining Hall. This will be the 10:30 food service move."

This move is to get the day shift food service workers to the Dining Hall to prepare the noon meal. It is a five minute one way movement. Argus stands in the corridor as the food service workers exit his unit. There are only a half dozen.

The Corridor Officer announces on the radio at the end of the five minutes, "Corridor to the housing units, close your doors. This move is over. They missed it."

Argus closes his door and locks it. He is on his way to his office to check the cell search log and plan his searches for the day when Inmate "Hat" comes running down the stairs from the upper tier yelling, "Hold the door! Hold the door!"

Argus looks at the inmate standing at the door. "Hat" is looking at Argus as if he expects him to open the door. This inmate has a food service hat he wears with the bill bent straight up. He is a middle aged inmate with a solid build. He is also a mouthy inmate with an attitude of entitlement.

Argus tells "Hat," "Corridor closed the move. You missed it man."

Hat says, "You got to call and get him to let me go to work."

The inmate could, at the Food Service Foreman's discretion get an incident report for being late for work.

Argus looks at the inmate.

"I can't call. Someone cut my phone cord."

"Hat's" mouth drops open as he looks at Argus and then at the range telephone. "Stop fuckin' around man. Use the one in your office."

Argus looks at the inmate directly, "I ain't going to my office right now."

Argus then walks down the flat as he hears "Hat" say under his breath, "Motherfucker."

Argus turns to see "Hat" heading back up the stairs to his cell on the upper left across from Argus' office.

Argus thinks, "As long as you're walkin' away, you can keep runnin' that mouth."

He also hears the telephone in his office begin to ring. Argus keeps walking and enters a cell midway down the flat on the right for a search. Argus performs the search in the usual manner without finding anything notable.

He thinks, "No squirrel gets all the nuts."

As he exits the cell, he sees "Hat" standing on the upper tier outside of his cell. He is watching Argus.

Food Service calls Argus on the radio, "Food Service to Eleven."

Argus answers, "Eleven, go ahead."

Argus is looking at "Hat." The inmate is smiling.

"Would you send Inmate "Hat" to Food Service?"

Argus goes to the corridor restraining door. "Hat" has heard the transmission and meets Argus there. "Eleven to Corridor, one to Food Service called for."

The Corridor responds, "Send him."

Argus keys the door and as the inmate walks past he looks at Argus and smiles. Argus shakes his head. "That was odd."

Argus locks the door and heads for his office to log the cell search. He grabs the handle to his office and knows immediately why the inmate was smiling. He pulls his hand away and sees the oily brown substance that had squished between his fingers. It is human feces on his door handle and hand.

Argus takes a breath and exhales slowly. The inmates on the flat are all looking at him. Argus looks at his hand and then at the inmates.

Inmate "Coffee Cup" approaches and says, "Boss, I'll clean your door."

He actually looks sorry for what happened. Argus looks at him and speaks in a low tone but still loud enough to be heard. "Don't touch my door. This is my mess to clean up."

Argus is seething. There is a darkness rising in him. The dragon is looking at him with those yellowed eyes and its lips have pulled back to expose its razor sharp teeth. Argus upper lip twitches. He turns, exits the unit and goes to the staff bathroom.

As he walks, he thinks of all of the diseases that could be in the feces.

"Hepatitis, aids, who the fuck knows coming from these dirt bags."

Shitting an officer's door down is one of the vilest things an inmate can do. Argus goes into the mop closet and finds the cleaning fluid they use on the floors for blood spills, takes it in the bathroom and douses his hand with it. Then he turns the water on as hot as he can stand it and washes. He repeats this process three times. He dries his hands and puts on the pair of rubber gloves he carries in his pocket and heads back to his unit with the solution to clean his door.

A bucket of water and a cleaning rag are sitting by his office door. Inmate "Coffee Cup" is trying to soften the blow. He knows what is about to happen. Argus takes the rag and cleans the door handle with the solution. Once he's satisfied, he rolls the bucket to the deep sink and dumps the water then he throws the rag in the trash. He can feel the inmates watching him. Argus leaves the unit once more to wash his hands three more times with the solution and then with soap. He returns to the unit, puts a dip in and spits. Argus decides he is going to think about this for a bit. It's always better to take a deep breath and use your brain and he knows this. He also wants the inmates to wonder what he'll do. Sometimes anticipation of the storm is just as bad as the storm itself. Argus doesn't call the lieutenant.

He stands at the door and looks at the inmates, looking at him and thinks, "This is my block. I'll run it."

The Corridor Officer announces noon mainline is open and begins calling the various units for chow.

Unit Eleven is called and Argus keys the door yelling, "Mainline!"

The inmates file out only glancing Argus' way. During mainline, Argus pat searches inmates coming back to his unit and takes a fair amount of food which goes into the trash can he's pulled out of the unit. Where before if an inmate had an extra apple or a cheese sandwich, Argus would usually let it pass but today, he doesn't let anything pass. He is pretty sure Inmate "Hat" is the one who shit his door down but he can't prove it. They are all suspects and the telephone thing, who knows. Argus remembers a line from a movie he once watched. "Be nice until it's time not to be nice. This is that time."

As he thinks these things the Corridor Officer announces, "Corridor to the housing units, mainline is over. Clear the corridor and secure your doors."

Argus sees three stragglers coming down the corridor and lines them up on the wall for a pat search. He confiscates a half loaf of bread as a result then he enters his unit and locks the door.

His plan is simple. It is policy that between the three shifts, the whole unit must be searched on a weekly basis. Argus intends to accomplish this himself. He goes to his office and makes a list of all the cells in the unit on a three by five card then he gets a large black trash bag from the bottom drawer of the desk. Today will just be a cursory mass shakedown.

As Argus exits his office, he looks around and thinks, "All within Agency policy."

Argus mentally splits the unit into quarters. If he just goes from cell to cell one right after the other, the inmates will just move the contraband while he's in a cell. Argus plans to hit half a range at a time without setting a pattern.

He starts at cell one and takes a government issued scrub brush which has been fashioned into a hair brush. From the next cell he takes some extra fruit and so on. Argus takes one piece of nuisance contraband from each inmate in the unit and throws it in the big black bag. He makes it halfway down the left side of the flat before the next move is called. Once the Corridor closes the move, he gets the bag from his office and goes to the upper right tier and works his way back. He finds two plastic bags of water the inmates are using to work out with, takes them to the deep sink and empties them. He finds containers taken from Food Service, a tattoo gun and extra perishable food that all go into the bag. He finishes the back right quarter by the time the next move is called.

The inmates do nothing but watch as Argus just does his job according to policy. After the move, Argus goes to the end cell on the right off the flat and finds Inmate "Television" sitting on a folding chair. "Step out, I'm going to search your cell."

Inmate "Television" looks at Argus and says, "Snoop, what're you doin' man?"

Argus just raises his eyebrows and gives the inmate a slanted grin. "Why, I'm just doing my job Inmate 'Television'. You guys wanna cut my phone cord and now shit my door down? I'm not going to replace that phone because I liked the telephone that was there. I want that one back and until I get it, I'm going to shake this unit down every day. Now step out."

An impossible demand, Argus knows. That telephone receiver probably went out with the trash shortly after the line was cut. One thing Argus does note as a result of the search is the contraband portable TV in Inmate "Television's" cell. Each unit has three portable televisions that are awarded to the cleanest cells for the month. Inmate "Television's" makes four. Argus doesn't confiscate it. That is his hole card. He'll get it if he needs to turn up the heat even more.

Argus goes on down the line and enters a cell housing one of Inmate "Television's" lieutenant's. Inmate "Lifer" is lying on the bottom bunk. Argus takes a gallon bag of makings from under his bunk and pours it down the deep sink. SEG is still full. Throughout the rest of the afternoon Argus works his unit as always and searches between the moves and callouts. His bag is three quarters full by the end of the shift. Inmate "Television" and some of his crew are standing at the table on the flat as Argus heads to his office at 3:20 to get ready for the 3:30 recall move. They look at him as he passes with the bag. Argus returns the look. Sometimes conversations require no words.

Argus hopes they'll be stupid enough to move their contraband into the common areas of the block. He has a surprise for them. He ties and marks the bag with some tape that says "hot trash" so the Rear Yard Officer will directly supervise it going into the compactor on the hot trash run and puts it in the office. Argus logs the search as "mass, whole unit" in the search log, locks his office and goes to his spot at the door to monitor the inmates. Tomorrow, more detailed searches. Argus knows this game has just started and he has two more days to play before his days off.

∞∞∞∞

It is Argus' last day before his weekend. He arrives at work with his usual everyday carry items including his "Uncle Henry" pen knife, a small empty makeup compact he uses for a shakedown mirror and his three cell flashlight. Argus makes his relief in Unit Eleven and finds out that Inmate "Hat" initiated a verbal altercation with the Evening Watch OIC and got himself placed in ADSEG. It wasn't long before Inmate "Hat's" cellmate, an inmate about the size of "Red" the orderly requested protective custody. The day prior, Argus searched the unit all day with the common areas first. He read the inmates correctly and bagged a gallon of wine in the bottom of the dryer, a bone crusher shank hanging in the washer drain on a shoe lace and another pick shank in the dryer vent. Argus closed the television room for an hour while he searched it.

The inmates complained to Mr. Gaylon who asked Argus to come up to his office. "What's going on Antrim? The inmates are telling me

141

you're sitting on them pretty hard."

Argus explains what happened and what he's doing. To Argus' surprise, Mr. Gaylon supports him. "I see. Well, I know there might be extra portable televisions in the unit. Why don't you confiscate any you find and bring them to me."

Argus thanks the Unit Manager and heads to the last cell on the right off the flat.

Inmate "Television" is sitting in the cell. "I'm gonna need that TV per the Unit Manager."

Inmate "Television" stands up and says, "I paid good money for that Snoop."

Argus looks at the inmate, "Yeah, well its agency property. I guess you made a poor investment."

Inmate "Television" steps aside as Argus takes the TV. Argus is running out of time to make an impact before he leaves for two days.

He stands at the corridor restraining door thinking, "Time to shake the tree one more time and see what falls out."

Argus puts a fresh chew in and heads for the upper right tier. Cell forty seven will be Argus' last search before the weekend. The inmate in forty seven is the same inmate that was involved when Argus took Inmate "Dustpan" down. Argus steps to the cell and sees that Inmate "Bed Post" is not in the cell. Argus steps through the door and closes it behind him. This inmate is a low level lieutenant in "Television's" gang. Argus stands and looks around the cell and sees it immediately. There is a crescent shaped scrape on the wall starting at the upper bed post. He can almost picture the bed being lifted and scraping the wall.

He thinks, "Now why are they lifting the bed that high. Working out or something else?"

This is when Argus sees the small metal trash can with two dents in the lip.

It all comes together in his head now. How many hacks are in good enough shape to lift this steel bunk bed. Not many Argus guesses. He positions the trash can next to the end of the bunk and lifts by the bottom rung. It turns out to be as heavy as Argus imagined and he struggles to get the can underneath the center bar. The dents line up perfectly. Argus knocks the lower cap off of the leg of the bed and out drops a bone crusher shank at least six inches long. It is a wicked looking weapon about one inch wide and one eighth inch thick with a black coating. The naked metal gleams in the light where it has been sharpened to a razor point on some rough surface. Probably the

142

concrete of the Recreation Yard urine stalls. He moves to the back leg and finds another. Argus can't believe it. This inmate should have enough standing not to be holding weapons in his cell.

Argus murmurs under his breath, "How fucking stupid can you get."

He makes sure that there are no more lodged in the leg then moves to the head of the bed and finds one more in the outside leg. He drops the bed down and finishes the search without finding any more items of hard contraband. With the shanks wrapped in a towel, Argus exits the cell and deadlocks it before heading to his office to call the Operations Lieutenant.

He dials the extension and Lieutenant Mack answers, "Operations."

Argus smiles as he looks at the find, "Hey LT its Antrim, you ain't gonna believe this but I just found three shanks in one cell."

Mack laughs, "Yes Antrim. Yes I would. Who's the inmate?"

Argus gives Lieutenant Mack "Bed Post's" name and number. "He's the only inmate in the cell and he's not in the unit right now. I'll snatch him if he comes back before you find him. In the meantime I'll bring the shanks down and process them."

Argus calls Officer Grass once again to watch the unit as he heads to the Lieutenant's Office.

After he photographs and bags everything, Argus returns to the unit but Inmate "Bed Post" does not. He hears the Corridor Officer clear the corridor to move one in restraints to ADSEG. Argus thinks, "Those guys in Segregation probably hate my guts right about now." He bags the property and moves it to the office where he starts to inventory the contents of the bags. This is what he's doing when his relief shows up at the door. When his relief sees the property, he just looks at Argus and takes a deep breath.

Argus says, "If it makes you feel any better, I'll be in the Lieutenant's Office for another hour writing the incident report. Sorry brother."

He gives a short pass down brief on the day and heads to the Lieutenant's Office to do the paperwork. After he's done, he has Mack look over the report to make sure it is complete.

Lieutenant Mack says, "Good work today Argus. Have a good weekend."

Argus gives the lieutenant thumbs up, "Oh I plan to LT. Gonna spend it with my girls."

Argus heads out for the Training Center. The dragon is hungry today.

∞○○○∞

He's looking through the window of the corridor restraining door from the outside and he's pissed. There on the wall is a brand new range telephone receiver.

Argus taps on the door with his flashlight and yells, "On the door!"

The Morning Watch OIC comes out of the office and heads to the door to key him into the unit.

Argus gestures to the telephone, "Phone fixed huh."

The officer Argus is relieving laughs, "Yeah, yesterday per the Unit Manager. It was the damndest thing. That fuckin' telephone receiver they cut showed up tied to the office door day before yesterday."

Argus smiles and says, "Good, good."

He thinks, "Maybe I'm making some headway down here."

Argus trades the chits he is carrying for equipment and prepares to start the day. He keys the off going officer out, locks the door and turns to face the unit. It is a small victory but he'll take it.

He thinks as he puts a dip in, "Well, at least they'll believe me next time when I tell them I'm going to do something."

He goes to his office to start the logs and grab his pass book when he hears the door being keyed.

It's Mr. Gaylon coming into the unit. He sees Argus and steps over to the office, "Antrim, you're doing a great job down here. I'd like you to stay next quarter if you want."

Argus smiles, "Sure sir. I'm in the flow."

The Unit Manager claps Argus shoulder and smiles then heads to his office.

Argus thinks, "It's nice to be appreciated."

Argus is glad the situation with the phone has been resolved. Now he'll go back to his regular routine.

Later in the day Argus is filling out the search logs in his office when Inmate "Television" shows up at the door. "Snoop, you bout caused some shit. I sent a delegation down to Unit One to get that phone back. Just so you know."

Argus looks at the inmate and smiles, "Well, I'm glad whoever it was decided to return my phone. I always liked it."

"Television" laughs as he turns to walk away shaking his head. "Damn. You somthin' Snoop."

The bag swings in a slow arc to the right. Argus throws a jab cross combination, ducks and bobs then throws two powerful hooks to where the kidneys should be. He's sweating profusely as he purges himself of the dragon. Argus thinks about the whole situation with the telephone and the feces. To someone who's never entered a place like Tarragon, the fact that Argus wouldn't just open the door and let "Hat" go to work might seem unreasonable but penitentiaries run on a schedule and that schedule is controlled by the Corridor Officer. If you allow one inmate to be late today, it will be five tomorrow and then ten the next day. That's just the way it is. Before long, your whole program is shot to shit and that is the whole idea of rehabilitation. Having a program that they have to follow and taking responsibility for their actions.

It pains Argus to know that someone from the outside looking in won't consider what type of man will defecate in his hand and rub it on a door handle or cut a telephone cord when he doesn't get his way. What type of psyche does a person have to have to spend hours sharpening a piece of steel with the intent on stabbing another to death over nothing? An insult? Cutting in the chow line?

Society says, "Lock him up" but they don't consider what that entails.

As Argus pounds on the bag, he thinks these things and smells the smoke from his dragon. If they've never walked the corridors of a maximum security penitentiary, they have no idea what the rules are and therefore Argus decides, their opinion doesn't mean shit. He looks at his watch on the dividing wall and is glad to see he has plenty of time to punish the heavy bag and punish it he will. It is the ark he rides to transition from Tarragon to his family.

Chapter 7
That lizard of old with his stony heart

The water is cool after lying out in the sun as Argus steps down into the pool where Olivia is already swimming around like a little fish. He was on the swim team in high school and taught her how to swim at an early age. She took to the water naturally and has become a real challenge for Argus in the games of water tag they play. Lynn is lying out on her beach chair enjoying her favorite pastime, reading one of her treasured books and soaking up the rays. The grass is green, the sky is blue and he is with his girls. Argus couldn't ask for anything else.

Lynn gets up from her chair as Argus and Olivia splash around in the water. "You guys want anything from the kitchen? I'm going to make a sandwich."

Argus and Olivia both say yes and Lynn disappears to the inside. Argus never fails to notice how beautiful she is in a bathing suit and watches her go inside. This gives Olivia the opening to jump on his back and try to dunk him. He goes under the water dutifully and she's overjoyed at dunking daddy.

Lynn returns a short time later with a tray of sandwiches and chips. Argus feels the hunger in his belly and lifts himself out of the pool. Swimming always makes him hungry. He gets a towel and helps Olivia dry off and they set down in the sunroom for lunch. Argus looks at Lynn and Olivia and feels good. This is the life he had envisioned for them. The benefits of being an Agency Correctional Officer are good. Two weeks paid vacation a year starting out, medical insurance and a good rate of pay with plenty of overtime if he wants it. He thinks back to all the long hours on the moving truck and is thankful he made the decision to leave. They would have none of this if he hadn't.

They aren't going anywhere. He has taken a week vacation just to stay at home and be with Lynn and Olivia. No cell houses and no inmates. His SWAT pager is sitting on the table but he takes no notice. Hopefully, it won't go off.

They finish their meal and Lynn and Argus head to the beach chairs as Olivia begs him to come back in the pool. "Just give me a minute to sit with mommy. I'll come back to the water in a second."

Olivia watches him like a sentinel probably wondering how long a daddy second is going to be. Argus opens his eyes after a few minutes and sees that she's still bird dogging him.

He laughs and says, "Okay, okay. I'm coming back already."

He gets back in the water and promptly dunks her. Now the fight is on but he feels at peace.

∞∞∞∞

Lynn is excited. She and Argus have a babysitter for Friday night and they have tickets to a comedy show in Indianapolis. Argus has also booked a room at a hotel within walking distance of the comedy club as well. They're both looking forward to going out and kicking up their heels a little bit. Lynn packs a bag for Olivia and one for herself. Argus throws some clothes in a bag and their set to head to Grammy's house. Olivia loves to spend the night at Grammy's. They drop her off with the usual hugs and kisses and get back in the car for the hour long drive to Indy. Traffic is light heading east and they make good time, finally weaving their way through the streets of downtown until they reach the hotel.

As they get out of the car, Argus looks at Lynn. He's looking forward to spending some time with her as a couple. It has been too long since they've been away together. He notices how nice the hotel is as they ride the elevator to the seventh floor. The fact that he can afford the night's stay in this place is just another indication to Argus that the Agency was the right choice for him and his family. The room is immaculate and spacious with a queen size bed and sitting area. This is much nicer than he could have imagined. There is even a small fridge in the room. A small placard on the top of the fridge reads, "Continental breakfast."

Argus is feeling very continental right about now. He smiles. They get changed and walk the two blocks to the comedy club. They're early for the show but the club also serves dinner and drinks so they duck inside and get a table to have dinner before the show.

The restaurant is nice with an old world feel. Down on a lower level from the street, it is decorated with hanging plants and dark, rich wood. The hostess grabs two menus and leads them to a booth on the street side of the restaurant. Lynn grabs a seat so Argus can sit facing the door. The waitress is friendly and takes their orders without much delay. She is a young girl with a bounce to her step. Argus wonders how long that will last once they get busy. Argus and Lynn both get the prime rib. She adds a baked potato and mixed vegetables, Argus a sweet potato and asparagus. He looks over the table at Lynn. She is gorgeous.

He asks himself, "How did I get so lucky?"

She looks at him, "What?"

He smiles, "You just look pretty."

She smiles back, "You're just horny."

They both laugh. They talk about everything and nothing during dinner. The food is extraordinary. Argus feels like he did when they first met and he had plenty of money to show Lynn a good time. He hasn't felt that way in a long time. It's a good feeling.

After dinner they head upstairs to check in for the comedy show. It is a packed house. The waitress comes around to get their drink orders and both order a seven and seven. Tonight is a well-deserved party. Their second drink arrives just as the lights go down. The comedian is funny and Argus laughs harder than he has in a long time. They are seated in the center near the stage which is usually a target zone for a comedian. Argus is thankful the comedian leaves him alone. Others near him are not so lucky. After the show, Lynn and Argus stop in the bar for another drink where they see the comedian. Argus buys Lynn one of his CD's. He was hilarious.

They finish their drinks and walk around the corner to a local bar. They step in and immediately feel the energy of the place. It is packed so Lynn approaches a couple sitting at a table and asks if they would mind sharing. They are friendly and agree. Both seem to be in their early thirties as Lynn and Argus are. Argus excuses himself and goes to the bar for two more drinks. When he gets back, Lynn is talking to the couple like they're old friends.

Argus thinks, "With her bubbly personality, no one is a stranger."

Eventually, the couple leaves and they have the table to themselves. The music is good but there's no room for a dance floor. Lynn dances in her seat and Argus watches amused. She brightens any room she is in and it's easy for Argus to fall in love with her every time he sees her. Both of them are feeling the liquor and the two block walk back to the room seems much longer as they weave back and forth laughing the whole way. Lynn gets confused about which way the hotel is. This causes them to laugh harder.

Argus thinks," It's good to laugh with her."

They make it back to the room after a couple of detours down the wrong hallways. They are happy and in love. The night is just beginning.

∞∞∞

He climbs the stairs on the right side of the unit to the upper tier without using the handrail. His steps are smooth and slow as he makes the right turn to move around the upper tier. He walks a quarter of the way down the right side and turns to check his six. The inmates watch as he moves around the tier holding his spit cup. Argus looks up at the lights in the unit. They seem dim and harsh at the same time. He makes the round and walks past the stairway on the left of the unit, walking to the front corner blind spot. His sixth sense kicks up as he reaches the corner, the hairs on the back of his neck rising. Argus turns to check his six again and sees the inmate. He has a shock of black hair and is dressed in the olive drab uniform. Long sleeved shirt and composite toe work boots. He's stocky and has come to fight.

He's moving toward Argus in a low stance, just under the line of sight.

Argus thinks in that instant, "He must've come out of the stairway to get behind me like that."

The inmate is looking at Argus with a malevolent glare as he moves slowly forward. Argus can see the knife in the inmate's right hand. It is made of stainless steel and glints off the lights as the inmate moves it at his right hip.

Argus thinks, "He knows how to fight with a knife. He's keeping it close to his body. It's tougher to disarm that way."

Argus is in the corner of the unit in the blind spot and he's mentally running through his options. Running is out of the question. You always get run down because the pursuer is always faster because of the pursuit. He turns to face the inmate and squares his shoulders. The inmate is smiling now and taking his time. Argus looks out of the corner of his eye to the right.

There is a large range trash can in the middle of the crossover but it's full. "Way to slow. He'd be on me before I got it in the air."

There is only one option as Argus sees it. The adrenaline has kicked in and he is sweating even though he feels the coolness from the range fans. Argus accepts the fact that he'll be cut or stabbed as he assumes a fighting stance. An orthodox defense isn't the smart move here

149

because the inmate knows how to use the blade.

He thinks, "It's almost like we were trained by the same motherfucker. No, I've gotta think outside the box. He'll see me coming otherwise."

The inmate is within three meters now. His left hand is up in the guard, weapon at the right hip so he can lunge, stab or slash and get back out. Argus knows he'll try to bleed him.

He feels the anger rise, "Who the fuck does this dude think he is to come at me like this."

Argus accepts it. This is going to happen so he'll make it happen on his timeline. He won't just stand and wait for it.

He thinks in the second before he moves, "Alright motherfucker, c'mon" and shoulder rolls toward the inmate kicking out at the inmate's knees but he doesn't connect.

Argus gets to his feet immediately with only four feet separating him and the inmate. He throws a spinning back kick and feels the impact. He also hears the crash as the unit goes dark. For a split second he panics because he can't see the inmate at all.

Then he hears Lynn yelling at Olivia, "Don't go in there, honey!" Argus stands in his bedroom, the closet doors hanging off the tracks. He runs his hand through his hair and blinks.

He hears Lynn at the door. "Honey, are you alright?"

She doesn't try to come in.

Argus clears his throat and swallows hard trying to get rid of the lump he has there, "Yeah baby, I'm fine."

He looks around once more and sees he'll have to put the closet doors back on the tracks

Argus stands alone in the darkness of his bedroom and thinks, "They're afraid of me."

∞∞∞∞

The tower is four stories tall and made of thick wooden beams. It's closed in on three sides with two windows on the rappelling surface. One window being on the second floor and one on the third. The window on the second floor has a steel cover on it with a prison lock. There is a metal ladder on the left side with accesses to all the floors. There is a ringed cage around the ladder covering all forty feet of the climb with no landings on the way up. Once you're on the ladder, you're on for the whole ride to the top. SWAT competition is coming up in a few months and the team is practicing the rappelling entry drill. This is a timed event and challenging. The SWAT member starts thirty yards from the tower and sprints to the bottom of the ladder where he climbs as fast as possible to the top.

Once the operator is on top of the tower, he moves hastily to the hooking point where he hooks the rope to his figure eight attachment on the rappelling harness. It's quickly checked by the Rappel Master and then he steps off the side. Ideally, he's in a semi free fall to just above the window where he sets his break and swings in. Once inside, he engages two targets with his pistol and then climbs back down. The challenge is to get inside and get your aimed shots off quickly enough to get out of the way of the next guy coming in. Five team members ascend the tower at once and Tarragon SWAT moves quickly.

Argus and his friend Harry Haddin are relatively new to the team and haven't made the competition team. This isn't unusual as a lot is riding on the competition and Lieutenant Sena wants the most experienced members to compete. Lieutenant Sena is a good team leader and still wants to include Argus and "Double H" in the practice. Harry and Argus have been friends since coming on to the team. He is a big guy at six foot and two hundred forty pounds but moves his bulk well. Years at the coal plant shoveling coal before joining the Agency have made him as strong as a bull. Lieutenant Sena announces that Argus and Harry will be running a practice exhibition run.

This is where Harry and Argus find themselves now. They are standing at the starting line in the sand which encircles the tower. Lieutenant Sena looks at the runners and asks if they're ready. This he says around the whistle clenched in his teeth with his stop watch in hand.

Argus and Harry nod as the LT says, "Ready, ready, ready, go!"

They take off at a full sprint toward the tower. Harry quickly outdistances Argus by three meters and hits the ladder running. Argus hits the ladder at a sprint as well and looks up as he climbs as fast as he can. Each time Argus looks up he gets a face full of sand from Harry's boots. Argus legs are pumping hard up the ladder as the rest of the team cheers the runners on. The cheers are muted because he is breathing hard. His arms and legs are burning as he pulls himself up onto the tower. Harry is already getting prepared to step off and Argus feels like he is miles behind. He gets the rope and pulls the loop through the figure eight and hooks it to the rappelling harness around his waist, adjusting the harness so it doesn't pinch his testicles.

The Rappel Master checks the hook up and gives Argus the thumbs up. The adrenaline is free flowing as Argus runs to the edge of the tower and jumps off backwards in a free fall. He sets his brake a fraction to late and has to pull himself through the window.

Somersaulting, Argus draws his side arm as he makes it to his feet and fires two quick shots into the targets. Immediately he hears Lieutenant Sena yell, "Time!"

Argus climbs down from the second floor and joins Harry with the lieutenant, "Not bad fellas. Respectable time."

Argus is still breathing hard and his heart is jack hammering but he feels elated. He feels like he's part of something. He feels like a Marine again.

∞∞∞∞

It's a month into the new quarter and Argus has two new orderlies. Inmates "Politeness" and "Crack".

He stands at the restraining door as he watches them work and thinks, "It's an improvement. The common areas of the unit look better and the floors are shining so well they could blind a person when the sun hits the windows to the East. Sometimes, change is a good thing."

The new orderlies were hired on Argus' days off to fill the vacancies left by Inmates "Coffee Cup" and "Red". Both had requested protective custody and are now housed in ADSEG under a PC investigation. If the rumor is correct and Argus believes it probably is, they won't be back on the yard. According to the prison grapevine, someone wanted "Coffee Cup" to share "Red" and he wasn't strong enough to be able to say no. It was really the only course of action for the couple. Whoever wanted "Red" would have eventually taken him. There will always be someone willing to fight over a punk in a prison, therefore there will always be violence. Argus thinks, "That's just the way it is."

Inmate "Politeness" is an extremely athletic inmate. Six foot and two hundred twenty pounds, he is lean and works out two hours each day. He is also the most polite inmate Argus has ever managed. Before Argus assumes the post in the morning, "Politeness" does his required morning cleaning then heads to the Recreation Yard as soon as it opens. The inmate keeps a low profile but is always there to clean up any sanitation issues before Argus has to ask.

152

He is, Argus thinks, "The perfect orderly."

Inmate "Crack" is about Argus' size and keeps to himself. He does his job and only speaks to Argus if the job requires him too. Inmate "Crack" lives on the top tier three cells from the end on the right. Inmate "Politeness" lives in the first cell on the left side of the flat.

Argus thinks, "I can't argue with the choices. They don't pester me with useless conversation and do the job well."

As Argus stands at the corridor restraining door of the unit watching his orderlies, he also notices the obvious discomfort of Inmate "Television" and his gang. There are five of them standing down at the end of the flat near "Television's" cell and are bird dogging the cell of a younger associate who Argus believed was holding weapons for the gang. The young associate is with them as well. They're having a conversation that looks serious. "Television" is looking at Argus and there is no friendliness in his eyes. Argus has searched the cell of the young inmate numerous times always coming up empty but his instincts are telling him the inmate is holding. Sometimes a unit officer just doesn't have time to spend all day in a cell, so Argus called the Special Investigative Office this morning and spoke to his friend Dan Lessen who runs the office shakedown team.

"Danny, I'm telling you, my gut is saying he's got something in there. Would you mind sending a couple guys down to check it out for me?"

Dan laughs, "Sure Argus. I've got nothing better to do right now but you'll owe me a cup of coffee."

Argus laughs, "You got it buddy."

The team has been in the cell for over two hours and "Television" isn't a bit happy about the in depth search. Argus hated to give up on finding the contraband but, frankly, he was out of ideas and the main goal is to find the stuff. Argus is thinking about this when Dan steps out of the cell and waves Argus down to the cell. He has a smile on his face. Argus spits in the trash can and walks down to the cell and looks in. Dan's partner, Officer Hannah Depps is sitting on the lower bunk and photographing eight shanks of varying sizes and shapes. Argus also sees a flat steel square standing against the wall. He is incredulous.

"Holy shit Danny, where were they?"

Dan smiles a big smile, "Your gut was right. They were behind a false back in the locker. It's good work. The only way we found them was to measure the outside of the locker then the inside. The discrepancy told us there was a two inch compartment in the back of the locker and bingo. We'll secure and inventory the property in a bit.

It's an SIO case now. Would you deadlock the cell? We're gonna take the inmate down to the Lieutenant's Office and button him up under investigation."

Dan and Hannah step out of the cell and Argus deadlocks the door. He looks over at "Television" and smiles. Argus points at the young inmate and makes a gesture with his head that says, "Okay, c'mon."

The inmate walks to the restraining door where Hannah does a pat search. Argus keys the unit door and the SIO Shakedown Team takes the inmate and shanks with them. "Television's" meeting concludes. The show is over. Argus goes into his office and logs the search in the log with Dan and Hannah's names as the searching staff. Argus feels good. His instincts were right and he learned something today.

As he exits his office, looks up, steps out from under the tier and thinks, "Well, it pays to know your inmates. I've got to start carrying a small tape measure."

∞∞∞∞

Argus stands at the starting line and looks down at his dusty boots thinking, "Fuck it's hot."

He's already regretting the buffet lunch he had just an hour ago. He mutters under his breath, "This shit is going to hurt. What a dumbass. I should've passed on lunch."

Lieutenant Sena is standing to the right with his clipboard and whistle, Big Franks is to the left with dry heaves. He had the buffet too. Argus stands in the middle of the pack and the only thing that has him worried besides dumping his lunch on the obstacle course somewhere is that Nash is right behind him. Lieutenant Sena starts the motivation speech.

He's a good team leader. "Okay guys, competition is coming up. Let's leave it all out there. Let's show these motherfuckers what Tarragon is all about. Ready! Ready! Ready! Go!"

Sena blows the whistle and Argus hits the first obstacle, side hopping each lateral pole like a fence. He can already feel the practice paying off.

He hits the balance beam with his arms stretched out to the sides for balance. Nash is right on his ass, "Fucking go Ant!"

Argus hits the horizontal ladders and pumps his legs hard and fast. Last rung and he drops to the ground almost losing his balance. His lungs are burning but so far, his arms are not. He climbs up the inverted ladder, swinging over at the top with Nash in his back pocket.

Around the turn and Argus goes airborne trying to get as high on the rope as he can.

His pulse is jack hammering as he talks to himself out loud and climbs, "C'mon, don't quit. You got this. You got this."

He reaches the top, grabs one of the platform timbers and swings over from the rope. Argus gets to his feet and steadies himself.

He's elated and pumps his fist up and down as he hears Lieutenant Sena yell, "Okay you made it now get the fuck off the platform!"

Argus picks his way across the timbers to the other side, looking down at the ground twenty feet below, sits down with his legs dangling and wraps the rope around his leg once.

He swings out and descends as fast as he can, the rope burning a nice hole in his shin. You can tell who's on the Tarragon Swat Team by this scar. Argus will be proud to wear it. He hits the ground, unwraps and sprints to the horizontal rope bridge. His arms are toast by now but he keeps the pace.

Hand over hand he pulls himself to the other side as he tastes the bile in the back of his throat thinking, "Baked chicken. What the fuck were you thinking?"

He hits the other side and sprints to the rope swing. Over the ditch and on to the last balance beam. The sweat is pouring into his eyes as he runs down the beam, almost losing his balance but recovering. The sprint to the finish and Argus is done in more ways than one. His arms are screaming their disapproval and his breath is ragged but he's made the course. He squats in the shade of the rappelling tower and makes himself two promises. Keep training with the flak vest on the course and no more buffet lunches.

∞∞∞∞

Argus stands outside his unit speaking with Officer Pickle. Dane Pickle is a friend and is working Unit Thirteen. Argus trusts Dane and enjoys working with him. Noon mainline is in full swing with the Main Corridor full of inmates moving to and from the Dining Hall.

Argus pulls an inmate over for a pat search, "Step over and grab the wall."

Before he can begin the search, Argus hears the Corridor Officer yell, "Stop!"

Keeping his hand in the middle of the inmate's back, Argus looks toward the Dining Hall as he hears the Operations Lieutenant call on the radio in a breathless voice, "Operations to East End, stop that inmate running toward you! He has a shank!"

Argus and Dane forget the inmate he is searching and start getting inmates against the wall. A young inmate with curly blonde hair is running toward them at full tilt. They look at each other in an unspoken, "Okay, let's do this" as the inmate gets closer. The inmate sees the road block and realizes he has no place to go. He stops and stands in the corridor by the inmate soft drink machines, looking back and forth as officers box him in on all sides. The inmate is hemmed in and he knows it.

Lieutenant Atkins says, "You better be on the ground by the time we get to ya." The meaning is clear.

The inmate pauses and then throws the shank at the wall above the drink machines. It strikes with a clatter as it falls behind the machines then the inmate lies down in the middle of the corridor.

Argus thinks as he watches this, "That's going to take some work to get that knife out from behind there."

The soda machines are surrounded by an expanded metal cage. Argus grabs the inmate's right arm and places it behind his back as Dane does the same with the left. Another officer puts handcuffs on the inmate. The three of them stand the inmate up as other officers watch their backs and clear inmates from the corridor. Once the corridor is cleared of inmates, Lieutenant Atkins grabs the inmate's elbow and leads him to the Lieutenant's Office. He posts a rookie at the drink machines until the Investigative Office can get someone there to fish the shank from behind the machines. Argus and Dane head back to the East End shaking their heads.

Argus says laughing, "Wonder where he thought he was going to go."

Dane smiles, "I don't know. Guess he forgot about the fence around this place."

∞∞∞∞

It never ceases to amaze Argus at what lengths the inmates will go to in an attempt at smuggling food into the unit. Food Service is serving baked chicken breast for noon mainline. Each inmate gets one large chicken breast. Only chicken breasts are served to avoid any long bones the inmates might sharpen and use as a weapon. The policy states that all food must be consumed in the Dining Hall. The only carry out is one piece of fruit.

As Argus has said many times, "It's not personal, just policy."

He has pulled the large trash can from the door of his unit into the corridor because he knows what is coming. The Corridor Officer announces mainline and calls the first unit. Argus and Dane stand ready at the door of their units. Dane also chews snuff and is using Argus' trash can to spit into as well.

It isn't long before the East End units are all called to chow and the game begins as the inmates start returning from the Dining Hall. The cover inmates as usual, are trying to clear the way for the mules. Argus and Dane are taking a good amount of chicken from the inmates as a result of some good pat searches. The inmates hide it everywhere to include the armpit, crotch, socks and pockets. Each time a piece of chicken is found, it goes into the trash can where Argus and Dane are spitting. Argus looks into the can and feels certain the contraband chicken is being destroyed well enough with the snuff spit.

"Grab the wall. You know the drill."

The inmate looks at Argus, "Oh man, c'mon boss."

Argus has seen the bulge swinging at knee level on the inmate way before he arrived at Argus' door.

He pats the inmate down and asks, "What is that?"

He points at the bulge. The inmate laughs, "It's a dick sandwich. What do you think it is?"

"Haha, very funny. Well pull it out," Argus says as he lifts the inmate's sweatshirt exposing the bread wrapper the inmate has tied to his belt with the chicken dangling in his pant leg.

The inmate looks at Argus as if he might have a chance at keeping it. "It's just chicken boss."

Argus replies, "No, it's a sanitation thing. Give it up."

The inmate huffs and pulls the chicken out of his pants. Argus takes the bag and holds it at eye level. "Three pieces. I got to hand it to you, you're ambitious."

Argus tears the bag open and dumps the chicken in the trash and spits. The inmate shakes his head and walks into the unit. By the end of mainline they've confiscated a fair amount of chicken.

The Corridor Officer announces on the radio, "Corridor to the housing units, mainline is over. Clear the corridor and lock your doors. They missed it."

Argus and Dane clear the inmates from in front of their units and head inside. Argus drags his trash can back into the unit containing the spit covered chicken. He keys his door and heads to the office to update his logs which only takes about five minutes then exits the office and locks the door. Argus makes one round in the unit and then assumes his spot at the corridor restraining door. He puts a fresh dip in and spits in the trash can. Argus can't believe what he sees. Most of the chicken is gone.

∞∞∞

The house is dark and cool with only the sounds of the night echoing through the quiet rooms. Argus opens his eyes and listens to Lynn's soft purring as she sleeps next to him. He looks at the clock by the bed, three hours. He's been asleep for three hours.

Argus thinks, "Right on time."

He's totally alert as his mind races. It's become a pattern for Argus to sleep two or three hours and then awaken as if his internal clock alarms every one hundred eighty minutes. He slips from the bed trying not to wake his wife and creeps from the bedroom, quietly shutting the door behind him. It is a short walk down the hallway into the kitchen where he checks the sliding glass door to the sun room and finding it locked, heads to the back door checking that lock as well. Next he moves to the front door to make sure it is secure. He pours a cup of milk and heats it in the microwave, bird dogging the countdown to stop it before it quits with that annoying "ding."

He looks in the cabinet and finds that he's out of chocolate powdered drink mix, but knows there's some chocolate syrup in the fridge so he makes do. He leaves the kitchen and goes into the living room, sitting on the couch with his steaming cup of cocoa. His legs are bothering him. Not a pain but a deep ache, from standing on the concrete all day he figures. The discomfort is just enough to make not moving them intolerable so he flexes his ankles back and forth, round and round. Argus knows this feeling will subside in a bit. He takes a drink of cocoa and listens to the pop and cracks of his home and his legs wondering if this insomnia will ever resolve itself.

He thinks about his unit and what is scheduled for today, looks at the clock again and thinks, "I'm up in six hours. God I need to get some sleep."

Standing from the couch, he feels the tightness in his calves and arches as he walks to the picture window and looks out at the empty street. He sees movement under the street light on the corner. A cat is making its nightly rounds of the neighborhood. It slinks athletically

158

across the street using no wasted motion. Argus watches it admiringly and wishes he could move like that. Scanning the scene outside, he focuses on each area of shadow, examining it for anything out of place. He hears a soft moan from Olivia's room and goes to check, opening her door slowly and quietly. She's just dreaming and is lying with her covers thrown half off the bed. Argus enters her room and gently pulls the covers back up over her.

After a moment of looking at her and making sure she's okay, he creeps back out of her room and rejoins his cup of cocoa in the living room. "Five hours and I'm up. Better drink this chocolate and try for some sleep."

He sits down on the couch and takes a sip, still totally alert as he stares into the darkness. Argus takes the last sip of cocoa and heads into the kitchen turning the tap on just slightly to keep the noise of the water down as he rinses his cup. He looks out of the kitchen window, watching for any movement in the back yard but it is devoid of anything out of the ordinary. He stands for a few more minutes thinking about the blind spots. The North corner of the house has always worried him. It's extremely dark in that area.

Checking the doors once again to make sure they're secure, he looks out the picture window one more time and thinks, "There are monsters out there."

He returns to the bedroom and slips back into bed. He feels more than sees that Lynn hasn't moved as he tries to match his breathing to her restful breaths. He closes the eyes that have been opened. Opened to the fact that true evil does exist and the only thing between it and his family is him.

∞∞∞∞

The inmate sits in his cell in Unit Three and looks at the six inch piece of plexiglass he's scored from an inmate who works in the Construction Shops thinking, "Four fuckin' books of stamps but it'll be worth it. I got somethin' for that motherfucker."

He's been at Tarragon for a month and was just looking to lay low. Do his bit and run his hustle but "Television" and his set aren't going to let him. "It ain't happening again. They ain't doing this to me again."

He puts the piece of plexiglass in his tennis shoe and waits for the first move of the day.

The officer opens the unit door and yells, "Rec move. Eight o'clock recreation movement!"

The inmate steps out of his cell and walks with a shuffling gait so both legs match. A limp will draw attention. Forty yards and he's in the indoor Recreation Center stairway. Four flights up and he heads into the bathroom, steps in a stall and locks the door.

He takes his trousers down and takes the shoe off containing the plexiglass, then slips his leg out of the trousers and sits on the toilet. He'll have to be quick. He takes the plexiglass in his left hand, wrapping one end in a wash rag and gets to work, grinding one end on the concrete surface next to the back of the toilet. He's working up a sweat, his heart pounding as he sees the beginnings of a spear point begin to form.

He thinks as he files, "I paid the tax. They said the tax would be the same as my last joint so I paid it but that wasn't good enough. It's that motherfucker's own fault. They should've just left me alone. Now they say I gotta give them half my commissary every fuckin' week to earn my way and stay on the yard. I ain't fuckin doin' it. Motherfuckers gonna see."

The inmate looks around listening as he works. He looks back down at the shank forming in his hand. He feels the sharpness of the point as he tests it on his right palm. It isn't a slashing weapon, but one meant to stab. He's satisfied with his work, puts his leg back into the pants, wraps the point of the shank in the washrag and puts it back into his shoe. He stands up, pulls his trousers up and buckles his belt. Wetting a piece of toilet paper, he cleans the filings off the floor and rubs the wet paper on the wall getting rid of most of the scrapes. He looks at the clean up and is satisfied so he drops the paper in the toilet and flushes. Now, just lay low till the next move.

The Recreation Specialist comes out of his office and yells, "Nine o'clock move!"

This is what he's been waiting for. The inmate walks down the stairs to the Main Corridor and walks toward his unit. The officer is on the corridor telephone and pays him no mind. The inmate walks past in a relaxed way. Even if he gets pulled up for a pat down, some officers don't make inmates take their shoes off or even flex their feet. He isn't worried. He heads up the stairs and goes into his cell, closing the slider. He's been planning this for a week and has a box of crackers and a few candy bars to eat. He takes the shank out of his shoe, wraps the wash rag around the squared end and uses a shoe lace to wrap it tight with just enough left over to wrap around his wrist. He puts the weapon underneath his locker, lies down on the bed and gets ready for a long wait. He won't leave the unit for the rest of the day and night. Tomorrow he'll leave this cell for the last time.

After lock down, the inmate shaves his head, flushing the long hair down the toilet in his cell as he thinks, "Television' and his bodyguard won't even see my ass coming."

At 5:00 am the main unit lights go on and the officers count. The inmate is already up and dressed standing at the sink with a towel draped over his head, brushing his teeth. He hears the officer's radio from the far end of the unit. Control is clearing the official count then he hears the lock on his door disengage. He is ready. Tarragon runs on a program just like any other joint.

The inmate knows what comes next as he hears the unit officer announce, "Mainline! Mainline!"

The inmate looks at his small bag of property then he steps out of his cell, the knife taped to his right forearm.

He steps out of Unit Three and walks down the Main Corridor toward the Dining Hall, walking swiftly to blend into the other inmates by matching their pace. He walks through the entry door to Food Service and gets in line, getting a tray and his food without making eye contact with anyone then picks a seat close to the chow line with his back to the entry. He eats slowly, biding his time. Looking at the line every once in a while, waiting for his target. He hears Inmate "Television" before he sees him and tries to stay relaxed. He's changed his appearance and isn't worried they'll recognize him. To hide in plain site is the best disguise. He dips his arms under the table and readies the shank, tightening the shoe string around his right wrist.

He sees Inmate "Television" and his bodyguard just a few steps away. "Motherfucker won't be so smug in a few," he thinks.

Three steps and a small leap over the dividing railing and the inmate is on his target. He stabs the bodyguard in the back first as he falls over the railing in an attempt to escape the attack. The bodyguard is lying on the ground screaming. Dark blood gushes from his right side.

"Television" looks at the inmate in astonishment with the knowledge he has no place to go. Other inmates are separating, not wanting to be involved in a wreck in Food Service. "Television" knows none of the other inmates are going to come to his aid. The inmate can hear the officers screaming at the inmates to get on the floor. He only has a few seconds left to do his work before they get to him. He also knows the officers at Tarragon won't hesitate to dump his ass onto the concrete, shank or no shank. The inmate rushes "Television" as he puts his hands out trying to ward off the attack. Again and again, the inmate plunges the bloody knife into the soft flesh of "Television's" abdomen and chest. The inmate is hit hard from behind. Someone grabs his arm and twists causing his shoulder to pop.

Through the pain he thinks, "It doesn't matter, that motherfucker can go to hell. I put my work in."

Argus pulls onto the main drive of Tarragon Penitentiary and notices the ambulance sitting at the main entrance. His heart quickens slightly as he presses the gas pedal of his truck. He parks and exits his vehicle, grabbing his lunch box and thermos before locking his truck and heads toward the entrance.

As he nears Tower One, the officer yells down to him, "Antrim! LT has your unit covered. He wants you geared up for a high risk escort. Says he'll be up in a minute."

The tower officer buzzes his door open and Argus puts his lunchbox and thermos in the base of the tower then turns around and heads down the ramp to the Armory where he bangs on the door. Mr. Farmer opens the door and lets Argus in. Mr. Farmer is a big man with forearms like trees with sinewy vines wrapped around them. Years of working on Tarragon locks have given him muscles as hard as his attitude. He already has the weapons and equipment laid out on the counter for Argus.

He hands Argus the clipboard and simply says, "Sign."

Argus signs the inventory form and begins putting on the equipment. Argus puts the bullet proof vest on and straps the belt and holster around his waist. He uses the belt keepers from his duty belt to better secure the holster. Argus picks the nine millimeter pistol up, does a function check and loads a magazine into the weapon. He racks a round into the chamber and holsters the weapon. Harry Haddin arrives and starts gearing up as well. Neither speaks as they get ready for the trip. They are SWAT brothers, no conversation is necessary. Two more magazines for the pistol go on the belt and then Argus loads the shotgun for duty carry. Once Haddin is geared up, they exit the Armory. Argus draws a set of sedan keys from Tower One and retrieves the vehicle from the line in the parking area. He pulls behind the ambulance then takes a position at the driver's door with the shotgun. Haddin will ride in the ambulance with the inmate.

Tower One yells down, "LT wants to know if you're ready." Argus gives the thumbs up.

As he waits, Argus sees Lieutenant Grant escorting the ambulance

162

crew with a gurney out of the Tower One Sally port. He looks like he's in a hurry. The inmate on the gurney is covered with a blood soaked sheet. Argus thinks, "That's a bad sign." They load the inmate on to the ambulance then Haddin climbs in behind and shuts the door. Lieutenant Grant meets Farmer at the door and gets his pistol and belt.

He looks at Argus and says, "Ant, let's go. This one's bad. Stay right on their ass."

The ambulance pulls away with lights and sirens blaring as Argus puts the sedan in their back pocket. They rocket off of the institutional grounds headed for Abhaile General Emergency Room.

As they weave through the streets of Abhaile, Argus asks Grant, "What the fuck happened LT?"

Lieutenant Grant looking straight ahead replies, "Dude hit Inmate 'Television' at mainline this morning. Stuck him up real good."

Argus is astonished, "Television's' out of my unit. Who did him?"

Grant replies still without looking, "Some dude out of Three. Don't know why yet."

"Did any staff get hurt?"

This time Grant looks at Argus, "No thank God, but we got a dude in medical stuck who was shanked in the back and this dude who probably won't make it.

Argus is concentrating on his driving as he whips the sedan around traffic trying to keep up with the ambulance. "Who else got stuck?"

Grant is looking at the packet, looks up and says, "Inmate 'Puma', 'Television's' body guard. His wounds aren't life threatening so he stays behind the fence."

They arrive at the Emergency Room and exit the sedan, Lieutenant Grant moving up near the stretcher as they unload, Argus keeping his distance holding the shotgun. They all roll into the ER and find a team of doctors and nurses waiting on them.

As they enter the trauma room Argus hears a nurse say, "No pulse. Start CPR."

There is a flurry of activity as the medical personnel work on the inmate. Two nurses are cutting "Television's" clothes off as another performs CPR.

A doctor says over the noise, "EPI in. Sandy get me an EJ and get some saline going. Mark, secure that airway. His pressure's in the toilet. Get me an EPI drip going and start O negative."

The medical team works on Inmate "Television" for thirty minutes as Grant, Haddin and Argus look on. Finally, the doctor who is obviously in charge says, "Okay everybody, let's go ahead and call it. He's gone."

Lieutenant Grant goes to the Nurse's Station to call the institution and advise them of the inmate's death. An officer from Receiving and Discharge will have to come to the hospital to fingerprint Inmate "Television" and photograph him. Argus and Haddin will stay with the body until it is released to the proper authorities. He and Haddin stand outside the room and wait. A nurse brings them a couple of stools and some water.

She smiles and says, "You officers need anything else, let me know." Then she walks away.

They set on the stools and prepare for a long day. Argus looks into the room from the hallway at what used to be a human being he had interacted with many times.

Haddin says, "Wonder why the dude stabbed him."

Argus looks at his friend and raises his eyebrows, shaking his head.

"Falls under the rattlesnake legend."

Haddin asks, "What's that?"

Argus grins and looks sideways at his friend, "Well, there was an old medicine man walking through the desert when he came upon a rattlesnake caught in a cactus. The medicine man being a friend to all life forces on the earth, untangled the rattlesnake from the cactus needles. The rattlesnake responded by promptly biting the medicine man on the hand. The medicine man grabbed his hand, knowing he would soon die from the venom and asked the rattlesnake why he would bite him after he'd just helped the snake. The snake looked at the medicine man with his little beady eyes and said, What the fuck did you expect. I'm a rattlesnake dumbass."

They both chuckle. Argus looks in the room again at all the medical equipment, the copious amounts of blood and the body thinking, "What a fucking mess. I could really use a cup of coffee."

He dumps the ice from his water cup in the trash can, puts in a dip of snuff and spits.

Chapter 8
Forked Tongue

The mood in Unit Eleven is tense today. As soon as Argus hit the door, he knew. It was palpable and in response he has been on high alert all day. Not jumpy. That would be the wrong term. It is more like a quiet smoldering resolve. The death of Inmate "Television" has created a shuffling of the deck in regards to his set. They are making a show of presence at the far card table on the flat. At least five have been at the table all day. It's not out of the ordinary to have inmates at the card tables and nothing for Argus to address, but he has noticed. He makes a round in the unit, looking in each cell as he passes. The inmates are low and slow. The orderlies are on the job. The flat is quiet. The Corridor Officer announces the 1:00 pm ten minute movement on the radio.

Argus walks around the upper tier and descends the stairs on the left hand side, making sure not to touch the handrails. As he hits the bottom, he looks left and right noticing Inmate "Television's" set are all standing and facing toward the door.

Argus thinks, "A show of force, interesting."

He moves to the corridor restraining door, keys the door and steps into the Main Corridor. Argus pulls one over for a pat search and comes up with nothing. The other officers on the East End are doing the same. It's just another day at the office. He hears what sounds like an argument coming from the direction of Unit Ten and starts moving that way along with the other officers. Before Argus has moved ten steps, he sees an inmate run from the unit with a carton of cigarettes, another inmate in pursuit.

The inmates are past Argus before he can utter a command to stop. He follows the inmates into the unit to where they have stopped ten feet from his office door facing each other.

One of the inmates is holding the carton of cigarettes while the other inmate is yelling, "Gimme my cigarettes motherfucker!"

As Argus starts to intervene in the apparent squabble he checks his six and realizes there are twenty inmates surrounding him and the two inmates. He sees in an instant what is getting ready to happen and realizes he is right in the middle of the impending wreck.

Argus' stomach tightens as he thinks, "Oh fuck, this is bad. I'm so fucking out of position."

In looking around, he also sees the other officers have stayed in the corridor to handle the inmates there. Argus has made a tactical mistake. His positioning sucks and he is grossly outnumbered.

Argus makes three decisions simultaneously. The most acute decision is to get out of the middle of all these inmates. He moves away from the two inmates through the crowd and puts his back against the wall while pulling his flashlight from his waistband at the appendix where he normally carries it. Next in order of importance, Argus decides not to call for assistance because in his mind, pressing the button is just going to make this thing pop off. He wants to try and deescalate the situation.

Argus metaphorically grabs his nut sack and yells, "If you don't live in Unit Eleven then GET THE FUCK OUT!"

It is his second mistake. Argus sees one of the inmates motion with his head to leave the unit but instead of half the inmates leaving, they all leave and are now in the Main Corridor. The number of the inmates has doubled in size.

Argus thinks, "You dumbass! Encapsulate. What the fuck Argus!"

Argus moves into the corridor and grabs the East End Corridor telephone dialing the Operations Lieutenant. The phone is answered immediately, "Operations, Lieutenant Hanks."

"Hey LT, Antrim in Unit Eleven, we've got approximately fifty inmates in the East End about to throw hands."

A microsecond of silence then Lieutenant Hanks blasts out of the Lieutenant's Office, walking to the East End at a brisk pace. Lieutenant Hanks has just finished a tour in the Investigative Section and has returned to regular duty as a shift lieutenant.

He walks up to the crowd and points at two of the inmates, "You and you! Come here. You're going to put your heads together and fix this. Get the fuck in the gymnasium. Now!"

Lieutenant Hanks has pointed out the leaders of the two groups. Lieutenant Hanks then snatches the cigarettes from the inmate who is holding the carton and hands it to one of the leaders. The two walk into the Gymnasium and Lieutenant Hanks starts walking back to his office glaring at Argus.

Pickle calls, "Hey LT, what do you want us to do about this?" as he motions at the crowd of inmates.

Lieutenant Hanks yells over his shoulder. "Fucking handle it!"

The three officers look at each other and then start trying to disperse the fifty odd inmates who comply after a moment of indecision to Argus' relief. The Corridor Officer had ended the move minutes before so after clearing the inmates from the corridor, Argus locks his unit door and goes to his office to make a notation in his confidential log regarding the incident. As he writes, he mentally derides himself on how monumentally he'd let the situation expand out of control.

"How fucking stupid can you get? You should have locked your door dumbass. Why didn't you press the fucking button? What the hell Argus?"

As he is finishing his notation, an inmate appears at the door. "Hey boss, can I get a roll?"

Argus reaches down and gets a roll of toilet paper from the box behind him and hands it to the inmate. The inmate looks at Argus "You got sack Snoop, but there was more steel in that corridor just now than you all could have took."

The inmate walks away as Argus thinks, "Tell me something I don't know."

∞∞∞∞

Argus jumps up and down to make sure his tactical vest is tight. The Corps taught him that on a long run, you don't want anything bouncing around. It'll just wear you out. The weather is sunny and humid which doesn't please anybody but Inspector the blood hound. He seems anxious to get started. Lieutenant Sena has arranged a special training for SWAT as well as the Canine Officer today. Inspector will run a track through the river bottoms adjacent to Tarragon. SWAT will run security for the track. Everybody knows the pace for the track will be dictated by Inspector and his handler. The handler, Officer Lang is also a member of Tarragon SWAT and has been working with Inspector for over two years. Everyone is geared up and ready as they stand in the knee high undergrowth. The mosquitoes are already working hard on finding a way up Argus' nose as Lang gives some final instructions for the track that he's set up for the hound to follow.

"Okay guys try to stay with me but about twenty five yards back. Don't fuck with the dog, he knows what he's doing and stay in a single file line. Everybody ready?"

Everyone nods, shifting in their gear. In addition to the full tactical

167

vest, everyone is carrying their Sig Sauer nine millimeter in a tactical holster of their choosing and an SMG in the same caliber. Argus likes a chest rig for his pistol and wears it across the base of his sternum. It stays out of the way when he's moving through obstacles and isn't on his legs when he needs to move fast. Everybody has their own thing. This is what Argus likes. Lang gives the dog some lead and he takes off like he's been waiting for a whole year. His nose is to the ground as he zigzags through the undergrowth of the mosquito infested river bottoms of the Silurus River. Abhaile, Indiana where Tarragon is located sits next to the Silurus. The undergrowth is heavy and hard to negotiate as Argus and the others slog through the muddy ground at a trot.

Inspector is baying away with his deep mournful voice as he runs from tree to stump, following the track Lang has run with the scented bait. Argus and the others are breathing hard as they work to stay up with the dog.

Argus thinks, "Holy shit, is this dog ever gonna get tired?"

He's already sweated through his vest after only an hour into the track. At the five mile mark Argus can see that they're starting to make a loop to head back. Inspector hasn't shown any signs of slowing down. He's a big hound at around a hundred pounds with long legs and ears to match. The pace stays the same all the way back to the starting area. As they arrive, Lang throws the dog's reward toy for Inspector to retrieve and to Argus' amazement the dog still wants to play. He's impressed with the dog's stamina as well as his own. It was a good workout.

Back in the ready room, Lieutenant Sena asks Lang what he used to bait the track for Inspector.

Lang tells everyone, "When I took over the Canine Handler's duties, I started meeting the prisoner transports every week and getting the shirts and socks that the escape risk inmates were wearing when they arrived. I put them into an evidence bag and then into a freezer. If one of these inmates escapes, I've got their scent already. I just went down to receiving and discharge and got a shirt from the incoming bin of clothes. Inspector is used to tracking on that."

Argus thinks, "What a great idea. He's got his own file of inmate scents."

As Argus finishes up with his gear he thinks, "I wouldn't want inspector tracking me. That dog has no let up."

∞∞∞∞

Sometimes it pays to keep your ear to the ground. The penitentiary grapevine is full of useful information. It's also full of bullshit but even that can sometimes give you understanding into what you might be looking at on a given day. The word floating around among the officers is that a hit had been put on an inmate for debriefing from one of the disruptive groups at Tarragon. The inmate who had been selected by the group to do the hit is now residing in ADSEG due to some intel work done by the Investigative Office. The inmate that the contract had been put on is now also in ADSEG under protective custody status.

Argus stands by the corridor restraining door of Unit Eleven and watches the inmates on the flat. He has his right arm propped up on the window bar and leans over the trash can to spit. The day is sweltering and the range fans are deafening as he feels a bead of sweat run down the side of his face and lodge in his beard.

Argus thinks, "I've still got some searches to do. I might as well get on it cause this day's gonna run away from me if I don't."

He moves away from the door and makes a round in the unit. Moving from the flat to the upper tier, he can almost feel the change in temperature as he gets higher in the unit. As he walks, looking into each cell, he sees more than one inmate lying on their rack with a battery powered fan blowing over a cooler full of ice. A prison air conditioner.

Argus thinks, "These guys are if nothing else, ingenious."

He finishes his tour of the upper tier and starts on the left side of the flat looking in each cell and observing much of the same thing. There aren't many inmates out on the flat. Everyone is laying low and trying to deal with the heat and humidity of Abhaile, Indiana in the dead of summer. Argus stops at the third cell from the end on the right and takes notice of the particularly clean condition of the cell. The floors are clean with the shoes lined up neatly under the bunk. There's no excess property lying about or laundry bags hanging from the rack. Even the items of property on top of the lockers are aligned as if for an inspection. "Every 'T' crossed and nothing left to chance," he thinks as he steps into the cell.

His sixth sense awakens and whispers, "We're so clean you can just pass us right on by Snoop."

He stands in the middle of the cell and looks around. The bunks are on his right and the lockers on his left. There is a towel spread out on the floor

169

next to the bunks that the inmate is using as a rug. The racks are made military tight.

Argus wonders, "I bet I could bounce a quarter off of them." He resists the temptation to try.

If he's wrong, he'll be messing up the cleanest cell he's ever seen and makes a mental note, "These guys got the cleanest cell of the week and get a small television if I don't find anything."

Fair is fair and Argus is going to give them the benefit of the doubt. With a tinge of regret, Argus starts on the locker side of the cell and begins the search. He tries to be professional and respectful when searching a cell. Putting yourself in the place of an inmate mentally is a two edged sword. He'd want an officer to be respectful with his stuff if it were him.

He goes through each locker with a fine tooth comb, even checking the inside of the dental floss containers for narcotics and comes up empty. He moves the property on top of the lockers to the bed and tips the lockers up slightly, looking underneath. He notes that there is no dust under the lockers either. The inmates are either clean freaks or serial killers. Both display that kind of attention to detail. Argus checks the gaps in the radiator and pipe insulation for anomalies. He checks the shoes under the bed, bending each sole but finding nothing. He lifts each side of the bed and knocks the end caps off. No shanks fall out. He rolls the mattresses finding nothing and makes an effort to put the linen back in a semblance of order. He uses his mirror and checks under the lip of the toilet and makes sure it flushes. Argus is beginning to think these guys are going to get that television. He stands up and looks around, his shirt wet with sweat due to the heat in the cell.

Argus shines his flashlight in the air vent and sees nothing unusual. "Was I wrong? Maybe I'm losing my touch."

There's only one other idea Argus has. He takes the property back off the locker nearest the door and stands on top. The fluorescent light fixture ballast cover is attached by two wing nuts. Argus removes the bulbs and unscrews the wing nuts, freeing the cover. He grabs his flashlight and looks inside the box containing the wiring of the light and hits pay dirt. It is the most beautiful shank he has ever seen. Argus pulls it out of its resting place and turns it over looking at it. The knife is made of solid oak and has been carved into a spear point. It's thick and strong with a carved handle of ridges to improve the grip when it gets bloody and it's around eight inches long. It is a knife meant to stay in the victim's chest.

A knife meant to send a message, "We were here," and Argus has found it.

He doesn't put the light back together because this is something unique and Argus figures, they may want pictures of where it was found. He wraps the shank in the towel from the floor and exits the cell, dead locking it before going to his office.

Once inside the office, Argus dials the Operations Lieutenant, "Hey LT, this is Antrim in Unit Eleven, I've just found the damndest knife you've ever seen. Its hand carved out of wood."

Lieutenant Grant replies, "Where'd you find it?"

Argus is looking at the knife on his desk, "In the light fixture. I figured you'd want some pictures so I didn't reassemble it."

Grant says he'll send the Activities Lieutenant down with the camera and an evidence form.

The Activities Lieutenant arrives and photographs the cell and light fixture, then the knife. Argus fills out the chain of custody form and places the knife in an evidence bag. "I'll go ahead and secure the property lieutenant."

The lieutenant looks at Argus shaking his head, "No, just dead lock the cell. I'm going to show this to the Investigative Lieutenant. I'm sure you've heard the scuttlebutt."

Argus nods, "Okay LT, I'll log the cell as deadlocked until the Investigative Section releases it."

The lieutenant claps Argus on the shoulder, "Good fuckin' job Antrim. You earned your money today."

Argus smiles and thinks, "Well now I gotta figure out somebody else to give these damn televisions to for the week."

∞∞∞∞

The inmate sits in the grass at the center of the gravel running track stretching after his run. He's been coming to the Recreation Yard twice a day for six months. Once in the morning to run and once in the evening for two hours of body weight exercises. He does burpees by the hundreds, pull ups, pushups and crunches until his muscles scream in protest. When the lactic acid builds up and the pain becomes unbearable he thinks, "I'll need every ounce of my strength for what's coming and it still might not be enough."

This one thing drives him on. The chance at freedom. He looks around the Recreation Yard as nonchalantly as he can and tries to focus on the plan once more.

It first came to him eight months ago out of desperation more than anything else. Right after he had first arrived at Tarragon. The place was more than a gladiator school, it was a slaughter house.

He thought, "I can't do all this time here, not here."

Slowly the idea had taken shape as he began to pick out the weaknesses of the place. The key was the Metal Shop. It is inside the fence line. He began to study the makeup of the bars in the windows and committed the exact dimensions to memory. They're old with none of the new enhancements in the construction. The officers are a downside because they do their job. The fence line is what you'd expect from a maximum security joint. Fence alarms, towers and razor wire but those things can be beaten with the proper planning and a little luck. The fuckers have a blood hound which is also a pain in his ass.

He's looked at the plan seven ways to Sunday and always comes to a point where he and his crew will have to take at least three officers off the count. No getting around that but they stand in the way of him getting out. It's just too bad for them. The mental checklist began to form and lengthen. For each tiny detail he had to come up with a counter move just like playing a game of chess. Except this is no game. It's his fucking life. The trick was maneuvering at least one other guy into an orderly spot in Unit Thirteen. That was tricky and just took some time. His guys in Thirteen are set.

He thinks with a smile, "I got these motherfuckers snowed in Eleven. They think I'm the perfect orderly."

The locking mechanisms on the cells are Alcatraz vintage so jamming them at lockdown won't be a problem. The trick is securing the door good enough that the hack pulling the doors at lockdown won't know that they're unsecure. He had to pay a dude from the Construction Shops six books of stamps for the wedges. He also had to get one of his guys to apply for a job in the Metal Shop to make the head and handle of the bar breaker. That took a while. He looks at the junction of the Recreation Yard fence and the perimeter fence. The fence alarm will be the point at which the clock starts ticking on them. Once they short it out at the wire junction box and it goes down, they'll have only a few minutes to clear the fence. It would have been less had he not decided to kill the Rear Yard Officer. It'll take them some time to send someone else when he doesn't answer the radio to go and check the problem. The fence will provide cover until they reach the top of the first one.

The towers will be on them after that but they'll have already cleared the first fence. He finishes stretching and picks up his gym bag to head back to the unit on the next move. The Morning Watch Officers for Units Eleven and Thirteen will have to go. It's too bad really. They'll just be in the wrong place at the wrong time. Two guitar strings from Recreation will take care of this nice and quiet. All they have to do is get through the midnight count, kill the unit officers and it's on. He closes his eyes and pictures snapping the bars to his window. Once he's out, he'll get his guys out of Unit Thirteen from the outside of their cell window then move along the inner Recreation Yard to the breezeway where the Rear Yard sits until the next count. Once their done with him, they'll take his keys and cross the man barrier fence to the perimeter. Tonight will be a moonless night.

He thinks, "Everything is in my cell ready to go, the bar breaker, wire, shanks, pepper and stuff to change what we look like. Tonight I taste free air."

It has been one shitty day. Argus moves around the unit chasing down what seems to be the hundredth call out who's not where he's supposed to be. When he started his shift this morning he saw the writing on the wall. Two pages of medical appointments and at least half were from his unit. He thought as soon as he saw it, "I'm going to be chasing fucking inmates down all day."

He was right. To make matters worse, Medical obviously couldn't read the column for job assignment on the sheet because half the inmates they were calling his unit about were at work and not even in the unit. He's been on the telephone all day calling the work foremen to get the inmates to the callouts. To top it off, today is the hottest July day he can remember, its unit inspection day and the cells look like shit. He sweated through his uniform shirt fifteen minutes into the shift and he is not in a good mood.

Argus exits the second cell he's "cleaned" for the inmates and moves down the flat with the trash bag full of nuisance contraband. One of the inmates meets him halfway to the office. He's new in the block and obviously doesn't know where he is yet.

He squares up with Argus and says, "You can't do what you're doing officer. It ain't right."

Argus is in no mood, "You better find the place you were five minutes ago, convict."

The inmate turns and walks away yelling, "You ain't right man. You can't do that shit."

Argus thinks, "I most assuredly can *do that shit*. This motherfucker needs to check himself and the policies."

He puts the bag in his office and logs the two cells as searches in the log. That makes four searches out of the five he has to do by policy. He checks the unit television list for the cells where the TV's were awarded last month and goes to retrieve them. Once he gets them in the office, he checks his notes and does the math for the cleanest cells in the unit. Argus adopted the practice early on of checking certain aspects of each cell. The cell starts at ten and loses a point for every aspect of cleanliness that isn't met. In his opinion, that's the fair way to do it.

The telephone rings and Argus answers it, "Eleven, Antrim."

"Officer Antrim, this is Sheila in Medical, I'm looking for an inmate."

Argus thinks, "Holy shit. What a surprise."

He gets the inmates name and number, checks the callout sheet and calls the Plumbing Shop to ask them to send the inmate to Medical. As Argus is heading back to his office from distributing the televisions, he realizes that he still has one cell search to accomplish for the day. He stands on the flat and considers this and the amount of time he still has in the shift.

Argus looks over at the orderly's cell and thinks, "I've been busting my ass all day I deserve an easy one."

He walks toward the inmate's cell and finds it empty. "Politeness" is sitting in the television room. His cellie is at Medical on a call-out. Argus steps in and closes the cell door while simultaneously looking around the cell. It is well organized but full of personal property. He sits down on the lower bunk and thinks about the inmates who live here. They don't cause any problems, are respectful and follow the program.

Argus thinks, "This should be an easy one."

Starting in the front left corner, Argus begins the search. As he works his way around the cell, he only finds minor nuisance contraband. At the back of the cell, he nonchalantly grabs the steam pipe insulation and raises it slightly as he shakes it, immediately noticing the extra weight. It feels like it's full of water. There is a small clothes line tied from the bunk to the insulation. Argus removes the clothes line and raises the insulation again. He thinks, "Still heavy. What the fuck."

As he spins the insulation around the piping, he immediately sees the tape on the back that has been painted over. Argus checks his six and then opens the insulation with his pen knife exposing a steel bar approximately eighteen inches long. It is two inches wide and one quarter inch thick with three holes drilled in the end.

Argus exits the cell, dead locking it behind him. He looks at the bar and realizes that he has no idea what he's found. As he stands on the flat, Argus looks around the unit and sees Inmate "Politeness" standing on the upper tier at the far end of the unit with two other inmates. He realizes that almost all of the inmates are watching his every move. Argus steps out into the corridor and dials the Lieutenant's Office from the East End Officer's phone.

Lieutenant Mack answers, "Operations."

Argus says, "Hey LT, Antrim. I've just found the damndest head knocker in one of the cells down here. Not really sure what it is. Can I bring it down so you can see it?"

Lieutenant Mack says, "Sure Ant. Have Ten cover your unit."

Argus enters the Lieutenant's Office with the bar and Mack jumps out of his chair. "Ant, tell me you deadlocked that cell."

Argus is incredulous, "LT, did you forget who you're talking to? Of course I dead locked it."

Mack is visibly excited as he looks at the bar. "Ant, there's going to be a head that bolts to the bar you have there. The head is designed to break the bars."

Officer Morris is sitting on the bench in the office but is now also on his feet. Morris is a new officer and Argus doesn't know much about him but he seems like a competent hack.

Mack says, "Argus take Morris back down to your unit and tear that cell apart until you find that head. What are the inmate's names who live in the cell?"

Argus gives Mack the names and numbers of the inmates and tells the lieutenant that one of the inmates is his orderly and in the unit then he and Morris exit the office.

As they head back down to the unit, Argus tells Morris, "Let's do this the smart way. We'll start the search over. You start where I started before and hit all the areas I already searched. A second set of eyes doesn't hurt. I'll start in the other corner and work my way around. We'll meet at the back. Everything gets disassembled in the cell. Sound good?"

Smiling, Morris nods in agreement. As they get to the unit, Argus sees his relief standing at the restraining door. Argus keys the door as the Corridor and another officer arrive to escort Inmate "Politeness" out of the unit. Argus looks up at "Politeness" and motions for him to step down. His friends are nowhere to be seen. The inmate walks around the tier and descends the stairs arriving at the door and the five officers. He's escorted out of the unit and placed in handcuffs as the Corridor Officer transmits, "Corridor to the housing units, clear the corridor and lock it down. No inmate movement."

Before being led away, "Politeness" looks over his shoulder at Argus and says, "You have no idea how much trouble you've caused me Mr. Antrim."

Argus has an idea that he does.

The relieving officer and Argus exchange equipment for chits as he gives his relief a rundown of what is going on. Argus tells him, "Me and Morris are going to be a while. Can you key us into the cell?" They enter the cell and Argus looks around with a fresh perspective. He immediately sees the cardboard tray under the bed with the pint sized container of pepper and thinks, "For Inspector I bet."

Morris has already started on his side of the cell. Argus doesn't hurry. He moves with purpose in a methodical manner. When he gets to the bed, he rolls the mattresses then checks the bed posts. There he finds the garrote after removing the caps. Argus is a Marine and knows all about this weapon and its purpose. The hair rises on the back of his neck. Argus looks under the bed and finds in addition to the pepper, a plastic bag containing ace bandages, a razor, band-aids and a pair of sunglasses.

He is going through the shoes when Morris exclaims, "Found it!"

Argus turns to see Morris, who is six inches taller than he is reaching into the air vent up to almost his shoulder. He hears the sound of tearing tape as Morris, now sweating pulls the item from the vent. It is the head for the bar and the bolts, covered in black tape and secreted in the vent. Both officers are ecstatic. They finish the search, inspecting everything with a fine tooth comb. Nothing is left assembled in the cell that can be disassembled. In addition to what they'd already discovered, two nine inch pick shanks and a length of wire are found. They exit the cell and have the Evening Watch OIC deadlock it. Argus looks at the weapons, especially the garrote and realizes Inmate "Politeness" wasn't going to leave without spilling blood. Once in the Lieutenant's Office, everything is photographed and bagged as evidence. Hannah Depps shows up and takes the evidence to the Investigative Office. After she's gone, Argus and Morris sit down to complete the paperwork. Morris will write a supporting memorandum to be attached to Argus' incident reports.

Argus looks at Morris, "I really appreciate your help brother. It was nice to have you on my six and I don't think I would've been able to reach that far in to that vent. Good job today."

Morris looks at Argus and shrugs with a smile, "All in a day's work."

The following day Argus' is supposed to be on his day off but he has grabbed an easy shift of overtime in Tower Two from 8:00 am to 4:00 pm. As he sits in the Captain's chair and looks out over the fence line and the institution, he mulls over the events of yesterday and the inmates involved. He had interacted with Inmate "Politeness" a hundred times and had misread him ninety nine. He thinks about the garrote and what it meant. Argus wonders which one of his brothers or sisters they were going to kill. A garrote isn't an "in case I need it" weapon. It is perfect for killing a sentry quietly. In a tower, you have plenty of time to contemplate things.

Argus wonders, "If I hadn't had such a shitty day and been behind on my searches, would I have gone into that cell?"

He thinks about God and if He sent Argus that day so he could stop the evil that was coming. Argus knows one thing as sure as he knows God exists, evil exists too and it doesn't stop itself.

These dark thoughts fill Argus' mind as he hears Tower One come on the intercom, "Heads up Ant, Captain's on his way to your tower."

Argus thinks, "Oh crap, a fucking tower inspection?" He starts tidying things up as quickly as he can. He's wiping the counter off when he hears a pounding in the door forty feet below.

It's Captain Rodriguez. "Tower Two, on your door!"

Argus goes to the window and looks down then buzzes the Captain in. After moving the chair to the corner, he opens the trap door and waits. Argus feels a nervous twitch in the pit of his stomach as he listens to the Captain's echoing foot falls as he climbs. The tower isn't inspection ready and he knows it.

Argus thinks, "Why did I pick today for overtime? Just my fucking luck."

The Captain appears at the bottom of the ladder, climbs up and makes his way into the tower.

He smiles at Argus. "Officer Antrim, I heard you were up here on duty and wanted to come up and see you."

Argus raises his eyebrows in surprise, "Sorry about the mess sir. I was just cleaning up."

The Captain knows this is bullshit but doesn't let on that he knows. Captain Rodriguez has been with the Agency for a long time. He was a hostage in the riot Argus learned about at the Training Center in Georgia during the hostage class. Whatever evil Argus thinks he has seen, it is nothing compared to what this man has experienced. Captain Rodriguez is a thin man with a stoic demeanor. His salt and pepper hair is never out of place and he's always dressed in a suit and tie. Argus respects him most for the contemplative way he carries himself.

The Captain smiles a wry smile, "No, no, I didn't come up to inspect. I came to see you and congratulate you on your work yesterday. Excellent job, just excellent."

Argus looks down at the floor and nods, "Thank you sir. I'm glad we found the stuff before they could use it."

The Captain smiles, "Indeed."

The Captain looks out over the institution as Argus closes the trap door and joins him at the window, "You know Argus, they'll be some big changes coming because of what you and Morris found yesterday. I'm moving the Metal Shop outside the wire. All of that work will be done at the satellite camp where the trustees stay."

Argus raises his eyebrows again and nods. The Captain looks at him and continues, "I also want you to know, they planned on killing some people. There are some officers still alive today because of what you did."

Argus looks at the Captain and smiles, "I kind of got the feeling that might be the case sir when I found what I did."

With that, the Captain shakes Argus hand, "Well, I'm going to get back inside. Keep your eyes open Mr. Antrim and if you have any other ideas on enhancing the security of this place, please don't hesitate."

Argus opens the trap door, "Thank you sir, I will."

The Captain makes the descent back to the ground leaving Argus to his thoughts. Before the Captain's vehicle even pulls away, the intercom lights up, "Well now, guess we know who the Captain's new kid is. HAHAHA!"

Argus smiles. He was expecting this, "Yeah, yeah, have your fun assholes."

Chapter 9
Look into the eyes of the dragon

He walks the upper tier of Unit Thirteen and feels the beginnings of fatigue nag at his psyche. Looking in each cell as he passes, he sees that most of them are occupied. He smiles as he thinks how he ended up here tonight working the 4:00 pm to midnight shift. You might say he was tricked but it is his willingness to take any assignment that really sealed his fate. Argus was making preparations for the arrival of his relief and the end of his 8:00 am to 4:00 pm shift in Unit Eleven when Lieutenant Atkins had called on the telephone. "Antrim, I just got a bang in. Easy overtime if you want it."

The next logical question would have been, "Where's it at LT?" but that's not Argus and Atkins knows it.

Argus replies too quickly, "Sure LT, what have you got?"

That was all it took. Unit Thirteen is a zoo on Evening Watch. One of the larger units at Tarragon with a solid body count of one hundred and fifty inmates at a minimum and it is anything but easy overtime. Especially on the tail end of a sixteen hour shift.

As soon as Argus said, "Sure LT" Lieutenant Atkins had replied, "Unit Thirteen, I'll put you down for it."

He then hung the phone up before Argus could say anything. Argus thought, "Easy overtime my ass."

It's not as bad as it used to be. Officer Pickle is the Day Watch OIC in the unit so the inmates know the program at least. Even though the cells have inmates in them, the flat is full and loud.

He takes a deep breath, shifts into low gear and thinks, "One more count and I'll lock these guys down for the night. Just five more hours. I can stand on my head for five hours. Nothing to it but to do it."

It would help if he was able to get a full night's sleep but the insomnia still plagues him. When he does sleep, he is visited by the dreams. Not always, but enough.

His searches are completed for the night, yielding nothing but nuisance contraband and a tattoo gun made from a beard trimmer motor, toothbrush and a piece of wire. The inmate was using a regular ink pen for ink. Argus spent fifteen minutes and wrote the incident report for tattoo paraphernalia. The sanction won't be much but tattoo needles pose a threat to every correctional officer. Diseases are rampant inside this place, the scariest being Hepatitis and HIV. A needle stick is a ten year sentence of testing every six months. Nobody wants that. Argus gave the Corridor Officer the paperwork and gun to take to the Lieutenant's Office. It'll be up to the LT what he wants to do with it. Argus finishes his tour of the unit and assumes his spot at the door next to his trash can, puts a fresh dip in and spits.

He just gets comfortable when Control transmits over the radio, "Control to all portable radio units, we have a medical emergency in the Linen Factory. Medical emergency in the Linen Factory."

Argus turns to see the Unit Ten OIC emerge from his unit at a sprint. Argus exits his unit into the Main Corridor to monitor both units.

The Corridor Officer is mid corridor and transmits, "Corridor to the housing units, ensure the corridor is clear of inmates. No inmate movement."

Argus then hears the Operations Lieutenant transmit from the scene, "Operations to Control, lock it down and get me a bus."

Argus thinks, "Well, I might as well get ready. An ambulance means somebody is going to the hospital. This night just keeps getting longer and longer."

Lynn is used to this by now and knows that he isn't always able to call. Sometimes, she knows when he'll be home when he walks through the door. The Activities Lieutenant, Lieutenant Atkins steps out of the Lieutenant's Office and turns toward Argus and circles his finger in the air.

Argus thinks, "Well, at least he's pulling a double too."

The meaning is clear. "Get ready for a high risk escort."

Argus goes into the unit and collects his lunchbox and thermos and steps into the corridor just as the Unit Six Number Two Officer shows up at his door. He is a heavy set officer who isn't happy at all about being pulled from Unit Six to take over Thirteen. The units are as different as apples and hand grenades.

Argus thinks, "Oh well, we all have our crosses to bear. You need the exercise anyway."

He gets his chits, stops by the Lieutenant's Office and signs the escort paperwork before heading through the Control Room grills in the direction of the front of the institution and the Armory. Once at the Armory, he waits for Lieutenant Atkins.

Argus almost laughs as he thinks, "Serves you right, you sneaky fucker."

The Lieutenant signals for the Tower One Officer to pop the Armory door just as Eli Stephens arrives. He is a SWAT member as well and a friend of Argus'. The Unit One Number Two Officer has been pulled to relieve Stephens from Unit Four.

Argus thinks as he steps up, "Good. I've got someone I trust to watch my six."

The three gear up with Stephens taking the shotgun. He and Lieutenant Atkins will ride chase. Argus will be in the ambulance with the inmate. They take up security positions and signal Tower One that they're ready. The Ambulance crew and Lieutenant Jennings exit the Front Entrance and head down the walk to the Tower One Sally Port. As the ambulance crew loads the inmate into the ambulance, Argus notices his right hand is secured with a flex cuff and bandaged. It's bloody and looks like it might be pretty bad.

The Linen Factory manufactures cotton blankets for the entire agency. They receive the raw cotton and process it into cotton thread which is then woven into the blankets used by the inmates. This particular inmate was working on a machine that rakes the raw cotton of debris using a high speed belt with large metal tines resembling oversized sewing machine needles. The belt is wide with a dozen needles in each row and hundreds of rows long. The inmate is loaded and Argus enters the ambulance positioning himself at the back doors with his weapon holstered on the left side of his body and away from the inmate. From what Argus gathers as he listens to the EMS crew speaking to the inmate, the inmate had tried to clear a jam in the machine without cutting the power and his right hand had been pulled into the belt.

The belt had chewed his right ring finger and pinky completely away along with most of the meat from his hand. As is the case with most of the inmates at Tarragon, Inmate "Malmano" is doing a lengthy sentence for possession with intent to distribute methamphetamine and felon in possession of a firearm during a drug crime. He'll be an old man before he ever sees the street again. It is Argus' job to make sure of this. The injury is too severe for Abhaile General to handle so the ambulance will be transporting the inmate to Indianapolis.

Argus thinks, "This just keeps getting better. I can forget sixteen hours, this is going to be a twenty hour shift."

Argus is happy that he at least thought to bring his empty water bottle for a spittoon. Argus pulls his snuff, puts a chew in and spits.

The inmate who is very alert asks Argus, "Hey boss, what brand is that?"

He looks at the inmate and says without emotion, "Mine. The brand is mine." The inmate looks away.

The ambulance and chase car pull away from the institution with lights and sirens going. Argus tries to get comfortable for the long ride by shifting in the seat but the gear deters him from reaching any semblance of comfort. As they ride along the highway, the long hours and lack of any decent sleep starts to wear on Argus. It's called the "Z" monster and it attacks when you least expect it. He feels the tentacles attach themselves to his eye lids and begin to pull them toward the floor. The hypnotic rocking of the ambulance doesn't help in the slightest. Argus realizes this and fights himself to a middle ground of a thousand yard stare before popping back into alertness and cussing himself inwardly. Argus looks at the inmate who is looking at him intently. The look in the inmate's eyes is that of a wolf watching its prey, waiting for a chance to pounce.

He stares back at the inmate until the inmate breaks his stare and looks away.

Argus thinks, "This guy's hand is mangled, he's in shackles and he's still waiting for a chance to take my weapon. Better get on point Argus. This fucker will kill you if you take your pack off."

Now he's pissed off at himself and the inmate. Being alert isn't a problem for the rest of the trip. They arrive at the Trauma Ward where the physician orders the restraints removed.

Lieutenant Atkins tells the physician who is obviously used to getting his way, "That ain't going to happen doc. I'll adjust them so you can work on the hand but the restraints don't come off till he's in surgery and unconscious."

The doctor looks at the LT and then at Argus and Eli realizing, he won't win this battle and nods at the LT. Lieutenant Atkins removes the flex cuff and attaches the handcuff to the belly chain so that the only loose appendage is the inmate's right hand.

The medical staff does their work while Argus and Eli provide security at the door. The inmate is moved to surgery where his hand is repaired as best as it can be. He'll have to learn to function with just three fingers on his right hand.

As they work on the inmate, Argus observes through the window of the operating room and thinks, "What would possess you to put your hand in a machine like that without cutting the power? You are some kind of major dumbass."

He wishes he had a cup of coffee and hopes Lieutenant Jennings is able to set up a relief crew otherwise it is going to be a long night. The surgery is completed around 11:00 pm and the inmate is admitted to a room on the third floor. Once in the room, Inmate "Malmano" is secured to the bed with his leg irons. Lieutenant Atkins calls Tarragon from the Nurse's Station and lets Lieutenant Jennings know what room they're in.

Eli and Argus provide security just inside the door while Lieutenant Atkins is inside the room to monitor the inmate as the nurses make their rounds and tend to the inmate. The relief crew arrives at 1:45 am with Lieutenant Jennings as the OIC. After passing on information and some good natured ribbing Argus, Eli and Atkins leave. The drive back is a long one but traffic is light. By the time they return to the institution it is 3:30 am.

As they head to their vehicles, Argus tells Lieutenant Atkins, "See you in a few hours LT and grins."

The lieutenant looks at Argus sideways and says, "Yeah, I better see you." His shift starts in four hours.

∞∞∞∞

"Tarragon Penitentiary has changed me. There's no getting around it. To stay ahead of a predator, you have to think like a predator and in so doing, darkness grows inside you. Evil doesn't stop itself and to stand in its path it has to be part of you. When you are surrounded by violence, a part of you becomes violent. Someone crosses a line and they'll feel what is inside of you. That's just the way it is."

These are Argus' thoughts as he looks at the pair of burgundy lace panties that someone has stretched across the steering wheel of Lynn's Jeep Wrangler at Walmart. He knows what this is. It's almost as if he is looking at the panties and also looking at the scene from above at the same time. The deviant is watching them, he knows. Looking for the reaction and probably jerking off while he watches. Argus begins to form a plan.

Lynn and Argus had made plans to do their weekly grocery shopping after work today. He'd passed on hitting the bag so he could meet her at Walmart. She was still in her skirt, blouse and high heels and Argus was in his uniform minus the duty belt. As Argus had pulled into the parking lot, he had spotted Lynn's jeep at about the middle of the lot. The store is busy today so he pulled into one of the end spaces one row over and parked. He walked to the jeep which was empty and looked around spotting Lynn waving at him from the store entrance. As he reached her, he kissed her as they headed into the store.

Lynn said, "There was some creep that was staring at me just a few minutes ago."

Argus asked what the guy looked like. "He was a big guy with a bright blue T-shirt. He was creepy and gave me the eeby-jeebies the way he was looking at me."

Argus looked around, "Do you see him anywhere?"

Lynn shook her head and said, "No."

Argus looked around again, "Well, if you see him, point him out."

They went into the store and began shopping. His attention wasn't on shopping because he was constantly scanning for anyone fitting the description but didn't see the guy. Lynn is a planner and had a grocery list that they followed as they collected their purchases.

He commented, "Shit is getting more expensive."

Without saying it, Argus was thankful that they didn't have to use a calculator anymore to make sure they didn't go over at the register. When he was moving furniture, the money for groceries was the money they had. No extra, so a calculator was a must. They followed the most expedient path through the store, picking out items, searching for deals and crossing the items off her list. He is thankful for her talent of stretching every penny.

They paid for their groceries and exited the store into the bright sunshine. As they approached Lynn's jeep, they kissed and Argus headed for his truck. As he finished loading the truck, he looked over and saw Lynn standing by her vehicle. She motioned for him to come over.

He walked the twenty yards at a hastened pace and as he got nearer, saw the worried look on her face. "What's up babe?"

She motioned into the vehicle and pointed at the steering wheel.

Now Argus is looking at the panties and feeling the blackness grow as he thinks, "You don't fuck with my girls, I don't care who you are."

This deviant spider is watching. Argus is as sure of it as he is sure that he can out think this piece of shit.

His plan is simple. "Lynn, stay calm. He's watching us right now. He picked you out the minute you got out of your jeep. Do you know where the stop and rob is over by the high school?"

Lynn nods, a worried look on her face. She may see what is behind Argus' eyes. He takes the panties off of the steering wheel and puts them in his pocket. "Get in your jeep and drive to the stop and rob and pull up to the pump like you're going to get gas. Make sure you stop right in front of the store. It's just down the street about four blocks. Don't leave this street. I'll be right behind you. If I'm reading this guy right, he'll follow you and I'll be right behind him."

There is no doubt in Argus mind, he is going to squash this spider with his tactical boot and after he's finished, he plans to put the panties in the guy's mouth for good measure. There will be no mercy or a 911 call. Lynn looks at Argus with a worried look.

Argus smiles and says, "It'll be alright. Don't take off until I get into my truck."

Lynn gets in her jeep and Argus heads for his truck. Once inside, he starts it up and watches as Lynn leaves the parking lot. Argus puts the truck in gear and follows. There are several cars in between the two as Lynn pulls into the gas station. She pulls up to the pumps as instructed while Argus pulls nose in to a parking spot facing away from the pumps.

As he exits his vehicle, a late model LTD pulls next to the pumps on the opposite side of Lynn's vehicle. She reacts immediately, pointing as if to signal, "That's him!"

Argus begins to trot toward the pumps as the man in the blue T-shirt turns to look at Argus. He turns back around, puts the LTD in gear and accelerates out of the lot, tires squealing in a cloud of oily smoke. Argus spins to go back to his vehicle and give pursuit but he'd pulled into the spot and has no chance of catching the pervert.

Argus thinks, "I read that motherfucker like a book. He's lucky he got away."

Argus throws the panties into the trash knowing the next time he works the bag, in his mind it will be wearing a blue t-shirt.

∞∞∞∞

It's the last day of the quarter and Argus' last day in Unit Eleven.

As he stands at the door and looks down the flat he thinks, "It was a good two quarters. I did some good down here."

He would've stayed for three had it not been for Lieutenant Mack pulling him up and asking him to come to ADSEG as the Recreation

185

Officer. Mr. Gaylon wasn't happy about it but the days are Saturday and Sundays off which is what Argus has been looking for.

Mack is taking over Segregation right in the middle of a gang war and he pushed the right buttons. "Ant, I need someone I can trust to get it right."

That's all it took. He likes Lieutenant Mack and also likes being the one who is known to take on the tough assignments. If Argus is truthful with himself, he's proud of the officer he is and likes the reputation. He is standing at the door watching his unit when an inmate exits a cell half way down the flat and shuffles toward him. Argus leans over and spits in the trash can.

"Officer, I'm sick."

Argus looks at the inmate and thinks, "This dude looks sick."

The inmate has dark circles under his eyes. "Alright, let me see what I can do. You missed sick call. Why didn't you go to sick call this morning?"

The inmate has been here long enough to know that unless you have an appointment, the time to go to Medical is right after morning mainline.

The inmate looks at Argus, "Please boss, I overslept. I'm really sick man."

Argus says, "Wait here. What's wrong with you?"

The inmate grabs his stomach. "I don't know man. I'm just sick. My gut hurts."

Argus goes to the range phone, picks it up and looks at the receiver to make sure no one has put shit on it, then dials Medical. "Hey this is Antrim in Unit Eleven. I've got a sick inmate down here. Can you see him?"

The Hospital Desk Officer says, "Yeah Ant, let me check."

Argus waits on the line for what seems like ten minutes, "Sorry Ant. The Doc says he'll have to come to sick call tomorrow. They're booked up down here."

Argus says, "Okay buddy. Thanks for checking for me."

He looks at the inmate, hangs up the telephone and shakes his head. "You're out of luck. They said you'll have to come to sick call tomorrow."

The inmate looks at Argus and vomits a puddle of baby crap yellow fluid onto the floor. Argus shakes his head and thinks, "Wonderful. Thank goodness I wasn't standing in front of this idiot."

He has seen this before. Someone has sold the inmate some wine that wasn't fully fermented. The fermentation process has continued in the dumbass' stomach. That's why he slept through breakfast and sick call. Argus smells the familiar rancid odor of hooch. "Well, I might as well end the quarter like I started."

The inmate has sunk to his knees in front of the corridor door. Argus steps over to him and says, "Stand up. I'm going to get you some medical attention."

The inmate doesn't look up, "I can't man. I told you I'm sick."

Argus looks at the inmate, reaches down and grabs him by the arm. "Stand up. If you want me to help, get the fuck up."

Argus looks down the range. "Crack!"

The inmate steps out of his cell.

Argus yells, "Clean this up for me man."

He takes his radio off his belt and calls the Corridor Officer.

"Eleven to Corridor, escorting one to the Lieutenant's Office." Dane steps out of Thirteen to check on Argus and says he'll watch the unit. Argus walks the inmate down the Main Corridor, holding his elbow as he shuffles. The inmate is made to face the wall as Argus pat searches him.

Once he finishes the search Argus says, "Stay right here and don't fuck up."

Argus knocks on the door and hears Lieutenant Grant yell, "Enter!"

As Argus steps in Lieutenant Grant smiles and says, "What ya got Ant?"

Argus grins sideways, "DWI Lieutenant. Looks like he got part of a bad batch and he's vomiting all over my block."

Grant raises his eyebrows, "Okay bring him in."

Argus brings the inmate in and retrieves the alco-sensor from the file cabinet to test the inmate for intoxication.

The inmate looks at the device. "I'm sick man, not drunk."

Lieutenant Grant says, "Okay, prove it. Blow into the tube."

The inmate blows through the tube and the numbers start climbing. They stop at well over the minimum limit for intoxication.

Grant gets on the telephone and calls Medical, "This is the Operations Lieutenant. I need a Physician's Assistant in my office for a medical assessment on an inmate."

For it to be a legitimate test, the inmate will have to be tested a second time after waiting five minutes. As they wait, the PA arrives to look the inmate over.

After assessing the inmate, the PA says, "He's fine. Heart rate is a little up but nothing to worry about."

The inmate looks at Argus. "I thought you said you was gonna get me some medical attention, now you're locking me up?"

Argus looks at the inmate with a sad smile. "Look in front of you my man. That PA is from Medical. Now blow into the tube."

Argus leaves the office to return to his unit and secure the inmate's property thinking, "Consistency is truly a beautiful thing."

∞∞∞∞

Argus is cleaning up his office in Unit Eleven in preparation of leaving the unit to a new Day Watch OIC next quarter. He never did like turning a unit over to someone without squaring it away first. He's dusted, swept and emptied the trash as well as cleaned out the junk from the desk which somehow accumulates throughout a ninety day period. An inmate appears at his door. He is an older inmate in his mid-fifties Argus guesses. The inmate has a beard and a wizened look in his eyes. Almost like a fox. He has a half grin on his face. Argus hasn't interacted with the inmate too much over the past quarters. In fact, he can't remember the inmate exchanging more than a few words with him. The guy just stays out of the way.

Argus thinks, "This guy is smart. He knows how to do his time."

Argus looks at the inmate expectantly. "Something I can do for you?"

The inmate puts his hand up on the door facing and smiles. "You coming back next quarter boss?"

Argus knows damn well the inmate already knows the answer to that question.

Argus cocks his head to the side. "C'mon man, you know I'm out of here next quarter."

The inmate looks around and says, "Well, since your headed out, I got a confession to make."

This peaks Argus' attention. "A confession?"

The inmate smiles that cagey smile again. "Remember that day about a month ago when you was searching all over the unit for that wine. All up in the pipe chases and everything but you didn't find anything?"

He remembers the day clearly. The whole unit smelled like wine but Argus couldn't find it.

Argus raises his eyebrows. "Yeah, I remember."

The inmate looks down at the floor, taps his foot and then looks back at Argus. "Well, I had me a spray bottle with some wine in it and I

188

went around the unit spraying it all over."

Argus gets it now. A practical joke is no fun unless the target knows he's been gotten.

Argus pictures the day and laughs. "Good one. You got me. That's funny."

The inmate laughs and starts to leave. "Well, we thought it was too. No hard feelings boss. Take it easy."

The inmate leaves and Argus chuckles again thinking, "I got to hand it to him, that's creative." Argus always liked a good practical joke.

∞∞∞∞

He sits at the kitchen table and looks at the small one inch by three inch box over his bowl of cereal and feels a sickness in his stomach. Guy Fealltoir is due to be at Tarragon Penitentiary as a Factory Foreman in two hours. He'd started at the penitentiary nine years ago as a correctional officer and soon figured out that he would rather be anyplace but inside those cell houses. He wanted to quit within the first month and had even talked to his wife about it but couldn't come up with a good reason for leaving the pay and benefits. He had one but couldn't tell his wife. He just couldn't bear the thought of how she would look at him if he told her the truth. The fact is, Guy is a coward and he knows it.

He takes a bite of cereal without tasting it and thinks, "No sane person could blame me. The fucking place scares me to death."

The inmates had recognized the smell of fear on him from the start and had begun testing different ways he could be turned.

In the end, it was his fear that had done it.

Guy thinks, "I should've quit when I wanted to. Oh God, how did I get to this point?"

From the first, several inmates consistently gave Guy a problem every day, each day escalating the disrespect and disruptive behavior. He just didn't have it in him to put a stop to it. Then one day an inmate stepped into his office and seemed to understand his problem.

The inmate said, "Boss you're a good officer. We can all see that. Those assholes giving you the trouble should be put in their place. A few of us could take care of it for you if you wanted. We hate to see them disrespect you like they're doing. Just say the word and it's done."

It was like a weight had been lifted from him because he knew someone finally understood and Guy didn't feel alone anymore. He looked at the inmate and nodded his head.

The next day, the problem inmates showed up at his office and apologized. Guy couldn't believe it. After that, things got a lot easier in the unit. He really didn't even have to leave his office much because the place was practically running itself. That was over eight years ago and now Guy knows that the problem inmates and the inmate who helped "fix" the problem were all in the same gang. He'd been tricked but didn't know that then and in gratitude, started giving his new friends extra privileges. The inmate who'd first approached him asked for a pack of gum that they didn't sell in the Commissary.

Guy thinks, "I didn't see any harm in it back then. It was just a fucking pack of chewing gum. I was fucked the minute I brought it in, now, they own me."

He thought bringing the contraband into Tarragon was all over when he'd landed the job in the Linen Factory. The job was just perfect for Guy. He was the only one in the Scouring Shop with just one inmate worker. He could go in his office and lock the door and work his numbers all day while the inmate scoured the raw cotton.

He looks at the half eaten bowl of cereal and thinks, "There's no way out now. If they tell on me like they've threatened to do, I'll end up in the cell next door to these animals."

Guy thinks back to the day the inmates he worked for made contact with him in the factory. The inmate worker had knocked on his door and motioned that he needed to tell him something. Guy unlocked the door and the inmate walked into the office like he owned it.

Before Guy could protest, the inmate put a slice of the gum Guy had brought in on the desk and said, "Your boys down in the block miss you Guy. Some packages are going to start arriving at your house. Don't look inside them. You just be a good boy and bring them in here to work and give them to me."

Guy had told the inmate, "I'm done with that. You guys need to leave me alone."

That's when the reality of what Guy always knew hit him full force.

The inmate worker looked at Guy and said with a grin, "Well boss, that's fine. Wonder what your wife will think when the gum and a list of everything you've brought in shows up on the Warden's desk? Your fingerprints covering the cigarettes, candy bars and that little pipe with the weed. All that shit."

The inmate laughed, "We own you motherfucker."

Now Guy sits at the table contemplating the position he's in. If he's

190

found out, he and his family are ruined. He takes the box and puts it in the side pocket of his trousers. He wonders what's inside and immediately regrets the thought. Best to go along for now and hope he can figure a way out of this mess. His wife and son are still asleep as he creeps from the house and gets in the car. The drive to work is over much too quickly. He walks through the front of the penitentiary and nods to the officer in Control. Guy walks straight to the factory and walks into his office. His stomach is roiling as he hears the Corridor Officer announce work call over the radio.

He thinks, "Maybe they'll let me pay them off to let me out of this. I can't keep this up."

The inmate worker shows up at Guy's office door and looks around. He knocks and smiles at Guy through the window.

Guy opens the door and the inmate steps in while looking around the office. "Well, where is it?"

Guy looks at the inmate then quickly at the floor and rubs his hands together, "Five thousand dollars. I'll pay you guys five thousand dollars to leave me alone."

The inmate looks at Guy, "Man, you are pathetic. Do you know that? Gimme the fucking box."

Guy hands the inmate the small box from his side pocket.

The inmate puts the box down inside the front of his trousers and smiles at Guy. "That'll be all for now. I'll let you know when to expect more. We know where you live now. Awful pretty wife you got. You're doing a good job Guy. I think we'll keep you."

The inmate laughs and walks out the door. Guy feels like he is going to vomit.

∞∞∞∞

Tarragon Penitentiary is like any other maximum security institution when it comes to the inmates. All have earned their way inside the many rows of concertina wire and fences. Whether that came as a slow progression through many years of disruptive behavior or the commission of a crime so egregious the individual earned a place at the head of the line from the start varies according to the specific inmate. Inmates at Tarragon are given a program which if followed will allow some to eventually work their way down to a lower level institution. Following this program is a fact of life for an inmate here. Another fact of life for the inmate is finding a way to successfully negotiate day to

191

day life while trying to follow that program and that includes the many gangs inside the penitentiary. To survive, most of the inmates are at least associated with some group for protection. Very few walk the yard alone.

All out wars between the gangs are a rarity. Sure, there are isolated incidents which are squashed afterwards through various means. In truth, war is bad for business. Every gang is running some type of hustle and it's hard to get business accomplished when you're locked down. Wars are rare but they do occur occasionally. They can start over something as little as a matter of disrespect or something larger. An inmate's world is very small which makes small things very big. For some, their self-respect is all they have.

As one inmate told Argus long ago, "It's hard to walk away and forget someone disrespecting you. You'll see the dude every day after that and he'll keep disrespecting you because he thinks you're weak. There's a fence around this place boss, so there ain't no walking away."

This is the place Argus finds himself in on his first day as the Segregation Recreation Officer at the Maximum Security Penitentiary Tarragon. Two gangs are at war and the segregation unit is busting at the seams with a body count of one hundred eighty four inmates. The war started over a matter of disrespect. As a result of the disrespect, seven fights have occurred in the last week, some involving weapons. The administration at Tarragon made the decision to round up all known members of both groups and place them in ADSEG pending investigation and possible transfer. It is Tarragon's policy to handle its trouble and not send it someplace else. They'll be in ADSEG for a while and it is Argus' job to run the recreation program without allowing any of the opposing members into the same recreation cages together. This is what Lieutenant Mack recruited him for.

Inmates in the ADSEG at Tarragon are locked in their cells for twenty three hours a day. They are afforded one hour of recreation in a twenty four hour period, five days a week. Anytime they are not behind a restraining door, they are restrained with handcuff restraints and escorted by an officer. Argus has two large recreation yards that can hold fifteen inmates each. There are also four single recreation cages for inmates under protective custody status and those who don't play well with others. These cages are smaller but still sufficient in size for one or two inmates to exercise in. It is Argus' job to compile a recreation list by going to each cell in the unit and asking if the inmates want recreation that day. Then he uses the list to create the recreation yards for the day, making sure that all inmates who are to be kept separated are not on recreation at the same time. It is a monumental task due to the abundance of separation issues.

He has a list of the members and associates of both gangs as well as notations on his recreation list regarding individual separations, "PC," protective custody and "OSO," out self only. From this, Argus compiles the lists of inmates who will go into each recreation cage at each hour of the day. On his first day in the unit, he looks at the paperwork and already has a headache. It is 5:45 am as Argus begins his tour of the four ranges in ADSEG with his recreation list in hand. At each cell he stops and asks the inmates if they want recreation. This is their only chance to give him a yes or no answer. Once the yards are compiled, there will be no adding of names. If an inmate decides he doesn't want to go out later, that is allowed. These are the rules and there is no deviation and no room for mistakes.

The Segregation Unit is comprised of four ranges with eighteen cells each. All the cells are at full capacity according to inmate status. Ranges "B" and "C" are on the main floor. Ranges "D" and "E" are upstairs. Argus starts at B-Range with Officer Brown at the restraining grill to cover his walk. Brownie and Argus are friends and he was glad to see Brown would be working with him this quarter.

At each cell, Argus stops and asks, "Recreation?"

He makes the proper notations according to the inmate's response. Some inmates have signs hanging on the bars made from notebook paper and pen which read yes or no to recreation. At these cells, Argus doesn't have to ask. He makes the rounds of B, C and D ranges without incident, slowly building his recreation list.

Argus and Brownie arrive at E-Range not knowing that the inmate drama is about to start. Brown keys Argus on to the range and he begins his walk. As he reaches cell ten, Argus looks into the cell and sees Inmate "Cigarette" sitting on his bunk. He is the lone occupant of the cell because he is on protective custody status. Inmate "Cigarette" looks at Argus with recognition. "Cigarette" is the inmate who tried to intimidate Argus during a cell search so long ago in Unit Thirteen. Argus asks "Cigarette" if he wants recreation.

"Cigarette" gets up and steps to the bars. "Yeah, I want rec."

Argus makes the notation and then moves on. After completing the tour, Argus formulates the inmate names into the various lists for the different recreation cages and at what times. There will be three yards or three hours of recreation to get completed today. With any luck, he'll have recreation completed by 1:00 pm.

He takes his list and tells the Segregation Number One Officer, Officer Grange that the list is ready. Argus and Officer Phan will start handcuffing inmates and moving them to the stairway while Brownie runs the cell control box. Today the upper ranges will go to recreation first. Tomorrow the lower ranges will go first. The two warring gangs are separated, one on the upper ranges and one on the lower ranges. Argus will fill the large recreation cages first, then the small cages. The three start on E-Range and handcuff the inmates going to the large cage. After the inmates are cuffed, Argus and Phan call out to Brownie for him to open the various cells. The inmates are lined up on the wall. Argus double checks the inmates in the line against his recreation list. Once this is completed, Brownie opens the restraining door and the inmates are led down the steps to the Recreation cages.

As they are leaving the range, Inmate "Cigarette" yells at Argus, "Hey! Antrim! What about me? I said I want rec."

Argus looks at "Cigarette" and says, "Yeah man, I'll be back in a second for you."

After the inmates are in the first large recreation cage, Argus and Phan go to D-Range and repeat the process with Brownie on the control box. The second large cage is filled. Now all Argus has to do is get the four single cages down and he'll settle in to watch the inmates exercise for an hour.

As the three officers hit the upstairs, Argus says, "Phan, would you go get Inmate 'Cigarette'? I'm going down D-Range and rec cell twelve in a small cage. Then we'll grab the last two singles."

Phan nods. "Sure thing Ant."

Brownie keys him onto D-Range and then Brownie and Phan head to E-Range.

Argus is about to put handcuffs on the inmates in cell twelve when Brownie yells from the restraining door, "Hey Ant! Better step over to E-Range."

Argus walks to the door and asks Brown, "What's up man?"

Brown keys the door and rolls his eyes. "It's 'Cigarette.' He says he's not going into a small cage. He wants to rec in a big cage."

Argus steps over and Brown keys him onto E-Range where he sees Phan standing in front of cell ten.

As soon as Argus is on the range, Inmate "Cigarette" begins yelling, "You ain't putting me in no small cage Antrim! Why I gotta go in a small one?"

He steps up in front of cell ten and looks at "Cigarette."

"You know why you have to rec in a small one. I'm not putting your business out on the walk man."

Inmate Cigarette looks at Argus with hate in his eyes. "That's bullshit man! You're just fuckin with me you bitch. I ain't goin then! Fuck you!"

Argus looks at "Cigarette" with disdain. "You're sure about that?"

Inmate "Cigarette" turns and walks toward his bunk. "Fuck you. Get from in front of my cell bitch."

Argus looks at Phan and says, "Okay, guess he ain't goin'."

The two start walking away.

Inmate "Cigarette" comes back to the bars and screams, "Antrim! I ever get ahold of you, I'ma beat the bark off your bitch ass! Just you wait motherfucker!"

Argus doesn't say anything in response as he and Phan exit the range. Over the next several days Argus runs the recreation without any major incidents. He encounters the usual complaints regarding the alternating schedule for the two gangs and whether it's fair that one group gets to exercise in the sun in the morning and the other has to exercise in the rain in the afternoon as if Argus can control the weather. Inmate "Cigarette" continues to refuse recreation and threaten Argus. It is Friday and Argus is looking forward to the weekend as he walks E-Range with his recreation list stopping at each cell with the usual question. As he reaches cell ten, Argus looks at Inmate "Cigarette" and asks if he wants recreation.

"Cigarette" looks at Argus with hate in his eyes and says, "Are you deaf motherfucker? I don't want your recreation. Why you keep askin' me?"

Argus sighs and looks down the range then back at "Cigarette". "I have to ask. It's my job. Why do you hate me so bad? I haven't done a thing to you man."

"Cigarette" gets up off the bed and approaches the bars. "I don't like the way you carry yourself Antrim. You disrespecting me with that small cage shit ain't gonna go unanswered. I'm gonna get your ass. Watch and see."

Argus looks at the inmate. "Well, that small cage shit is policy. Know what else is against policy? Threatening me every time I come on the range. Don't do it again."

"Cigarette" smiles and says, "What you gonna do bitch. Nothin' that's what."

Argus turns to continue his walk and replies over his shoulder, "Okay, don't say I didn't try to talk it out."

The inmate huffs and says, "Fuck you."

Argus has been thinking about this inmate's fixation on him. "Cigarette" is an unverified protective custody inmate. He refuses to go back to general population so he'll eventually have to be transferred which will solve this problem but Argus can't continue to allow this disrespect to go on. In fact, it's gone on too long as it is. He decides to start writing incident reports every time "Cigarette" threatens him, starting with this morning. Threatening an officer is a level two offense. The lieutenant has no choice but to send it to the Disciplinary Hearing Officer. Officer Phan is on the cell control box and has heard the whole conversation.

Argus exits the range and looks at Phan. "You hear him threaten me?"

Phan nods and says, "Yeah, every word."

Argus replies, "I'm going to put paper on him. Will you write a supporting memo for me?"

Phan smiles, "About time Ant. You put up with too much from that dude already."

Argus walks toward the stairs. "Yeah, well that's dead and stinking."

∞∞∞∞

Guy sits at the table holding his wife's hand as she looks at him in disbelief. Another box had shown up on his porch this morning just as his inmate worker forewarned. His confession to her is like a weight being lifted.

His wife looks at him with tears in her eyes and says, her voice thick, "Guy, you're not actually going to take it to them are you? Think about the other people working there. For God's sake, there could be anything in there."

Guy looks at his wife, "I have to. Don't you see, they'll turn me in and then I'm finished."

She looks at him, the tears having disappeared. "If you do this, we're finished."

He stands in the middle of his office waiting on the inmate. His wait ends with the sharp knock on the door and the inmate's smiling face in the window.

As he opens the door, the inmate walks in and smiles. "Guy, next time, I'd like you to have it in your hand so I don't have to keep asking for it. I'm starting to get annoyed."

Guy looks at the inmate and says, "There isn't going to be a next time. There isn't going to be a this time. My wife will leave me if I don't quit. I'm done. Do you hear me? Fucking done!"

The inmate looks at Guy and lowers his chin. "You sure about that my man? Because once I pass this message along, there ain't no turning back."

Guy nods and says, his voice low, "Now get the fuck out of my office and get to work or I'll have them put you in ADSEG and take the consequences."

The inmate leaves the office shaking his head. Guy sits in his chair and tries to take a sip of his coffee but his hands are shaking so badly he spills it on his shirt. He can barely hold back the tears. That night an envelope goes out in the unit mail to the Investigative Office with a letter, a small packet of marijuana and a stick of gum. The next day, Guy enters the Front Lobby on his way to the Linen Factory carrying his lunch box and thermos. At the Front Desk, he's met by the Investigative Agent and two Investigative Technicians. He is not surprised and will never see the inside of Tarragon Penitentiary again.

∞∞∞∞

It is 1:45 pm and Argus has just escorted the last of the recreation yards back to their cells and retrieved the handcuff restraints. As he puts the restraints back into the expanded metal box made to hold the ADSEG equipment, Phan grabs his lunchbox and waves goodbye. His relief has arrived. Argus has no relief but before he can depart the unit, he has to complete the paperwork documenting each inmate's recreation or refusal and the times this occurred. Argus is mentally tired and his uniform is soaked through from the heat and humidity of the unit. Today is shower day for the lower ranges. As he prepares to finish this last step of his day he'd like nothing more than to be finished, but as the saying goes, "If it's not written down, it didn't happen." Argus grabs the binder which holds the segregation sheets that document everything about an inmate's stay in seg to include meals, separations, recreation and status reviews by the lieutenant. Using his recreation lists, Argus begins to notate the recreation participation of each inmate in the proper column.

As he turns the page to notate the next inmate's information, he

197

hears Control transmit, "Control to all portable radio units, staff needs assistance in Unit Three. Inmates have officer trapped in his office."

Argus closes the book and gets ready to respond. In the event of a call for "additional assistance" staff from ADSEG will respond as a second wave.

He waits by the door as he hears several garbled transmissions and thinks, "This sounds bad."

Argus adrenaline starts to flow as he and Grange wait by the ADSEG door. Grange is the Segregation Number One Officer and will have to key Argus out of the unit.

Argus and Grange look at each other as they hear Lieutenant Jennings transmit, "Operations to Control we need additional assistance, multiple inmates with weapons. Tone SWAT."

Grange keys Argus out of the unit and he runs down the stairs two at a time as his pager starts going off.

He hits the bottom of the stairs and starts pounding on the door yelling, "Staff on the door!"

The West Seg Officer keys the door and Argus begins to sprint to Unit Three along with additional staff. What he sees as he enters the unit is not something he will soon forget. Two inmates are holding the Unit Officer's Office door closed. Argus would later find out they did this to keep the Unit Officer from being injured while they put their work in. The noise is deafening as the additional officers enter the unit. Several melees are occurring at once throughout the unit between multiple inmates. There are inmates on the upper tier throwing fire extinguishers and trash cans at responding staff. Argus sees an officer using a range fan to fend off the projectiles. He has learned through experience that it is never wise to run head long into an incident. Exit doors have a way of disappearing when you find yourself in the middle of the wreck. Argus steps to the side before heading out from under the upper tier walkway with a sick feeling in his gut. This is a habit he has developed to keep from getting anything dropped on his head from above. Today, the habit has paid off.

Argus steps out from under the walkway and looks up to see an inmate holding a large range trash can on the upper rail.

He points at the inmate and yells, "I got your face motherfucker! Put that down!"

Argus bolts for the stairway to the upper tier and looks into the Laundry Room as he nears the stairway. There he sees an inmate sitting against the washing machine with blood coming from his eye. The inmate looks back at Argus as he pauses for a second but the unit has to be secured before any assistance can be given. As he mounts the stairs, other officers chase the inmates away from the Unit Officer's Office. The Unit Officer uses his keys to rack the ranges so the inmates can be locked down. Argus reaches the inmate with the trash can and orders him to place his hands on the wall. The inmate smiles at Argus and throws the trash can on the ground in between him and Argus, trash spilling everywhere.

Argus advances toward the inmate who continues to smile as he backs away. For a brief moment, Argus expects the inmate to run but realizes he is backing toward the end cell on the upper tier. The inmate backs into the cell and continues backing until he is all the way inside. Argus looks at the inmate with disgust and closes the door, hearing the satisfying sound of the lock engage.

Argus tells the inmate, "I'll be back for you later."

The inmates are realizing that staff have arrived in the unit in sufficient numbers and are doing the math as they begin to step into their cells, their work completed. Several inmates are being handcuffed by other staff members and led from the unit. Once outside in the corridor, they are lined up against the wall.

Argus starts at the end of the upper tier and begins to close cell doors, hearing the snap of the lock. Other staff members are working their way around the upper tier on the opposite side of the unit. More staff members are working their way around the flat. After the unit is secured, Argus descends the stairs to the flat and sees Pete Wicker talking with Lieutenant Jennings. Argus looks into the Laundry Room but the inmate with the bloody eye is gone.

Argus thinks, "Probably already in Medical."

He steps over to the two and says, "Excuse me LT, I got one upstairs who was going to drop a trash can on our heads as we came in. He's locked in the end cell."

Lieutenant Jennings motions with his head. "Okay, Wicker, go with Ant to take the guy to the ADSEG Annex."

The ADSEG Annex is a unit with twenty cells located above the Hospital that is utilized for just this sort of incident. Lieutenant Jennings has made the call to open the additional unit. Pete Wicker is one of Argus' best friends and also a mentor. He is also a former Marine. They ascend the stairs with the Unit OIC and find the inmate sitting on the bottom bunk of the cell. The Unit Officer keys the door and Pete orders the inmate to stand and back toward the door to which he complies. Once he reaches the door, Argus applies handcuff restraints behind the inmate's back and grabs the inmate's elbow.

As he does this, the inmate looks over his shoulder and says, "You got it all wrong officers."

Argus looks at the inmate and says, "I don't want to hear it. I know what I saw."

Pete and Argus escort the inmate from the unit. As they exit the unit, Argus looks down the corridor and sees seven members of the SWAT team coming down the corridor in civilian clothes and tac vests. He smiles at the sight of his brothers and is glad they are here.

As they pass, Nash says, "Hey Ant, what's going on?"

Argus motions with his head over his shoulder. "Major wreck brother. Lieutenant Jennings is in the unit."

As Argus and Wicker get to the top of the stairs, they find Officer Skim and Grass in the unit getting it ready to be occupied.

Skim says, "I'll be with you in minute, guys. I've almost got the sheets and towels in the cells." Argus and Pete stand and wait until Skim is ready, and then they have the inmate strip so a visual search can be performed. Once that is completed the inmate is given underwear, socks and a jumpsuit to put on. Argus bags the clothes the inmate was wearing to take back to the unit and place in his property. Other staff and the inmates in their charge are arriving at the door. Each inmate will go through the same process to be admitted to the unit. Throughout the afternoon and well into the evening, Argus and the other officers escort inmates to the ADSEG Annex and pack inmate property. The inmates who are not escorted from the unit are fed bag lunches for the evening meal and remain locked down for the rest of the night.

As Argus drags a bag of property to the flat, he hears an inmate inside a cell remark, "Man, I been at a lot of joints but I ain't never seen no shit like that."

Argus thinks, "Yeah? Welcome to Tarragon."

∞∞∞∞

It has been a month and a half since Argus assumed the duties as Recreation Officer in ADSEG and as with most things, time has made the job easier. He has a process and the process has worked successfully. Over time, various members of each gang have been filtered back out into general population which has also eased the overcrowding in the unit. The situation with Inmate "Cigarette" has continued to be an issue but Argus has a plan for him too. He'll use policy to, if not manage this inmate then manage the situation. Argus has written at least ten incident reports on the inmate for threatening an officer. The inmate discipline policy and the sanctions imposed by the DHO haven't curtailed Inmate "Cigarette's" threats. In fact, the threats have escalated from physical beating to threats on Argus' life, but Argus knows that with each incident report, the inmate's security level rises. Tarragon is a maximum security penitentiary, but there is one type of prison that is higher in security. A Control Unit Prison is basically a giant segregation unit. All prisoners at this type of facility are locked in their cells twenty three hours a day. Argus' goal is to help Inmate "Cigarette" with a transfer to one of these facilities and he'll get it accomplished by the inmate's own hand.

This is the situation and the plan as Argus escorts the last two recreation inmates back to their cells on E-Range. There is a new officer on the control box. His name is Officer Dunsel and he is young and new to segregation. He has drawn a relief post in ADSEG and works on Brown and Phan's days off.

As Argus reaches the inmate's cells, he calls out, "Open eight and nine!"

Cells eight and nine open and the inmates step into the cells.

Argus calls out, "Close eight and nine!"

The cells close and Argus removes the handcuff restraints from the inmates.

As he is completing the removal of the set of handcuffs from the last inmate, someone from down range yells, "Open ten!"

To Argus' surprise, cell ten begins to open with a mechanical whine. He isn't angry at Dunsel because the inmates try this all the time and usually the officer on the box knows to ignore the inmate's ruse, however, Dunsel is new. Argus is standing just to the side of ten. It is Inmate "Cigarette's cell and he is not restrained.

The inmate has been threatening Argus for weeks and now his cell door is fully open. There is nothing in the way of him trying to make good on his threats and whichever inmate called for his cell to be opened is trying to help him with that. Argus stands at cell nine and decides to wait. If the inmate comes out of his cell, Argus will deal with him but that isn't what happens.

Inmate "Cigarette" begins to scream, "Close this motherfuckin' door! You tryin' to get a motherfucker's ass kicked! Close this fuckin' door!"

Over the course of many weeks, Argus has put up with a great amount of disrespect from this inmate and in a penitentiary respect is everything whether you are an officer or an inmate. Argus steps in front of "Cigarette's" cell and calmly looks in. He has decided, if it's going to happen then it will happen. What Argus sees causes a chuckle to escape.

Inmate "Cigarette" is flattened against the right wall of the cell, screaming as he looks at Argus, "Shut this motherfuckin' door!"

Argus looks in at the inmate for another second to let him know that he is in no hurry nor is he the least bit intimidated.

He turns his head in the direction of Dunsel and calls out, "Close ten!" The door closes with a grinding mechanical sound as Argus stairs at "Cigarette." The inmate sits down on his bunk and looks at the floor. Argus shakes his head and walks off the range. As he exits, he hears what he knows will follow from the other inmates on the range.

A chorus of cat calls and insults begin. "You check in, PC motherfucker! You had the man and you did nothing! You coward cocksucker!"

Argus smiles as he thinks, "Be careful what you ask for Inmate "Cigarette." Now you've gone and got your nuts clipped."

He knows the inmates will ride "Cigarette" for the rest of the time he is at Tarragon.

Argus looks at Dunsel as they walk away from the range and says in a low voice, "Only my voice. Unless you see me call for the cell to open, never flip a switch. No big deal. It happens but always take a second to be sure before you open a cell in here."

Dunsel looks at Argus apologetically. "Sorry Ant."

Argus claps him on the shoulder. "No big deal brother. Dead and stinkin'."

∞∞∞∞

It is Thursday and has been two weeks since the incident on E-Range. The threats from Inmate "Cigarette" have stopped completely which is fine with Argus. He isn't trying to beef with anyone. Argus is like every other hack in this place, it's just his job to be here and enforce the rules. As Argus stands and watches the inmates do burpees, he considers Inmate "Cigarette." The inmate has stopped communicating at all. He won't even look at Argus or respond when asked if he wants recreation. This is fine with Argus but also eerie. Argus can't help but feel that the sudden change in behavior means something and he is missing it.

He looks at his watch and yells to the yard at the end of the cages, "Five minutes fellas, start wrapping it up."

He gives them this warning in case they have something special they want to do at the end of their workout. As the inmates finish up, Argus starts organizing the handcuff restraints and radios ADSEG, "Antrim to Grange, cuffing the first yard."

Brown and Phan show up just as Argus finishes applying the last set of restraints. He takes a final check and makes sure all the inmates are properly restrained then keys the yard. The inmates step out one at a time and are pat searched then lined up along the wall. Once all the inmates are out, they are escorted upstairs to ADSEG and their respective ranges. This yard is off of E-Range. Argus and Phan go down range with Brown on the cell control box. The inmates are put away in their cells and then the trio head back down and repeat the process for the D-Range yard. These inmates are also put away without anything out of the ordinary.

Argus thinks as he does this, "Just the way I like it. No wrinkles." They make one more trip downstairs and escort the three single cages back to their cells. Phan escorts one inmate to E-Range and Argus escorts two to D-Range.

Brown is once again on the box as Argus yells, "Open four!"

Cell four opens and the inmate walks into the cell while the other inmate stands facing the wall.

Argus yells, "Close four!" The cell closes and Brown heads over to E-Range to control the cell for Phan as Argus removes the handcuffs then escorts the other inmate to cell seventeen. By the time Argus makes it to cell seventeen with the other inmate, Brown has returned and the process is repeated.

As Argus removes the last set of handcuffs for the day, he feels the extra tension release and thinks, "One more day and I'm off for the weekend."

One more day without an incident where the bar is zero mistakes. If the wrong guy goes in the wrong cage, it could mean someone being hurt or killed. He feels drained from the heat of the unit and the stress of the post and is glad to turn to exit the range.

As he heads for the restraining door, the inmate in cell nine holds a paper up which reads, "I need to talk to you."

Argus keeps on walking and exits the range on his way downstairs to the office. Brown and Phan stay upstairs to continue running showers for the upper ranges. As Argus starts completing the segregation sheets, he thinks about how he will get the inmate off of D-Range so that they can speak without the other inmates becoming suspicious and settles on using the Law Library in the unit as a ruse.

Every inmate in ADSEG is afforded the use of the Law Library just the same as an inmate in general population. This is a privilege that cannot be denied to the inmate and holds the same importance in policy as food and recreation. When an inmate wants time in the Law Library, they put in a written request to staff and are afforded one hour with each request. Their name is placed on a list which staff uses to ensure all inmates wanting the privilege are afforded it equally. After Argus finishes his paperwork for the day, he returns to D-Range and steps to cell nine. Inmate "Sapo" is the only occupant of the cell and has the status of out self only.

Argus looks at the inmate. "Sapo,' your name came up on the Law Library. Do you want to go?"

The inmate realizes the ruse and steps right into role. "Yeah boss, let me get my stuff."

The inmate collects a pen and notebook then backs up to the bars to be handcuffed.

Argus yells, "On the box, open nine!"

Brownie flips the switch and the cell grinds open. The inmate backs out as Argus puts a hand on the cuffs to guide him.

Argus yells, "On the box, close nine!"

The cell closes with the same mechanical grinding. He escorts the inmate off of the range and down the stairs to the small expanded metal cage that serves as the Law Library in ADSEG. Argus keys the inmate into the cage and secures the door before removing the restraints. The Law Library is in the back of the unit past the supply room so Argus and the inmate are alone. The inmate turns around and looks at Argus expectantly.

Argus raises his eyebrows and asks, "Okay, what's on your mind?"

What comes next is anything but what he expects.

The inmate lowers his voice, instinctively looking around. "They're planning to kill you, boss."

He looks at the inmate in disbelief, smiles and says, "Bullshit."

The inmate lowers his chin slightly and says, "I'm being straight with you Officer Antrim. They've got a zip gun and that bitch in cell ten on Easy Range is the shooter."

Argus looks into the inmate's eyes and his gaze doesn't waiver as he recalls the change in "Cigarette's" behavior.

Argus takes a deep breath before asking any questions. "Okay, how do you know?"

The inmate leans forward. "I heard them talking through the vents. They smuggled the gun into the unit in the bottom of the laundry cart. It's in the unit now but I don't know where. The orderly's going to pass it to him when they're ready."

Argus mouth tightens. "Who's they and why me?"

The inmate half grins and says, "What do you mean why you? Fuck man, you took that dude's manhood Antrim. He'll never be able to walk any yard after that shit. Those dudes on the range hooked him up. I don't know why unless it was for the money. He paid big for the gun."

Argus takes another deep breath. The story is tracking so far but he knows from experience a prison zip gun isn't a run of the mill item found inside and usually not very powerful. Argus looks at the inmate and says, "So they shoot me with the end of a pen. That's not gonna put me down."

The inmate shakes his head, "No boss, this one's made with a bullet."

Argus laughs, "You think I'm an idiot. A bullet? Okay, how did they get ammunition inside Tarragon?"

Now the inmate raises his eyebrows and looks straight at Argus. "Ain't no secret why they walked that factory foreman out boss. The ammunition wasn't the right kind so they had to take it apart but, the zip is made with a bullet and powder. They're going to end you."

Argus looks around trying to make sure he asks everything he should. "When are they going to do it?"

The inmate replies, "Don't know but the thing is in the unit so it's going to be soon."

Argus looks sideways at the inmate. "So, why are you telling me. What's in it for you?"

The inmate looks down at the floor. "I didn't figure you remembered me. I brought you the message from 'Bellychain' when you was working the East End. Remember? 'Bellychain' said you was a stand up dude and your word was good. He respected you for that. You don't deserve what's getting ready to happen man. That punk brought this shit on himself. You just do your job. I ain't no snitch but this ain't right."

Argus looks at his watch and realizes that their hour is up. "Okay, time's up. Thanks for the heads up. If you hear when they're planning on hitting me, let me know. Just show me a sign like you did today."

The inmate nods and turns around to be handcuffed.

As Argus escorts the inmate out of the rear of the unit, he finds Brown and Phan in the office. "Hey Brownie, mind taking this guy back to D-Range for me, I still got some paperwork before I leave."

Brown nods and along with Phan takes the inmate back to the range. It would've looked suspicious for Argus to take the inmate back. He sits down in the unit office at the typewriter while still trying to put everything he's learned in some type of lucid order. The tale is outlandish but also has a ring of truth. Argus tries to think of the angle for the inmate in telling him and can't come up with one. The inmate is going to be transferred. He didn't ask for anything. The inmates know Argus won't be intimidated off of a unit so, why, other than the reason given?

Argus types a memorandum detailing his discussion with the inmate for Lieutenant Mack.

He adds every detail and suspicion, also adding, "This information is still unsubstantiated, therefore, it is my sincere request that I be permitted to remain at my post."

Argus thinks as he signs the memo, "Mack knows I'll pitch an absolute fit if he tries to pull me. They can't let any officer be pushed out of a unit. If they did, the inmates would be making threats all the time. No, Mack won't pull me. I have to believe he won't do that to me."

Brown and Phan walk back in the office as Argus is getting ready to leave. Grange walks in behind the two, making the office seem more crowded. Argus stops. These are his friends who he trusts with his life. He needs to let them know a zip gun might be in the unit. He looks at the three and says in a low voice, "Close the office door. I'm going to let you read something but it stays in this office. Understand?"

They nod and Argus produces the memo. After they finish reading it, they look at each other in disbelief.

Argus looks at his friends and says, "I got to bolt fellas. Remember, that shit's just between us. See you tomorrow."

Grange keys Argus out and watches as he descends the stairs, a look of concern on his face. Lieutenant Mack is in the Operations Lieutenant's Office when Argus enters.

He looks at Mack. "Hey LT, can we talk for a minute?"

Mack smiles at Argus and says, "Sure man, step in my office."

The two go into the Segregation Lieutenant's Office and Argus lays the information out for Mack.

Argus finishes by saying, "It could be a bunch of bullshit LT."

Lieutenant Mack strokes his handlebar mustache, "I'll pass this up the chain Ant. Did you let the other guys know?"

Argus nods. Lieutenant Mack leans back in his chair, "Okay Ant, see you tomorrow."

Argus leaves the Lieutenant's Office and heads toward Control wondering what tomorrow will bring. He's rolled it over and over in his mind and knows the inmate's information tracks.

Argus thinks, "So if they have it in the unit, it'll be soon, maybe tomorrow. The orderlies are in on it because they helped smuggle the thing in. Then again, maybe this is all bullshit and they're trying to see if I got sack."

He starts his truck and heads for the Training Center to punish the heavy bag. The dragon is always hungry at Tarragon and he was fed well today. He arrives home in his sweaty t-shirt as the sun is setting. Sixty minutes on the bag has exhausted the rage for now and he feels fit to be around his girls. Lynn meets him at the door with a kiss and ushers him inside to the smell of nachos for dinner. With what transpired today, Argus had forgotten that this was Thursday and therefore, "Nachos night." Olivia is sitting on the couch watching television. He looks at her and wonders where the time has gone. She is growing up and he feels like he has missed a large part of it somewhere. The nachos are ready so Argus goes into the bathroom and splashes cold water on his face then returns to the table where Lynn and Olivia are waiting. Nachos night has become a tradition and Argus looks forward to spending this time with his wife and daughter. Lynn always out does herself with a large plate of chips piled high with salsa and sour cream. The vegetables are cut fresh and the various cheeses give the meal a special touch.

Argus looks at his girls as he eats and silently hopes that they know how much he loves them. He hopes that he has done a good job of being a husband and father. The danger of not coming out of Tarragon is just a part of the job every day that you walk through the grills but tonight, that solemn fact is more pronounced for him. The weight of the fact that this might be the last meal he shares with them almost brings tears to his eyes. He pushes these thoughts down into the box where everything else goes and tries to act normal.

Lynn looks across the table and asks, "Is everything alright Argus? You look like you've lost your best friend over there."

Argus looks at her and smiles, "Oh yeah babe. I'm just a little tired.

I'm thinking how good these nachos taste."

After dinner, the three of them watch a movie on television and Argus has a second beer which is a rarity.

They spend the evening as a family and all the while Argus is thinking, "This is where I am happiest."

The next morning, Argus gets ready for work as usual. Before he leaves, he kisses Lynn and whispers in her ear that he loves her more than anything.

She replies sleepily, "I love you too Argus." He steps into Olivia's room and kisses her on the head then heads out the door. On the drive to work he feels tension in his gut like he's never felt. With each passing mile, his anxiety builds. As he passes the Training Center, Tarragon comes into view. Argus looks at the place like he hasn't looked at it in a long time and notices the malevolence it exudes. His rage builds as he thinks of the men waiting for him there and what they are planning. As he pulls in to the penitentiary drive, Argus realizes he is clenching his teeth. His grip on the steering wheel is so tight his arms ache. Argus pulls into a parking spot and turns his truck off. He takes a deep breath to calm himself and looks in the rear view mirror.

What he sees there is defiance as he says to his reflection, "You can't let them put you down. If they shoot, you've got to stay on your feet. You will walk off that range Argus."

He takes another deep breath of the morning air, gets out and walks toward Tower One thinking, "Today I show them who I am."

As he enters ADSEG, Brown is already in the unit. Argus looks around. "Where's Dunsel?"

Brown shrugs his shoulders, "Not here yet."

Argus looks at Brown and motions with his head toward B-Range. "Okay Brownie, wanna key the grill so I can run this recreation board. It's my Friday."

Argus grabs the clip board and Brown follows him to the range. He looks at Argus as he keys the door. No words are exchanged. Argus walks the range with a stoic demeanor, stopping at each cell and asking the usual question. Inside, the adrenaline is flowing which only serves to strengthen his quiet resolve. Argus feels mean. It is something that has grown inside him through the years in this place. It is an ugly, dangerous thing. Argus tours B, C and D Ranges in this manner with Brown on the door and Argus on the range. As they approach E-Range, Brown reaches for the clipboard.

Argus quickly pulls it out of Brown's reach. "What the fuck you

208

think you're doing?"

Brown looks at Argus and says in a low voice, "C'mon man, let me run the board on this range."

Argus shakes his head and smiles, "No way in hell brother. Key the fuckin' door."

Argus motions with his head. Brown unlocks the door and swings it open as Argus leans toward him and whispers, "If they shoot me, I'll get off the range on my own. There's no reason for you to get shot too."

Argus thinks about Lynn and hopes she knows how deeply he loves her.

He steps inside the grill and thinks, "Well, I've always heard God hates a coward."

He walks the range slowly, head erect and stops at each cell, looking in and asking the question. Argus gets to cell ten and asks "Cigarette" if he wants recreation. The inmate is standing with his back to Argus and refuses to answer. Argus stands on the range looking in the cell, then turns and moves to cell eleven, then twelve and on down the range. With each step, he expects to hear the sound of the round going off.

With each step he thinks, "That's right, shoot me in the back. You ain't even got the nuts to face me and do it you coward piece of shit."

At the end of the range, Argus puts the clipboard under his left arm and walks back toward the restraining door. He walks slowly and looks in each cell as he passes.

He feels the heat in his face and thinks, "Now's your chance you fucking cowards."

He makes it to the door but no shot comes. Argus steps off the range having proven his point. He isn't going anywhere and he isn't afraid. Throughout the rest of the day, Argus is in such a state of heightened awareness that his skin almost tingles. He runs the recreation as usual without a hitch.

As the last inmate is escorted to his assigned cell Argus thinks, "Well, if they're going to do it today, they're running out of time."

He removes the handcuffs and steps off the range to do his paperwork.

Grange comes into the office. "You okay Ant?"

Argus looks up and smiles. "Doing good brother. How 'bout you?"

Grange smiles back and says, "Yeah man, I already knew that." Argus looks at the clock, only a half hour over today.

He thinks, "Not bad. Not bad at all."

Argus finishes filling out the last form and closes the book with a sigh. "You can stick a fork in me Grange I am done."

Grange laughs and moves to the door to key Argus out of the unit. "See you on Monday brother. Have a good weekend."

Argus looks back, "Yeah man, watch your six."

It is Sunday morning and Argus is sitting at the kitchen table watching Lynn make breakfast. The smell of bacon and eggs makes his stomach growl as he sips his coffee.

Lynn looks at Argus and smiles. "Want to go get the kid up? It's ready."

Argus gets up and starts for Olivia's room when the phone rings. Argus and Lynn look at each other. No one ever calls on Sunday morning. Lynn gives Argus the look. "If its work, the answer is no. I want us to spend the day together."

Argus picks up the phone. "Hello."

It is Officer Omar on the other end of the line. "Ant, its Omar."

Argus looks at Lynn and shrugs his shoulders. "Hey Omar, what's up man?"

Omar chuckles and replies, "They found that zip last night. Thought you'd want to know. It was on E-Range in between the ceiling and the metal duct work that runs down the length of the range."

Argus looks at Lynn and winks. "How far down the range?"

Omar sighs, "About midway. I'm not sure."

Argus wrinkles his eyebrows. "Where are you working today?"

Omar laughs, "Control man. I got a bird's eye view of everything today. Lobo was working morning watch in ADSEG last night and found it when he shook down the range. Now the Investigative Office is in here jumping through their ass. They brought one inmate straight from ADSEG this morning and marched him right out the front grill and into a van. Warden to Warden transfer to the Control Unit down South. He didn't look happy."

Omar laughs again. Argus smiles at Lynn. "Thanks buddy. I appreciate the info."

Argus hangs the telephone up. He likes Officer Lobo. The guy is all about business. A former cop from Ohio, he'd joined the Agency a few years before Argus started. It hits him that his friend may have saved his life. Lynn looks at Argus expectantly and asks, "Well?"

He looks at her and grins. "Just some bullshit work stuff babe. Let me get Olivia. I'm starving."

Argus spends the rest of the day with his family. Today, his heart is lighter.

It has been two weeks since that Sunday telephone call. Argus is walking through the Front Lobby of Tarragon on his way to the Training Center to work the heavy bag.

As he passes the desk, Hannah Depps steps out of the Investigative Office and says, "Hey Argus, got a second?"

Argus turns, "Sure Hannah, what's up?"

She motions him to come over to the office door and leans in confidentially. "Thought you'd be interested. We sent the zip off to the ISP Crime Lab. They tested it and it fired. They said it discharged with a fair amount of force."

Argus thanks her and heads out of Tarragon. As he drives to the Training Center, Argus thinks, "I came close. The reaper's always on your shoulder in this place. If Lobo hadn't been on the job, there's no telling what might have happened."

He thinks about "Cigarette" and the dirty factory foreman and feels the seething rage inside. Argus peels off his shirt and puts on his bag gloves. He smells smoke and the dragon roars.

Chapter 10
The talons are sharpened

He presses the button on the coffee pot starting the machine on its journey to producing the brain jarring elixir Argus depends on. The aroma of the coffee reaches his nostrils making him unconsciously inhale. He'll need all the help he can get. An hour ago, Lieutenant Grant had phoned him with the offer of an overtime shift in Disciplinary Segregation as a third man. Apparently, the inmates are unhappy with the choice Lieutenant Mack has made for range orderly and have been trashing the range all night. They have set several small fires out on the range and have been throwing fruit at the officers intermittently. Lieutenant Grant is putting a third officer in the unit for the weekend.

The inmates in DS are inmates who have been seen by the Disciplinary Hearing Officer and have received sanctions for allegations of misconduct. As part of those sanctions, they will be locked down for a certain period of time with reduced privileges and less personal property. In this unit, there is only one range orderly that cleans the range and folds laundry. This inmate is housed in the first cell on the range. Historically, the way the inmates on the range mess with the orderly is to trash his range. From what Lieutenant Grant has told Argus this morning, they are definitely unhappy with this orderly. Argus will work from 8:00 am to 4:00 pm today as an extra in the unit which in his opinion is gravy overtime. He puts on his uniform and makes some peanut butter sandwiches and a thermos of coffee, goes in and kisses Lynn and then Olivia goodbye and heads out the door to his truck.

The drive to the penitentiary takes Argus about fifteen minutes. He pulls into the Staff Parking Lot and exits his vehicle like he's done hundreds of times before. Officer Laundry greets Argus at Tower One in his usual jovial manner. "Antrim, what are you doing here?"

Argus looks up and grins as he yells, "OT my friend!"

Laundry looks down and the gate buzzes. "Well, pull the fucking gate! I got things to do!"

Argus just laughs and shakes his head thinking, "Laundry is a fucking classic."

As he enters the Lieutenant's Office, Argus sees Lieutenants Grant and Atkins. Grant has worked from midnight to 8:00 am and Atkins is his relief. They are in the middle of passing down information so Argus doesn't stay and just lets them know he is there. He heads across the Main Corridor and has the West Seg Officer key him into the DS Unit sally port.

He steps in and yells, "Staff on the door!"

Rob Odenburg steps around the corner and keys Argus into the unit.

Rob is one of Argus' best friends at Tarragon. They went to high school together but weren't friends then. They are friends now and Argus likes working with Rob. They think alike and have the same way of doing the job. As he enters the unit, he looks down the range and sees a small insidious fire about midway down the range. It looks like a few pieces of notebook paper.

Rob looks at Argus and smiling says, "Welcome Argus, it's your turn friend."

Argus looks at Rob quizzically. "My turn for what?"

Rob chuckles, "We've been taking turns going down range and putting the fires out."

He smiles, "Remember to duck."

Argus takes his lunch box and thermos around the corner and deposits them in the office, saying hello to Hibben, then comes out and goes to the range door where Rob is waiting.

He looks at his friend, smiles and motions with his head as if to say, "Okay, let's get this party started."

Rob keys the door and Argus picks the fire extinguisher up and steps down the range staying up against the wall away from the bars.

As he walks, he hears an inmate from one of the cells say, "Get ready, here he comes."

They are laughing and having a good time with this. Argus sprays the fire with the water extinguisher successfully extinguishing the flames.

As Argus turns to leave the range, a cup full of water comes out of the cell he is in front of. He dodges it and keeps moving.

Odenburg yells from the grill, "Duck Ant!" Argus instinctively ducks his head and raises his shoulders. An apple smacks the wall in front of him showering Argus with the pulp. This is how the morning progresses. Argus, Rob and the Number One, Hibben covering each other as they take turns walking the range. Hibben calls the

Lieutenant's Office and reports that the inmates are assaultive as a unit. Lieutenant Atkins consults with the weekend Duty Officer and authorizes Hibben to feed bag lunches for the noon and evening meal.

Argus is happy about this development thinking, "I sure as fuck wasn't looking forward to passing out sixty six plastic trays full of food they can throw on us."

Rob tells Hibben, "Good call man. Bologna isn't near as messy as mashed potatoes." They all laugh.

The inmates call a halt to the demonstration long enough to receive their noon meal of bologna and cheese but once fed, they resume the shenanigans. All three of the officer's uniforms are a mess. Sometimes they're successful in dodging the fruit and water, sometimes not. Hibben reports the continued disruptive behavior to Lieutenant Atkins who responds to DS. He sees the condition of the unit and the officers. Without saying a word, he goes into the office and calls the weekend Duty Officer. The WDO is the Warden's designee on the weekend and is usually a Unit Manager. Atkins returns from the office and joins Argus, Hibben and Odenburg at the grill.

Hibben looks at the Operations Lieutenant and asks, "What's the word LT?"

Atkins looks at Hibben with a grin as he says, "Man said this is a group demonstration. He's going to contact the Associate Warden of Custody. He said he'll call me back."

Argus looks down the range and sees a small fire near the box car restraining door.

He picks up the extinguisher and nods in that direction. "Well boss man, time to get back to work."

No call comes and Lieutenant Atkins returns to his office, but an hour later the Associate Warden of Custody arrives in the unit. He is wearing blue jeans, a polo shirt and loafers. AW Law is a former hack who rose through the ranks. He knows what it is like to work a housing unit and he hasn't forgotten where he came from. Argus likes the man. He is personable and treats an officer with respect. The AW steps in the unit and looks at the three officers. Their uniforms are wet and stained and their eyes look tired but they still have smiles on their faces.

He thinks, "Resilient motherfuckers" and smiles.

He feels a sense of pride and regret at the same time. They're Tarragon hacks with a reputation of being the toughest throughout the agency and he is proud of them but he sees that this situation has been allowed to go on too long. The agency is changing and not for the better. Too many "administrators" moving up in the ranks and making policy decisions about things they have no real world experience in. Staff shortages, overcrowding and the constant violence that comes with it all make for a recipe that can bring a correctional complement to its breaking point.

He smiles at the three, "I heard you guys have had a pretty rough day today."

They all nod and smile Hibben saying, "That's one way of putting it sir."

He looks at Hibben, "Okay, give me a report of what's gone on up to now."

Hibben looks at Argus and Rob then back at the AW.

"Well sir, the inmates have been disruptive and assaultive in a coordinated effort all day. The assaults have been minor and the fires they've started have been small but they refuse to stop. They're mad over the choice of the range orderly. It seems they don't like him."

Hibben raises his eyebrows and shrugs his shoulders. The AW nods his head and steps to the grill, "This is AW Law! This crap stops now!"

Then a voice comes from down range. "Fuck you Law! You ain't runnin this unit, we are!"

Argus smiles as he thinks, "That has got to be the stupidest thing I've ever heard an inmate say."

The AW doesn't respond but just walks away from the grill saying, "Excuse me gentleman, I need to make a call."

Five minutes later Argus' SWAT pager begins to buzz. The AW comes back from the office and tells Argus, "Go to the Armory with Lieutenant Atkins and get enough progressive restraints for the entire unit. Also get enough soft restraints for every man in here."

Hibben keys Argus into the sally port and locks the door.

Argus pounds on the door and yells, "Staff on the door!"

Within minutes the West Seg Officer keys Argus out of the unit. Lieutenant Atkins meets Argus in the Main Corridor and they head for the Armory. Inside the Armory, they fill two large equipment bags with the restraints. The SWAT Team starts to arrive and helps with carrying the bags into the institution. Nash looks at the LT and asks, "What's going on LT?"

Lieutenant Atkins gives the members a rundown of the situation. "The inmates in DS have finally fucked up enough that the AW is going to roll on the whole unit."

Lieutenant Sena has arrived and starts organizing the responding

215

members into three teams of five. Argus is kicking himself because he is working the unit so it is against policy for him to participate in the actual use of force. He knows that Hibben is feeling the same way. Their role will just be support for the entry teams. They all enter DS in a group and start suiting up. The plan is a simple one. Starting at cell two, the teams will start making calculated use of force entries into each cell. There will be two teams on point and one team in reserve which will rotate after each entry thereby providing a fresh group of operators with each entry. Paperwork for every inmate in the unit is generated. This will be used in one briefing as the calculated use of force will be ongoing from start to finish.

Lieutenant Atkins looks at Hibben. "Make sure we have plenty of fresh batteries for the cameras."

The use of force will be filmed in its entirety. They all know that a camera is a correctional officer's best friend when it comes to use of force. As the staff entered the unit, the inmates saw the writing on the wall. Now as Argus looks down range, he can hear the sound of ripping fabric and sees the inmates tying the doors to their cells shut. A 911 rescue knife is produced from the equipment cage so the teams can cut their way into the cells as needed.

He hears AW Law tell Lieutenant Sena, "If they fight, four point them on the bed with soft restraints. If they lie down when ordered and comply with the entry, they go in progressive restraints."

Progressive restraints are simply a belly chain, handcuffs and leg irons. Argus starts getting the restraints lined out. He'll go down range with the teams and hand restraints to the operators as needed. Officer Hibben being the one with the most experience will be on the cell control box. When the Lieutenant yells for the cell to be opened, there will be no room for a delay or a mistake. The inmates in a cell midway down the range pull a sprinkler head loose and the range starts flooding.

Argus hears a voice from down range yell, "How about a warning you stupid ass!"

The inmates start scrambling to get their personal property off of the floor. Odenburg is smiling as he runs for the laundry room to get a few blankets to lay on the floor as a dam to slow the water from its inevitable arrival in the Main Corridor. Argus opens the pipe chase but Atkins holds up his hand.

"Hold on Antrim, let it run for a few seconds."

Almost immediately the stench of the oily water from the sprinkler system reaches the nostrils of staff and inmate alike. From behind

Argus, he hears someone yell, "Staff on the door!"

He turns and sees his relief, Ken Shelter standing in the DS sally port.

Ken looks at Argus and mouths, "What the fuck?"

Argus doesn't have time to respond because at that moment Lieutenant Atkins tells him, "Okay Antrim, shut the water down."

Argus enters the pipe chase and turns the valve, stemming the flow of water. He exits the pipe chase and looks around. It can only be described as organized chaos in the unit as twenty staff members try to accomplish individual jobs in a space usually occupied by two or three.

Lieutenant Sena yells, "Okay, team one and two line up!"

Argus sees AW Law speaking with Lieutenant Sena but he can't make out what they are saying. Lieutenant Sena nods and then Hibben keys the AW out of the unit. Lieutenant Atkins leaves with him.

Before the LT exits the outer door, he yells at Argus, "Antrim, you stay until the moves are complete then you can leave. Shelter, you grab a camera."

Ken nods and the two head for the laundry room for the briefing. Lieutenant Sena is in charge of the unit now. The preparations for the calculated uses of force aren't very different from others that Argus has been involved in. The only differences being that there will be multiple inmates in multiple cells and instead of moving the inmates to a clean cell, they will be restrained in the cell they have been housed in. Lieutenant Sena goes through the pre-move briefing in front of the camera Ken is holding. Argus does a final check on the restraints he has hanging from his belt, making sure that he'll be able to access the proper type without having to look. He closes his eyes and touches the soft restraints on his left side and the belly chains hanging on his right. The handcuffs are hanging from a d-ring on the front of his belt.

Hibben keys Odenburg on the range to handcuff the orderly in cell one and take him upstairs to ADSEG. For his own safety this inmate will not have a place on the range after today. The teams are lined up and the briefing is completed.

Lieutenant Sena goes down range to cell two and says, "I'm going to give you men one final order to cuff up. The inmates in the cell laugh and say, "You're out of your fucking mind Sena. You know as well as us we can't do that."

The incident is driving itself now and the only way it will be finished is to arrive at the end.

Lieutenant Sena nods and yells over his shoulder, "Teams up!" Ten operators, a cameraman and Argus carrying thirty pounds of restraints slosh through the fetid water to cell two and line up on the door. The inmates have tied the door closed with a torn sheet and have strung a spider web of sheet rope in the cell in an attempt to impede the team's entry. The number one man on the first team starts to cut the sheet rope from the slider when one of the inmates grabs the bar, putting his hand in front of the knife. Double "H" palm heel strikes the inmate's hand until he is forced to release the bar.

The rope is almost cut when Lieutenant Sena yells, "On the box, stand by for two!"

One of the inmates in the cell moves into the corner of the cell between the bunks and the bars and begins to throw cups of water from the toilet at the members of the entry team. The other inmates on the range are yelling encouragement for the inmates in cell two, telling them to go hard.

The noise is deafening as Lieutenant Sena yells, "On the box roll two!"

The lock on the slider releases and Double "H" rips the door to the side and leaps into the cell driving the first inmate into the wall with the second operator peeling off to pin the second inmate. Eight more staff members enter the cell and drag the inmates on to the range because there is simply no room to work inside the cell. The inmates are placed on their bellies in the fetid water. Argus hands the restraints as needed to the team members and the inmates are taken back into the cell and restrained to the bunks with the inmates facing up. Their wrists and ankles secured to the four corners of the bed with the soft restraints.

The officers back out sounding off as they exit, "One out! Two out! Three Out!" and so on.

The PA enters the cell and examines the inmates who are still breathing hard and yelling obscenities at everyone. The PA exits the cell and Lieutenant Sena instructs Ken to enter the cell and video document the condition of the inmates. Ken does as instructed and then exits the cell. Cell two is closed with a satisfying click of the locking mechanism.

Lieutenant Sena looks at the camera. "Team one will now exit the range. Team two will assume point. Team three up!"

As team one exits the range and team three sloshes down the range Lieutenant Sena continues addressing the camera. "I will now go to cell three and give the inmates one last chance to submit to handcuff restraints."

Lieutenant Sena approaches the cell and says, "I'm ordering you to back up to the bars and be handcuffed."

Argus sees a cup full of water come out of the cell as Sena ducks sideways. The question has to be asked because it is policy but everyone on the range knows the rules in this place. Once cell two went "hard," they'll all have to do the same even if they want to let themselves be cuffed. Argus knows they'll all fight now. No one is going to bitch up. The rest of the cell entries go as the first with little variation. Some of the inmates are more challenging to restrain than others but in the end, the whole unit is four pointed in their cells. Everyone is wet and tired, officer and inmate alike. Argus' uniform is wet and stained from being pelted all day with fruit and toilet water not to mention working the entries with the range flooded. His boots make a squishing sound as he walks. As he stands in front of the camera and details his part in the calculated uses of force, Argus feels tiredness so deep it reaches the souls of his feet. He wonders if his brothers feel the same.

Argus finishes his memorandum detailing the day's events and his part in the calculated use of force and drops it by the Lieutenant's Office on his way out of the institution. The squishing of his boots seems unusually loud as he enters the Control sally port.

Tarp is in Control and laughs, "What happened Ant, forget your rubbers?"

Argus smiles and flips him off before getting his brass chit for the radio he's just turned in and walking out.

He thinks, "It says something about a person who can smile after a day like today. I'm not sure what though."

His truck is a welcome sight as Argus clears the Tower One sally port.

He thinks, "My uniform is a mess. I'll have to put a towel down before I get in the seat."

Argus carries extra towels in the truck for just this kind of day. He considers passing on the heavy bag but dismisses the thought almost immediately. Argus realizes that to go home after this day without burning this thing out of his soul would be a monumental mistake. He refuses to force Lynn to deal with that and turns into the Training Center parking lot. He gets out of the truck and thinks about the shift he's just worked.

The inmates had started off with just trashing the range but as time wore on, they became assaultive.

219

Argus says to himself, "Give them an inch, they'll try for a mile."

He gets his bag gloves and heads inside. Once in the basement, he peels his shirt off and puts the gloves on

Argus looks at the gloves and thinks, "Already time for another pair. I need to buy stock in the glove company."

He squares off with the bag and begins to rid himself once again of the dragon who feeds so well at Tarragon. As he works, Argus knows that the shift he and his brothers had just worked will dissolve from memory into one of many. Argus throws a jab, cross, elbow combination, switches his stance and throws a wicked slashing kick.

As he watches the bag swing in a slow arc he thinks, "Fuck it. It means nothin'." and squares up again.

∞∞∞∞

He looks around the cell block but it is unfamiliar to him. Argus doesn't even know how he got here but instinctively knows that this is his block and he'll have to run it. The first thing he notices is the configuration of the unit is all wrong. There is no wide flat with the cells positioned around it making supervision relatively easy. In fact, there are no cells at all. There is a common area around a control pod but the pod is unoccupied. Branching off of the common area are several hallways. He starts down one of the halls, trying to get a feel for the unit and finds that they twist and turn with blind corners everywhere. The inmates are sitting along the walls. Some are sleeping on the floor and Argus has to step over them to get down the hall. The unit is extremely crowded.

He thinks, "How am I ever going to keep track of these guys in this place. It's an accountability nightmare."

He moves through the unit but doesn't encounter any other staff members. Argus realizes he is alone but it's his job to work the unit so he presses on, trying to find his way through the hallways of the unfamiliar building.

Argus walks each hallway of the unit, trying to organize it in his head. Count time is coming up. Somehow he knows this. There will have to be an organized method to the count and he tries to rectify this in his mind but can't see any organized way to approach it. Argus finds an exit and steps out into a rear area with a small walking track. He starts around the track, walking with several inmates to try and clear his head. The sun is bright and the sky is blue as he walks the gravel track. Argus

220

has to figure this out because count time is getting nearer and it's his job to keep track of these inmates. Argus walks across the track to the door he exited from and proceeds down the hallway to the commons area. He has still seen no other staff members. He feels alone and lost in the unit with too many inmates to account for.

Argus steps over an inmate and thinks, "How can I even count the unit? I need two fucking staff members for the count."

He stands at the control pod and looks around at the inmates on the floor everywhere knowing that they'll move before he can count the unit. There is no way he can do it. Count time is coming soon.

Argus is at a loss as he thinks, "How can I do my job in a unit like this?"

The ringing of the alarm wakes him with a start. He shuts it off and looks around the bedroom, relieved to see the familiar surroundings. The angst that he felt in the cell house is subsiding but a ghost of it still remains in the back of his mind. Lynn is lying next to him and he finds comfort in the soft purring noise she makes as she sleeps. He gets out of bed quietly and leaves their bedroom, wondering about the dreams. What do they mean? Argus knows that they are random but always have some of the same elements. He is always outnumbered and there is always an underlying sense of dread. He wonders if his friends have the same dreams. He dismisses the line of thinking and starts the coffee pot. He'll have to be at work soon.

∞∞∞∞

Argus stands at the seven yard line with his back to the target. His sidearm is affixed to his left hip in a low profile holster. Argus switched to this rig a few months ago because of how well it holds the pistol to his side. It is also ambidextrous. Will East, the SWAT firearms and self-defense instructor is standing behind the line of operators with a whistle clamped tightly in his teeth. Today the SWAT Team is qualifying with some extra shooting drills on the side. Argus along with everyone else on the line have their hands on their heads and eyes closed. The object of the drill is to improve reactionary shooting and is one of Argus' favorites. The operators wait as Will looks at his stop watch. There will be no warning prior to the whistle. Argus breath is low and steady as he mentally wills his muscles to relax.

He goes through each element of the draw in his mind and thinks, "Slow is smooth and smooth is fast."

A sharp blast of the whistle startles Argus out of these thoughts as he instinctively pivots on his right foot, turns to face the target, drawing as he turns. He accesses the front sight and fires two rounds into the chest of the target and then puts a third round into the head. When it's real, there is no negotiation at this point. He ensures his weapon is safe then re-holsters to examine the target.

Argus thinks, "Not too bad, I pulled a little to the left on the head shot. Gotta tighten that up. The cheek bone will do as good as the nose I suppose."

Will steps up behind Argus and looks at the target. "Tighten up with your support hand grip Ant and slow down a little on the chest, head transition. You hurried that third shot."

Argus nods and says, "Yeah, I felt like I rushed my head shot. Thanks."

Will is a tactical expert and a black belt in various martial arts. Argus has a lot of respect for the man and values his advice. The team runs the drill three more times with Argus getting slightly better with each round but still not where he wants to be.

He thinks, "I'll practice some more on my own time."

The day is a beautiful day to be on the range with a mild temperature and a blue, cloudless sky. Argus loves being at range and perfecting his shooting skills. He feels a slight westerly breeze as he squats to pick up the spent brass casings and deposit them in the bucket sitting at the center of the firing line.

Lieutenant Sena walks out of the range shack and yells, "Okay ladies, play times over. Will, go ahead and get them qualified!"

East puts his hand to his brow to shield his eyes from the sun and gives the LT the thumbs up. The Tarragon SWAT tactical pistol qualification consists of a course of fire at the seven, fifteen and twenty five yard line. Total possible score of three hundred.

It is anything but easy to qualify which Argus thinks is good. "If you can't shoot, you have no place in hostage rescue."

Argus heads to the range tables with everyone else and tops three magazines off with fifteen rounds each. He puts two extra boxes of rounds in his BDU pockets to reload for each stage of fire. This course is nothing new to Argus and he smiles as he steps up to the seven yard line. He is wearing his pistol on his left side for a left hand draw.

As the day wears on, all of the SWAT members do well on the course. Argus comes away with a respectable score of two hundred eighty seven. Will yells for everyone to get ready to run the course one more time. As Argus loads his magazines, he gets a crazy idea and decides to shoot the course right handed. He switches his holster to a right hand draw and heads to the seven yard line with his weapon and loaded magazines.

As he waits for the rest of the team to get done loading up, Argus practices his draw a few times and thinks, "Slow is smooth and smooth is fast."

He smiles as he holsters the weapon and shakes his arms to get them relaxed.

Will yells, "Ready!" and then the whistle blows. Argus draws in less than a second and finds the front sight, lining it up on the target. He puts three rounds in the ten ring in less than four seconds. The rest of the second qualification goes on in this manner with Argus ending up in the group of top five shooters on the team with a score of two eighty six. He feels a sense of pride as he picks up the brass shell casings at the end of the day. Shooting is one of his favorite things to do and he's good at it.

As Argus stands up to walk over and deposit his brass in the bucket, he sees Lieutenant Sena walking toward the firing line. "Ant! Doble! Step over here please."

Argus and Doble double time it over to where the LT is standing.

Doble says, "What's up LT?"

Lieutenant Sena looks at the two. "The Agency is starting a law enforcement sniper program and I have two slots to fill for the qualification in Louisiana. You guys interested?"

Argus smiles, "Hell yes LT."

Sena looks at Doble, "What about you?"

In true Doble fashion, he smiles and nods, "Yeah LT, That'll be great."

Stephen Doble has been on SWAT a few years longer than Argus and is also an excellent shot. He is a quiet, introspective man who works in the Accounting Office at Tarragon. Although, he and Argus aren't close other than being on the team together, Argus has always liked Doble.

Lieutenant Sena smiles and says, "Alright, you guys have got it. You leave in a week. Instead of reporting to work tomorrow, I need you to report out here to the range so you can zero your rifles and get some trigger time. This isn't a school you're going too. They'll expect you to be able to shoot when you get there."

As Argus drives home after training, he is elated.

223

He has skipped the heavy bag today and headed straight home to give Lynn the news. As he walks in the door, Lynn comes around the corner from the bedroom and greets him with a smile and a kiss. "How was training?"

Argus looks at her and smiles. "Good. I shot pretty well today. Everybody did."

Lynn is going around the room, tidying up. "That's good honey. Are you hungry?"

Argus nods and says, "Yeah. Hey I got some good news today."

Lynn stops her cleaning and looks at Argus. "Really? What news?"

Argus goes into the kitchen with Lynn following. "They want me to be a sniper on the team. Me and Doble. It's a new program and we have to go to Louisiana for a week to qualify."

Lynn is used to this although it's been a long time since he has had to deploy. Argus was a Marine when she'd first met him. She moves up to the counter beside him. "When do you leave?"

Argus looks at her. "We drive down in a week. We'll leave not this Sunday but the next."

Argus can see the reservations in her eyes. "I'll be back before you know it."

He hugs her to him. Argus can understand why she would have reservations about his leaving for a week. Her career is a demanding one as well and Argus leaving for a week puts everything on her with regard to Olivia. Argus looks around and asks, "Where's Olivia?"

Lynn motions with her head. "She's over at her friend's house on the corner. I was just about to call them to send her home for supper."

Argus takes Lynn's hand in his. "I know its short notice honey. I probably should have talked it over with you first but when Sena offered it to me, I just said yes. If nothing else it'll look good on my resume"

Lynn gives Argus that sweet smile. "It's okay Argus. If it's something you want to do, we'll make it work."

The next day Argus arrives at the range looking forward to shooting his new rifle. As he arrives, he sees that Lieutenant Sena and Will are already in the range shack getting things ready. Argus parks his truck in the gravel parking area and gets out with a hot cup of coffee in hand. He puts a dip of Copenhagen in and walks toward the shack. As he enters, Sena and Will look up from the boxes of ammunition and targets they are separating. The rifles are still in the cases and it is all Argus can do not to open them to take a look. Doble arrives and all four of them move the ammo to the hundred yard line then walk down to the target line and put up some targets. Once this is done, they all walk back to the shack.

Sena looks at Argus and Doble. "You guys are going to love what I brought you this morning. Go ahead and take a look."

They move over to the cases on the counter and open them up. For someone who isn't a shooter, it might seem ludicrous that a weapon might hold any beauty at all, but for a lifelong shooter, what the cases contain is something very beautiful indeed.

Argus and Doble look into the cases and then at each other. Inside the cases are Macmillan TAC- 308 rifles. They are fitted with Leopold optics and they are absolutely beautiful. Argus lifts the rifle from the case and works the bolt, opening the chamber. The rifle feels good in his hands.

Sena smiling says, "Okay, go ahead and give it a kiss Ant so we can start shooting the fucking thing."

Argus looks up embarrassed. It is another beautiful day with a cloudless blue sky as they make their way to the firing points. Argus and Doble lay down at their respective points in the prone position and adjust the sand bags to bolster the rifles at the proper height. Sena is with Argus and Will is with Doble to call their shots by looking through spotter scopes. The target is a football field away but through the scope, it is incredibly clear. Argus has never fired such a high end rifle and can't keep from smiling. He drops three rounds into the magazine and closes the bolt driving one of the heavy shells into the chamber. The rifle is tight into his left shoulder as he brings the cross hairs onto the ten "X" ring. Argus was a rifle expert in the Corps and knows that body position is everything when shooting at greater distances. If you're trying to muscle the weapon on target it will tell on you when you start to fatigue.

Argus makes sure of the positioning of the cross hairs and then closes his eyes. When he opens them after a second, he sees that the cross hairs are slightly to the right of the bull's eye. He scoots his chest slightly to the right bringing the cross hairs back on target and repeats the process. This time when he opens his eyes, the cross hairs are on target. He takes the safety off and mentally rechecks everything before putting the tip of his left finger on the trigger. Argus takes in a long slow breath and watches the cross hairs move then he slowly lets it out until he is on target and holds the breath while taking the slack up on the trigger. The report of the rifle surprises him which is just what it should do.

Sena says, "Low four inches and right two."

Argus fires two more rounds creating a pretty good grouping. He clears the weapon and puts it on safe before making the proper changes to the scope. At twelve rounds Argus is punching the bull's eye consistently. Doble is doing the same from his firing point. Argus marvels at the weapon's accuracy. He feels like he's driving a Porsche. The rest of the morning is spent putting rounds down range so Argus and Doble are completely at ease with the weapons. They knock off in time to clean the rifles and pack them in the cases with the required ammunition for the qualification then break for lunch.

An hour later they meet back at the range to fire the secondary weapon that Argus and Doble will have to qualify with. A standard ArmaLite rifle in 5.56 caliber with open sights. They are a sniper team and in an actual deployment, they will work together with one operator carrying the AR and the other carrying the MacMillan. The marksman on the sniper rifle will always be covered by the marksman with the AR. Argus and Doble will switch off on the primary gun so the qualification with the open sighted rifle is a must for both. As he lies on the ground, Argus looks over the open sights at the much smaller target and misses the Leopold optics. He qualified at five hundred meters in the Corps with much the same weapon so the football field distance does not intimidate him. After sighting the weapon in, Argus manages respectable groupings.

Sena leans over and says, "Tighten it up Argus, you'll be shooting at a two inch circle when you get to Louisiana."

He reevaluates his body positioning and base before taking a few breaths. Argus relaxes his legs and completely concentrates on his trigger finger. He feels the contraction of each of the muscles in the finger and the pressure of the trigger on the pad of the finger.

In his mind he chants the mantra, "Nice easy trigger squeeze. One shot. Only one shot to shoot today. Nice easy trigger squeeze" and the weapon fires, bucking against his shoulder.

Sena leans in, "That's what I'm talking about Ant. Ten X. Now do it again."

Throughout the afternoon Argus and Doble put round after round down range into the targets. Lieutenant Sena seems satisfied as the four clean the rifles and pack them in the soft carriers. Again, enough ammunition for the qualification is also packed.

Lieutenant Sena looks at Argus and Doble and says, "Don't fuck this up. You guys are representing Tarragon SWAT down there. There is nobody better. You only get one shot at this so make it count."

They both nod. Argus feels a great sense of pride that he has been entrusted with this opportunity. He also feels a knot in the pit of his stomach.

∞∞∞

Argus walks down B-Range with a set of ten handcuffs affixed to his duty belt. It is the end of the quarter and the end of the Segregation Units as they once were. For the past two years, construction on a new Segregation Unit has been ongoing. The new unit has double the capacity and is completely computerized with a secure control pod. The doors are solid steel with handcuff ports and it is air conditioned. Today is moving day for the inmates and as with any inmate movement, the staff are very busy. Inmates are to be moved in sets of ten from the old unit to the new unit. They have been given plastic bags to hold their personal property from the cells. These bags will be moved on a cart. The inmates will be handcuffed as usual.

Extra officers have been placed on the roster to assist with the move so Argus is only one of many handcuffing inmates and escorting them to the front of the range. Brownie and Phan are working the cell control boxes on two ranges at once. The correctional officers are operating in standard Tarragon fashion, economically and efficiently. As the day wears on, the inmates from ADSEG are moved to the new ADSEG and then the inmates from DS are moved. Their property is searched and then returned to them. The new unit has five ranges making what was once overflowing now manageable with a great deal of empty cells. All of the recreation cages are inside and climate controlled. Argus steps into the control pod and is impressed with the technology. The officer inside can control everything from the doors to the water in the cells.

He thinks, "No more running into a pipe chase when they decide to flood the range."

Argus has bid for the Special Housing Unit or SHU Property Officer position next quarter. He was selected but will miss the first week of the assignment due to the sniper qualification. This position also has weekends off so that he can spend more time with his girls, something he always enjoys. He will be responsible for picking up property from the units when an inmate is locked up and issuing the inmate what he is allowed in the SHU as policy dictates. It will be a good job but challenging. The Agency has adopted a new inmate

227

property policy and Argus will be tasked with bringing the personal property into compliance through attrition.

He walks into the property storage room and looks around thinking, "Home sweet home."

Argus is looking forward to the new assignment. He has a new mission.

∞∞∞∞∞

The classroom is a nondescript wooden structure located at an abandoned military range in Louisiana. The white paint is chipped and peeling giving some of the wood a feathered look. Inside, the walls are bare except for a white erase board hanging at the front of the room. Two men stand at the front of the room facing fourteen sniper teams from around the Agency. The two men are as different in appearance as night and day. One has a compact build attached to a five foot nine inch frame. He has short cropped black hair and his name is simply McGill. The other is tall and wiry with a solid muscularity. He has the facial features classic to a Native American with the strong jaw and high cheek bones. His name is Mr. Rainwater. Both of the men are clothed in BDU's and have the same serious eyes. They are private contractors out of Chicago and are here to share the realities of being a sniper or as the Agency prefers, "Law Enforcement Marksman."

They will also decide who achieves the certification to take a surgical shot in a hostage situation.

As the participants sit at the old folding tables, McGill presents the training outline, "Gentlemen, by the simple fact that you are in those seats, we're going to assume that you can shoot. This isn't a class on being a marksman. You should already have those skills. This is a qualification course with some wisdom and training mixed in. The target you'll be engaging at one hundred yards with your MacMillan rifles is a two inch circle on the face of a *Bad Guy* target which is the approximate size of the medulla oblongata. You're here to prove that you can separate the brain from the body with one shot consistently. We'll have two days of classroom training covering the psychological aspects of being a shooter as well as ballistics, etc, etc. On day three you will qualify with the open sighted ArmaLite. On day five you will qualify with the MacMillans. Qualification will consist of five rounds in a ten inch circle at one hundred yards with the ArmaLites and a two inch circle with the MacMillans on *Bad Guy* targets. If you miss, you go

228

home. It's that simple."

The participants are silent as Argus feels a bead of sweat begin to inch down his spine. The lack of air conditioning in the building becomes more pronounced as the day goes on. Yesterday Doble and Argus had arrived at the motel they would stay in for the week. There were no armory accommodations for their weapons so one of them would have to stay in the room at all times. The motel was anything but high end with two beds, a desk and night stand. The television was secured to the desk with a cable as was the television remote to the night stand.

The class room portion of the training is presented by McGill exclusively. Mr. Rainwater does not say much but just stands to the side nodding and adding points here and there during the classes. The training is extremely interesting to Argus and he soaks the knowledge up like a sponge. The subject matter verifies that the two instructors have real world experience as marksmen. The attendees learn out of the ordinary things like the fact that a piece of shattered glass travels at the same speed as the bullet for eleven feet after the bullet pierces a window. The training opens up a whole new world to Argus involving long range shooting. Things he'd never thought about like the ability of two marksmen to coordinate their shots. What is most interesting to Argus is the mental aspect of the duties.

McGill tells a personal story of a deployment in which a high risk warrant service had gone horribly wrong with a police officer being taken hostage in a residential neighborhood.

McGill looks at the students, "I was positioned on a roof top adjacent to the house where they had this guy tied up. They'd controlled the environment and had the windows blacked out. I didn't have a shot so I was feeding command intel. The hostage takers were still talking to the negotiators so command wouldn't authorize an entry. I spent the night on that roof listening to them periodically beat that cop with his own mag light. He didn't survive. You've got to be able to handle that mentally. Sometimes looking someone in the eye and pulling the trigger is the easy part. You've got to be able to hold your shit together no matter what you see or hear."

Doble looks over at Argus and raises his eyebrows. It is a sobering story.

McGill looks around the room, "Any questions before I go on?"

A man from one of the teams to Argus' left raises his hand. "Yes sir, Uh, I'm a Christian and wondered what your thoughts were on the commandment thou shall not kill."

McGill looks at the man with a stoic look. "Everyone has to rectify that for themselves. As for me, I believe God uses man to complete His will and frankly, some people need killing."

This is met with a few chuckles. McGill isn't laughing.

∞∞∞∞

It is the beginning of day three as the alarm goes off at 5:00 am. It is Argus' turn to go out and get breakfast at the only restaurant in town. It is a small diner that opens at 6:00 am every morning and is within sight of the motel. Doble will stay and watch the weapons and ammunition. Argus returns a short time later with egg sandwiches, home fries and a large coffee that he is thrilled about. Doble isn't a coffee drinker and has a coke. They eat hurriedly and load the Agency van to go to the range. As they arrive as part of a convoy of various agency vehicles, Argus sees McGill and Rainwater standing at the range building.

He thinks, "They're up early. Wonder what's up."

As the SWAT members gather their equipment and form up at the building, McGill makes an announcement, "As planned, this morning you'll be firing the ArmaLites. We're going to give you all morning to get that nice, fuzzy, warm feeling on the gun. After lunch will be the open sight qualification. You'll fire five rounds, you miss, you leave."

One of the students raises his hand. "You mean we have to leave the range?"

McGill looks at the group. "No, I mean you're going home. Look guys, if you miss when it's real that equals a dead hostage. If you haven't got the mental capabilities to qualify with no misses here, I don't want you shooting out there. I'm doing you and your agency a favor. Trust me."

Argus and Doble look at each other. Things just got real in the short period of time it took for McGill to make his speech. The operators put their MacMillan's back into the vehicles and prepare the ArmaLites for a day of shooting. All morning long they fire the open sighted rifle at the extremely small scowling face of the bad guy down range. Argus tweaks his sights click by minute click bringing his groups to dead center, just under the nose. His stomach is in knots in anticipation of the qualification. There will be no second chances. At lunchtime, the group is relatively quiet as each shooter is absorbed in his personal thoughts. Argus doesn't have much of an appetite but manages to eat

230

part of the MRE that has been provided as part of the training package.

He takes a deep breath thinking, "Okay, it's just one shot times five. One shot at a time. I've been punching the bull's eye all morning. I can do it this afternoon."

His nerves calm slightly as he takes a pull on the bottle of water. Doble is wiping his rifle down as if in deep concentration. Neither of them wants to go back to Tarragon a failure.

After lunch, Argus receives his five qualification rounds and wipes each one down with a cleaning rag before loading them into the magazine. This is probably a useless gesture but it helps him mentally to leave nothing to chance. A misfeed or jam could easily throw him out of the zone he'll need to stay in to make these shots. Everyone walks to their respective firing points with the sound of their boots on the gravel being the loudest sound on the range. No one is talking. As Argus lies down at the firing point, he brushes any random stones from the ground giving himself another second to brush away any random thoughts. He gets in a relaxed prone position and brings the rifle to his shoulder, bringing the target into the sights.

He looks at the target a football field away and thinks, "Fuck me, that's a small face."

The heat waves shimmer in between Argus and the target. He tries to relax and consciously wills his breathing to slow. His focus is total as he closes his eyes and breathes in deeply then letting it out, opens his eyes to find the front sight slightly off target. Argus adjusts his body positioning and repeats this process twice more before he is satisfied. He is ready.

McGill has the bull horn while Mr. Rainwater is walking up and down the line.

Argus hears McGill give the command, "Gentlemen, this will be a five round qualification string of fire. You'll fire five rounds at your own pace. You will have ten minutes to do so. Once you begin firing, you will remain in the prone position until completed. With a magazine of five rounds, lock and load!"

Up and down the line the sound of twenty eight magazines being inserted and the same number of bolts being brought home on live rounds is heard.

Another announcement before the final outcome is revealed. "Is the line ready?"

Rainwater gives the thumbs up. "Gentlemen, you may commence firing!"

Argus looks at the target, resisting the urge to pull the trigger.

He completes a mental check list regarding all aspects of taking this one shot and then thinks, "Okay, fuck it. It either is or it isn't. I'm here now, so I might as well get it done."

Argus breathes in then out then in again. As he exhales, he stops when the front sight reaches the point just under bad guy's nose so far away and takes the tension up on the trigger. The gun booms and bucks against his shoulder, the charging handle punching back against the tip of his nose.

The distance is too great to actually see where his round went.

Argus takes a deep breath and thinks, "One down, one to go." He lines up his sights as before, taking his time and fires the second round. With each round, Argus conducts the same ritual as if the only shot is the one before him. Nothing else exists except that one shot. He is the only one on the range and his world has collapsed to the target, sights and trigger. He fires the last round and it surprises him when the bolt locks to the rear. There are still shooters firing so Argus stays prone and looks over at Doble a few feet away.

They both raise their eyebrows in the unspoken question. Argus shakes his head and smiles. Inside he is a wreck.

Everyone has fired their string and McGill clears the range by announcing, "Cease fire, cease fire."

Each shooter shows Mr. Rainwater a clear chamber and an engaged safety before the shooters are allowed to rise up off the ground. Only Rainwater and McGill are allowed down range to inspect the targets. Everyone gathers around as McGill calls off the names of those who qualified. Argus doesn't realize it but he is holding his breath. He releases it in relief as his name is called. There will be two less shooters tomorrow. In no instance are both of the shooters from any team eliminated so the remaining member will continue with the training while the member who didn't qualify will have to wait at the motel. Argus pities these guys. They'll have two long days to second guess every shot they made today.

∞∞∞∞

It is day four and the Louisiana sun is high in the sky. The high humidity causes Argus to sweat through his t-shirt, a drop of sweat creeping down his nose and dropping onto the ground in front of him. He is lying in the prone position on the firing line along with all the

232

other would be marksmen. Each team is firing from a respective firing point. The exercise this morning is to practice synchronized shooting. Synchronized shooting is a method of coordinating two individual shots from two shooters to ensure the hostage is unharmed from, for example, shrapnel from a breaking window. One shooter will shatter the window at an angle which isn't in the direct gun target line thereby minimizing the flying glass directly at the hostage while the second shooter takes the decisive shot. Argus and Doble's shots must be simultaneous to make sure the hostage taker doesn't react when the window explodes.

Argus thinks, "Easier said than done."

They have been at it all morning and are just now getting it fine-tuned enough that their individual shots sound like one. Argus shifts his body trying to move the tiny piece of gravel that has been wearing a hole in his chest for the last hour.

He hears McGill's voice over the megaphone. "Shooters, dial it in!" Argus focuses on the crosshairs and lines the target up.

McGill again, "Ready, Ready, Ready! Fire!

As Argus hears the beginning of the "F" sound, he pulls the trigger. Although twenty eight shooters are firing, it sounds like only a few shots. Everyone is getting better. Argus racks the bolt on his weapon clearing the chamber and feels someone lightly kick his boot.

Argus turns to see Mr. Rainwater standing above him. From Argus position on the ground, Rainwater looks even taller and more imposing. He motions with a relaxed wave of his hand. "Antrim, hip shoot."

Argus thinks, "Shit!"

A hip shoot is an impromptu shooting challenge. There's no telling what it might be, no way to practice and it is a cold shot. There will be no warm up. Once Argus gets to the firing point that the instructor designates, he'll have sixty seconds to dial the target in, make any adjustments using Kentucky windage and punch the target. This won't count against Argus if he misses besides the fact that he'll have to look himself in the mirror and know he failed to perform. Any SWAT member knows this outcome is just as bad as having the shit kicked out of you. Argus makes sure his rifle is safe, then gets up off the ground and stands in front of Rainwater expectantly. He glances at Doble who is looking at Argus and smiling. Argus mentally flips him off.

Rainwater smiles an easy smile. "Double time to the second floor of the tower. Cross angle shot into target twenty nine. Go!"

Argus takes off running toward the building behind the firing line with several elevated firing points. The run is approximately thirty yards before he gets to the staircase.

He hits the staircase with Rainwater behind him and ascends to the second floor. Rainwater points to the left window.

Argus thinks, "Fuck, that's a completely cross angled shot."

Rainwater's smile widens as Argus looks at him. The stop watch is ticking and Argus hears it in his head like the thudding of a heartbeat. It feels like he is moving painfully slow as he puts the barrel of the MacMillan on the sandbags just inside the window. His heart rate and breathing are up as he looks at the target. His body feels like it is at an obscene angle as the crosshairs bounce with each heartbeat.

He thinks, "Fuck me, I'm running out of time. C'mon Argus, line this motherfucker up!"

He takes several deep breaths while working the bolt. Argus looks at the target and takes the safety off, willing himself to take a slow breath in. As he slowly exhales, he waits until the crosshairs are even with the center of the mouth and smoothly pulls the trigger. He pulls the bolt to the rear and swivels to look at Rainwater who is looking at the target with his binoculars. Argus cocks his head to the side in the question.

Mr. Rainwater takes a deep breath in and looks at Argus, enjoying the suspense. "Good shot. It is a kill for sure but not dead center. I like dead center. There are two things that I want you to remember. All stress is self-induced. You made that a stressful shot yourself. I had nothing to do with it. Secondly, you have to tune everything else out. The only thing that exists is your rifle and the target. You have to get in that zone every time but it takes practice. Okay, clear your weapon and head back down to your partner."

Argus gets up and heads back down the stairs to where Doble is lying on the ground smiling. "Well, how'd you do?"

Argus looks at Doble, "It wasn't dead center. He likes dead center." Doble chuckles.

∞∞∞∞

The next day, Argus and Doble rise early from a fitful night of tossing and turning. Argus feels like shit and probably looks it.

As he looks over at Doble, he thinks, "No way I look as bad as him."

Argus volunteers to get breakfast and both of them eat light with just a bacon and egg sandwich on toast. Argus eats without tasting as the toast clings to his dry throat. Today they will qualify with the

MacMillans. All morning long the shooters fire at the two inch area between the nose and the mouth, fine tuning their weapons. Argus feels much better about today after he's looked through the Leopold. The target seems so much larger through the scope. They break for lunch and set down near the range shed to consume the daily MRE.

No one is speaking as McGill comes over and stands in the middle of the shooters. "Well, does everybody feel all warm and fuzzy about today?"

There are a few nods and one yes sir.

McGill walks off saying, "Good, good. You guys look all warm and fuzzy."

Then he laughs. Argus is thinking about the men at the motel. He doesn't want to have that mill stone hanging around his neck when they return to Tarragon. His stomach rolls and he puts the food to the side.

On the firing line, Argus kicks pebbles away from where he will lay and starts making his world smaller. He lies down in the prone position behind the heavy barreled rifle and looks at the target's face which seems so far away now. The ballistics for the gun are running through his mind like a ticker tape. He checks the range flags and is happy to see them flapping calmly. A low value wind is good. He tops the weapon off with five rounds and waits, looking down range and focusing on his target completely.

From behind him, Argus barely hears the bull horn over the beating of his own heart. "Shooters, this is your final qualification. The course of fire is five rounds at your own pace. You will have ten minutes to complete the course. Mr. Rainwater is the line ready?"

Rainwater gives the thumbs up.

McGill speaking again with a flamboyant flare, "Shooters, you may commence firing!"

Argus takes a deep breath and settles in thinking, "You got all the time in the world Argus. Ten minutes is a lifetime."

He works the bolt chambering a round and looks down range at the target. Argus takes a deep breath in and lets it out. The cross hairs fall slightly left of the nose. He adjusts his body so they fall on target, closes his eyes and takes another breath. When he opens his eyes, the cross hairs are on target.

He takes another breath, watching the cross hairs rise and fall. As he does this, he lightly touches the trigger feeling the smooth metal against a finger sensitized to each stage of the trigger release. When the cross hairs reach a point just beneath the bad guy's nose, Argus holds his breath and smoothly takes up the tension on the trigger. The rifle booms and recoils against his shoulder blurring the view of the target.

Argus thinks, "One down."

He repeats the ritual as sweat begins to drop from his forehead across his eyebrows and into his eyes. He blinks the drops away, keeping his body alignment. Again the gun booms.

With each shot he talks to himself, "Smooth easy trigger squeeze. Remember to follow through. This is the only shot today. Relax."

He works the bolt forcing himself to keep the pace slow and methodical. Nothing exists in the world besides the target and his rifle. He is completely in the zone. Argus looks at the target for the last time and pulls the trigger. The gun booms sending his fifth round down range. He works the bolt sending the final empty cartridge through the air and over his right shoulder. He feels empty. Win or lose, the contest is decided and Argus lies on the ground, waiting in a void. He doesn't look around and realizes that he is tired.

Argus hears McGill from behind announce, "Cease fire! Cease fire! Mr. Rainwater, please make sure the line is safe."

As Rainwater walks the line, the shooters show him an empty chamber and an engaged safety.

McGill once again, "Is the line safe? Shooters you may gather you weapon and gear and head to the range shack."

Argus stands up and arches his back in a stretch. He looks at Doble and asks, "How do you think you did?"

Doble shakes his head, "I don't know Ant. Guess we'll see."

They head to the range shack to wait as McGill and Rainwater grade the targets. The next fifteen minutes are excruciating as the shooters wait. Finally, the instructors enter the range shack holding a stack of targets with each shooters name written at the top.

McGill starts handing out the targets and says, "You guys can take a look but I'll need these back for record keeping in case you ever have to take a live shot."

Argus holds his target up and looks at the group. Four of the holes are touching with one hole a half inch above. The group is well within the two inch circle. Argus feels a great sense of pride and shows Doble. His partner did just as well and Argus claps his smiling friend on the shoulder. All of the shooters have qualified today and the noise rises as the tension releases.

McGill yells over the talking and laughter, "Alright, listen up!

Gimme the targets back and get your certificates. We've got to police these ranges up. Brass and trash fellas, then you're free to travel home. Everybody did a great job. I appreciate your attention and work."

∞∞∞∞

Argus pulls into the staff parking lot at Tarragon and his pulse quickens as he spots the ambulance parked at the Tower One Sally Port. He is anxious to get started in the Property Room of the Segregated Housing Unit but sees that he might be assigned to an emergency escort and adjusts his focus accordingly. He silently prays that the ambulance isn't for a staff member as he walks with his lunch box toward the prison entrance. Argus reaches the sally port without hearing the usual call that would re-direct him to the Armory.

The gate buzzes and he steps through thinking, "They must have this one covered. Good, I've got a shit load of work to catch up on."

Sniper qualification was a rewarding experience but it has put him a week behind in getting the Property Room set up the way he wants it. Argus exits the sally port and walks toward the Front Lobby, passing the desk and heading toward Control. At the Control Sally Port, Argus stands at the grill and sees that the Main Corridor is locked down. He is not surprised. Officer Grange is in Control and nods as he sees Argus. The metal grill opens with a metallic grind. Argus steps through and tells Grange through the key slot that he'll get his equipment in SHU. As the inner grill slides open, Argus steps through and sees Lieutenant Grant, Hibben and Skim escorting an ambulance crew toward Control.

Argus stands in front of the open grill until everyone is properly identified. It is indeed an inmate on the gurney and Argus sees that he has been assaulted. It looks like he has several wounds to his midsection. The gurney and ambulance crew are stopped at Control while Grange properly identifies the inmate from the escort paperwork Lieutenant Grant has prepared. Argus steps closer to the gurney and looks at the inmate. He is writhing on the gurney and his abdomen is a bloody mess. Bandages can only do so much. The inmate is saying something in Spanish which is well beyond Argus basic understanding of the language. Argus asks Hibben what the inmate is saying.

Hibben is fairly proficient in speaking Spanish and says, "He's begging to God."

Argus thinks, "Smart, he might be meeting him soon."

Grange verifies everyone's identity and motions them into the sally port.

237

Argus steps aside as Grange yells through the key slot, "The escort crew is good to go LT!"

Skim and Grant escort the ambulance crew in to the sally port and Hibben stays behind. He is an Acting Lieutenant today. Argus and Hibben begin walking toward the East End and Argus asks what happened.

Hibben looks at Argus and says, "Found him in the Recreation Center stairway all stabbed to shit this morning after mainline. Not sure what happened but he pissed someone off."

Argus nods his head. "Hmmm. You're right, definitely not a good day for him."

Hibben claps Argus on the shoulder. "Heard you did well at sniper qualification."

Argus smiles, "Yeah, it was good training. They weren't messing around."

Hibben and Argus reach the Lieutenant's Office.

Hibben stops and says, "I'll see you later when I make rounds in SHU Ant."

Argus smiles and nods. "Yup, see you in a bit."

Argus keeps walking down the corridor toward SHU thinking about the inmate and the absurdity of that being normalcy.

Argus thinks, "I'll come back with my cart this afternoon and get his property from the unit."

He doesn't give a second thought to whether the inmate will survive or not. Argus has become calloused to the violence of this place. As calloused as his knuckles have become from punishing the heavy bag day after day.

He feels nothing and puts the incident into a tiny box deep inside thinking, "Fuck it. It's just another day."

Argus' only true fear is that on some dark night, when he is alone and his guard is down, the memories of these things will escape the prison he has built for them and come drifting back to pay him a visit.

∞∞∞∞∞

The SHU Property Room is designed in a manner that Argus can review the inmate's property with them without compromising security. Argus has a door that he enters the Property Room by and a half door that he opens with a large countertop in between the holding cell and the Property Room. When an inmate is sent to SHU, Argus retrieves the property from their assigned unit and brings it to SHU where he searches it and reviews the property with the inmate. Argus issues the property that the inmate is allowed to have in the more secure unit and completes the necessary paperwork to notate this. In addition, the Agency has adopted a new inmate property policy to minimize the amount of property an inmate may possess. The Segregated Housing Unit is the choke point where this policy is put into place. Go to SHU and your property is brought into policy guidelines. It is Argus job this quarter to implement this policy and the inmates are not happy. He has been working the post for two weeks and has found each day to be full of confrontation regarding the new policy. This is where Argus is today as the inmate across the counter stares at him with hate in his eyes. Argus has searched the inmate's property, gone to his cell and brought him down to review the property and has given him the bad news regarding the extra property that must be disposed of including the eighty seven photos above the twenty photo limit.

Argus looks at the inmate with resignation, "Look, its policy. This pile of property is what you can either mail home on your dime or you can donate it. Donate means I confiscate it and in ninety days it gets thrown away. You can pick twenty photos out of the one hundred and seven to keep."

The inmate looks at Argus with rage in his eyes, "So, why can't I have the Polaroid of my girlfriend? Because she ain't got no clothes on?"

Argus sighs, "That has nothing to do with it. Polaroids are against policy. You'll have to mail that with this other stuff."

The inmate takes a deep breath in, "Who the fuck am I supposed to mail it to? My wife? Are you fuckin crazy? Gimme the fuckin' picture. I'll rip it up in front of you, you prick."

Argus hands the picture to the inmate and tells him he can send it to another address but the inmate is well into his tantrum and does his best to tear the photo to bits. Argus marks on the property form, "Destroyed by inmate" and initials. He hands the inmate the bag of basic hygiene items and current legal work he is allowed to retain along with his radio and four batteries.

Argus looks at the inmate and shakes his head. "You sure you don't want to mail this stuff?"

The inmate shakes his head and bares his teeth in a tight scowl.

Argus shrugs his shoulders. "Okay, I'll confiscate the stuff. For the next ninety days you'll get a review every thirty days if you change your mind. I'll bag the other stuff and it'll be waiting when you go back to the yard."

Argus goes around and unlocks the holding cell where the inmate is waiting in handcuff restraints and a belly chain. He is holding his small bag of property in front of him. Somehow Argus thinks they will never be friends. He puts his hand on the inmate's elbow and they walk back toward the range where the inmate is housed. As they pass the admission holding cells where new inmates are strip searched and processed into the unit, Argus sees a familiar face. It is Inmate "Percolator." Argus is familiar with this inmate from the old ADSEG and knows this inmate to be a mule. He will insert contraband into his rectum and then get sent to segregation on a minor infraction to smuggle the contraband into the unit. Once in his segregation cell, he simply sits on the toilet and has a bowel movement, depositing the contraband tobacco or drugs into the commode. Inmate percolator has been waiting in the holding cell for a while because the segregation crew is extremely busy today.

As Argus passes the inmate who has his head down and is leaning on the door, he says, "Hey 'Percolator,' you're looking a little green man. You okay?"

The inmate looks up at the sound of a familiar voice. "Antrim, can you help me man? Can you get me in a cell? I gotta take a shit real bad Officer Antrim."

Argus thinks, "I bet you do" and smiles then says, "Yeah man. Hold on 'til I get this guy put up and I'll be back to get ya."

This is a new state of the art segregation unit and "Percolator" isn't up to speed yet. Argus knows the inmate has a rectum full of contraband and Argus has a plan. Argus escorts the inmate he has just issued property to back to his cell on B-Range.

Once at his cell, Argus keys his radio, "Antrim to Pod, open Bravo-8."

The cell door opens with a mechanical whine. "Close Bravo-8."

The cell closes and Argus removes the restraints from the inmate and closes the cuff slot. As Argus walks away, he can hear the inmate complaining to his cell mate.

Argus thinks, "I ain't the one who fucked up on the yard. Wanna keep your property, don't come to SHU."

He exits the range and finds his friend, Ron Conner who is the Number One Officer in SHU this quarter. He is about Argus height and slightly overweight but a good officer and a man Argus calls friend. Ron is in the process of putting recreation inmates back in their cells and Argus jumps in to help.

Once the inmates are back in their cells, Argus says, "Hey buddy, you got 'Percolator' out there in a holding cell. He says he has to take a shit."

Conner looks at Argus and smiles, "Yeah Ant, you know the guy as well as I do. He's packing something."

Argus looks at Conner with a sideways grin. "Well, let me run something by you. The Pod can disable any toilet in the place but if we do that and he figures it out, 'Percolator' will just dump it then reinsert it but the Pod can also flush any toilet in the place."

Conner looks at Argus and smiles as the idea takes shape and says, "We'd have to time it perfect."

Argus chuckles, "We can pull it off man. Go strip him and get him in the cell, then walk around the range and come back to the cell. If he's on the shitter, just radio me. I'll flush his contraband for him."

Conner heads out to the holding cell and Argus steps into the Control Pod to wait. In a few minutes, Conner passes the Pod escorting Inmate 'Percolator'.

It only takes a few moments before Argus hears on the radio, "Conner to Pod, open Charlie 10."

Argus finds C-10 on the plumbing control board and gets ready. Officer Grass is the SHU Number Two Officer and works in the Pod.

He looks at Argus smiling and says, "What are you up to Ant?"

Argus smiles back and says, "Just wait, you'll see."

Conner transmits, "Close Charlie 10" and Grass punches the buttons to close the cell. He turns back around to look at Argus with his eyebrows raised in the question. Argus is smiling on the verge of laughing in anticipation.

In a few minutes Conner transmits, "Conner to Antrim, ten four."

Argus pushes the button to flush the toilet in cell C-10 and immediately hears, "AHHHHHHH! You motherfuckers!"

Argus guffaws as Grass breaks into his "hee hee hee" laugh. Conner walks off the range laughing as well. Argus heads back to his property room laughing all the way. He always loved a good practical joke.

Chapter 11
Tattooed Soul

Argus drives his truck toward Abhaile from the new home he and Lynn have built in the Southerly outskirts of town. It is a beautiful place on six wooded acres that Lynn designed herself. Argus looks over at her as he drives not believing how lucky he is. She is absolutely beautiful. It is their anniversary and they are going to their favorite Italian restaurant to celebrate. As they drive, the conversation is light and playful. Argus' mother has Olivia for the night which is a welcome opportunity for them to enjoy a night out as a couple. As they enter the city limits, he is looking forward to the plate of chicken alfredo that he always orders.

It is his favorite and as he always tells Lynn, "Once I find something I like, I stick with it."

This always makes her smile. They are within minutes of the restaurant when his SWAT pager begins to chirp. Argus looks at Lynn with an unspoken apology as he takes it from his belt and looks at the lighted display. His stomach tightens as he reads the three digit code directing him to report to the SWAT Ready Room located behind the Training Center immediately. When this happens, it is usually something big and never good. He looks over at her as he makes a left turn to head to the prison.

Without looking at her, he says, "I'm sorry honey, I have to report. Maybe it won't take long and we can still get a late dinner."

He knows as well as she does that this is wishful thinking. It always takes a long time no matter what it is.

She looks at him with a sad smile and touches his arm saying, "I know. Don't worry about it. We'll have dinner some other night."

Right at this moment Argus hates that pager.

As they arrive at the Training Center and drive around back, Argus sees that there is a flurry of activity. Several members of the SWAT Team have already arrived and are gearing up. Argus puts the car in park and gets out just as Franks exits the building headed for his truck.

Argus yells to Franks, "Hey brother, what's the game?"

Franks looks at Argus then at Lynn then back to Argus. "They took a unit. The officer is out and safe. I'll brief you in the room."

Franks walks away and Argus looks at Lynn, "No big deal sweetie. This'll take a while though. You should probably just head home. I'll see you when I see you."

He looks in to her eyes and sees the worry there. Argus gives her a sideways grin in an attempt to ease her mind but inside he knows that taking back a unit could always go sideways. He consciously really looks at her. She is beautiful.

He kisses her and says, "I love you sweetie."

He hopes she knows how much. Lynn drives away and Argus heads into the Ready Room where everyone is getting dressed in black BDU's.

Franks yells, "Listen up! The inmates have Unit Four. They've armed themselves and are barricaded. This will be a less than lethal entry. Gear up with Flak vests, helmets, gas masks and thirty six inch batons. Everyone carries ten sets of flex cuffs. We'll get the other shit when we get to the Armory. You got five minutes then we're heading over to the institution."

Argus literally jumps into his uniform and finishes gearing up as the team starts out the door. He starts toward the door then runs back and grabs his Copenhagen, spinning and running out the door in time to jump on the back of Stephens' pickup. The sun has set and a damp chill descends on the Silurus River Valley as the team makes the short drive to the Armory. Mr. Farmer is waiting with a bag of munitions that he hands to Franks. Argus looks around and notices that Lieutenant Sena and a third of the team hasn't arrived yet. As they enter the Front Lobby, Associate Warden Law stops Franks by lightly grabbing his arm. Argus can see Franks nodding as the AW gives him instructions. As the AW walks away toward the Warden's Office, Franks pulls out his notebook and begins to write. Hibben has arrived along with sixteen members of the Disturbance Control Team and is issuing the munitions to SWAT. The Disturbance Control Team is another team at Tarragon which handles a myriad of crowd control scenarios. Tonight, they will supplement SWAT's numbers. Hibben hands Argus a sting ball grenade and as he takes it, Argus instinctively checks the pin. A sting ball grenade is a less than lethal distraction device which sprays rubber pellets in all directions when it explodes. The concussion and noise reach approximately two hundred forty decibels. It is enough to get your attention. Argus deposits the grenade in his side pocket and leans against the wall to wait. The Front Lobby is full as Argus watches the flurry of activity. The AW is back at Franks' side, nodding as he takes the sheet of paper from the big man and heads back toward the Warden's Office.

Argus realizes that in the absence of Lieutenant Sena, Franks had been tasked with writing the operations order which will detail how the entry will be conducted.

He looks at Franks thinking, "He looks tense and I don't blame him."

From his place along the wall, Argus realizes that the conversation has died down to a low mutter as the operators wait for the Warden's approval. The Lobby telephone rings and is handed to Franks.

Argus hears Franks say, "Yes sir, right away."

Franks hangs the telephone up and looks around the Lobby. "Okay listen up. There are one hundred twenty three inmates in Unit Four. It is unknown if they are all participants but we have to assume they are. They've taken the unit and armed themselves. They've told the Captain that until the unit OIC is replaced, we can't have it back. Warden wants this taken care of ASAP so we go with what we've got. I want four squads, two upper, two on the flat. Squad order is three SWAT operators on the front of each stack, four DCT on the tail end. We make entry, deploy munitions and then move through the cell house front to back in tactical column, moving the inmates into the cells and locking them in. Once we take the front of the unit, I'll key the boxes and put the cells on lock. If you have to enter a cell, then convert to centipede dump and keep moving. Remember use of force policy. If they fight, pound'm and ground'm. Squad leaders are, Antrim, lower right squad, Nash, upper right squad, Stephens, lower left and Hibben, upper left. Okay, let's form it up!"

Argus raises his hand and yells, "Lower right, form on me!"

The other squad leaders do the same and in short order, the squads are formed and ready.

Once formed the left and right squads form into two columns and face the direction of the interior of Tarragon. Argus will be one of the first through the door and the pre-action resolve has kicked in. His heart becomes stone as he goes through the steps of the entry plan which will more than likely go to shit after the first minutes if it turns into a melee, but you have to start somewhere.

He looks back at his squad and says, "Stay together. Don't let yourself get separated off."

He knows they already know this but, it makes him feel better to say it. The word finally comes down to move out. Once past the Control Room Sally port, they will double time it down the Corridor toward Unit Four. The inmates are expecting a negotiation and they'll get it, just not the type of negotiation they are expecting. This is Tarragon Penitentiary and the taking of a unit by the inmates cannot be tolerated. The Warden knows this as well as every staff member here. The entry team is outnumbered four to one but they have force multipliers which even the score. Plus, they'll have the element of surprise. Once everyone is through the sally port, they form up on the other side and wait. Franks gives the command to move out and the operators start running down the Main Corridor toward Unit Four in two single file lines. The institution is locked down and the empty corridor makes the sound of the team's boots hitting the floor sound like much more than their numbers actually are. Argus feels the thrum of his own heart in his ears as he tries to control his breathing as they run. He can see that there are correctional officers standing outside of the adjacent units with large sheets. As the team comes into view, the sheets are held in front of the doors of the units to impede the inmates from seeing what is passing. Officer Stepford is the Unit Four OIC and keys the unit door as the entry team rounds the angle in the corridor. From the operator's throats comes a collective deep throated roar.

It is at this moment that the inmates realize what is about to come through the door. Argus sees two inmates run across the flat and then he is through the door. Several inmates are massing at the far end of the flat and Argus pulls the pin on his grenade and side arms it into their midst. It explodes joining the concussive force of twenty more being thrown. The concussive explosions come one after the other. An overhead light explodes and the cell house fills with the acrid smell of flash powder. Argus' ears begin to ring as he moves with his squad and quickly takes control of the area up to and just past the stairway on the right as Eli does the same on the left. Nash and Hibben peel off and head upstairs. The smell of powder smoke is thick in the unit and Argus' eyes begin to sting. Some inmates make for their cells right away. Some need further convincing. The inmates that refuse to go into their cells are driven into them with batons, grenades and pepper spray. Inevitably, the unit is taken back and secured. Argus steps to the first cell and orders the inmates to lie down on the floor of the cell face down.

One of the inmates looks at Argus in a scowl and says, "There ain't enough room."

Argus face is emotionless and his eyes are cold as he says, "Well you guys better work it out because when I open this door you'd better be on the ground and trust me, I'm gonna open the door."

The inmates slowly lower themselves to the ground. Argus keys the door and swings it open while simultaneously giving the order, "Inmate closest to the door, crawl out of the cell."

The inmate follows Argus orders and crawls from the cell where he is flex cuffed on the flat. This process is being followed by all four squads. In cells where the inmates still have weapons and want to fight, pepper spray is deployed and the inmates still crawl out on their bellies and get cuffed. As the inmates are secured with flex cuffs, they are assisted to their feet and escorted to the old ADSEG. Once in the old segregation unit, the inmates who chose to receive pepper spray are washed off in the shower before being processed and put in a cell. All inmates are medically evaluated by a PA. The noise is deafening and the air is still thick with the smell of smoke and pepper spray as inmates are escorted out of Unit Four. After all of the inmates are removed from the unit, the teams shed their tactical equipment and begin the arduous process of searching the entire unit and packing property. Argus flak vest is soaked completely through with sweat and makes a slapping sound as it hits the floor. The adrenaline dump is fully upon him as he grabs three property bags and picks a cell to work in. He fills one bag for each locker and one bag for the common property. After the property is secured and inventoried, everything left in the cell is disassembled. All contraband is confiscated and a master list is compiled by the officer designated as the record keeper. Throughout the night, the staff members search, secure and pack property while outside the unit, normal operations have resumed. It is 3:00 am when the job is finally completed. On the table that has been designated as the "contraband depository" there lies seven shanks of various sizes, two tattoo guns, four broken mop handles, two gallons of wine, three padlocks affixed to the ends of belts and a myriad of nuisance items.

Argus looks around at the mess and thinks, "What a fucked up way to celebrate an anniversary."

The inmate is a big man at six foot three and at least two hundred fifty pounds. He stands in front of the Operations Lieutenant's desk and glares at Lieutenant Spires. The inmate has forty pounds on the lieutenant and he knows it. He is also drunk which makes him volatile. He is housed in Unit Three and the officer has brought him to the office for refusing to cell up for the 4:00 pm count. Now he stands in the office and has decided that he is not going to be tested for alcohol or be handcuffed. Officer Dunsel, the unit officer stands by the door and looks back and forth at the two men staring at each other.

Lieutenant Spires stands up in his usual resigned manner and tells the inmate, "Look partner, you are going to turn around and be handcuffed."

The inmate huffs and says, "Yeah lieutenant, what if I don't?"

Lieutenant Spires smiles and shakes his head. "Well, if you don't, we're gonna rock."

The inmate cocks his head to the side then looks quickly at the unit officer. He pulls his hair back and ties it with the rubber band he takes from his wrist.

Looking back at the lieutenant he says, "Okay motherfucker, I think I wanna rock."

He hits Lieutenant Spires with his right fist in a powerful arching punch causing the lieutenant to stumble backwards into the book shelves directly behind him. Officer Dunsel reaches for his radio.

Argus exits the Special Housing Unit with a sigh of relief. The SHU Property Officer Post isn't what Argus would call good duty by a long shot. Every day he listens to first pleas and then insults regarding the property policy. It is in a word, monotonous. He enters the Main Corridor and walks briskly to the Control Room Sally Port. Argus thinks about stopping in the Lieutenant's Office to say goodbye but decides against it and walks past. As he heads for Control, he sees Omar standing at the window smiling. Argus smiles back as he wonders what rude comment Omar has ready for his arrival. As Argus reaches the sally port, the grill opens with a mechanical grinding sound.

Omar abruptly runs for the radio console and transmits, "Control to all portable radio units, staff needs assistance in the Lieutenant's Office."

Argus throws his lunch box and thermos into the sally port and motions for Omar to shut the grill as he spins and takes off for the

Lieutenant's Office at a sprint. It is a short run and Argus has plenty of wind left for the fight when he blasts through the door to the office. He is fully into the office when he realizes he'll be fighting a giant. The Unit Three OIC, Officer Dunsel has his arms wrapped around the inmate's waist and is trying to pull him away from Lieutenant Spires who is being soundly pummeled.

Argus thinks as he dives into the melee, "This shit is going to hurt."

He hits the inmate with his shoulder right at the right hip and wraps his arms around the inmate's knee. It is like hitting a tree. Argus pulls hard and the inmate goes down on his belly.

The big man is scrambling to get his feet under him again when Argus jumps on his back and digs his thumbs in just behind the ear, finding the pressure points. These points are usually very effective for pain compliance, usually. The inmate roars and does a pushup with all of Argus' two hundred pounds riding on his back. Dunsel is pulling on the inmate's left leg as Argus drops a hammer fist on the inmate's right shoulder causing him to roll. More officers arrive and Argus feels someone grab his right leg and pull. He looks down in time to see a rookie officer trying to apply leg irons to his ankle.

Argus can't remember the guy's name so he shakes his leg and yells, "That's mine, motherfucker. Cuff the inmate."

The officer releases his ankle and attempts to put the leg irons where they should go.

There are six officers in the fight when the inmate begins to tire saying, "Alright. You motherfuckers got me. I'm done."

The inmate is laughing as he is handcuffed behind his back with two pair of cuffs linked together. Eight officers, four on each side carry the restrained inmate from the Lieutenant's Office to the SHU. Argus holds the inmate's right arm as clothes are cut off, leaving only his boxers. They place the inmate in progressive restraints and leave him in a holding cell. He'll remain there until he sobers up. Argus enters the Pod to write his memorandum detailing his actions in the incident. Once finished, he walks toward the exit for the second time today.

As he passes the holding cell, the inmate yells through the door, "Hey, how long do I hafta stay in here?"

Argus looks at the inmate and smiles, "You have to sober up before you can go in a regular cell. It's policy. You gotta take an alcohol test so we can tell if you're sober. See how that works? You shoulda just took the test."

The inmate grins at Argus, "Hey officer, go fuck yourself. Nice shirt."

Argus looks down at his torn uniform shirt.

The inmate holds up a full urinal and says, "What should I do with this?"

Argus shrugs his shoulders, "Not my problem."

As he starts to walk away the inmate opens the urinal and drinks the contents. Argus just shakes his head and walks away while the inmate pounds on the door and laughs. Argus makes it to the Control Sally Port and finds his lunchbox and thermos where he threw them.

As he picks up the thermos, he hears the ominous tinkle of broken glass and thinks, "Why not. A broken coffee thermos tops this day off perfectly."

He heads out the door on his way to the Training Center for his appointment with the heavy bag. Today he fought a giant but before he goes home to his girls, he must fight a dragon.

∞∞∞∞

It has been a long eleven weeks in the SHU Property Room and Argus is tired. His alarm went off this morning and he realized for the first time since starting at Tarragon Penitentiary, he wasn't ready to come to work. Now as he pulls into the parking lot and looks at the familiar sight of the institution, he realizes that he's done everything that he can do here as an officer. For the past couple of years, he's been bidding on posts not for the challenge, but for the days off. From somewhere deep in Argus' psyche, he hears the phrase, "Better is good's worst enemy," but he declines to listen. He looks at the reflection in his truck rearview mirror and sees a man in his prime and at the top of a game he has chosen, yet the eyes are those of an old man.

The coldness is unmistakable.

He breaks from these thoughts and grabs his lunch box saying under his breath, "Fuck it. Ain't nothing to it but to do it." He closes his truck door and locks it, then heads for the Tower One Sally Port to face what no one on the outside of these fences will ever see.

Argus thinks as he walks, "Even if you want to talk about it, there are no words. This is something you have to see for yourself."

As he reaches the base of the tower, Officer Skim sticks his head out of the window forty feet in the air and yells down, "Don't bother Ant! Bus is on the way. LT wants you to gear up. Argus looks up and sighs as he does a one eighty and heads for the Armory. He bangs on the door and is greeted by Mr. Farmer's smiling face. "Gear's on the table.

Do you know who else is going?"

Argus gives Farmer a stoic smile and says, "Nope, just walked up."

Argus is just clearing his weapon when Haddin shows up.

He looks at Argus with a smile and says, "You want the bus or chase Ant?"

Argus looks back as he loads a magazine into his pistol and says, "Lady's choice "H." What do you want.?"

Harry grabs his gear and starts getting dressed out saying, "I'm too big to ride in an ambulance all the way to Indy. I'll take chase."

Argus raises his eyebrows. "Indy? What the fuck happened?"

Harry speaks as he works the action on the shotgun, "Some dumbass pissed the wrong guy off. They took a fire extinguisher and crushed his head. I don't see how he's still breathing. Found him in the restroom in the Shops right after we closed work call."

Argus shakes his head and thinks, "Dude must have looked at someone the wrong way. It doesn't take much in here."

Harry looks up from his gear with a smile. "Hey, Sena is the LT on the trip. It'll be a good shift."

This makes Argus feel better about the trip. He likes Sena and anytime the whole crew is SWAT, the escort is always smoother. They exit the Armory into the bright sunshine. Harry heads over to Tower One and draws a vehicle key, Argus stands in the sun and waits.

They don't have to wait long before Skim opens the window and yells down, "You guys ready?"

Argus gives him the thumbs up. As Harry and Argus look through the razor wire, Lieutenant Sena and an ambulance crew hurry down the front walk to the tower. Skim buzzes the trio through the sally port and Argus takes over the escort of the inmate while the ambulance crew loads him on the rig. The LT heads for the Armory to quickly put on his gear. Harry and Argus have readied it for him. They are all SWAT so there is no need to check it. Argus looks at Harry and Sena and nods then closes the ambulance door.

Argus looks at the inmate from his usual spot at the rear of the ambulance.

The ride is smooth and controlled as he thinks, "Driver knows what he's doing."

The inmate is moaning and his hands clench in a rhythmic pattern. His head is bandaged in white trauma pads and gauze bandages, leaving only his eyes, nose and mouth visible. There is plenty of blood. The inmate's face resembles a raccoon's with the eyes and nose completely purple. He looks, swollen. As the ambulance gently rocks back and forth along the highway, Argus wonders what the inmate did to whoever did this. Did he deserve to be beaten almost to death? Then the stoniness returns and Argus realizes that "deserve" has nothing to do with it. The minute the inmate worked his way to Tarragon, he chose the rules of the game. His mood is sour as he rides along and ponders the inmate. He puts a dip of Copenhagen in and looks around. The EMS crew member in the back hands him a vomit bag to spit in. Argus nods a thank you. They ride in silence, racing to save a dead man.

As they pull into the ambulance bay at the hospital in Indianapolis, the medic starts shifting the tools of his trade on to the stretcher. Argus opens the door slightly and ensures Harry and Sena are posted and ready. They give him the thumbs up so he opens the door all the way and watches as the EMS crew extracts the inmate from the back of the ambulance. All three of the SWAT Operators have their heads on a swivel as they rush into the Trauma Ward of the hospital. What awaits them there is a flurry of activity as the medical staff plies their trade in attempting to save the inmate. Sena, Harry and Argus stand at the door of the room and watch both the room and the hallway leaving nothing to chance. Chance will get you dead. To Argus' surprise, the doctors and nurses are able to stabilize the inmate. Lieutenant Sena goes to the Nurse's Station and calls back to Tarragon, letting the Operation's Lieutenant know their status. The inmate will be moved to the Intensive Care Unit. There is no timetable and no prognosis.

Argus and Haddin tell Sena that they are good with spending the evening so Sena tells Lieutenant Hanks, "We're here for sixteen. I'd start setting up crews for at least a week. This guy's not going anywhere soon if he lives."

As Sena returns to the room, Argus asks, "Hey LT, mind if me and Harry call our wives and let them know we won't be home for dinner?"

Lieutenant Sena smiles a wry smile. "Yeah Ant, go ahead and call."

Argus looks at Harry and motions with his head for him to go first. Haddin walks toward the Nurse's Station. He returns a short time later and then Argus goes. He dials Lynn's Office phone which is answered in two rings. He tells her that he is at the hospital on an escort and won't be home until late.

She is silent for a moment then says, "Do you have enough food?"

Argus laughs as he says, "I've got plenty baby. You know me."

It is a little lie so she won't worry. He's gone without eating before.

Argus tells her that he loves her and they hang up. He returns to the room where Sena says with a grin, "She's got you whipped Ant." Argus can't deny it. They spend a long day standing at the door of the room, watching nurses come and go. Finally, late in the afternoon, the inmate is moved from the Trauma Ward to ICU. The inmate is hooked up to even more wires and hoses while Argus and his companions are given nice comfortable chairs. It is a welcome gift. The nurse assigned to the room asks if they have eaten and all shake their heads. She orders three additional trays for the evening meal. She brings the trays and ice water to a chorus of gratitude, then leaves with a smile.

After she is out of ear shot, Sena says, "I think I love her."

They all three laugh. At around midnight, Lieutenant Mack, Stephens and Lang show up at the room. They are a welcome sight. It has been a long day and Argus isn't looking forward to the hour drive back to Abhaile. He is left to his own thoughts as they travel the highway back toward home. Sena and Harry are asleep as Argus drives and thinks about water and what happens to it if it stops moving forward. It stagnates. An idea is forming. One in which it is time to move forward with his career. It is time to have a conversation with Lynn about their future.

∞∞∞∞

The only sound is the October wind blowing through the hardwood trees that surround the house. It is just three hours past midnight and a full moon is high in the night sky pouring its light through the bedroom windows. Argus lays with his eyes wide open, listening to Lynn's soft breathing. It is technically his day off, but there is no danger of him sleeping in. The insomnia still plagues him as his mind races. His thoughts are a mixture of mostly inconsequential nothings which is why he is so frustrated.

He stares at the ceiling and thinks, "Why can't I turn it off?"

He doesn't have time to answer the question before his SWAT pager begins to chirp.

He sits up in bed and swivels, putting his feet on the carpeted floor thinking, "Just fucking great."

Lynn rises up on one elbow and asks sleepily, "What's going on Argus?"

He looks at the pager and sees the triple digit code to report to the Ready Room. "They've toned SWAT. I've got to go. Don't know what it is yet. Go back to sleep sweetie."

252

His breath is wasted in saying this. Lynn gets out of bed and says, "I'll throw you some breakfast together while you get dressed."

He smiles and shakes his head thinking, "I couldn't have picked better."

She goes downstairs and Argus throws on a sweat suit and his duty boots. He grabs his radio and turns it on to dead silence.

Argus looks at it to make sure it is turned on and then wonders, "Nothing going on inside the joint. I wonder what the tones are for."

By the time Argus has made a large cup of coffee and put two cans of Copenhagen into his pocket, Lynn is handing him a scrambled egg sandwich. He picks up his keys and wallet off the kitchen counter, puts his radio on the waist of the sweats and heads toward the door. Lynn follows and kisses him whispering, "Be careful. I love you."

Argus tells her he loves her too and kisses her. He looks at her one more time and then steps out the door. He waits until she locks it behind him and steps off the porch. Argus warms his truck up and watches the leaves drift toward the ground as the cold Indiana wind hastens the onset of fall. He's glad he is wearing a thick sweat shirt. He pulls down the drive and makes a right turn to begin the ten minute drive to Tarragon. As soon as he sees the garish flood lights of the institution, his dragon awakens. He pulls into the parking area of the Ready Room and parks. Inside, several members of the team are getting dressed. Argus goes to his locker and joins them. Lieutenant Sena is standing by the door with his ever present clip board, checking the members off as they arrive. In between this, he is looking around the room and tapping the pen on his leg.

Argus thinks, "Something's got him wound up."

Finally, everyone has arrived and are standing around waiting for instructions.

Sena finally speaks after double checking the roster. "Listen up! Gear up for a lethal entry. Minimal equipment."

Argus stomach tightens as Sena continues, "At around midnight several lower level Agency institutions experienced major disturbances. The inmates were housed in dorm settings that lacked the control of a higher level institution. At several of the institutions, buildings were burned. At all of the institutions, staff were surrounded and beaten. Lethal weapons had to be introduced on the compounds to keep from losing the facilities. No escapes have been reported and the institutions are locked down. This appears to have been coordinated."

The team members are silent and look around at each.

Harry raises his hand and asks, "LT, what's the situation inside Tarragon right now?"

Lieutenant Sena nods and replies, "I was getting to that 'H'. It's quiet for now. We just took back Unit Four a few months ago when they got out of hand so they know we won't hesitate. The Warden is hoping that will keep things quiet. As a safe guard, we're going to go in under the penitentiary through the tunnels and stage under the Main Corridor. If they do decide to jump, we'll already be there. DCT will be on standby at the front of Tarragon. We're taking a wait and see if they fuck up approach."

The team members start moving and grabbing gear as Sena yells, "One more thing, rounds will be issued at the armory. Make sure you verify the count because you'll be responsible to bring the same count out. Antrim, Doble, Hibben and Nash on the Benelli's. Everybody else draw Mossbergs."

They arrive at the Armory where Mr. Farmer has the weapons and ammo staged and ready. Argus draws his shotgun and ammunition, signing on the dotted line for Farmer. Argus likes the Benelli. It functions well as far as he is concerned with only one caveat. The shooter must keep a firm stance with the weapon or it won't cycle properly. The team is quiet as they move single file into the sally port. It is fall in Indiana and the sun is far from showing itself. They make their way to the tunnel entrance where Farmer unlocks the hatch. It opens with the heavy groan of unused hinges.

As they descend the steep stairs, Sena tells each operator, "Remember your noise discipline."

They move through the dark maze of tunnels with the only sound being the scrape of boots on wet concrete and the hiss of steam escaping from the old pipes overhead. The heat from the pipes makes the tunnels much warmer than the brisk air Argus dressed for. He is soon sweating in the tactical gear. The team finally reaches the stairs which will lead to an access door midway down the corridor. Argus mounts the stairs and climbs as far as the three operators ahead of him allow room for. He picks a step and sits, the muzzle of his shotgun in the air.

Argus and his brothers wait in silence in their tactical stack. Sena calls on his radio and notifies the Command Center that they are in place and standing by. Argus pulls a bandana from his vest and wipes the back of his neck. He hears the Corridor Officer in his ear mike announce mainline.

Sena whispers, "Okay, be ready."

The operators ripple with an almost imperceptible shift. They can hear the inmates moving past only feet away on the other side of the heavy steel door. Argus sees Lieutenant Sena look at the heavy key hanging from his vest. They wait on high alert for an hour as mainline is conducted. It is a relief when the Corridor Officer announces that mainline is closed. Lieutenant Sena is on the Command Center channel speaking with someone. He motions for everyone to quietly gather around.

As he kneels, he whispers, "Okay, I just got a report that only about twenty five percent of the inmates went to mainline. The Warden is going to partially lock Tarragon down. They are going to announce an inmate recall for an emergency count. Once the count is complete, the inmates will be let out in the housing units only. No work calls or mainline. They'll eat bologna in the block. We're here until they get the place locked down and then we'll shag ass to the Rear Gate and standby. Everybody tracking?"

They all nod and resume their places on the stairs.

Argus sits on his stair and focus' on the slow descent of a bead of sweat rolling down his spine. He wonders what Lynn and Olivia are doing. He pictures running through the door just feet away into the corridor. He thinks of past mistakes. Argus mind goes to many things while he waits, yet he is still alert and cognizant of the present. It is a skill learned and perfected by every correctional officer to be able to fill the monotony while still being ready to respond in an instant. The inmates are recalled to the units without any problems and the count clears. Sena decides to stay in place for another hour before departing to make sure no problems arise in the units. Finally, the LT circles his finger in the air signaling the team to start moving out. They negotiate the dark tunnels in the opposite direction this time and find Mr. Farmer standing with the hatch open in anticipation of their arrival. They make their way out of the secure perimeter just as they had entered without having to fire a shot. As Argus exits the sally port, he puts a dip of Copenhagen in and spits. The sky is a clear blue although the air is chilly. He looks around and smiles. It's a good day.

∞∞∞∞

The SWAT Team has been at the Rear Gate for two weeks pulling eighteen hour shifts. They are there from the time the cell doors unlock in the morning until they lock at night. As Argus sits in a chair in the gatehouse, he thinks about the money he's making. This paycheck will be a sizeable one. Officer Benell is the Rear Gate Officer and has warmed up to the presence of the team in his tiny kingdom. He's still not happy about the extra company but he's at least friendly now. The atmosphere of the Agency is changing and Benell is one of many older hacks who has foreseen the future and have headed to the perimeter to finish their careers. Ricky Oak also started riding the towers. Argus sees the change as well and it scares him. Agency leadership has changed from administrators who have worked a cell house to politicians and social workers who wouldn't know how to turn a key.

Waiting for a wreck to occur is mentally taxing especially for a type "A" personality. Early on, a football was introduced which has given birth to several games of touch football. The institution has provided meals which consist of the same bologna sandwiches the inmates have been getting. Argus reads a book he has brought. He watches television. He plays dominos. He is monumentally bored. There are just so many pushups you can do and he's working on breaking the record. Argus is not alone in his pursuit of things to combat the boredom. Everyone is fighting the same battle. This is why the news that the Warden had made the decision to open Tarragon back up and bring the inmates off lockdown is so welcome to the SWAT Team. The plan is to run mainline as normal for the evening meal and if there are no issues, Tarragon Penitentiary will resume normal operations on the following morning. The team will spend one more day at the gate after today.

Argus thinks as he hears the news, "Okay everyone, just play nice."

Lieutenant Sena calls Argus and Doble to the side after making the announcement. "Ant, I want you and your rifle in Tower Four tomorrow by 6:00 am to cover the Linen Factory and Construction Shop work calls at eight. Doble, you need to be in Tower Six to cover the Recreation Yard at the same time. Command Center is still active so they have authority. Keep them updated on the command frequency."

The next morning Argus rises at 4:30 am to the annoying buzzing of his alarm. He is tired having only had a few hours' sleep. He quietly gets out of bed without disturbing Lynn and goes into the bathroom to get dressed in his black BDU's. Once he's dressed, he heads down the stairs and turns the coffee pot on to start loading his body with caffeine. The nicotine load will start in his truck. He makes some toast, fills his thermos and throws a few cans of tuna into a bag then silently creeps back upstairs and kisses Lynn on the cheek. She stirs only slightly. He descends the stairs and sneaks out the front door, making sure to lock it then he is in his truck for the short drive to the prison. He stops at the Armory and draws his rifle and one box of .308 shells then takes the back road to Tower Four and pulls into the parking space next to the Morning Watch Officer's car. He pounds on the door and Officer Thoms looks down from high above. He does not acknowledge Argus' greeting, just disappears back into the tower shortly before the door is buzzed open. Argus climbs the stairs round and round until he reaches the ladder directly under the main platform. He hitches his gear up and makes the final ascent through the trap door. Thoms does not offer to help with the load. Over the years, Argus has gotten to know Thoms and even saw him laugh once. The old hack isn't unfriendly, he just isn't overly friendly. Argus figures it is just his way and leaves it at that.

As Argus starts getting his firing position arranged, Thoms makes small talk in his deep voice. "Guess they're gonna open up today huh."

He looks at Thoms with a sideways grin and nods. "Yeah, that's the plan. Hopefully it will go okay."

Thoms raises his eyebrows and takes a deep breath before saying, "Well, I guess we'll see."

Argus senses that this will be the extent of the conversation. He continues setting his gear up. Argus puts a small sandbag in the window sill of the tower and props the barrel of his weapon on it. He glasses the target area and realizes if he does have to shoot, the shot will be relatively straight forward. He does the calculations in his head and figures a two inch drop on the round at maximum range past zero. It will be an alley way with no cross wind considerations. His only concern which becomes apparent almost immediately is the short time he'll have to engage the target if things go bad. Will Command even have time to authorize a shot before the inmates have their hostage in a building and out of his sight? This thought makes his stomach tighten. For the next ninety minutes, Argus and Thoms occupy the small tower platform with only short snippets of conversation and grunts being exchanged.

At 7:30 am Thoms stands and says, "Well, I guess I'll leave you to it."

He picks up his lunchbox and descends the ladder. Argus closes the trap door listening to Thoms' footfalls echo up through the belly of the tower. The door buzzes and he is gone. Argus looks at his rifle and considers his mission today then looks around the tower and feels the silence.

Argus has been monitoring the radio since his arrival. His tactical radio is set on the Command channel and the tower radio on the institutional frequency. Mainline has been completed with no incidents. He glasses the area where the inmates will emerge one more time then loads five rounds into his rifle, closes the bolt and double checks the safety. His stomach growls as he pulls a protein bar from his pocket while sipping his coffee. Argus finishes inhaling the protein bar as several Factory Supervisors walk across the alleyway and enter the factory leaving a lone female Factory Supervisor in the alley to monitor the inmates as they cross. She is blonde and petite. Argus doesn't know her name but that's not unusual. He doesn't know a lot of the Linen Factory personnel. She turns and looks at Argus, giving him a slight wave. He raises his hand in return.

The Corridor Officer announces over the radio, "Corridor to the housing units this will be the Linen Factory and Facilities work call."

Argus stomach tightens and he feels his pulse quicken. He spits into the trash can and pulls his balaclava down over his face, grabbing his rifle. Argus sits in the captain's chair and braces his right foot against the counter while resting the butt of the rifle on his left thigh and waits for the inmates who he knows will soon come into view.

He sees the Factory Supervisor look his way one more time and thinks, "You're nervous and that's okay. Just don't lose your head and run like hell toward me if they decide to jump."

The first of the inmate workers start to trickle from the breezeway into the alley between the main institution and the factory.

Argus keys his microphone on the tactical channel and says, "Tower Four to Command, inmates in the alley."

The female supervisor has positioned herself so that she is on the tower side of the mass of inmates. Argus is happy that she is already thinking ahead. He is totally focused on the stream of inmates coming from the breezeway and examines each one for signs of tension or abnormal behavior. His senses heighten with the adrenaline and he becomes acutely aware of the musty smell inside the tower compared to the cool breeze entering the window. He notices the movement in his peripheral vision of a small spider making its way up the window framing and almost senses the vibrations in the air from its efforts. The supervisor's blonde hair contrasts sharply against the olive drab of the inmate's uniforms as they file past in a haphazard mob. Some look up at the tower and see Argus with the rifle. They look quickly away. None of the inmates pass close to the supervisor, not wanting any misinterpretations of intent. Argus is wearing a balaclava so the inmates cannot identify who the snipers are on the SWAT team but the fact that he is in the tower on this morning is enough for them to know, he'll do his job and pull the trigger if needed.

As he watches he thinks, "Just keep walkin'."

Finally, the last of the inmates file past the supervisor. She looks up at him once more, smiles and waves then walks into the factory taking her out of his view and protection. As the Linen Factory door closes, he lowers the rifle and leans it in the corner within easy reach then picks up the binoculars and starts scanning the windows of the factory.

He reaches down and presses the transmit button near his right collarbone and says, "Tower Four to Command, the alley is clear of staff and inmates."

His transmission is acknowledged immediately.

The Corridor Officer transmits, "Corridor to the housing units, this will be a ten minute recreation movement. Recreation Yard only."

In a few minutes Argus hears Doble's voice on the tactical radio, "Tower Six to Command, inmates on the yard."

At the same time, the tower intercom comes to life with Officer Laundry's voice, "Okay tower hacks, thugs on the yard. Look alive."

Argus spends the rest of the day monitoring his area of responsibility. There are no incidents which pleases him. He watches as the inmates file out for lunch and back, then out of the factory at the end of the day. Once the factory area is clear of inmates, Argus down loads his rifle with a sigh of relief. Ricky Oak arrives to take over the tower at 3:30 pm on the dot. Argus is glad to see him. They exchange their normal light hearted greetings.

He runs down the day's events for Oak who looks at Argus with his wry grin and says, "Well, sounds like you kept the place in good shape for me Ant."

Argus just laughs as he starts picking up his gear.

Oak stops him and says, "Hold up there young man. Go down the ladder and I'll hand you your stuff."

He nods in appreciation and descends the ladder, reaching up and taking the gear after he reaches the bottom.

He looks up as he hears Oak say, "Be careful my young friend."

Then the trap door is closed and Argus walks to his truck to make the drive around to the Rear Gate to join the rest of the team.

It has been two weeks since going back to normal operations at Tarragon and it is business as usual. The only incidents have been the normal isolated examples of depravity that are so common inside the walls of a maximum security penitentiary. The inmates learned the lessons of Unit Four many months ago. There was no riot at Tarragon. Other facilities were not so lucky. Those inmates that took part in the riots are to be transferred to Tarragon and held in the old ADSEG Unit to be reprogrammed. Some will stay at Tarragon, others will be transferred. All will have to earn their way out of lockdown. The SWAT Team will meet the buses carrying the men who burned institutions and assaulted staff. They will be processed and escorted to their new quarters. By the time the day that they arrive is finished they will know where they are. Since the end of the SWAT vigil at the Rear Gate, Argus has been assigned to the sick and annual roster. Although the posts are of greater responsibility since his promotion to Correctional Officer Specialist, they are still mundane. Argus has seen all the games before and rather than view them as a challenge, now he sees them as a never ending parade of inconveniences. It strikes him that rehabilitation is a myth and all he is doing is warehousing society's predators until they are freed to victimize again in a never ending rotation of crime and incarceration. He is standing in the Main Corridor during an open movement watching the inmates with these jaded eyes and thoughts when the Corridor Officer's telephone rings.

Argus picks up the telephone, "Corridor, Antrim."

Lieutenant Sena is on the other end of the line. "Ant, we're meeting the first bus tomorrow at around 7:30 am. Be suited up in the Ready Room by 6:00 am for the briefing."

Argus looks down the corridor at an inmate who is running toward him. "Hold on LT. Hey! Stop! Grab the wall and don't move. Okay LT, I'll be there."

Lieutenant Sena asks, "Everything okay?"

Argus looks at the inmate, "Yeah LT. Just the usual."

Argus hangs up the telephone and walks over to the inmate. "Where's the fire my man?"

The inmate looks at the wall and says, "Trying to get to Education boss man."

Argus grunts. He pat searches the inmate finding nothing and says, "I run a full ten minute move so you ain't gotta run. Consider this your only warning. You can go."

The inmate looks at Argus for a microsecond and then continues down the corridor.

Argus takes his radio from his belt and announces, "Corridor to the housing units, this move is over. Clear the corridor of inmates and lock your doors. They missed it."

Argus awakens at 4:30 am having had little sleep the night before. The insomnia causes him to wander the quiet house like a ghost. It is almost a steady routine now. He goes downstairs where he has staged his clothes and gets dressed. Using the downstairs bathroom to wash his face and brush his teeth before eating some buttered toast and drinking the first cup of coffee of the day. He ascends the stairs to kiss his girls goodbye and heads out the door barely disturbing them. They have become used to the odd hours of his comings and goings. He starts his truck and shivers in the November cold.

He thinks, "Fuck, I hate winter."

His arrival at the Ready Room is like a hundred others. A flurry of activity as team members get suited up in the equipment specific for the mission. Today it will be riot gear. Today will be about sending a message.

Everyone is pretty well geared up when Lieutenant Sena stands up by the door and yells, "Listen up! First bus will be rolling up between 7:30 and 8:00 am. Franks, line everyone up for an equipment check. You guys need to look sharp and look alike. No bandanas. We'll line up in formation facing the drive. Remember, unless you're giving these fuckers an order, no talking. We'll escort to Intake and process them hands on. Be professional. There'll be cameras. All eyes are on us so don't fuck it up. Okay, let's get this done. We're expecting four buses today."

Big Franks turns to the room, "Okay, everyone line up outside! Let's go!"

After the equipment check and a few adjustments, the team heads over to the penitentiary in several pickup trucks. They park in the staff parking area and move to the center of the circle drive, forming themselves into a line stretching across the front of Tarragon. The Captain, Associate Warden of Custody and two camera operators are also there.

Franks yells, "Squad! Align to the right and cover!"

Several members make slight adjustments to their positioning. Franks orders the team, "Parade rest!"

The squad stands with feet shoulder width apart and their sticks held across their bodies at the waist. It is 7:30 am. The first bus arrives fifteen minutes later and pulls slowly around the circle stopping right in front of the team. Argus can see the inmates looking at them through the windows.

As the bus doors open, Lieutenant Sena quickly mounts the three stairs and faces the inmates. "What are you looking at? Eyes forward! When I call your name and number you will step to the front! You will follow all orders immediately! Failure to comply will result in you being helped to comply!"

Lieutenant Sena sees an inmate looking out the window at the squad and grinning. "What the fuck are you looking at?"

Sena sticks his head out the door and motions for Hibben and Pinolo to board the bus. "Go and get that asshole."

The big men move down the aisle and stand the inmate up, escorting him to the front.

Sena looks at the inmate, his jaw tight as he says, "Congratulations asshole. You just volunteered to be first."

Hibben and Pinolo grab the inmate by the arms and escort him off the bus, quick walking him to the Intake area. The other inmates learn from the example and shuffle forward looking at the floor when they are called. Each one is escorted quickly from the bus to Intake where they are ordered to sit on a bench in a holding cell and told not to move. The camera operators roam through the Intake area filming as the last of the inmates are brought into the cell and assisted in sitting down. Argus is assigned to monitor the "clean cell." This is the cell the inmates will be placed in after being processed. Argus takes his position and waits. The inmates are escorted everywhere by two team members. They have no fight in them now. Argus sees fear in their eyes as they are escorted from one processing station to the next where an order is given. The quiet is deafening as SWAT complete their duties as automatons.

The team members are stoic and only communicate if an order is required. This is not what these inmates are used to, having come from lower security level institutions. No one is asking nicely for their compliance. No friendly smiles. This is a different place and they are realizing it. In short order, Argus' cell begins to fill with inmates. They look straight ahead and no one speaks, their bravado gone absent the violent mob. Argus stands like a statue by the door but his eyes never stop roaming. Three more buses arrive throughout the day and each one is processed in the same manner. By the time the last inmate is escorted into the old ADSEG, all of the ranges are full. The sun has set as the team heads back to the Ready Room in the trucks. The cold wind penetrates the sweatshirt he is wearing and cools the perspiration underneath until a shiver crawls up his back.

Lieutenant Sena stands by the door as he did this morning and yells, "Listen up! Outstanding work! Today was a good example of why we're known throughout the Agency fellas. Everything went like clockwork which is nothing less than what I expected. Get your gear off and go home."

Argus stands in the room among his brothers feeling the camaraderie he thought he'd left at Lejuene long ago. It is a good feeling.

∞∞∞∞

Argus stands at the Corridor Officer's desk which is just a two square foot counter affixed to the wall right outside of Food Service and works on his orderly's pay sheets. As he looks down the list, deciding which inmates should receive a bonus for outstanding work, the telephone rings. Argus reaches for it. "Corridor Antrim."

It is Ron Conner on the line. He is the SHU Number Two Officer and is working in the Pod.

Ron says, "Hey Ant, Got one of your old friends to release back to Unit Four. Can I pop him out?"

Argus smiles, "Yeah man, kick'm."

Argus goes back to his paperwork and hears over the radio, "SHU to Corridor, one to Unit Four."

Argus answers, "Corridor to SHU, send him."

A short time later, the inmate comes walking down the corridor past Argus. It is Inmate "Worm" once again making his rounds out of SHU. Argus glances at him as he drags his property bag past. He smiles as the inmate starts with the mouth. Argus knew "Worm" wouldn't be able to walk past without saying something.

Argus turns as the inmate says, "Hey Antrim, I can't believe nobody's cut your head off and shoved it up your ass yet."

Argus grins at the inmate and shakes his head. "I ain't met nobody up to the task yet. Why don't you drop that bag and grab the wall."

The inmate let's go of the bag and walks to the wall saying, "I just got released from SHU. You know I ain't got nothing."

Argus moves up behind the inmate and says, "Yeah, you still got that mouth though."

He does a quick pat search and waves the inmate on down the corridor.

263

Inmate "Worm laughs and says, "You still fucking with my worm Antrim. Bad shit happens to people who fuck with my worm. HA! HA!"

Argus smiles and walks back to his desk thinking, "So fucking predictable."

∞∞∞∞

It is mid-December and the snow is already on the ground. Lynn is sitting in her usual place in the garden tub located in the Master Bath as Argus eases himself into the water. When Lynn designed the house, the garden jet tub was a luxury they had allowed themselves and it has turned out to be the place they have all of their deepest conversations. This place of total openness is where they make their plans. The subject tonight won't be a new one. They have talked about moving before but never seriously pursued it. Tonight, they have all but decided.

Argus looks at Lynn as the steam rises from the water and the heat invades his muscles. "I talked to AW Law today about a lieutenant's spot at Tarragon."

Lynn leans forward and asks, "Oh yeah? What did he say?"

Argus shakes his head. "He said that he would love to have me and that I'd make a good one but, there won't be anything coming open for a while. So, I'm shot in the ass on that route."

Lynn wrinkles her brow. "Well, that's disappointing. What about the other place in North Carolina?"

Argus smiles. "Well I got a call from the Captain down there and he wants us to come down and take a look around. If I want it, there's a lieutenant's spot at the new prison they've built that's mine. It's a paid move. I just wanted to give Tarragon a chance before I took it. They want me to run the Disturbance Control Team down there as well."

Lynn leans forward and grabs Argus' hand. "Oh Argus, that's wonderful. Is that something you'd want to do?"

He wrinkles his brow. "Yeah. I think I could make something out of it for sure. Frankly, I'm ready for something more."

Lynn smiles and says, "Me too. I'm really sick of all this snow."

Argus leans forward and gives her a quick kiss. "Okay, I guess it's settled. I'll call tomorrow and set the trip up. All three of us will go down and take a look. If it looks like a good place for you and Olivia, I'll take the position."

∞∞∞∞

The telephone rouses Argus from a fitful sleep. He is disoriented at first as he looks around and wonders what time it is. The display on the clock says 2:06 am. At first he just looks at the telephone blankly and then he picks up the receiver wondering who the idiot is that's calling at this hour. The minute he says hello, he knows it is a mistake.

Lieutenant Atkins cheerful voice comes through the receiver, "Antrim, we got fog at the institution and you got mandatory fog patrol. See you as soon as you can get here."

Argus doesn't have time to reply before Atkins hangs up.

Argus mutters under his breath, "How in the fuck does he do that?"

Lynn roles over so she is facing him and asks sleepily, "Who was that?"

Argus moves to the window and looks out at the eight inches of snow covering his yard, "It was Atkins. I have to go in for mandatory fog watch. How can there be fog in all this snow? This is some crazy shit and on my day off."

Lynn rises up on one elbow "What do you have to do for fog watch?"

Argus sits on the bed and scratches his head, "I gotta walk back and forth along the fence line with a twelve gauge shotgun and pop anyone who tries to come over it."

Lynn lies back down, "Make sure you wear your long underwear. It'll be cold out there."

Argus looks at her and smiling shakes his head. He gets up and puts on his thermal underwear and wool socks, then his uniform. He takes gloves, scarf and hat. He kisses Lynn goodbye and heads out into the snow storm. At two-thirty in the morning, the plows have not started really working the rural roads yet so the driving is treacherous. As he pulls on to the penitentiary drive, Argus looks at the fence line and sees to his amazement that it is shrouded in a thick blanket of fog. He parks his truck where he thinks there might be a space and walks into the new lobby building under Tower One. Argus picks up the telephone and dials the three digit extension for the Lieutenant's Office.

Atkins answers on the second ring, "Operations."

Argus says, "I'm here LT. Where do you need me?"

There is a slight pause and then Atkins comes back on the line, "Hmmm, well I need you to take the fence line between Towers One and Two."

Argus hangs the phone up and steps to the Tower One entry and is

265

buzzed inside. He fills out the paperwork and draws a fog patrol shotgun from the lock box the tower officer has opened. Argus checks the chamber to ensure it is empty then closes the slide and inserts four rounds into the magazine. The other four go into the side saddle. He puts his gloves on and cradles the gun in his right arm before walking toward the stretch of fence line he is responsible for. Argus was a Marine and has been to Norway twice. He knows how to operate in cold weather. He sets a good pace and trudges through the snow following the same path each time to make a walkway. He knows he'll be out here for a while and knows to move is to stay warm but to stop is to freeze your ass off. It takes only an hour before he is covered in the freezing snow and ice has formed in his beard but his core is warm and that is the most important thing. As Argus is making his way towards Tower Two, June Walker drives up beside him in a van.

She roles down the window and says, "I'm supposed to relieve you guys every once in a while so you can get warm."

June is a new correctional officer and a nice girl. She is young, just a wisp of a thing and a good officer.

Argus looks over at her and smiles thinking, "There is no way in hell I'm going let her walk in this shit while I sit in a van."

Argus looks around and then up at the cold night sky. "You know June, I'm really kind of enjoying the walk. I'm good. If you come across any coffee somewhere, I could use a cup, otherwise I'm straight."

The relief on her face is evident as she drives off. Two hours pass before June makes her way around to his post again. By this time, Argus' trousers and boots are covered in snow. His beard and the front part of his cap are covered in ice where his warm breath has frozen. He blows on his hands to keep them warm and stomps his feet to combat the stinging in his toes.

She stops the van and roles the window down holding out a small paper cup of coffee. "It's from Tarp in Tower Five."

Argus takes the warm cup of liquid as if it might disappear if he moves to quickly. It is the best coffee he has tasted in a while.

Argus holds the cup up. "Thank him for me."

All through the night, Argus walks the fence line. As he walks, he thinks about why he and his fellow hacks do the things that they do.

What it comes down to is very simple in Argus' mind. "It's not the Agency or the paycheck. It's my girls. I'll walk this fence line till hell freezes over if it means none of these inmates escape and have a chance at getting to my girls. It's that simple."

By seven the fog has lifted enough to call off the fog patrol. Argus acknowledges the transmission and along with the other hacks that have been on the fence line, he walks to Tower One on sore frozen feet. His pants below the knee are stiff and frozen. He is covered in a fine powder of snow. Argus turns in the shotgun, radio and rounds and walks into the lobby where he finds a broom. He walks back out front and starts cleaning the snow off of his pants and boots but sees it is a lost cause almost immediately. He returns the broom and walks along with his brothers to the parking lot. Light hearted exchanges are made with some profanity then he is in his truck and heading home.

As he drives down the icy roads with the heater on full blast he thinks about North Carolina and says to no one in particular, "I really hate this fucking snow."

∞∞∞∞

Argus stands in their family room in the dark. The house is quiet with only the pops and groans he has become accustomed to emanating from the home he and Lynn built in the South end of town. Lynn and Olivia are fast asleep as he surveys the room full of their belongings neatly packed in boxes stacked in every corner. Over the years, the darkness has become almost comforting as he's wandered the house during the night. He holds the plaque at eye level to read the inscription one more time. "To Argus 'Ant' Antrim. Thank you for your dedication and consistent pursuit of excellence in service to Tarragon Penitentiary, 1991 to 2001."

It is a beautiful award with a picture of Tarragon taken from the air and mounted on varnished oak with brass plates shined to a mirror finish. At the bottom is a piece of granite carved into the shape of the state of Indiana.

As he looks out of the sliding glass doors into the inky blackness of the forest that surrounds the house, he takes stock of the past ten years and thinks, "It was a good run."

All things eventually come to an end as has his time here in Indiana. He and Lynn simply outgrew Abhaile, so Argus started searching for their next opportunity. His search was answered by the offer of a supervisory position at a prison in North Carolina. The position came with a pay increase and the chance to run his own Disturbance Control Team. He just couldn't turn it down and frankly, who could blame him.

A few days ago, he and Lynn had attended his going away party. It consisted of the usual things one might find at a party to celebrate the departure of a comrade. There was dancing and drinking, the usual speeches and recollections of funny anecdotes. Argus kept his speech short and heartfelt as he suppressed the lump in his throat.

They had jokingly accused him of having something prepared and it probably sounded like that but in truth, he came up with it in the moment. "Most people go through life with many acquaintances and few friends. I stand here before you blessed with many friends and few acquaintances."

His friend, Pete Wicker had poured shot after shot of whiskey and Argus had downed them dutifully. It is a memory he's sure he'll always cherish. His brother was saying goodbye to him. Finally, Lynn had led him from the party to the car. It was his night and she had agreed to be the designated driver although it was usually the other way around. By this time, the partiers would not notice his absence. As Argus stands in front of the glass doors, looking into the expanse of nothingness, he starts to take account.

He had arrived at Tarragon with no experience at all and had quickly learned that he loved the work and the people there. He had been trained by some of the best and hopes that he had lived up to their expectations of him.

Argus wonders how many lives he had saved by finding the many weapons he'd discovered and asks himself, "Was it enough?"

It is a question that only the universe might answer. How much good had he accomplished just by doing his job? He thinks of all the time away from Lynn and Olivia and wonders if it was worth it. He knows for sure that the escape plot he'd thwarted at the apex of its fruition had saved three of his brother's lives but he will never know exactly who Inmate "Politeness" and his crew might have killed. That too can really only be answered by God Himself. Argus had watched one man take his last breath and had survived two attempts on his own life.

He had been involved in two major incidents at Tarragon, countless minor ones and a series of riots that had cascaded throughout the Agency. He and his sniper rifle had provided over watch from Tower Four to the reopening of Tarragon's Linen Factory after the riots. Argus thinks of the lone female factory supervisor standing in the breezeway as hundreds of inmates passed by. Her blonde hair standing out against a sea of olive drab is indelibly etched into his memory. He also knows, given warrant, he would have pulled the trigger. There is something sobering in that knowledge. He has stood the line with his brothers and sisters and has put his life in their hands. He knows there is no greater bond that can be formed and he feels privileged as he thinks of them. Argus thinks of all of the times, outnumbered with only the wall at his back, he questioned whether he would make it home, hoping Lynn would remember how much he loved her. He wonders what all these things have cost him.

Argus looks at his dark reflection in the glass and knows that Tarragon has changed him forever. It will always be a part of him and him of it. He soon found after his arrival the camaraderie he'd left at the gate of Camp Lejeune so many years ago. He mentally walks the corridor of Tarragon with its many nuances that only a seasoned veteran might discern and thinks of the ways the place had tested his mental and physical tenacity.

Argus thinks of the many times he has repeated the mantra into the rearview mirror of his truck, "You'll be as tough as you need to be each and every second of the day, one second at a time."

He hopes he was. During his time here, he has also lost something. The hundreds of shifts equating to thousands of hours at a heightened state of awareness have changed him. A part of him has died over the years in this place. The final lesson from so many teachers found Argus and embedded itself in him.

Whether this was an epiphany or a slow awakening, he cannot say for sure. "You have to be able to suppress the human part of yourself, putting emotion and weakness into a tiny box shoving it down so deep it never sees the light of day. This is what feeds your dragon."

He looks into the eyes of his reflection and ponders the coldness he sees there. When had they changed? These are the eyes that have seen too much of naked humanity and the evil it can give rise to. Argus ponders this stranger to the young man he once was and thinks of the amazing story he has been a part of. He wonders what happens to a story left untold when the teller is no more.

Epilogue

It is 4:00 am and Argus is silently walking the ranges of the Segregation Unit in the prison he had opened so many years before. As he walks, he silently prays for a quiet shift. It is his last shift. In exactly four hours his retirement becomes effective and he wants to end his career quietly. The officers on his shift only found out that he was retiring a few hours ago. Argus prefers an Irish goodbye. He finishes the tour and tells the officers, his officers to call him if they need him. They are good men and will only call as a last resort. He exits the large steel door and walks across the open compound to assist the Food Service Foreman in counting his workers because once again, Argus is shorthanded on his shift and has only one Compound Officer.

Twelve staff members to watch fourteen hundred inmates is more than challenging but, Argus and his crew get it done. After the count clears he stands at the front of the Dining Hall and monitors the inmates as they make their way through the line for breakfast. This is where he always stands unless he is walking around telling inmates to remove their hats or stopping them from cutting in line. He and the Food Service Foreman are the only staff members in a Dining Hall full of inmates. Argus' remaining Compound Officer and the Activities Lieutenant are outside pat searching inmates as they leave. As the Operations Lieutenant, Argus fields the usual complaints and confiscates a belt buckle the inmate has carved his gang affiliation into. He won't back off just because it is his last day. That's just not how he's built.

After the morning meal is complete, Argus walks across the compound to the Lieutenant's Office where he meets his relief. They exchange some light hearted banter before shaking hands. Argus picks up his lunch box and walks through the Control Room Sally Port, waves at the officers then proceeds to the Warden's Office where she is waiting with the Captain. She is in a hurry because she is due at a meeting. They shake his hand, wish him luck and give him his plaque and mantle clock. Argus senses their urgency to leave and makes his exit.

As he is about to walk out the door, the Captain says, "Hey Lieutenant, thank you."

Argus just nods and walks out the door of the institution for the last time. The parking lot is full of empty cars and no one to witness the end of his career. Argus turns to look back at the prison and thinks about all he has given to this "thing". He realizes that it has always been a machine of which he was only a small part. It will keep running without him. He is no longer Lieutenant Antrim, the leader of the DCT Team, Tactical Trainer, SHU Lieutenant or the Investigator that foiled an escape plot and in so doing saved a pilot and his family's lives. He is none of those things now. As he opens his car door, he looks back one more time and feels used up. Empty to his soul.

He asks himself, "How do you stop being what you've been for so long?"

No answer comes. When he arrives home, Lynn is waiting and throws her arms around him. They walk into the kitchen and Argus takes comfort in the familiarity. He hangs his duty belt on the kitchen chair for the last time and wonders what he will do now briefly thinking of his dragon. He stands in the middle of the kitchen feeling the warmth on his face from the sunlight coming through the windows and sees Lynn standing in the doorway. She has her arms crossed and is giving him that beautiful smile. Her eyes are bright and as he looks into them, he hears the answer from somewhere deep inside. It is what should have been the answer all along. "Whatever it is, I'll do the next thing, for her."

"He who fights too long against dragons becomes a dragon himself; and if you gaze to long into the abyss, the abyss will gaze into you."

Friedrich Nietzsche

About the author

Arthur Sappington II is a veteran of the United States Marine Corps. At the end of his enlistment, he embarked on a journey which led him to a career with the Federal Bureau of Prisons. He served dutifully in Correctional Services for twenty three years until his retirement. He is still active as a public servant and enjoys a quiet life with his wife of forty years, his daughter and granddaughter.